LILY FROM LINCOLN

OPERATION BIG ROCK BRIDES - BOOK 6

NORA NOLAN

Published by Blushing Books
An Imprint of
ABCD Graphics and Design, Inc.
A Virginia Corporation
977 Seminole Trail #233
Charlottesville, VA 22901

Nora Nolan
Lily from Lincoln

eBook ISBN: 978-1-63954-029-7
Print ISBN: 978-1-63954-030-3
v1

PROLOGUE

BIG ROCK, WYOMING TERRITORY, MID 1880S

*T*he woods weren't quiet that day. They were full of the sounds of saw blades against wood, loggers yelling warnings and good-natured obscenities at each other, and the satisfying noise of huge trees crashing to the ground. A team of lumbermen from the local sawmill was out in force trying to get enough trees felled to meet the lumber demand for new orders. They'd already been through surrounding forests cutting down the standing dead trees, which were prized because there was no moisture in the wood and shrinkage wouldn't be a problem in the completed project. While the weather was cool and clear, they decided to go ahead and cut taller trees. The green wood could be drying and curing while the lumber from the standing dead trees was used first.

The owners of the sawmill, Angus Kelly and Henry Tucker, worked right alongside their men; it was one of the reasons the men held them in such high regard. Besides, Angus was a giant

1

of a man who stood at six feet and eight inches and he was a handy man to have around. He'd once lifted and held a loaded wagon while the wheel was changed. To his embarrassment, and admittedly to his amusement sometimes, his strength had become almost legendary in the town.

Will Wharton and Amos Cameron made one sawing team. Both were big and beefy men whose muscles seemed to enjoy the workout. Equally yoked, they had their saw strokes down to a rhythmic cadence; it was only interrupted when a knotty eye in the wood got in the way.

They were best friends in their off hours, too. Often one would be found at the other's house, usually working on improvements. They'd helped each other build their houses, tables, chairs and swings to go on the porches. They'd helped each other build barns. At the time, Amos was helping Will put the finishing touches on his house. Next, they planned to build a handsome wardrobe for Will's fiancée, Lily. She was one of the town's mail order brides and was on her way there from Lincoln, Nebraska. Lily was scheduled to arrive within a week.

The two men had felled a sky-high oak and had just finished cutting off the limbs. Amos called out to the men with the horses to come pull it out of the way. Another group of men sorted through the limbs, saving the ones that were large enough to get smaller lumber pieces from and the rest they set aside to be cut for firewood.

Will wiped his brow and took a big swig from his canteen before offering it to Amos. "Here. I need to go over that ridge and find a place to drop my own log. I won't be long."

Amos nodded and took the water from him. He sat down on a stump for a quick rest while his friend went to relieve himself. He closed his eyes for a moment to rest them and nearly fell asleep sitting up. He splashed a small handful of the canteen water over his face.

Before too long a scream of "No!" that quickly grew

into a chorus of them drew his attention toward the side of the ridge. He dropped the canteen and stood while the scene before him unfolded in what seemed like slow motion. He felt like he was trying to run in water. Or maybe molasses.

As he was walking back to the gathering place, the giant tree fell before Will could get out of the way. He'd been hidden by the ridge when the men checked before the tree fell. He was alive; his scream filled the forest for a moment, then his sounds died down.

"Will! Will!" Amos yelled out as he finally made it to where his best friend lay under the tree. There were branches on top of him holding him down, but it appeared the main problem was the thick tree trunk that landed across his legs. Men with hatchets and saws scrambled to cut away the limbs so they could reach him.

Angus and Henry were in the middle of the men as they worked. Angus tried to move the tree, but its branches dug into the ground and prevented any progress.

Another couple of men unloaded a wagon and pulled it up as close to the tree as they could so Will could be transported to Dr. Larkin's office in town. One man rode ahead to make sure the doctor was there. If not, he'd find him.

THE WAGON NEARED the home of Dr. Elliott Larkin, whose office and an examination/surgical room took up the front of the house. The doctor ran out to greet the wagon carrying a wooden stretcher he'd devised himself.

Henry summed up the injuries. "His legs were crushed, Doc. Branches were across him so I suspect he has internal injuries, too. He passed out when we pulled the tree off him."

"All right, let's get him inside. Go in and take him into the room on the right. Put him on top of the exam table, stretcher and all."

Dr. Elliott's wife, Sadie, came in to help. She brought a bucket of steaming water and a bucket of cool water and set them beside a table that held a couple of deep metal bowls. She opened a closet and pulled out fresh cotton dressings. The doctor asked her to fetch her sewing shears so they could cut off Will's clothes. In short order, they had him uncovered down to his underwear.

His torso was already splotchy with red and bluish bruises. "Crushed" was a good word for Henry to have used for his thighs, as they were flattened. The doctor told the men that if Will survived, he'd have to amputate both legs. The men already knew that, but even so, they didn't want to hear it. Amos turned away to silently pray again. He'd prayed most of the ride there as he'd cradled his friend's head.

As Dr. Larkin began to work on him, Will opened his eyes. At first he was disoriented but remembered when he saw the faces of his friends. He looked down at his body and he knew.

Amos jerked back around when he heard Dr. Larkin's voice. "It looks like you lost a fight with a tree, Will. Where does it hurt the most?"

Will's voice was soft. "I can't feel anything, Doc."

The doctor nodded. "I'm glad you aren't in pain."

"I'm dying, aren't I, Doc?"

The doctor looked him straight in the eye. "You've been hurt very badly, Will. I can't tell exactly how much internal bleeding is going on. I fear multiple organs are damaged. I believe your back's broken, too."

"My back?"

"Yes. Can you move your hands for me?"

They waited a few moments but there was no movement.

"Can you move anything?"

The look on Will's sunken face answered for him. "Amos,

come here." His voice sounded weakened but resolute. "Amos, see to it that Lily gets the house and the money in my account."

At that, Henry sped out the door, yelling behind him that he was going to fetch Ross Bailey, the attorney. His office was in the next block.

"Amos, promise me you'll take care of Lily for me. It'll be hard enough on her to get here and find out I'm gone." Will's voice was becoming weaker and the discolored skin now covered most of his torso. His breathing was more labored by the minute. "Hell, marry her if she'll agree to it. I can't think of another man I'd trust with her more. I know you'll take good care of her."

"I'll do that, Will, I'll take care of her. I'll see to it she has everything she needs," Amos said.

"And marry her. Tell me you'll make an effort to see if the two of you would make a match."

Amos felt conflicted, but he agreed.

Henry and Ross Bailey entered and stood at the foot of the table. "Will, the attorney's here. Tell him what you said so we'll have everything all legal."

Will looked toward the attorney and forced his eyes to focus. "I want all my worldly goods and the money in my bank account to go to Lily Holt. I want Amos Cameron to see that it's done. I want him to see that she never wants for anything."

Bailey nodded as he made notes.

"Amos, get my clothes and personal things out of the house before she gets here. I don't want her to have to deal with them. She'll need as much of a fresh start as she can get. If she wants to sell the house and move back home, that's all right, too. Or move anywhere else, but please, Amos, try to make it work between you two. You and I are so much alike, I think it's possible."

"I promise, I will." Amos turned to the attorney. "He's paralyzed. Does it matter that he can't sign his name on that paper?"

"No, not with all these witnesses, it won't. I'll have all the men here sign and that'll be sufficient," Bailey answered.

"Good." Will's voice was barely a whisper.

Amos was suddenly overcome with emotion. "Will, I'll miss you. You've been the best friend a man could have."

Will's reaction was merely a moan.

Dr. Larkin felt Will's pulse and quietly told them it wouldn't be long now. He was right.

THE NEXT DAY several men who worked with Will met at his house and began to collect his clothes and personal touches that might be painful for Lily to deal with. They agreed to each keep a memento, a remembrance of their friend. One of them kept a coat that Will wore on the coldest days. Another kept a fairly new pair of boots that fit him. Amos kept his shaving kit since it reminded him of the ribbing they'd given each other about who could grow the better beard.

Amos found a framed tintype of a young Will and his parents and set it aside. He thought Lily might be interested in keeping it. If not, he would. He found the letters Lily had written. Not sure what to do with them, he came back later with a small box and some pretty ribbon. He put the letters and the tintype in the box and tied the ribbon in a bow around it.

The men cleared Will's personal items from the house and barn and cleaned them both well. One of the older men commented that this was one of the saddest and most sobering tasks a man is ever called to do: take care of business left behind by a dear friend. They all agreed it was sad, and they wanted to make the house reflect as much happiness as it could for Lily's arrival. They worked hard to attain that goal.

CHAPTER 1

$\mathcal{L}$ily Holt didn't particularly enjoy riding trains or stagecoaches. She didn't enjoy travel much at all. It was pleasant enough, watching scenery go by, but the cold discomfort of the loud, clanging train and the horrid, dusty bumpiness of the stage offset any joy she felt. She'd be happy if she could get to Big Rock, settle down and never have to travel again.

She'd be even happier if she could get to Big Rock sooner. She smiled inwardly when she admitted to herself that she really meant she'd be happier if she could get to Will Wharton sooner. Will Wharton. *I'll be Mrs. Will Wharton. Lily Wharton.*

Her friends back in Nebraska couldn't believe she was bold enough to become a mail order bride for a lumberjack she'd never even met. She couldn't believe it either at first, but now she knew in her bones, in her very soul, that it was the right move for her.

There were eligible men in Lincoln, but she was never interested in them. Some had called on her, but she rarely agreed to see them a second time, and only one young man had called on her a third time before she tactfully explained that she didn't see the relationship growing. They were what she thought of as city men. Lily thought that might not be a fair assessment since she was a city girl, through and through. But she couldn't help it. City men didn't appeal to her.

Her father and her uncle had been big, burly, take-charge kind of men, raised in an isolated cabin and brought up to take care of themselves. They could fell their own trees, build a house, hunt and fish to feed their families, catch and tame wild horses, and outsmart grizzlies if the situation demanded. The men she met back in Lincoln all seemed inadequate compared to her father. She doubted if they'd ever even had a calloused hand. She felt sure they wouldn't fare well in a survival situation. They seemed small. At least that's how she thought of them, small and soft.

Lily had idolized her father. Although she wouldn't have criticized her mother aloud, she never thought it was fair that she had forced Lily's father to move to the city. Apparently, theirs was a powerful love, because he gave up the life he wanted to make her happy. It was tragically romantic in a way, but Lily always wondered what it would have been like if she'd been raised in his world instead of her mother's.

She might not have been able to get an education and receive a teaching certificate, for one thing. Although she hadn't had a teaching position yet, she looked forward to it. She knew there was an opening for a teacher in Big Rock, and Will had agreed to allow her to teach if the town wanted to hire her. In one of his letters, he said he'd be 'proud to be married to a woman who would mold young minds, teach them to think for themselves, and always be eager to learn more, even after they'd outgrown her classroom.'

Lily thought of Will's letters, now tucked away in the satchel at her feet. She'd read them so many times she had much of them committed to memory. They were a treasure to her. Sometimes she imagined one of her descendants, perhaps a grand-daughter, going through her personal things after her death and stumbling across the letters. Lily smiled and wondered if she'd be surprised that her grandpa had once been quite the romantic suitor. She imagined what the young woman might think when she read the intimate passages where Will expressed his desire for her, where he described what he wanted to do with her and to her, and how he wanted her body to respond to him.

Perhaps when they were married, she would store their letters together, so that her imaginary granddaughter could read her letters, too, and see the entire correspondence unfold. The poor thing might be scandalized to read about how eager Lily was to become one with Will, to surrender herself completely to the man she would vow to honor and obey for the rest of her life. She'd read how Lily told him she was eager to kiss his mouth and feel his touch on her skin, to take him inside her body and know the very heights of sensual joy that can be shared by lovers. The young woman would surely be surprised at the letters her grandma wrote. *I was surprised at myself when I wrote them!*

Lily heard the horses' hooves clip-clop the miles away. They would arrive in Big Rock soon. She took a deep, steadying breath and realized she wasn't nervous after all. She felt confident that her decision to come and marry a *real man* was the right one, and Will was the right man. If he'd been honest in his letters, she knew she would adore him.

She was eager to meet him and taste their first kiss. She'd wondered many times how his strong arms would feel around her, and even now with their meeting imminent, she yearned to feel that touch.

We're getting married this afternoon. Tonight, I'll know his touch and he'll know mine. We'll join the number of lovers through the ages who have felt that fullness of joy, the connection of hearts and souls that binds us together for eternity. Tonight, I'll be Mrs. Will Wharton, his wife in every sense.

∼

AMOS CAMERON DID NOT LOOK FORWARD to meeting the stage. As Will's best friend, he felt it was his duty to break the terrible news to Lily that her betrothed had been killed and buried while she was *en route*. He'd discussed it with Harriet and they agreed that he, Harriet and the pastor, Reverend Copperfield, should probably be the ones to greet her when she arrived. She might want to talk with the lawyer, but that could wait. Harriet wanted to be there since she represented the Ladies' Aid Society who arranged for Lily and Will to correspond. The pastor should be there to offer comfort and consolation at her time of loss and sorrow. Amos had to be there because Will asked him to take care of Lily. He wasn't going to tell her that Will wanted them to marry, and he hoped none of the others who knew would mention it. Even if he did decide to pursue a union with her, this wasn't the time to bring it up.

The mood was somber as the three of them waited for the stage. They stood on the street, away from the area where the coach would stop so they wouldn't block the sidewalk. It was decided that Amos would fetch her and bring her where the others stood so they could have a little spot of privacy to break the news. After that, they'd take her to her house, the house Will left for her. The Ladies' Aid Society members had brought food so there would be plenty to eat.

"How do you tell a woman the man she came halfway across the country to marry died before she arrived?" Amos asked no one in particular.

"You do it with compassion," the pastor said. "Then we take our cues from her. Will she cry? Will she be too stunned to cry? Will she get hysterical? Frightened? Remember, she's already tired and stressed from a long journey. Then to have this dropped on her, well, there's no telling how she might respond. The poor girl. What an awful position to be in. Having your hopes and a happy future ripped from you by strangers. Poor, poor girl. I hope she's a woman of faith so she can call upon the strength and comfort of God."

"Will said she is, Reverend."

"Good. Did he tell you if she was leaning toward accepting the teaching job? I hope she'll still be willing to do that. What if she wants to go back home?" Harriet asked.

"We'll all do our best to get her to stay," Amos said.

The sound of the approaching stage got their attention. Harriet put her hand on Amos' arm in a silent gesture of good luck for his unpleasant duty.

Amos stood near the door of the coach, far enough away so people could disembark, but close enough to step up and help Lily step down when he saw her.

Two older women stepped down, steadied by another woman who was obviously there to greet them. A very attractive young woman, eyes bright with expectation, stepped into the doorway. He stepped forward.

"Miss Lily?" He held up his hand to take hers.

"Mr. Wharton?" she asked with a smile.

"I'm afraid not, Miss Lily. I'm Amos Cameron, Will's best friend. Let's step over this way." He held her upper arm, gently pulling her.

She was willing to get out of the way of the stagecoach crowd, but not willing to get too far before she found out why Will wasn't there.

"Mr. Cameron, um, Mr. Cameron. Stop!" He stopped, not because she asked him to, but because she stopped walking. "Where is Will?"

"He won't be able to meet you. Come on over here and we can explain."

"No. What's going on? Why won't he be able to meet me?"

She wasn't going to wait until they reached the others. Amos turned to look squarely at her. "Will was badly injured in a logging accident. A tree fell on him. He lived long enough for us to get him to the doctor's office. He died four days ago and we buried him two days ago. I'm very sorry, Miss Lily, very sorry."

The color drained from Lily's face. "No! No, that can't be. What'll I do? I can't go back home now. I can't afford another ticket." Her voice was raised, shocked with a little panic.

"You don't have to worry about anything, Miss Lily," Amos said as he once again took her arm and propelled her toward Harriet and the pastor. "Will provided for you. My friends and I will explain everything when we get to your house."

"My house?"

"Yes. Will left it to you."

"My own house?"

"Yes, ma'am. Will was adamant that you get all his assets. You have a house and a modest bank account. Will put most of his money into building his home. But there's enough money to sustain you for quite a while, over a year, I imagine. Enough for your needs, enough to feed the horses, and I'm sure, for any other things you might want."

"He died four days ago?"

Harriet answered, "Yes, dear, he did. There was no way we could reach you on the train. We're so sorry to see you have to go through this. We were all looking forward to today being a happy occasion."

"Did he have to suffer much? Please tell me he didn't die in pain."

"He didn't," Amos said. "The tree paralyzed him. He couldn't feel anything."

"Thank Heaven for that. I can hardly believe it," Lily said. "I never even got to meet him in person."

"He was a good man," Reverend Copperfield said. "He was a church-going man, and as far as I could tell, he walked with God in his day-to-day life."

Amos let go of her arm, but she almost immediately took hold of it again. "I don't feel very steady right now. I need to sit down."

"We'll get you home. Right now." Amos helped her up onto the buggy, then excused himself to get her bags and two big boxes. Harriet in her own buggy and the pastor on his horse, rode on ahead.

"So, you're the Amos I read about in Will's letters. How long have you been friends?"

"Since we were boys in school. People said we were just alike. And I suppose we were."

"He said you're on the list of men who are seeking wives. But he spoke up first so he got a bride first."

Amos chuckled. "That's about right. I'm confident my time's coming."

"That's a long time to be friends, or a long time to stay friends, I should say."

"We got along from the very start. Our lives paralleled in interesting ways. When we were still in school, my mother passed away within a couple of months of his father passing. That was hard but we had each other to talk to. Then in our first year of college, both our remaining parents died in the same month. We took it hard, both of us. We quit school and drifted for a while. Landed here in Big Rock."

"Sometime you'll have to tell me how that happened. You know, I have several letters from Will and he told me his parents were gone, but he never told me the circumstances. I didn't even know he ever attended college."

"We didn't for long. We figured out that it prepares you for a life of staying inside and working at a desk, and neither of us wanted that. We both needed to be out in the open, not watching life pass by through a window. That wasn't how we wanted to live. So we never went back."

"And never regretted it, either, I imagine."

"Yes, ma'am, you're right about that."

"He told me you helped each other build your houses."

"Yes, ma'am, that's right. We didn't get to finish his front porch. Your front porch, that is. Or get a handrail on the back steps. I will finish that for you. I promise I will."

"I hate to ask that of you, but I suppose I'll need them to be completed."

"Yes. And I intend to. We were hoping to get it done before you arrived."

There was no more conversation until they arrived at her new home.

"Now, dear," Harriet said as she poured coffee into their cups, "The Ladies' Aid Society members have brought you food so you don't have to worry about cooking for a while. I know you must still be in shock. Now listen to me, Lily." Harriet sat and took her hand. "If it's too upsetting for you to stay in this house, I want you to come stay with me for a while. There's also the boarding house you could stay in. The town added extra rooms just for our mail order brides to stay in until they marry or find employment. We named it the Bride & Board. You wouldn't have to pay; our prospective brides stay there rent-free."

Lily looked around at the kitchen Will had built with her in mind. "It wouldn't seem right to live anywhere else. I don't think I would be honoring Will's memory if I didn't stay here. He built this place for us and he left it for me. It's a fine house. I want to live here and respect his wishes. I owe him that."

Amos and the pastor nodded their appreciation.

"I hope that means you intend to stay and accept the position as our schoolteacher," Reverend Copperfield said. "I'm on the school committee, and we sure are hoping you'll agree to teach our children."

"I can't go back home and I don't plan to go anywhere else," Lily said. "So, yes, I'll need that position."

"Wonderful!" both Harriet and the pastor said at almost the same time.

Reverend Copperfield reached into his vest pocket and took out a key. "Here you go, Miss Lily, this is yours. Amos can take you to see the schoolhouse anytime you like. I'd say the sooner the better so you can see what kind of supplies you'll need. You can let me know, or you can go ahead and purchase what you want at the mercantile and tell them it's for the school. They'll bill the town's account that's set aside for it."

"When you mentioned Will leaving you the house, it reminded me of something. You need to sign a paper at the bank to be on Will's account," Amos said. "I'll take you there tomorrow, too. We should probably check at the lawyer's office to see if there's anything you need to sign to have the deed transferred to your name."

"I appreciate that since I don't know my way around yet. You're being awfully generous with your time, Mr. Cameron. Don't you have to work tomorrow?"

"No, you're my priority for a few days. Will was my best friend, you know. He asked me on his deathbed to take care of you, look after the place, and make sure you don't need anything. Henry and Angus—they own the mill—were heartbroken that Will lost his life in their employ and while they were on the job. They want to help, too. When things have settled down, they'd like to meet you. In the meantime, I'm at your disposal."

"Oh, my," Lily said, "I don't want to be a burden to you."

"You aren't a burden. Besides, it wouldn't matter if you

were." Amos gave a rueful grin. "A man doesn't break a deathbed promise to his best friend."

Harriet stood and began to tidy the kitchen and put some of the food away. "I know you're worn out, dear, and you probably feel like a wrung out rag. I'll leave here in just a few minutes. Promise me you'll get some rest."

"I am tired. I think I'm going to need some time to let all this soak in. It's so much! But I thank you all for your kindness. Will said there were good people in this town. He was right about that."

Harriet dried her hands and leaned over to kiss Lily's forehead. "Anything, remember, Lily. If you need anything at all. Perhaps Amos can show you where I live while you're out tomorrow. You're always welcome."

Reverend Copperfield said a prayer asking blessings of grace and strength for Lily as she began her new life among new friends, then he and Harriet left.

Amos and Lily remained at the table, sipping their coffee.

"I should leave and let you rest," Amos said. "I'll get out of here and tend to the horses in a few minutes."

"I'm tired but I couldn't sleep now anyway. Too many thoughts and questions swirling in my head. Would you mind to to stay to help me sort things out? I think talking to someone who knew Will would help."

"Of course, I will," he said, then he smiled. "But I'm still going to have to tend to the horses before too long. You can go with me if you'd like. They're your horses."

"Then I should definitely go with you. I've never had my own horse before. I hope you don't mind teaching me how to take care of them. I'm a city girl, remember."

"I remember. And I'll be happy to teach you, but I don't mind taking care of both our stock. I live next door, you know."

"Oh, that's right. Will said you bought property together so you'd be neighbors. It's good to know I'll have a friend nearby."

"You haven't even seen the whole house yet. Let me show you your new home, then I'll show you the barn."

"All right, that sounds like a good plan."

Amos led her through the home, pointing out features as they went. The water closet held a nice tub and had a flushing toilet. Lily was glad to see that because she was accustomed to the one they had in their apartment back in Lincoln. She had running cold water but would have to heat water for bathing and cleaning. Will had included a mudroom, too, and Lily was impressed. It was roomier than she expected such a room would be. There was a closet, but there were also hooks on the wall to hang coats and other winter wear. In front of the hooks was a plain but sturdy wooden bench. Lily thought it would be an ideal place to put on and take off muddy boots. There was a huge sink, too, and she could picture herself using it to wash laundry items or clean up after having been outside getting dirty.

The two bedrooms and the parlor were all on one side of the house, and the wet rooms were on the other. When she commented on it, Amos explained that it made the plumbing easier that way. They had done the same thing at his house.

"Is your house just like this one?"

"In most ways, but mine's a few square feet larger. I added a third bedroom, another small one. I have one bedroom about the size of yours, and two smaller ones," Amos answered with a shrug. "You never know how many children you might have. Will figured if he needed more rooms, he'd build on later. Let's go jump on the buggy and I'll show you your barn."

On the ride to the barn in the backyard, Lily spied the outhouse. "Well, I know what that is. I don't need a tour of it. I like how he put a star on the door instead of the usual half-moon."

Amos chuckled. "That was the first thing we built when we got started. He wanted it to be just a little different from what

17

most people had. Next, we dug his well. After that, I insisted we build something for me, so we started on my house. For the longest time, I used his well water and outhouse. After that, we'd build on each other's things a while, than catch the other one up. Mine's all done. All we had left was the work on your place that I already told you about. Well, that and fences. We both wanted fences, at least around the barns."

"I'm very impressed that you both could do all this yourselves. Did you fell your own trees?"

Amos grinned again. "Yes, but not because we were big he-men who went out and tamed the forest. We work at the sawmill so it was our job. Didn't hurt that we get a discount on lumber," he added.

Amos hoped to change the subject. He didn't want to get into the territory of talking about Will's death on the job. "I'm proud of our barns. They're a good size. Nice and sturdy and built to be strong against winter winds. There's enough room for this buggy, too. It shouldn't stay out in the snow and ice."

Lily didn't know what barns normally look like, but she was impressed with hers. "It's so organized in here. It looks like a place for everything and at least right now, everything's in its place."

"Don't get too accustomed to that. I may well slip up and neglect to keep it that way all the time. Will didn't, either, to tell the truth." Amos hesitated a moment. "Before Will passed, he asked all of us, his friends with him at the time, to clean up the place and make it ready for you, so you could start over fresh. He wanted it to be clean, with his personal items removed so you didn't have to have sad reminders facing you every day."

"Oh, my. What a thoughtful man. It seems I would have been a very lucky woman if we could have married as we planned. It isn't ours to question, though, is it?"

"I questioned," Amos said. "I got angry. I was more angry

than sad he'd been taken from us. He was closer to me than a brother could be."

"Mr. Cameron, everyone has been so solicitous of me since I've been here. Now I'm almost embarrassed at the outpouring, considering your loss. The truth is I never even met Will in person, and you've suffered an even more terrible sorrow. I am so very sorry you lost your lifelong friend."

"Thank you, Miss Lily. I think the main thing helping me get through it is that he left me instructions." A grin showed through the sadness on his face. "There are things I promised to do, and I will do them. You might get tired of seeing me, but that's just going to have to be your misfortune."

"Perhaps not, Mr. Cameron. Maybe it'll be a good tonic for us both, mourning his loss together while trying to move on."

"Please call me Amos."

"All right. You don't have to call me 'Miss,' either. You aren't one of my students."

"I'll try, but I might slip up."

As Lily watched, Amos explained how he unhooked the team from the buggy. She watched as he moved the buggy out of the way and thought it would be heavier than it was. He explained that the weight was balanced over the wheels, making it easy to move. He showed her how to remove the tack from the horses, then he showed her how to comb and rub down the animals. She helped with the last part and enjoyed it.

"You can help anytime you like, but I'll be taking care of the animals myself for the foreseeable future."

"You don't trust me?"

"It's not a matter of trust. I like taking care of animals. I guess I still think of these as Will's horses."

Lily gave a little shrug. "I can understand that. Sometime I want you to show me how to saddle one, too, if you don't mind."

"I'll be happy to, but I don't want you going anywhere without me."

"Amos, I can't depend on you for everything. There will be times when I need to go to the store for something, and I shouldn't have to wait for you."

"In time. But for now, I'd feel better if I were with you. Humor me, please. I need to do this."

She decided not to argue. It would be nice to have company to show her the town and introduce her to people. She'd make the best of it. She'd do it for Will.

When they were through taking care of the horses, Amos mentioned there was something he meant to show her earlier when they walked through the house. Once inside again, he led her to the larger bedroom, the one Will had slept in and he presumed the one she'd sleep in.

He reached up on a shelf in the closet and handed her a box with ribbon tied around it. "These were on the table beside his bed and I figured you'd want to keep them. They're the letters you wrote to him. They were loose so I found a nice box to put them in."

"Oh." She hesitated. "Amos, did you read them?"

"No, no, of course not. I didn't let anyone else read them, either. There's one other thing in there I thought you would like to have. It's a tintype of Will and his parents. Looks like he was around twelve or thirteen when it was taken."

She untied the ribbon and took out the photographic image and gently ran her fingers across it. "So this is our Will. That face shows a little bit of angel and devil, I think."

Amos grinned. "That's an apt description."

"Something tells me you let the devil part of him lead you into temptation."

Amos laughed at that. "Yes, ma'am, I did, whenever I wasn't leading him. 'Two peas in a pod' they called us. Oh, before I forget, Will's guns are there in the corner of the closet. He has a rifle and two pistols. Do you know how to shoot?"

"I do," she said. "Daddy taught me how. He used to take me out to the country to practice."

"Good for him."

Lily set the box on the bed and led the way back to the kitchen. "Let's see what we have for supper in here."

"All right. While we're at it, pay attention to what you need from the mercantile. We can go tomorrow when I'm showing you around."

"Tomorrow's going to be another big day. Let's see, we'll go to see the lawyer, go to the bank, go to the schoolhouse, and go to the store."

"Maybe the restaurant for lunch, too. Mary's one of the best cooks around here."

"That would be nice."

Over supper they discussed plans for the next day and Amos told her about some of the people she'd meet.

"It's entirely possible we'll see Harriet and her husband Arthur at the restaurant. They eat there pretty often."

"That would be nice. I'd like to tell her how much I appreciate her kindness today."

Amos sported a broad grin and nodded. "That's the most subdued I've ever seen Harriet. It shows just how much she was concerned for your welfare. Harriet's normally much more outgoing and lively. Always in a good mood, always being the first to greet people. She knows everybody and usually, everybody's business. But people let her get away with it because she does it in such a charming way."

"I look forward to getting to know her better. She sounds like fun."

"She is. Our lawyer, Ross Bailey, is a quiet man, on the serious side. I think he's a widower. The people who own the mercantile, Shirley and Clint Keller, are good people, too.

Mary, at the restaurant, is a short little thing, and I'll warn you, she hugs. She's another one who never met a stranger."

"Amos?"

"Yes?"

"Before you bring me home tomorrow, will you take me to the cemetery?"

"Yes, ma'am, I surely will."

LILY UNPACKED her bags of clothes, then opened the crate that held other things. She had books and notebooks, her mother's teapot and teacups, her father's hunting knife, his six-shooter, and some embroidered tablecloths and napkins. She had a photograph of her mother and father that she knew she wanted to display prominently.

She realized just how tired she was and decided to put the items away at a later time. For now, she'd just set them out of the way. Too tired to heat water and prepare a bath, she took off her clothes and sponged off with cool water, then found her favorite nightgown.

Lily crawled in bed and opened the box that contained the letters she'd written to Will. She carefully checked the dates of each one and inserted his letters so they would be in proper order. As she read some of the passages again, she had a troubling thought.

I expected to marry this man. Only days ago he slept in this very bed. If he had lived, he'd be in bed with me right now, and I would be his. Did I love him? I thought I fell in love with him through these letters. Is that even possible? Maybe I didn't love him. Maybe love would have grown between us after we were together. No, perhaps I wasn't in love after all. How else can I explain not shedding a single tear for the man I was to wed?

Amos sat at his table with a small whiskey, thinking about what an emotionally exhausting day it had been. His eye caught the light in the bedroom of the house across their massive yards.

Will, my friend, I wish you were still here with us. You'd be with your wife in that bedroom enjoying your wedding night. Instead, you're in the cold ground and she's mourning your loss, as am I. You were right to send for her. She's a pretty thing, and smart, and she's touched by how you thought of her in your last moments and provided for her. She knows what a good man you were. Lily would have made you a fine wife, Will, a fine one. You should still be here. That damned tree.

Amos downed the last few sips of whiskey and slammed the glass down on the table. And just as he had done the night Will died, he sobbed.

CHAPTER 2

*L*ily woke when the bright morning sun fell across her
face. When she opened her eyes and realized whose
bed she was in, the memories of yesterday flooded
back. Will was dead and she was starting over. She crawled out
of bed and smoothed down the top quilt. She'd hung her robe
on a hook the night before, and while she put it on she slipped
her house shoes on her feet.

The morning had brought a chill so she decided to start a
fire in the kitchen stove before she even relieved herself. In the
kitchen she mentally thanked Amos for being thoughtful
enough to bring in the firewood for her the night before. She
put on a pot of coffee and a big pot of water for cleaning later
and went to the water closet.

She saw something she'd missed before and smiled, wishing
she could thank Will. There was a small stove on a stone floor
behind the tub. Her water closet back home didn't have one,
and that made for quick visits and short baths. Other than in
hotels, she'd never seen a stove in a water closet. This was a
luxury, especially in the west where accommodations were
generally much cruder. She knew people who, even back in a

24

big city like Lincoln, didn't even have water closets or stationary tubs with a drain. They brought in tubs and placed them near the fireplace and used chamber pots that usually sat in an unused corner when it wasn't convenient to go to the outhouse.

Will had built in some cabinets for storage and she opened the doors to take stock. He had a few towels and washcloths and a new bar of soap still wrapped in paper. Another opened cabinet door revealed a bottle of iodine and strips of cotton that looked like they were made from an old sheet or pillowcase. The cabinet closest to the toilet was empty and Lily knew she would use it to store her menstrual rags. She glanced around the toilet again to confirm there was space to put a bucket to soak the bloody rags, and there was. She smiled, remembering how her mother used the bloody water to feed their plants. *I need a plant or two. Next spring, I'll plant flowers out front and maybe a small vegetable garden.*

In the kitchen she sliced some bread to toast in butter in a skillet, then she heard a noise from the back yard. Lily ran to the back door and saw it was Amos coming out of her barn.

"Good morning," she called out to him, waving. "Have you eaten breakfast yet?"

"No, just coffee."

"Come on in. I was just about to scramble some eggs."

"Are you sure?" he asked.

"Of course, come on in. I have a fresh pot of coffee, too."

AMOS WENT in and washed his hands before sitting at the table. He took in the sight of Lily and felt just a little bit uncomfortable being there alone with her. Her robe covered everything a dress would, but something about it seemed intimate. Especially with her long hair still disheveled from lying in bed. That wasn't something he should be thinking about. If Will had lived, she would be his wife by now.

Lily brought him a plate heaped with scrambled eggs and fried bread. "There's jam there on the table and cream and sugar for your coffee if you like."

"Oh, I like my coffee strong and black," he said. "One time Will said the perfect coffee for me would be so strong it would keep its shape outside of the cup."

"I'm afraid I don't have that much coffee in the house. You'll have to settle for this," she said as she smiled and sat down.

Amos thought this must be what it would be like to be married. A woman to make breakfast for you, sitting across your table looking much like she did in your arms in bed just a little while ago. His heart ached for Will's loss.

I need to think of other things.

"I think we should go to Ross Bailey's office first. He's the lawyer. You may need to sign papers, and he can tell you if there are any other things we need to take care of," Amos said. "Then we can go to the bank. I can drive around and show you the town if you like. It might still be too early to eat lunch by then, so we could go ahead and stop at the mercantile." He looked up from his eggs and smiled at her. "Don't forget your list."

"I won't. It's already in my bag, along with a pencil in case I think of something else."

"Well, if you forget something, we can always go back. If it's lunchtime by then, we can go on and eat. If not, there might be enough time to go to the schoolhouse."

"I hope we can eat first. I don't want to be rushed when I check out the school."

Amos nodded at her. "I'll make sure you have plenty of time there. We aren't in a rush."

"Do you know who taught last year? Or the year before?"

"I'm embarrassed to admit I'm not completely sure. I mean,

I don't have any children so I didn't pay much attention. Seems like it was mainly one lady year before last, she's Angus' wife, and last year, I think two or three women took turns."

"I wonder how that worked out," she said.

"Not as well as they hoped, I don't think. But they didn't want to go a year without school at all, and it was the best they could do."

"No wonder they want a teacher so badly. I was surprised when I found out how much they were willing to pay a teacher. It's more than they pay teachers in Lincoln, especially inexperienced ones."

"That is good news. I didn't know they did that."

"Yes, it is very good news. Thanks to Will, I don't have rent to pay so I should be able to build up some savings unless something catastrophic happens." She paused. "I owe him for not only my home, but a secure future. I sure wish I could thank him."

Amos smiled, gratified that Lily recognized how much Will had done for her. "Will was like that. And I think, somehow, maybe he knows how much you appreciate it. I like to think so."

Lily took a deep breath. "Well, these dishes aren't going to clean themselves. If you want to go back to your house, just give me time to tidy up in here and get changed."

"No, let me clean up," Amos said. "By the time you're dressed, I'll have this kitchen spotless. It's the least I can do after you made breakfast."

"Are you sure?"

"Positive," he said as he picked up their plates.

"All right, then. I'll try to be quick."

"Take your time."

Amos watched her walk away, then chided himself for doing it. Her robe was form-fitting and he didn't feel right watching her form. She was Will's woman.

He finished in the kitchen before she was ready, so he yelled out that he'd bring the buggy around for her. She answered, and he left by the front door. He was afraid if he walked through the house to the back door, he might see her before she was fully dressed.

THEIR FIRST STOP was at Ross Bailey's law office. Mr. Bailey was a quiet, somber man who inspired clients to have confidence in him. He had some papers for her to sign and he took the time to explain what each paragraph meant. It lengthened their stay more than they had planned, but Lily felt assured when they left. Mr. Bailey said when he'd filed the papers, he would personally deliver the deed to her home.

As Mr. Bailey walked them to the door, he said, "You know, Miss Holt, I was there when your fiancé breathed his last. His thoughts were of you until the very end. You and Amos, that is. He instructed Amos to take good care of you and I trust he will. When he said Amos was the only man he'd trust to—"

"Yes, it was a sad day. I told Miss Holt already how I promised Will I'd take care of her and help her every way I can. Thank you, Mr. Bailey, we'll be going now." He shook the man's hand.

Lily looked at Amos as they made their way to the bank. *Did he cut that man off before he could finish his sentence? It sure sounded like it. Was Bailey about to say something that might upset me? Is Amos keeping something from me? Maybe he didn't cut him off. Maybe he was eager to get on with our business. Still, it surely did seem like he cut him off mid-sentence.*

"Lily? You seem a million miles away. Is something bothering you? Can I do something for you?"

"Oh, no," she said, brought out of her inner thoughts. "I was just thinking of the things I want to get done today. I can't wait to see the school building."

"You have a school with a steeple. It used to be the church, then it was both school and church. As the town grew, so did church membership, and we outgrew the building. So we built a new church house and you now have a dedicated schoolhouse. Good thing. Everybody secretly hated rearranging chairs and tables and pews before service every Sunday."

Lily smiled at that. "I can see how it would be annoying."

Their trip to the bank was a quick one. She just needed to sign one thing and she was done. The employee she dealt with first offered his sympathy for her loss, and she wondered if everyone who met her would do that. She was afraid the constant reminders might keep her from thinking thoughts of moving forward. Before they left, the clerk asked if she'd like to withdraw some cash, but she declined. She still had money left in her bag that she'd brought with her from Lincoln.

Amos decided to take a circuitous route to the mercantile so he could point out some homes and businesses she might be interested in. In the block next to the one with Bailey's office, he pointed to the shingle hanging outside Dr. Elliott Larkin's house.

"The front rooms are set up as his office and an examination room and surgery."

"So that's where... it happened."

"Yes." They were silent for a few moments. "Now up ahead is the boarding house. Since the town bought it from the previous owner, they've added several rooms specifically for our mail order brides. It's the place Harriet was talking about yesterday."

"I remember. The 'Bride & Board' is a cute name."

"Harriet chose it."

Lily chuckled. "That figures."

"If we were to turn around and keep on this road behind

us, we'd come to some of the bigger ranches around here. Some of them have children you'll be teaching." He took another turn and Lily noticed fewer houses and no businesses. "This is the one side of town that doesn't have much development. See that road? It's hardly a road. I guess it's a trail. Anyway, that trail leads to what we call the Low Quarter. It's about the only place around here that's good for any crops, because of the lower elevation. It stays wetter. The soil is more fertile than the rest of the ground around here. We think it's an old, mostly dried out lakebed. Everyplace else is too rocky to grow much."

"There are farms there?"

"A few, if you could call them that. They grow alfalfa mainly. It's where most of the hay for our horses comes from. They bring in bales and sell them to the mercantile in the fall. They grow a few vegetables. And fruit trees, some of them have fruit trees. They bring eggs, and the ladies make jams and jellies and such to sell, too."

"The way you describe it, it sounds like a whole other town. I would think the trail would be more established, then."

"Well, the hay is seasonal, as are the fruit products. They bring in eggs every week or two. There's a flip side to it being wetter and more fertile there. In the summer everything gets so overgrown it encroaches on the trail. When it comes time to bring in the hay in wagons, the men have to keep stopping to hack out a clear path wide enough to drive through."

"That sounds awful," Lily said.

"It's inconvenient and it's hard work. I don't envy them. I like it just fine where I am."

"Me, too. It's private but still close to town. You and Will chose well."

Amos took another turn that led back into the town proper. "The next street over has the saloons. I'm not going to drive by them."

"That's fine," she said with a big grin. "I don't get to saloons very often."

He grinned, too. "One of them is just a saloon. I mean, there aren't any upstairs women. It's called the Buckin' Bronc and it's actually a good place. Lots of men take their wives. Once in a while they book a traveling musical guest or an acting troupe and you can bring the whole family. They have more than just alcohol to serve. The other saloon, the Big Rock Poker Palace, is a bad place. Believe me, no man would want his wife in there."

"It's a safe bet that I'll stay away from that street."

"This is where you can take your laundry if you don't want to wash it yourself. I take mine there. It's run by a widow woman and her children. They do good work."

"Oh, that is good to know. When school starts, I'll have much less time to do things like that."

"All right, we're back to the main street now." He pulled the buggy to a stop. "Most of the town is to the right, but I want to point out a few things first before we head that way. This is the main street in and out of town. A few miles that way is the copper mine. You'll find a few houses between here and there. Most belong to the miners who are married. They have a barracks, or bunkhouse, for single men who don't want to drive back and forth to the boarding house every day. About a mile down, there's a road that goes off to the right, and it meets up with another road that goes up to Separation. That's another stop on the Union Pacific line. There are two or three other sizable ranches out that way."

He *hyahed* and gently whipped the reins, and the horses moved again. "You might appreciate that place," he said as he nodded his chin toward a white house. "It's the dressmaker, Mrs. Canfield. I hear she's good. She's also a tailor and can make men's suits."

"Are her things expensive?"

31

"Lily, I have no idea. I'm a simple man and I buy my clothes at the mercantile. We can stop in if you'd like."

"No," she said with a chuckle, "maybe another time. I don't need any clothes right now."

"We're coming up to where you got off the stagecoach, but I suspect you didn't get a chance to look around."

"You're right about that. The surroundings are just a fuzzy memory."

"Well, the hotel, jailhouse, and stagecoach depot are close to each other. The newspaper office is close, too. You can see it's a house. The rooms with the printing press and telegraph are at the front of the first floor."

"I see."

"And we're coming up on the general store and mercantile. Mary's Restaurant is right across the road. Are you getting hungry, or would you rather do your shopping first?"

"Let's eat. Is that all right with you? I know it's a little early still."

"It's fine with me. You'd be hard pressed to find a time when I won't be willing to eat."

"Well, you *are* a big bear of a man," she said, hoping she wasn't insulting him. "It probably takes a lot of food to keep you going."

He grinned and she was a little relieved. "My mother always said I was a bottomless pit. I've always been that way."

"I'll remember that the next time I make you scrambled eggs."

Amos helped her down to the ground and led her inside the restaurant. It wasn't crowded; they were a bit early. Mary came out of the kitchen and saw them. She held up her arms. "You must be our Lily. I'm glad Amos brought you here. Honey, I'm so sorry for what happened." Mary hugged her, hard. She looked over Mary's head at Amos and he gave a tiny shrug. When Mary let her go, she took her by the hand. "You must be hungry, so let's find you a good table. Here you go, by the window. Best seats in the house. Will you have tea to drink?"

Both of them nodded. "All right, I'll be right back then. Decide what you want to eat. Your choices are on that blackboard."

"Mary's a little whirlwind," Amos said. "An enthusiastic and demonstrative whirlwind."

"I believe you."

"But she loves everybody and we all love her right back. Oh, shoot, that reminds me, I forgot to point out Harriet's house. It's on this road, but back past the newspaper office. Two-story white clapboard house. Green shutters on the windows."

"I remember it," Lily said. "It had a red door."

"That's the place."

Mary brought their drinks and a basket of breads. They ordered their food, and then each of them relaxed and looked out the window.

"Oh, look," Lily said as she pointed. "I see two steeples over there, two or three blocks over. You didn't drive me down that road because we're going to go there last, right?"

"Yes, ma'am." Amos paused. "Remember I told you the school building used to be the church. Well, the cemetery is behind the school. I hope it won't bother you to see Will's grave every day."

"Maybe I can turn it into a positive thing. I'll think of the good things he did for me and make the sight of his grave a reminder of how grateful I am to him."

"Lily, that was a nice thought, and beautifully said. I surely do wish you could have met him."

"Me, too, Amos. Me, too."

It was a short ride to the other side of the street, and they shared a little laugh about it. Lily took out her list and started walking up and down the aisles, seeing what all they stocked. Occasionally, she picked up something on her list and put it in her basket that Amos carried. She picked up a bottle of carbolic acid and put it in the basket.

"Carbolic acid? Are you planning to get hurt?"

"No," she said with an embarrassed little grin. "Will had a bottle of iodine in a cupboard with some bandages. It reminded me of how my mom and dad swore by carbolic acid to clean a wound, and iodine mixed with sugar to treat it. Or honey," she added. "Now I'm ready when my clumsy side comes out."

"Always good to be prepared," he said with a nod. "I know where to go if I get hurt."

Lily picked up just a couple of other things and led Amos to the front desk to check out. There was no one there, so she tapped the little bell to alert someone.

Shirley came almost running through the door from the back storeroom. When she saw Amos, she knew who the young woman was. "You must be Lily. I'm Shirley Keller. I'm in the Ladies' Aid Society. Lily, we all felt awful about what happened to your Will. We're thrilled you decided to stay."

"Thank you, I appreciate it. I noticed you have some slates and chalk in stock, and some writing tablets, too. The reverend said I could get things for the classroom and let you know, and you would charge it to the town. Is that how it works?"

"Yes, it is. If we don't have what you need, we can order it. Let me see, I think I have a catalog of teaching supplies in here somewhere. Yes, here it is. Why don't you just take this and keep it? I can order whatever you need; you just let me know."

"Wonderful! Amos is taking me to see the schoolhouse when we leave here. I'll make a list of items we need."

They checked out and made their way to the school. Amos pulled up and stopped the horses, then he noticed something.

"It looks like Jeb got Will's tombstone out here already. I figured it would take longer."

"Let's go look at it now before we go inside," Lily suggested, and he helped her down.

When they reached it, Lily read the words under the dates of his birth and death. "William B. Wharton, a good man and a great friend." She looked back up at him. "You told him what to inscribe, didn't you?"

He nodded.

"Amos, it's perfect. So few words that convey so much."

"Will would have wanted it kept simple. He'd have been happy with just RIP on it. Hell, he'd have been happy with no marker at all."

"I'm glad you got one for him. I can't think of a better thing to say about a man than that."

"Come on," Amos said. "Let's go see where you'll be teaching those ragamuffins."

"Good thing you're smiling, talking about my students like that."

The room was fairly big as schoolrooms go, and Lily knew it was because it had been a church in the beginning. There was a cloakroom to the right at the entrance, with hooks all around the wall. To the left there was a bench against the wall. In the main room there was a pot-bellied stove near the wall on the right. There were a few single-unit desks with the writing surface connected to the chair. They had holes for inkwells and indentations in the wood at the top to keep pens or pencils from rolling. There was a place to store books under the seats. In addition to the desks, there were tables and benches and two unmatched chairs.

A table and chair were at the front of the room, offset to the left, and Lily surmised that was so it didn't block anyone's view of the blackboard. On the table were two piles of books, two or three composition notebooks and a stack of slates. There was another stack of books on the floor. Lily made her way to the front, hoping one of the notebooks was the teacher's gradebook from last year. One was, and she sat down to examine it.

Amos pulled one of the chairs to the table next to Lily and sat down. He pulled out the other notebooks and opened one. He chuckled and Lily looked up.

"I have in my hands an item that could secure my financial future. It's a whole notebook of tests and answers. I bet some of those students would rob the bank to get hold of this."

"Well, if I see you suddenly splurge on frivolous things, I'll know what you did, so you'd better be careful. Besides, I don't think these students are going to come up with that much money."

"Maybe not, but I'd still guard this notebook. It might be a good idea to keep it at your house."

"Do you really think someone would steal the answers?"

"Back in the day I knew a few who might, and I doubt if boys have changed that much since I was one."

"Would you have stolen the answers?"

"No, I was a good student. I enjoyed school. My teacher said I wrote the best essays she'd ever seen in her career. I wrote some of Will's essays, too. He was better at math and the sciences. But, bless him, he wasn't much of a reader, and he didn't like grammar or writing essays. Unfortunately, it was our teacher's favorite subject," he said with a wry smirk.

"Amos, you shouldn't have helped him cheat! You know, you should have become a writer. It's not too late, you could still do it."

He grinned and shook his head. "I wouldn't know what to write about." He nodded toward the notebook she held. "Did you figure out how many students you'll have?"

"At most, maybe a dozen. It's possible there could be new little ones, and older students might have moved on."

Amos picked up another notebook and a loose page fell out. "Nessa Kelly was one of the teachers. She's married to Angus

Kelly, one of the owners of the sawmill where I work. Sadie Larkin taught, too; she's the doctor's wife. And Amy Larkin, the sheriff's wife." He looked up at Lily. "The doctor and the sheriff are brothers, if you didn't figure that out by the names."

"I did, but I suppose one could have been a sister."

"True. Oh, and Marla Fields. I don't know her. But it looks like those four did the teaching last year. This is a ledger showing how they split the salary."

"This is good. I'd like to spend some time with these ladies before school starts so they can tell me about the children and their families. You know, I think I might like to visit with some of the children and their families before school starts. What do you think?"

"All right, I'll take you."

"Amos, really, I don't need for you to do that. You don't have to take me everywhere."

"I want to, and besides, all these families are spread out for miles around. I'll take you."

She grinned and threw up her hands in mock surrender. "All right, all right, I know when I'm defeated."

Amos cocked his head a little as though he was trying to understand her meaning. "Lily, this isn't a fight. You don't know this town yet, and especially the outlying areas. I would hate for you to get uncomfortable, maybe unsure of where something is, or whether you're on the right road. In time you will be familiar and I won't think twice about it. But for now, do this for me. I'd feel awful if I let you go by yourself and you ended up frightened or even lost."

Lily searched his face a moment and with a tender smile, said, "You and Will must indeed be very much alike. You're a good man, too."

Amos shrugged it off, but her words went right to his heart.

Lily stood and walked around the big room, surveying it from different angles. "This room desperately needs some bookshelves. Look at all the books just stacked up. I'd like to get even more books in here, and not just for the children. I didn't see a lending library in town, and I thought I might be able to set one up for the public. Eventually, that is. It's not the highest priority."

"I can build you some. Henry and Angus said they'd do anything to help you. They might even get the men to build you some. Where would you want them?"

"Along the back wall, I think. As long as I'm asking, I might as well ask for the sky. It would be wonderful to have that entire back wall covered in shelving. On both sides of that door."

Amos laughed. "I'd bet anything you get it." He saw a yard-stick hanging on a nail and used it to measure the wall.

On the ride home Amos asked Lily what she had planned for the next day, which was Saturday.

"I brought all these notebooks home to go over. I thought it would be a good idea to see what was in them before I talk to the ladies who taught last year. It would be nice if I could visit one or two of them tomorrow, but I hate to just drop in on them."

"If you're going to church on Sunday, you can talk to them then. Or at least schedule a time to get together."

"Oh, good idea. That would be perfect."

"If it won't bother you, I'll work on the porch in the morning," Amos said.

"Of course, it won't. Why don't you come for breakfast? I'll make it a big breakfast fit for a working man."

"I can't say no to that."

Amos drove the wagon back to her barn and let her help him see to the horses.

～

THE NEXT MORNING Amos showed up at Lily's house on horseback. She giggled when she opened the door and saw it.

"Please tell me you didn't saddle a horse to come next door. Saddling it would have taken longer than walking over here."

Amos laughed, too. "No, we ran out of screws and Clint didn't have any in stock so we've been having to use more sixteen-penny nails than normal. Now I'm low on those, so I'm going to run to the mercantile and see what they have in stock. If you want to go, we can both ride my horse. It's not far, you know."

"Oh, no thank you," Lily said as she closed the door behind him and led him to sit at the table. "I don't need anything. I think I'll just clean up and then sit down and study those notebooks." She went back to tend the food on the stove instead of getting a cup of coffee for him as he expected. "I hope you like onions. I'm frying the potatoes with them and scrambling eggs with them. Biscuits are in the oven."

"That sounds delicious." Amos saw that he startled her; she probably didn't hear him get up from the table and stop at the cup cupboard just behind her. He grinned. "I'm sorry. I didn't want to bother you for coffee. I know where the cups are. I can get it myself."

"Oh, now I'm sorry," she said as she slapped her forehead in a self-deprecating gesture. Lily shrugged. Amos thought her good-natured apology was endearing.

He sat down again and watched her cook. She was dressed already but her hair hadn't been combed yet. It looked like it had the day before, but a little wilder, as though she'd tossed in bed all night. She brought the butter dish to the table and smiled at him. He saw her walk back and stir the eggs and turn over the potatoes. She quickly grabbed a jar of jelly, brought it to the table, and rushed back to the stove to divvy up the eggs before they got overdone.

Lily folded a kitchen towel several times to protect her

hand from the heat and pulled the lightly golden brown biscuits from the oven. She folded another towel to protect the table and set them on it. "You can go ahead and butter yours while they're hot."

Amos watched, amused, as she went back and put the potatoes on their plates. He could easily tell which plate was his from the heaped up serving. She brought their plates to the table and set them down as she sat.

His grin grew wider as he watched her settle in at the table.

"Dig in!" she said.

His grin grew into a chuckle.

A look of confusion crossed her face just for an instant until she realized what he was waiting for. "Cutlery! I forgot the cutlery," she said, jumping up from her chair. "Oh my goodness, I forgot the napkins, too. I even forgot to bring my own coffee."

Amos laughed out loud at that point and she joined him, shaking her head at her own forgetfulness. "That does it. From this day forward, you are no longer company. If something's missing, you can feel free to get it yourself. Just play like you live here. It's clear I can't bear up to the strain of being a hostess."

"Yes, ma'am. I will. I'll play like I live here."

After breakfast he was going to help clear the table, but Lily shooed him off, telling him the faster he went to the mercantile, the faster he could get to work. He felt her watching him as he mounted his horse and headed down the road.

Will, you should be here. Lily is a joy to be around. She would have been the perfect wife for you. She seems to be settling in well. You'd be tickled at how eager she is for school to start. I'll bet she'll be a good teacher. I surely do wish you were here, my friend.

Outside the mercantile he spotted a familiar horse. It belonged to John Garrett, another man who worked at the sawmill. He'd always liked John.

Inside, he greeted him and shook his hand. "Morning, John. What brings you out here on this fine Saturday?"

"I wish I had a worthwhile reason, but I can't think of one right now. I just had to get out of the boarding house for a while. I was thinking, I wish you'd let me know when you'll be working on Will's house, and I can help you. He was my friend, too."

"Well, all right, that sounds good. How about now? I do wish I had more hands sometimes. Let me get some more nails and some screws if they have them, and I'll be ready to go."

"Do I need to stop off at the boarding house and get my tools?"

"No, no need. I have most of what we'll need, and you can just use Will's if you need to."

When they got back to Lily's house, they hopped down off the horses and loosely tethered them to a low tree branch. Lily stepped out onto the unfinished porch to see who Amos brought with him. "I thought you went for nails. I didn't know they sold workers, too." She smiled at the newcomer. "Hello, I'm Lily."

John tipped his hat. "Miss Lily, I'm John Garrett. I work at the sawmill, too, right alongside Will and Amos. I hated it when we lost Will, and I sure am sorry you had to get here and find out like you did. We'll miss him. He was a good man."

Lily glanced at Amos. "I'm learning that more and more each day, it seems like. John, I hope you'll still be here at lunchtime. If you'll join us, I'll whip up a big mess of something good. Will you be here?"

It was Amos who rushed to answer. "Yes, he will. Supper, too." He saw their looks and shrugged. "What? There's a lot of work we need to do."

❧

LILY CUT up what she thought was a huge amount of beef, potatoes, carrots, and onions. She seasoned and browned the meat the way her mother always did, then added the liquid and vegetables. Finally, she put the lid on the pot to let it simmer until the meat was almost tender enough to eat without teeth.

She sat down with the notebooks from the school and her own pencil and paper and wrote down the comments and questions she had. She got almost through three notebooks before it was time to put the cornbread in the oven.

Lily tasted the stew and decided to thicken the broth into a thin gravy. After that she put three settings at the table, complete with glasses, cutlery, and napkins. She got out three bowls and the ladle so she'd be ready to serve. Before she walked back to her notebooks, she folded a dishtowel to use for a trivet on the table and set another one by the oven for the cornbread. She timed it so that when she called the men to come and wash up, they'd sit down at the table just as the cornbread came out of the oven.

When the men were seated, she took their bowls to the table and joined them as Amos finished pouring cold water from the pitcher into their glasses.

Lily was pleased that the men weren't shy about eating. *Yes, this is how* real men *eat.*

Lily's eye was drawn to Amos. He'd waited until he saw John look down, picked up his knife and spoon and got Lily's attention. He widened his eyes and nodded just a little as if to tell Lily he was proud of her for remembering the cutlery this time. She managed to stifle her reaction and kept a straight face. Mostly.

"Lily, are you getting ready for school to start?" John asked.

"I'm not quite ready yet, but I'm getting there. I'm going through notes and lesson plans done by previous teachers and I'm excited about what I've come up with. Tomorrow at church, I'll meet the previous teachers and see if they have any advice for me. I hope one or two of them will be willing to sit down and tell me about the students. You know, let me know if I need to look out for anything special, or if any of them have problems at home or need special attention."

"It sounds to me like you'll be ready. I don't think I could teach school."

"Why? Don't you have the patience for it?" Amos asked.

"I have patience. I don't have the desire for it. I remember thinking some of the history and advanced math had to be the most boring topics ever taught," John answered.

Lily smiled indulgently. "I remember thinking that about a few assignments, too. There may not be much hope for advanced math, but I have hopes I can make history come alive for them. One day when I was in school, the teacher just seemed to spout off historical facts, one after another. It was so dry and disconnected it was hard to understand a timeline, or a political or social cause and effect." She paused and chuckled. "She talked about a war and I suddenly thought of the people in the old days and wondered what their doctors were like then. Did they even have doctors? What happened to wounded warriors? That led me to all kinds of other questions and I ended up doing my own research to find out. Later it dawned on me that if I can tie history in with the people and how they lived and struggled at the time, the students would be able to relate to it and even appreciate how far we've come in the world."

"Lily, that's brilliant," Amos said with genuine admiration. "That would indeed make it more interesting."

"It would; it definitely would," John said. "I wish I'd had you for a teacher. Who knows? Maybe I'd have gone on to college and been an intellectual instead of cuttin' down trees and livin' in a boarding house."

Amos laughed. "That's where we're obviously different. I'd rather be out in the woods in the fresh air dealing with nature, making the highest use of the raw materials God gave us. I don't think I could stand being cooped up inside to work."

"All right, you have a good point. I enjoy that, too."

"You mentioned the boarding house," Amos said. "Will and I lived there until we bought this land and had something built on it. How do you like it?"

"It's a nice place. I just feel so sorry for Miz Helen. Such a sweet lady, but she's not in as good a shape as she was. Most days she gets by, but some days she's hurtin' and has a hard time of it. She still insists on cooking our three meals a day, though. We've all started to take our own dishes into the kitchen so she won't have to carry them. A couple of nights ago, another boarder and I even washed the dishes and cleaned the kitchen because she was so tired and worn out. We told her to go on to bed but she insisted on keeping us company while we worked."

"She probably didn't think you'd do it right," Amos joked. "I remember she was a sweet lady. She kept telling Will and me we needed to meet some nice girls and get married. Her husband was alive then. He kept the place up."

"You know when he died, the town bought the place and built on to it to house the brides. They hired a man to do most of the things Tim Bonner had done. We all thought that was the perfect solution and it was, until now. I can see having to get more help in the next few months. Miz Helen will probably be both incensed and relieved."

BY THE END of the day, the men had completed the floor of the porch and cut most of the pieces they'd need for the rail. Lily came out to inspect it, joking that they wouldn't get to eat until she was happy with the work. She was thrilled with it and told them so, over and over.

Dinner was as enjoyable as lunch had been. Lily slathered butter on the leftover piece of cornbread and sent it home with John for him to snack on that night.

Before he left, she thanked him for helping Amos with the work Will hadn't gotten the chance to complete. "I'm happy to do it," John said. "Will would have done it for me."

When the suppertime mess was cleaned and the dishes put away, Lily and Amos sat in the porch swing to admire the work they'd done by the fading light of the sun.

"I still can't believe John just offered to come help do all this work," Lily said.

"He did. Will was highly thought of. People like to offer sympathy and support in the way they can do it best. For John, it's building something Will didn't get to finish himself."

"Like you," she said.

"I suppose so." He grinned. "It's what I know best."

"Amos, I want to thank you. You're doing so much for me. And don't say it's because you promised him. It's more than that, I think."

"I want to do it. I have to do it for him, it seems like. Sometimes I find myself talking to him. I tell him I miss him, and how he should be here with you." Amos paused and shifted in the swing. "I told him how easy you are to be with. How smart and pretty you are, and how the sight of your smile and the sound of your laugh stays with a man. Told him he'd have had a perfect wife, the ideal partner in this life, if only he could have stayed."

"Oh, Amos, I hardly know how to respond to that. Thank you for saying those things." A silence followed while she searched for the right words to say. "Maybe one day I'll be the perfect partner for someone else. My mother used to say that when God tells you no, it's because He has something even better in store for you. Maybe He wanted Will to come on Home, and He used him to get me here for another reason. We

45

just can't for sure know the why of it, why Will's gone so soon."

"That's a nice thought, that He's got something even better in mind." There was a pause. "You know, Will never told me what made you decide to come out west to marry. You're a pretty woman, and nice. There must be eligible men in a city as big as Lincoln. Why did you do it?"

She nodded and slowly smiled. "Yes, there are eligible men there. There were some who wanted to court me, but I wasn't interested in any of them. I hope you won't think me fickle or fanciful. You'll understand better if you let me tell you about my father. He was my hero."

Lily told him about her father, and how she always thought of him as a *real man* after once hearing her mother refer to him that way.

She explained that since that time, no other man she met measured up to her father in the qualities she admired most: beefy and brawny physique, rugged, outdoorsy, bold with the strength of his convictions, sense of humor, masculine, good character, a man of faith, resolute yet compassionate, loyal, adventurous spirit, romantic, passionate, resourceful, a man in command, and inherently capable.

Those men back in Lincoln, they may have been perfectly nice in other aspects, but she couldn't picture herself spending her life with them. She hated to think of any of them as less than a man; it wouldn't be fair. There were other women who would make ideal matches for them. Since she couldn't call them lesser men or small men, she called them city men. But in her mind they were soft and small.

"Lily, whoa," Amos said with his hands thrown up as if in surrender, but with a big smile. "That's a lot to ask of a man. Do you think a man like Will could measure up to that? Or I could?"

"I do indeed," she said. "You know what's funny? When I

46

imagined the real man of my dreams, he was almost always a lumberjack."

It was Amos' turn to laugh. "All right, I suppose we qualify there. Although, we're carpenters as much as we are lumberjacks, maybe more. Most are. After a time, you start to appreciate wood more. It feels good to build things with it, something useful or beautiful, to take it from a tree stage and turn it into a house, for example. I trust that qualifies as a real man thing to do?"

"Absolutely! What's more elemental, more fundamental to the human condition than to make with your own hands the home that'll protect the ones you love? It'll be their safe haven, the place where their bodies and their spirits will be fed. That's most definitely a real man thing."

"I can see that; it makes sense." Amos hemmed and hawed and made a little more small talk, then he stood. "It's getting dark. I should go. I'll pick you up for church at ten-thirty. We'll have time to visit a little before the service."

"All right. Amos?"

"Yes?"

"If you talk to Will tonight, tell him how much I appreciate what he did for me and how much I wish I could have met him."

"I'll do that."

CHAPTER 3

*T*hey arrived at church the next morning just as Angus and Nessa Kelly rode in.

"Lily, this is good timing. That's Nessa Kelly, one of the schoolteachers, and her husband Angus. He's one of the owners of the sawmill. Let's get down so I can introduce you before they go inside."

"Aw, they have a baby."

"They do. He's little Liam. The way Angus tells it, he's the smartest bairn who e'er drew breath," Amos said, mimicking Angus.

That got a chuckle from her. The introductions went well and Angus emphasized again that if she needed or wanted anything, to let him know.

Amos grinned at him. "There is something she wants. Bookshelves all across the back wall of the schoolhouse."

"Well, then, Miss Lily, ye shall have them," Angus said in his Irish brogue. "If I remember that room, there's nae point in having multiple bookcases because there are no' many places where they could be moved. Built-in ones would be the way to go. We'll need a key to the door so we can work in there."

"I can't thank you enough, Angus. I have the key in my bag. Would you like it now?"

"Aye, lass. Thank ye."

"Lily, that's a wonderful idea. I should have asked for them when I was teaching," Nessa said.

"I've been going over the notebooks and I'd like to sit down with you and the other teachers. I have some questions and I'd like to know about the children before school starts."

"We'd love to do that. Amy and Sadie should be here today. Let's get together after the service and pick a time when we can get together."

In his announcements, Reverend Copperfield introduced Lily and asked her to stand so the children could see their new schoolmarm. He mentioned the loss of her fiancé, but he framed it in a way that not only gently acknowledged her bereavement, but he signaled the start of a new and exciting future for her, in the schoolhouse, in the church, and in the town. He encouraged everyone to support Lily and 'do their part to make her know she's welcome and an important part of the community to us.'

During the sermon Lily's mind wandered back to his words. *I think he just gave us permission not to grieve anymore.*

The children who were in attendance ran up to her afterwards and introduced themselves, and Lily reveled in their enthusiasm. She recognized their names, from the gradebook and notes, and was glad she could now put faces to the names. Some brought their parents over to meet her, too.

In talking with Amy, Nessa and Sadie, she learned that the other woman, Marla, had moved back east to take care of her elderly mother. Marla hoped she might come back when she was no longer needed there. The teachers, current and past, decided to meet Tuesday morning at the school.

On the ride home, Lily asked Amos what he thought about the pastor's introduction of her.

"I thought it was nice. It sounded like he wants you to get a good start on your teaching career. It was nice that he mentioned everyone should do what they could to make you feel welcome."

"It was nice, but there was something about how he said it. I don't know, it seemed like it held a deeper meaning."

Amos thought a minute. "I can't imagine what it might have been."

"Maybe it was my imagination. I got the idea he was telling everyone to move on and not dwell on the past, or maybe he was just telling me that. That I should stop thinking about mourning Will and get on with my life. We should all get on with our lives." She waved her hand in front of her as if she was pushing the thought away. "Maybe I'm just being fanciful."

Amos nodded slowly. "I don't think that's fanciful. I've been pondering along those lines, too."

"How so?"

"I don't want to do anything that would dishonor his memory."

"Nor do I."

"You haven't, Lily." He abruptly turned to look at her. "Everything you've done has honored his memory. Staying in town, staying in his house is honoring him. I know how appreciative you are for the things he left for you."

"Yes, and appreciative that he asked you to look after me. You're living up to that promise to the fullest extent. Why, you could stop looking after me right now, well," she said, shrugging, "after the porch railings are up, and most people would think you'd lived up to your obligation."

"No, I want to do all those things for you. It just seems right. But there's more to it than that. What I want to do, what I think about, it just doesn't all settle well, deep down."

"Amos, I can't think of anything you might do or think that

wouldn't be honorable or would dishonor Will. What exactly worries you?"

He looked at her, smiled and shrugged. "It's not something I'm ready to talk about yet. I have an idea. Let's go to Mary's for Sunday dinner."

She flashed a smile that made his eyes linger on her lips a moment too long. "Now you know I won't say no to that."

As soon as they entered, they were flagged down by Angus motioning for them to sit at their table. Lily had to smile at the striking family the Kellys were; all three sported flaming red hair. "You are such a handsome little man," she said as she reached out to touch Liam's hand. "You're going to have to fight off the girls with a stick." She would have sworn she saw Angus sit up a little taller and puff out his chest with pride.

Before long, Nessa started talking about the bookshelves in the school and what a good idea they were. Angus wondered aloud how many students and how much time it would take to use all that shelving.

"Well," Lily said, drawing out the word. "I had an idea, but I wanted to talk to the other ladies and get their opinions. I noticed there's no lending library in town and I thought about setting up a small one in the school that would be open to everyone in town. The idea would be not only to have books available to them, but to teach the students how libraries work, and let them take turns being librarian. When someone comes in to check out a book, the student would make sure it's signed out correctly. When it's returned, he would make sure it's registered and he'd put away the book."

The men both nodded thoughtfully, but Nessa was visibly excited. She straightened in her chair, shifted Liam, and leaned forward. "That's a wonderful idea, Lily! It would be good to have a library, but it would be even better to involve the children, let them share in an important responsibility. Give them something to bolster their self-esteem. While they're learning that, they would be learning how to deal with adults with confidence. Oh, Lily, this is a good idea all around."

"Lily, that's a fine idea; I thought so when you mentioned it to me, but we didn't get the chance to talk about it in more detail. If the children are interested enough, they'll continue to read all their lives. They'll want to keep learning even after they've outgrown your classroom. Where will you get the books?" Amos asked.

"Good question. I hope a few people might have a book or two they'd be willing to donate. I'll go through all the books I can get my hands on and find out the name and address of the publishers. Then I can write to them and ask for donations," Lily explained.

"Or better yet," Nessa said, "you could make it a class project and let students write the letters. Oh, this is such a good idea! Will you let me help take this on?"

"Let you?" Lily said, laughing, "I was prepared to beg you for help."

Liam began pawing at Nessa's bosom. "He's hungry again. I'm afraid we need to leave before he gets too impatient. Angus, are you through eating yet?"

"Aye, I am." He looked at Lily and Amos and grinned. "She does no' mind if I get impatient from having to wait to eat, ye ken."

"Oh, Angus," Amos said, "I meant to tell you. I can come back to work when I've finished the porch rails on the front and back of the house."

"Do no' worry. Take care o' the lass first. When ye do return, ye' migh' work only part o' the day. She might find more for ye to do." He winked as he said that and walked away.

Lily and Amos finished eating their own meals. Amos went to the counter to pay, only to find out Angus had already paid for it.

Amos used the phrase "outgrown your classroom." I should tell him he's not very original, that Will used that same phrase in one of his letters.

On the ride home Amos asked her what she planned to do for the rest of the day.

"Rest some, I suppose. I want to study those lesson plans again, too. Maybe rinse out a few things. That might wait until tomorrow, though. Since you took me to lunch, why don't you come over for supper? It won't be anything special. Probably beans and cornbread."

"That sounds like a feast to me. I do like your cornbread. I'll be there."

Amos drove the buggy straight back to her barn. That had become their habit. They would use her horses and buggy, and she would help him unhook the team and unharness the animals. She enjoyed taking care of them and feeding them hay from her hands. They seemed to be such strong and noble beasts, and she commented once to Amos that she understood why Will had named them Atlas and Hercules.

They walked out of the barn together, but Amos told her he'd be back for supper and took off walking across their yards to his house. She slowed her steps so she could watch him. *He's as attractive walking away as he is walking toward me. Mmm... and those muscles. Sometimes his shirts seem strained to contain them. And those long, strong thighs. All those muscles rippling as he moves... Definitely a real man.*

She shook herself out of her thoughts and realized how eager she was to see him again. Once she'd changed out of her Sunday best, she went in the kitchen and put the beans on over a low fire.

When is he going to stop thinking of me as Will's fiancée? Lord, please make it soon!

Lily decided to wash some bloomers and shifts before she sat down with school things. She wrung them out as well as she could, then wrapped them in towels and stepped on them to try to get as much water out of them as she could. Realizing she had no clothesline, she shook them out and draped them over pieces of furniture to dry.

Lily, if only you knew what you're doing to me. Amos poured himself a cold glass of water and looked out his window as he swigged it down.

Will, my friend, it's getting harder and harder to remember she's your girl. Yes, I know, I know. You told me to marry her, but it's just too soon. If only you hadn't died, I wouldn't be in this mess. She wouldn't be anything to me except your wife. But you did die, and here I am. She would have made you a fine wife, Will. Now all I can think of is how much I want her to be mine. Hell, she might not even want me. This town's full of other men.

Amos put the glass down and headed outside to do some chores of his own he'd been neglecting. Several times that afternoon he realized he'd stopped working and was staring at her house, imagining he was inside it, doing with her all those things he'd helped Will write about in his letters.

Amos arrived early, or at least Lily thought it was early. She was still standing at the stove, fussing over the beans and getting ready to lift the cornbread out of the oven. "Come on in," she said when he knocked, her back still toward the door.

She heard the door open and close, then she heard Amos' voice. She could tell from his voice he was smiling even without looking at him. "Well, I'll be. Angus was right about you finding more for me to do. Is this your way of letting me know you need a clothesline?"

Lily's eyes opened wide and she had a sharp intake of breath when she remembered her dainties were draped over every piece of furniture in the parlor and bedroom. "Oh, no. Let me get those out of the way."

She hurried toward the parlor but he caught her arm and stopped her. "I've already seen 'em so there's no need to pick 'em up on my account. Besides, I know what ladies wear under their dresses. Although yours have more lace than usual, I think. Very nice."

Lily looked up at him in embarrassment, but the look on his face loosened her up some and made her laugh about it. She shrugged. "I like lace."

"Come on. Let me help you set the table and get the food served."

"All right."

After she'd eaten a few bites, she started the conversation. "You never did tell me how you and Will ended up here in Big Rock."

"No, I don't believe I did," he said. "I told you we quit college when our folks died. We each sold our parents' places and had more money than we'd ever seen. We decided to spend a little of it traveling around. So we flipped a coin to decide which direction to go, and we went. Late one afternoon up in Rawlins, we decided we wanted to play some poker, so we found a saloon. Weren't that many men who looked like people we wanted to sit with, but there was a table with three men playing who looked promising. We stood at the bar and watched a while. One of the men had to leave. We looked at each other, knowing what the other one was thinking, and went over to the table. When I asked if we could join them for a poker game, they invited us to sit. Even bought us beers."

"No, don't tell me they got you both drunk," Lily said.

"No, they didn't. We just played poker and talked. You know, you can tell when people are good friends. We could tell they were. We were all joking around, tellin' stories, and before long we knew how they became friends and they knew our story. We were all pretty decent players, staying fairly close in our winnings. But then Henry's luck turned south. Pretty soon he ran out of cash. Angus didn't have any on him to let him borrow, and he didn't want to go all the way back to his hotel. So he said, 'Boys, we already told you that Angus and I have a successful sawmill and furniture factory in Big Rock. If I lose, I'll pay the stagecoach fare for both of you to come with us tomorrow and we'll give you jobs working with us. I think lumberjacking and building things qualifies as working out in the open like you boys want to do. Will you accept that as my ante?' Well, we did accept, and I won that hand, and that's how we got here."

Lily was fascinated. "Amos, what an amazing story that was. Just imagine all the things that had to come together to make that happen. Think, what if the coin toss had sent you in the other direction? What if you hadn't wanted to play poker, or if they hadn't wanted to? What if Henry hadn't run out of cash? Or if Angus still had a full wallet and was able to lend him some? I'm glad it worked out the way it did."

"So am I, Lily. More and more every day."

What did he mean by that? Does he mean he's gladder each day because I'm here?

They finished the meal and cleared off the table. "Let's leave these dishes," Lily said. "There aren't many and I can do them later. I want to sit on the porch while it's still nice outside."

"All right."

Lily watched Amos' thighs flex as he controlled the gentle movement of the swing. *I need to speak before he realizes what I'm looking at. He might figure out what I'm thinking. Wait. Maybe that would be a good thing.*

"You know I cooked and did a little laundry this afternoon. What did you do with your time?"

He smiled at her. "I chopped enough wood to make my arms sore tomorrow. I'll bring it over and stack it with yours."

Lily laughed. "You should have brought it on over earlier this evening. Your arms are going to be sore tomorrow. Remember?"

"Well, you got me there."

"Amos, I do appreciate everything you do for me. I don't want you to think I take any of it for granted."

"I don't think that. I like helping."

"I know you do. Like you said, you'd be helping me even if Will hadn't made you promise. You're just honorable that way. Honorable down to the bone."

Lily saw the smile leave his face and the almost imperceptible tensing of some of his muscles. His whole demeanor changed.

"I'm not that honorable, Lily."

"Why would you say that?"

He didn't answer, but she knew there had to be something bothering him regarding Will. She tried again.

"Have you talked to Will recently?"

"I did. Today, as a matter of fact."

"What did you tell him?"

Amos blew out a long, deep breath. "I told him it's getting harder and harder to remember you came here for him."

"Amos, how long do I have to mourn a man I never met?"

"What?"

"I know he was a fine man and a good friend. I know he was thoughtful enough to see to it that I'd be taken care of. But, Amos, I haven't shed a single tear for him."

"That's not true. I saw you cry."

"I was so relieved that he didn't leave me stranded. I was thankful he left me a home and money to start this new life without him. They were tears of gratitude, Amos, not sorrow at his death. You can't mourn the loss of a relationship you never had with a man you never met. I hope that doesn't sound shallow. I'm baring my heart here. I tried to mourn as I thought I should, but I couldn't. You suffered the loss here. All I lost was a dream of what might have been."

"No, it's not shallow. I think I understand what you mean."

"Amos," Lily pressed on, hoping he'd share more with her, "back in Lincoln whenever I read the more tender parts of his letters, I imagined a man doing the things with me that Will wrote about. But the man in my dreams didn't have a face, and he didn't have a voice, all because I hadn't met the man yet. Ever since I got here, whenever I think of those same passages, the man in my dreams... has your face. He's you, Amos. He's been you since I got here."

Amos turned to her, searching her face and eyes... for what? She hadn't seen his eyes like this, with so much need, so much ache. Lily thought there must be an emotional storm raging behind those eyes. *Maybe he needs confirmation, a signal that I meant what I said.*

She put her hand up to his face and that was all it took. Suddenly she was wrapped in his arms and held tightly against him. He lowered his face, looking from her eyes to her lips until both their eyes closed and his mouth was on hers. She knew him with that kiss. She knew his need, his ache, his sorrow and guilt, and as his hold on her turned into a softer hug, she knew his relief and joy. She hoped he knew her joy, too.

He broke the kiss. Lily put her arms around him, afraid that he might remove his from around her, but he didn't. They held that embrace until the next kiss when their hands began to explore. She reveled in the feel of his hands, the taste of his mouth, and the playful dance their tongues performed.

"Sweet Lily," Amos whispered as he smoothed his hand across her cheek and into her hair. "My sweet Lily."

She smiled up at him and gently kissed his lips in response.

Amos pulled away and took her hands in his. "Well," he said, "I'm glad we got that settled."

Lily laughed, and he told her he loved to hear the sound of it. They sat like that for a while, with him holding and stroking her hands and wrists.

"I think I should go home now, Lily. It's getting late."

"Will you come back over for breakfast in the morning?"

"I believe I will."

"Will you kiss me again when you come back in the morning?"

"No army on this earth could keep me away from these lips," he said as he ran his fingers over them.

"Good. I'll see you in the morning. Sweet dreams," she said.

"I will definitely have sweet dreams tonight."

"So will I."

JUST A FEW MINUTES LATER, Lily stood at the kitchen sink with a silly grin on her face. She didn't even remember walking in from the porch; she might have floated in for all she knew. Maybe she was only remembering the important things, like the feel of Amos' arms around her, the feel of his hand on her face, his lips on hers. Mostly, she remembered that it felt so right.

With the kitchen clean again, she walked into the parlor and smiled even wider when she saw her dainty underthings strewn over the furniture. Amos had seen them when he first came inside. Now she relished the idea of him seeing them. It seemed playfully wanton, and she wondered if he'd imagined her in them.

Lily was caught up short by the sight of Will's letters on her bed, right where she'd read them again earlier in the afternoon. She put the pages back in their envelopes, stacked them in order, and clasped them to her heart briefly before putting them in their box and placing it on the shelf in her closet. She had the odd feeling that if she read them again, she'd be betraying Amos.

CHAPTER 4

$\mathcal{L}$ily woke with the sun again and a big, broad smile crossed her face before she even got out of bed. She ran her arm over the bed beside her and imagined what it would be like to wake and find Amos there. In her daydream, he wasn't ready to let her out of bed yet.

She got up and started a fire in the stove to let it get hot while she did her morning routine. She sponged with cool water because she didn't want to wait for any to be heated. When she was dry, she used the scented powder she rarely used. Her hair was perfect when she was through with it, and she smiled at the thought that Amos had never seen it quite this neatly done.

In the kitchen, Lily put a big pot of water on to boil; she always did that first. Next came the coffee. Then she remembered to put on an apron to protect her dress; she'd hate to be covered in grease and flour when Amos arrived. Biscuits first, she thought. Soon a batch of big ones were in the oven. Lily decided on ham instead of bacon this time and sliced several pieces to fry. Into one skillet they went. In the other skillet, she caramelized chopped onions in butter to await the eggs for scrambling. On a whim, Lily grated some cheese to top off the eggs, hoping Amos would notice that special touch.

There was a knock at the door, and Lily wiped her hands on the bottom of her apron as she walked over to answer it.

"You're earl—"

Amos kicked the door closed and grabbed her to him for a hungry kiss.

"Early, hell," he said. "You're lucky I wasn't over here before dawn to wake you up."

"Maybe I'd have been even luckier if you had."

"Lily, girl," he said as he pulled his head back to look at her. "As much as I love hearing you say things like that, we have to be careful. You're the schoolmarm, you know. People hold you to a higher standard because you have influence over their children. Most people know I'm finishing up all this work and helping you out, but there's no good reason for me to be here before dawn."

Lily sighed. "You're probably right. Besides, I was thinking that since it hasn't been very long since, well, Will, that maybe we shouldn't let anyone know we're on kissing terms."

"Kissing terms. I like that. I don't think anyone would think that's a bad thing as long as I don't take advantage and compromise you. But if you want to keep it secret for a while, we can do that." He grinned and tipped up her head. "It's a very sweet secret to have."

"I thought so, too. Oh! My biscuits!" She ran into the kitchen. "And I haven't even scrambled the eggs yet."

Amos chuckled and assessed the kitchen situation. He got two cups and poured coffee, then he got out two plates and two sets of knives and forks. Next, he got the butter and a jar of jelly, and before he sat down, he pulled out a spoon for the jelly.

He complimented her more than once on what a delicious

meal it was and how he was going to gain weight if she kept up this kind of cooking.

"Nonsense. As much hard work as you do, you need the energy. All those muscles need to be fed."

"I surely am glad you're concerned about my muscles. They do come in handy."

"I imagine so. I can think of times when they'd be good to have around."

Amos gave her a flirty grin.

"Speaking of meals," she said, only partly changing the subject, "what do you think John would like for supper?"

"I'd like some more of those beans and your cornbread. I'm sure he'd like that."

"Again?"

"Most men could live on that. And, Lily, yours are damn good."

"Oh, all right," she said, brightening. "I'll slice up some ham to go with them."

"That would be perfect. After breakfast I want to go to the mercantile and pick up some things. Would you like to go?"

"No, I don't think so. I'll tidy up and get focused on what I want to discuss with the other teachers tomorrow. And I'm trying to think of interesting ways to teach certain things so the children will be excited to come to school."

"That's a noble goal. If you can pull it off, my hat's off to you."

Amos left after they finished breakfast, but not before he pulled her to the couch and sat her down for several minutes of secret passionate kisses.

LILY HEARD Amos call out a greeting when John arrived, and she went out on the porch to greet him, too.

"And how was the old sawmill today?" she asked.

"I wouldn't know," John answered as he handed her the key to the schoolhouse. "I spent all day with Angus putting shelves all across the back wall of the schoolroom for you." He smiled. "We think they look pretty good."

Her eyes widened with excitement. "I can't wait to see them! I'm meeting Nessa and Sadie and Amy there in the morning. Ooh," she half-sang, doing a little jumpy-dancy thing.

Amos laughed. "If she gets that excited over bookshelves, I can't wait to see what she does when we finish everything on this house."

Later over dinner, Amos asked John how Miz Helen was doing at the boarding house.

"She seems to decline a tiny bit every day. One might not notice it from one day to the next, but I see her struggle with something and recall that she didn't have that trouble a week or so ago. Bless her heart, she doesn't want to admit she needs help."

"Do you think she's afraid of losing an income?" Lily asked.

"I don't know. I think she has some money from when the town bought the place from her. I don't know how much it was, but I can't see that she's spending any of it."

"Maybe she's afraid of not being needed anymore," she said.

Amos nodded at that. "You're probably right. She's worked at that boarding house since she and her husband built it. It means a lot to her."

Amos and John went on to other topics of conversation, but the problem-solving part of Lily's brain was trying to think of a solution to the boarding house issue.

WHEN JOHN LEFT, Amos helped Lily clean up the supper mess. He was quick and efficient and still managed to steal kisses and flirt. She enjoyed it so much, she suggested he could help with kitchen cleaning more often.

He pulled her to the couch again.

"Don't you want to go out and sit on the swing?" she asked.

"No, ma'am. We couldn't kiss out there because if anybody passed by, they'd see us."

"Oh," she said with an innocent look, "there's going to be kissing?"

He answered, but not with words. They kissed for a long time, with long, slow, tender kisses she didn't want to end. She felt transported to a different place, or maybe to a place inside herself she'd never experienced before. There was no other world outside their walls, maybe not even a world outside of his arms. It was the world she wanted to live in.

"Mmm... this must be what Heaven's like, kissing you," she said.

"It is heavenly, I have to agree. But in my Heaven, it goes a little further. Well, a lot further." He took her hand and put it on his fullness. "This is what kissing you does to me."

"I understand. It makes me," she paused a moment, then whispered, "want to feel this inside me."

"Lily, sweet Lily, you know I won't tarnish your reputation. I'll kiss you into oblivion, but I won't compromise you."

"Who will even know?"

"I will. And you will."

"I'm not that strong, Amos. I want you. I'm willing to gamble my reputation if it means we can be together as one."

"Then I'll be strong enough for both of us."

"Don't you want to, Amos? Don't you think about it?"

He laughed ruefully and spoke slowly. "I hardly think of anything else. I'd like nothing more than to take you to your bedroom and slowly remove your clothes, savoring each new sight as I go. I want to touch you, lightly, as more of your skin is revealed. And I'll follow those touches with kisses. Before I have all your clothes off, you'll beg me to go faster and to take my clothes off, so we can be one."

"I don't know about that begging part. That doesn't sound like me."

"No one's brought out that side of you before. I will."

"I'll have to make it a point not to beg."

"Won't matter. You'll beg me."

Lily thought that must be a common scenario for lovers. Will had described something very similar, but without the begging part. Maybe Will wasn't quite as cocky as Amos.

Then they started kissing again, and conscious thought fell away.

LILY FIXED breakfast for Amos again the next morning, but this time it was bacon and pancakes. He was pleased. And again, they kissed on the couch for the longest time before they started their workdays.

This time was a little different, though. Lily found herself caressing him more, all over. She stroked his face and neck, then she kissed his neck. She ventured more and rubbed the muscles on his upper arms, and the caresses strengthened into massages. Softening her touch again, she concentrated on his chest, and she was encouraged when it elicited moans of passion from him. Lily worked her way down to his hardness and rubbed it harder, in ways she hadn't before. Amos pressed harder into her touch. She loved getting such a reaction from him.

"Lily, honey, it's taking every ounce of strength I have to keep from taking you back to that bedroom. I think it's time to stop for now."

"I don't want to, but you're probably right." She touched his hardness again and grinned at him suggestively. "I really do like making this happen."

He chuckled. "I'm mighty glad to hear that. I like it, too. I think I'll go take care of it so I can get to work. If I don't, I'll be so distracted I might nail my thumb to the porch."

"Take care of it yourself? You mean—"

"Yes, I mean do it myself. Isn't that what you do when I leave?"

"No. I've never done that before. I've thought about it a few times, but I never, you know, made it happen. It just didn't feel right to do that to myself. Made me feel a little silly and awkward."

"Are you telling me you've never felt that kind of release?"

"That's what I'm telling you. I never have."

He touched her cheek, then kissed her lightly. "Maybe we'll have to do something about that."

"Oh my," she said. "I look forward to it."

LILY GOT to the schoolhouse early, and she enjoyed the walk. Her mind wasn't on the three R's, though. As she turned the key in the lock, she told herself to make a conscious effort to put thoughts of Amos to bed for a while. Then she laughed at her subconscious choice of words.

Schoolwork, Lily. Get your mind on the schoolwork.

The faint smell of freshly cut lumber greeted her when she entered. She walked all the way to the front of the room and put her satchel down on the table at the front before she let herself turn around to see the bookshelves. The sight of them nearly took her breath away. They were beautiful and grand. In her mind, they gave the room such an important feel. They silently said *knowledge and learning are in this place.*

"Now we're going to need some bookends," she said aloud. "And some books."

Nessa came through the open door and hurried to stand beside Lily so she could see them, too. "Oh, they did such a good job on those, didn't they?"

"They're so much nicer than I imagined they would be. You, my friend, better get to roundin' up some books," Lily said.

"I'm working on it. Opal's going to donate several books. She wanted to share some without donating them altogether, so she wondered if she could lend books to the lending library for, say, three months at a time, then they'd be returned to her at the end of the quarter. I told her I thought that was workable."

Lily considered it. "I don't see why not if it'll get us more books to share."

Sadie Larkin and Amy Larkin walked in together. Nessa grinned and motioned for them to come to the front.

"Those shelves sure do dress up this schoolroom," Sadie said.

They pulled up chairs around the table and settled in to go over Lily's questions. She took notes as they answered. The first question she asked was for noteworthy information about each student. She wanted to know what each child was like, what they needed help with, if she should be aware of any potential problems, that sort of thing.

Nessa answered first. "You met some of these at church. Rosemary McBride is about seven now, second grade. She wants to be a teacher when she grows up. Of course, she'll probably change her mind a hundred times before she grows up. Ben Wilkerson is a smart young man, ninth grade. He's determined to be a lawyer, and I suspect he will. He's the oldest of the children. There were times when I had to step out and I felt fine leaving him in charge to help the others with assignments."

Sadie piped in. "Elizabeth Woods wants to be a doctor. She caught a lot of criticism from a couple of the other students who maintained women shouldn't be doctors. As for being on guard and needing eyes in the back of your head, look out for Margie Meyer. She's thirteen and she's boy crazy. If you don't keep an eye out, you might find her in the cloakroom with Jed Culpepper. Oh, Jed's father is a rancher and he plans to be one, too. Now Ken White told me he wants to be a blacksmith, but he might have changed his mind. That's all I can remember about what they want to be when they grow up."

"Lettie Stewart is a shy little third grader. Being calm and positive and reassuring with her is probably the best way to gain her trust and get her to open up in class," Amy added. "I've wondered about her home life, but never had anything solid to base any suspicions on. I could be all wrong, but sometimes she just seems so skittish."

The others agreed with Amy's assessment of Lettie.

Nessa added information about another student. "Billy Simmons is a sweet third grader from the Low Quarter. He's the only one from down there. If he's occasionally late, it's understandable."

They discussed a bit more about the students as they thought of things, and they mentioned that the remaining ones on the list were good students, too. Lily was encouraged and relieved that she didn't have troublemakers in the group.

"Let me ask your opinions about something," Lily said. "I'd like to visit each one of the students in their homes before school starts. Is that a good idea or not?"

"Some of them live pretty far away," Nessa answered. "You shouldn't be going out on your own."

"Amos said the same thing, so he said he'll take me."

Lily could tell the other ladies wanted to say something.

Nessa finally did. "Well, if Amos takes you, then it should be all right. You know, it might be enough to visit the ones you already met at church. That would save a couple of long trips. So, I take it you and Amos are getting along well?"

Remember, it's a secret for now.

"Of course. I understand he promised Will to look after me and finish the work on the house. He's been so good about the work and about taking me places like church and the store. Will would be pleased."

"I'm sure he would. Amos is such a good man, don't you think?"

Lily wondered why they were fishing for information about her and Amos. Was he right? Were the townspeople watching her behavior with him? "He seems to be. He was Will's best friend, so he must be."

"I don't know if anyone told you," Nessa said, "but I was the town's first mail order bride. I still have the letters Angus wrote to me. Sometimes I read them now and I can't believe how brazen we were in our writings. It would have been scandalous if we weren't scheduled to marry."

Good. This is a chance to dispel any rumors about Amos and me.

"I know exactly what you mean," Lily said with a big grin and a gleam in her eye that wasn't quite genuine. "Whenever I reread Will's letters, I think how much I'd hate for anyone else to read them, especially all those romantic parts. That man waxed lyrical on some very intimate things. His descriptions were so vivid without being vulgar. Almost poetic." She finished that little speech with a slightly bowed head, her eyes cut upwards at them conspiratorially, and an impish grin.

"Will did? Will waxed lyrical?" Nessa asked. "I can't imagine Will waxing lyrical on anything. I knew him pretty well through Angus, and he never gave me the impression he was big on writing things. He didn't sound like it when he spoke, that's for sure. Now Amos, it wouldn't surprise me for Amos to do that, but not Will. I'm surprised to hear that about Will."

"Oh, yes, but you'll just have to trust me on this. You can imagine how personal they are."

"Well, we can all understand that."

Lily couldn't concentrate on what the ladies said for a few minutes after that exchange. "*...my teacher said I wrote the best essays she'd ever seen... sometimes I wrote Will's essays...*" *That fraud! Amos Cameron wrote those letters to me, not Will!*

She felt the tingles that indicated her face was flushing. Her tummy felt uneasy. She recovered the best she could and rejoined the conversation.

"Lily," Sadie asked gently, "do you think Amos would be the kind of man you might be interested in some day? He and Will are alike in so many ways."

"I don't know, perhaps, someday. Why do you ask that?"

"Well, the day of the accident when they brought Will to Elliott's office, I was there. I heard what he said to Amos. He was so concerned about your well being and your future. He was adamant that you get the house and his bank account. He asked Amos to promise he'd always look out for you, protect you. You may not know this part, but he told Amos to marry you. He said Amos was the only man good enough, the only man he trusted with you. It was very moving. Will's thoughts were of you until the very end."

"No, I didn't know about the marriage part. Thank you for telling me."

That monumental ass. All that talk about feeling disloyal to Will, and come to find out, he already had Will's permission from that very day. Not only his permission, but his urging. How dare he keep that from me?

"Oh, I had a question about supplies. Will there be a problem if I try to buy too many things?" Lily needed to ask the question, but she needed to change the topic even more. "What should I get to start out with?"

"No, nobody ever questioned us, so you're probably fine

getting anything you want. I'd go ahead and get three or four more slates, lots of chalk, pens and ink for the older ones, and paper. And felt for erasers. I don't know how, but they seem to disappear. But now's the time to buy whatever you want. I think they're in deep pockets mode right now. Angus said they're buying a piano for the community hall." Lily wrote down everything Nessa listed, then it registered what Nessa had said.

"Did you all ever include music in the school activities? Teach music or sing songs?"

"A little bit," Nessa said. "I know some silly children's songs and the younger ones love learning those. Sometimes I'd teach them a song suitable for any age. Why?"

"I don't sing that well and I know nothing about music except for what we sing at church. But I always thought a music foundation could be taught in school. It should be taught. At least a basic knowledge. When you said that, it occurred to me that we might be able to have a music lesson, maybe once a week, and since the community hall is barely a block away, we could walk there for the lessons so we'd have a piano."

"I think that's a wonderful idea, Lily," Nessa said. "Let me talk to Angus and see what he thinks. I'd love to come in once a week and do that."

"That's wonderful. It's going to benefit them so much, I know it will. Now I just have one more question, or one more topic. I'm certified to teach all twelve grades, as you are, Nessa. I know what they told us in school and what I've read in educational publications. Out here in the west, precious few students stay in school past the eighth grade. Is that what you see here in Big Rock? What might it take to get them to stay in school longer?"

Nessa answered, "I guess we'll have a better idea if Ben shows up for class. He completed eighth grade last year. If he shows up when school starts, we'll know if he's serious about being a lawyer."

Sadie pitched in her thoughts. "A lot depends on what the student wants to do in life. The truth is, if you're going to be a miner, a higher education might not be of benefit unless you plan to do some assay work. I don't mean that negatively. The copper mine owners pay a good wage to the miners. For those who don't mind being underground most of the day, it's a good, solid job. Those boys would rather be out bringing home money than staying in school. I can't blame them for that."

"No, I can't, either. I imagine it's about the same for the boys who plan to take over the family ranches. Although, I could make the argument that higher education would help them run ranches. What about the girls?"

Amy smiled. "That may depend largely on whether or not she has marriage prospects by that age."

"Fourteen?" Lily asked, thinking how young it sounded.

"Wait until you meet Margie. Unless the other girls are needed at home or are needed to help support their family by getting a job, they'll probably stay in school longer. Remember, one wants to be a teacher and another wants to be a doctor. Both of those require higher education."

"Well," Lily said, "that sounds marginally better than what was described to us in school. I'd like for us to figure out what the magic answer is to keep as many as we can as long as we can. At least in the cases where it makes sense."

LILY'S WALK home wasn't nearly as pleasant as her walk to the school had been. She worked up a fair fury over the men's deception in the writing of the letters.

I should have figured out that Amos wrote the damn letters. At least twice he used either a direct quote or thoughts that were uncan-

nily similar to the wording in the letters. He already admitted he used to write Will's essays. I guess I was just another homework assignment to him, except he could use grown-up words and ideas with me. How humiliating. What must they have thought of me?

Amos wasn't there when she got home, and she was relieved since he was usually around at mealtime. She didn't want to see him right now. She relit the stove to warm up the leftover biscuits from breakfast and put on a fresh pot of coffee.

The more she thought about the letters, the angrier she got. It wasn't just anger, though. Resentment was creeping in, and betrayal. Amos lied to her. He'd assured her he never read her letters. Then how did he know what to write? She pictured the two men sitting at the very table where she now sat, her letters spread out before them, laughing and scheming over what to write next, speculating about how the gullible girl in Lincoln might respond.

When she thought about how Will wanted Amos to marry her, her anger turned livid. Who was he to give her away, like she had no feelings or no say in the matter? She might as well have been on the same level as Hercules and Atlas, his property that needed to be taken care of.

Lily barely tasted her food, even with all the butter and honey she put on the biscuits.

Before long there was a knock on the front door and just as Lily made the split-second decision not to answer it, it was opened. Amos walked in with a look that told her he was happy to see her. That look changed when he saw her expression.

"Lily, honey, what's wrong? What happened?"

She threw down her napkin and stood so abruptly, her chair fall backward. She wanted to poke her finger in his chest, but that would be childish.

"You lied to me, Amos! You wrote those letters, not Will. Did you both think I'd never figure it out? Did you even care?"

"That's not exactly true, Lily. I didn't write them. All I did was help him put his thoughts in nicer words for the passages that meant the most to him."

Once she started to give voice to her feelings, the tears started. "I feel so humiliated. I thought I was the only one who would ever read Will's letters. And I when I wrote my letters, they were for Will's eyes only. I wrote what was in my heart and on my mind, and there were passages so personal, I never dreamed anyone else would read them. I'm so embarrassed." She turned away and wiped her tears with the bottom of her apron.

"I never read your letters to Will. No one but Will ever saw them," Amos said.

"Now I find out they weren't even Will's letters. I'm mortified. The deceit—I feel so foolish. I can just see you both. Two conniving little boys sitting there," she vaguely pointed to the table, "laughing while they write steamy and erotic messages to a naïve chump of a girl, just trifling with her emotions."

Amos turned her to face him. "Listen to me, Lily. Those were not the thoughts of a boy. They were the thoughts of a grown man. A man who spent hours trying to put into words the powerful emotion of a romance he expected to share with the woman who meant more to him than anything. A man who wanted the words and the message to convey what was in his heart. Some of the words may have been mine, but the message was his. We never laughed at you, and we certainly never intended to make a mockery of the situation. He thought he was the luckiest man alive, and I thought he was, too. I wanted to be writing those things to my woman."

Lily laughed ruefully. "Well, it appears you were doing just that. I don't even know which one of you I fell for through those letters. I guess it's fitting, since he practically willed me to you at the end, like I was another head of livestock, unable to make my own decisions. 'Here, since I can't use her, you marry her.'"

"Lily, I'm not sure how you learned about that, but the person didn't explain it very well. Will wanted to ease your way, to protect you and make sure you had everything you needed. He wanted you free from any worries about where you'd live, or how you'd support yourself. He wanted you to move on and start your new life. He wanted me to move on, too."

"I don't understand why all this time you've been hesitant about me when he told you himself to marry me. All this time you've been saying you felt you were dishonoring Will, but you had his blessing all along. Instead, you were taking your time deciding if I was good enough for you, or if I was the woman you want. Do you know how that makes me feel?"

"Where are these wild ideas coming from? Just because he gave me his blessing doesn't mean I was ready to act on it. Will's been my best friend for almost my whole life, and I knew how much you meant to him. Everything. You meant everything to him. I couldn't ignore that. I felt so much guilt for being the one who lived. It was even worse when I thought about how it would be to live the life that should have been his."

"You want to hear something funny?" Lily stepped away from him again. "That first night we kissed, I came in and put his letters up in the closet. I thought if I read them again, I would be disloyal to you. Look, Amos, I think you need to leave. I'm still upset."

"All right, I'll go. For now, anyway. Remember, neither he nor I had anything but the best of intentions."

When the door closed behind him, Lily stared at it for a long time. Had she been wrong? Had she jumped to conclusions? The wrong ones? There had been deceit, no question about it. If they were schoolboys and those letters were homework, she'd have called it cheating. It was just like the times when Amos wrote Will's assignments. Well, maybe not exactly like it. After all, Will did write most of the letters himself. Maybe she should have noticed the difference in writing styles. But handing her off to marry Amos? That was uncalled for. How could he do that without giving her a chance to have her own say? *Because I wasn't there, that's why.*

The whole time Will and I were writing to each other, Amos was watching Will fall for me as he planned the rest of his life. Our life. That's about the most serious thing a person can do. Amos knew how important I was to Will. I can understand the guilt. Even I know you can't turn feelings and emotions off in the blink of an eye. Damn, it would have taken anyone some time to do that. Damn, damn.

Lily went in the kitchen and pulled out the pie pan, rolling pin, flour, lard, salt, and the jar of apple pie filling Will had apparently purchased at the store. Then she got to work.

WHEN THE PIE had cooled substantially but was still warm to the touch, Lily wrapped it in tea towels and took off across their yards to Amos' house. She took a deep breath and knocked. When Amos opened it, she thought he looked a little surprised to see her.

"I came to apologize. With pie." She held it up for him to see.

He nodded slowly and stroked his chin. "Pie. I've often thought a good apology should start with pie. We should see if that's true."

Lily was grateful he wasn't going to make this too hard for her. He opened the door and let her in. It was the first time she'd been in his house and she noticed similarities to hers. The cupboards and cabinets had the same look but the layout was different. Both were good, she thought.

She put the pie on the table and watched as Amos fetched a knife, two forks, and two plates.

"Would you prefer coffee or milk?" he asked.

"Whatever you're having."

He selected two cups and put them on the table, then he brought the coffee pot and placed it on a folded towel. They both sat.

"Amos, I overreacted today. Unbelievably so. When I realized you'd written, well, all the good parts, my imagination got away from me." She noticed a softening of his lips, maybe even a tiny smile. "I managed to picture all the worst scenarios. Then when you explained, I knew you were right. I hope you can forgive me."

"I don't know yet if I can do that," he said. "I'll have to taste the pie first."

Lily smiled and picked up the knife to cut two slices and served them. "I should tell you, I used a canned filling I found in the pantry. I didn't make it from scratch."

"I think it still qualifies as an apology pie. Besides, I heard once that the crust is the hardest part."

"It is," she agreed. "You have to roll it out just right, on the right amount of flour. And you can't roll it too much or it won't be tender and flaky."

"Is that why you have on a different dress? Did you get flour all over the other one?"

"Yes. Let's say that's why."

His smile widened. "This is good," he said with his mouth full. "It's an excellent apology pie."

"Does that mean you'll forgive me?"

"Tell me why I should," he challenged as he lifted another bite on his fork.

"Because… it'll illustrate what a good man you are."

"You already think I'm a good man. You told me so."

"All right. Because it's not good to harbor a grudge and withhold forgiveness. It gnaws at the gut."

"I do like my innards. It would be a pity if a grudge got me so bad I couldn't eat your apology pies. Give me one more reason."

She leaned forward a little bit. "Because if you forgive me, I'll do my very best to show you how much I appreciate it."

Amos swallowed the last bite of his pie and set down his fork. "I can tell how heartfelt this apology is. It would be uncharitable of me to leave you hanging. You are forgiven. Now come over here." He scooted his chair back and patted his lap.

She practically ran around the table and sat on his lap. She was kissing him even before she got settled and steady.

"Now why did you think I meant for you to sit? I might have wanted you to lay across my lap so I could give you what you have coming to you."

"Is that what you wanted?" she asked as she absent-mindedly tickled his ear.

"Hell no. But it could have been."

Lily ignored it. Several nice, long kisses later she realized there were drawbacks to sitting on a man's lap. "Let's go to the couch. I can't reach my new friend here very well."

"We can't have that. Come on." Once at the couch, he turned and pulled her to him. "So I wrote the good parts, huh?"

They resumed their petting on the couch, his stiffened length readily accessible to her roaming hands. His hands roamed, too, more than he'd done before. Lily moaned softly when he caressed her breast, and she whispered his name when he leaned down and nibbled the hardened tip.

"Amos, I want you so badly right now."

"I know, but we can't. Let's stop for a while and just sit here."

She sighed, but resigned herself to it. He wasn't going to budge, so she leaned into the arm he held up to put around her shoulder.

"Amos?"

"Yes?"

"I was thinking. As much as I want us to remember and appreciate Will, sometimes it should be just you and me. When the time comes for us to go, you know, further, I want it to be here at your house. In your bed."

"I've had the same thought."

CHAPTER 5

The next day began as the previous ones had: Lily made breakfast, they ate, Amos helped with cleanup, and they spent as much time as they dared getting passionate on the couch.

"You do realize, Lily, that I've almost completed the work on the house. I'll be going back to work for half-days until school starts, then full-time. When I'm working and you're teaching school, we won't be able to spend our mornings like this."

"Maybe we can spend more time at night doing it."

"We can certainly try that."

"Why will you only be working half-days until school starts?"

"It's what Angus and Henry said to do. I'm not sure you realize how bad they felt that Will was killed on the job. They feel a huge responsibility. I think if Will hadn't left you a home and some money, they would have provided it. We'll never know for sure, but it would be like them to do that."

"I should think of a way to thank them."

"All right, if you want to, but they aren't expecting it."

～

THERE WAS a knock at the door midmorning, and Lily knew that wouldn't be Amos. She was surprised to find Mr. Bailey, the attorney.

"Good morning, Mr. Bailey. Won't you come in?"

"No, no, no. No need," he said with a smile. "I promised you I'd deliver the deed when all the paperwork was completed and filed. Here you go. This property is officially yours, Miss Holt."

"Thank you, Mr. Bailey. This means so much to me. But really, I could have come to your office."

"It's my pleasure, Miss Holt." He tipped his hat. "Good day to you."

As he turned to leave, Lily had an idea. She hurried out to join him on the porch.

"Mr. Bailey, do you think you might find a few minutes to come to my classroom and talk to them about your profession? I have a student, one student in particular, who I understand has expressed a desire to be an attorney."

"I can't imagine what I would talk about."

"It needn't take long; I know you're busy. I thought maybe you could explain what you do, or share an interesting case or two, I mean, to the extent that you're able to speak of it. You could talk about what education is required. I want to get the children to think about their futures."

"Well, I did have some noteworthy cases back east before I moved here. That might be interesting. How long do I have to talk?"

"I'll give you as little or as much time as you need," Lily said.

"I'll do it, ma'am. Just tell me when to be there."

That exchange excited Lily. What if she had other people come in and talk about their jobs?

～

John came over again to help Amos for a couple of hours, then he joined them for supper.

"Is there any work left to do, Amos?" John asked.

"No, that clothesline was the last thing. That means I can go back to work tomorrow and Friday for half-days. School starts Monday, doesn't it, Lily?"

"Yes, it does, but you said you'd be able to take me to my students' homes to visit with them before school starts. Will you be able to do that tomorrow?"

"Sure. I'll just work a half-day Friday, then on Monday, we'll both be working full-time."

"Oh, good," Lily said. "I was afraid I couldn't visit them after all."

Amos smiled at her reassuringly. "If it's at all possible, I'll make it happen."

Thank you, Lord, for sending this man to me.

Lily turned her attention to John. "How is work at the sawmill, John? Is it hectic since you've been shorthanded? I'm afraid I've monopolized Amos' time."

"It's not too bad, but I'll be glad to get Amos back. We got a lot of timber that day..." he caught himself before he finished the sentence.

"It's all right," Lily said softly. "You mean the day we lost Will."

"Yes. We got most of it cut and Angus was just about to schedule a team of jacks to go out again, but the Capp brothers felled their own trees while they were clearing land for a pasture. They sold us three big loads."

"Oh, is that common? For other people to bring you trees?"

"It's not as common for people to want to sell them to us. It's more common for people to cut their own, then bring them to us to mill, but they keep the final lumber. It's cheaper that way for people who are building and have the time to cut their own. I can see it happening more and more, though, as the town grows and more people move in."

"That's interesting how a business can change with growth, or have a different focus. Today, I asked Mr. Bailey if he'd come talk to my students about what it's like to be a lawyer. I wonder if Henry or Angus would come talk to them about the lumber and milling and furniture businesses?"

Amos laughed. "If you ask them, they'll do it. You seem to wield a lot of influence."

Lily laughed, too. "I don't want to overburden them, but I do have another request for the school. You two can handle it, though, I'm sure. When you get a chance, would you build some benches to go outside the schoolhouse?"

Both of the men grinned, but John answered. "We'd be happy to."

"Thank you. Both." She looked at each one of them and gave a nod of gratitude.

Amos changed the subject. "John, how are things at the boarding house?"

"Miz Helen badly needs help. I've tried to bring it up with her, but she doesn't want to talk about it very much. She tries to deny it, but that's not going to last for very long. If she still denies needing help after one more week, another boarder and I are going to go to the men on the town committee and see if they'll hire more help."

"Angus and Henry are both on that committee," Amos said. "Why don't you just talk to them about it? I'm sure the committee would handle it diplomatically. They're all fond of Miz Helen."

"I've come close, but I always thought it would be best for her to ask for help herself. I think I was overly optimistic. I thought I might talk to Harriet Smithers about it. You know how she can get the committee to do things."

Amos laughed and nodded in agreement. "That she does, my friend."

"Besides, I've about decided to ask her to find me a mail order bride."

Lily was so excited, a little bit of coffee came out her nose, causing her to sputter and grab a napkin. "John, that's so exciting! I can't wait until you have her here."

THE NEXT MORNING passed just as previous mornings had. But this time, since Amos had to work the following morning and their time would be limited, they spent extra time on the couch. Lily was getting bolder, touching Amos all over and bringing his hands to touch her. She even brought his hand up under her skirt and placed it mid-thigh. The sound he made was of both desire and torment. Lily lost herself in the sensations, knowing that Amos would stop them at some point. She couldn't fathom how he could have the strength to stop; she would have gone on until their final release.

When the time came to stop, she sighed and cuddled against him.

LILY PICKED up her notebook with the students' names to take with them. She went out to the barn with Amos and helped him hook up Atlas and Hercules to the buggy. She drove the buggy outside the barn while he closed the door, then he hopped up beside her and took the reins.

She rubbed his thigh while they were still in the yard; she wouldn't be able to do that when they were on the street among people.

"Oh, Amos," she said in a husky voice, "I just realized you

didn't get a chance to be alone to take care of things." She punctuated the statement by putting her hand on his crotch and felt that the hardness hadn't fully subsided.

He grinned and swatted her hand away. "So you don't need to make it worse right when we're about to be in public."

Lily gave him a mischievous look and grabbed it one more time before she behaved.

"Where to first?" he asked.

She opened her notebook and looked at her list. "I'm not sure, to tell the truth. I know that Billy Simmons lives in the Low Quarter, but that's about it."

Amos tilted her hand so he could read, too. "I know some of these, but not all of them. Here's a suggestion. Let's go first to the ones who don't go to church with us. I say that because if worse comes to worst and we don't get around to all of them today, you can always visit with the remaining ones on Sunday. As for the Low Quarter, we might want to go home and change to horseback. That road's a bear."

She nodded in agreement. "All right."

"I know where the Wilkersons, Meyers, Culpeppers, and Finns live. One lives out on the road to Separation and the other three are on the outskirts of town. Let's head to the Finns first; they might be the closest."

Lily was excited. She planned her introductory speech in her head so she wouldn't look too scattered when someone answered her knock.

Amos pulled up in the yard, jumped down, and lifted Lily out of the buggy and to the ground.

"Are you going in with me?" she asked.

"No, honey, this is your day. I'm going to stay out here and think of all the ways you're going to thank me for driving you around today."

"Don't think too much. We are in public, you know," she said, glancing down at the button placket of his britches.

When Lily knocked, the door was answered by a pleasant looking woman.

"Hello, I'm Lily Holt, the new schoolteacher. I'm trying to visit with each child before school starts so we can get to know each other beforehand. It might help ease the first day jitters on Monday. Is Curtis available to visit with me for a few minutes?"

"Come on in, Miss Holt. Have a seat at the table. I think the boy's out back. I'll go get him. The coffee's still hot and there are cups beside the stove. Pour yourself a cup if you'd like," Mrs. Finn said. The easy look on her face made Lily feel comfortable and welcome. She liked Mrs. Finn immediately.

Curtis came running in and sat at the table. "Hi, teacher. I've never had a teacher come to my house before."

"You can call me Miss Lily if you'd like. I'd like for you to tell me a little about yourself and how you feel about school. I have some questions to start us off. Will that be all right with you?"

"It sure will. You can ask me anything." Curtis leaned back in his chair and folded his arms, waiting for the first question.

After a while Lily called their visit to a close, but she could have talked to the child all day.

"You were in there over half an hour, sweetie. You might want to shorten the visits or we won't get very far on the list today."

"I can't believe we talked that long! We were both enjoying it so much. I need to write down notes on Curtis while they're still fresh. Otherwise, I'll get confused if I wait to write notes later. I hated to write down anything while we were talking. I want these to be nice conversations, not inquisitions. I'll try my best to be quicker, though."

"Good. The Wilkersons are a mile or so farther down this road. His dad works for Angus and Henry, too, mostly at the furniture factory."

"Oh, good information. I'll write that down. Do you know what Mr. Finn does?"

"He's a miner."

"Got it, thank you. Ben Wilkerson is the oldest one in class. He's the one who wants to be a lawyer. Nessa said he's studious and very responsible."

"Sounds like a good student to have."

They were silent the rest of the way to the Wilkerson place. When they arrived, a young teenage boy was in the front, playing with a dog.

"Hello, are you Ben?" Lily asked.

"Yes, ma'am," he replied. "My ma's not home right now. She should be back before long, though."

"That's all right, I came to see you. I'm Lily Holt, the new schoolteacher."

When she stood to step down to the ground, Ben hurried to the buggy to lend her a hand. Lily and Amos were both impressed with his manners. Lily and Ben sat on the front porch and had their discussion. She did her best to keep it short, but if it hadn't been for Amos discreetly giving her signals, she would have talked for far too long.

They left there and headed for the Meyer's home. Amos told her that Mr. Meyer was the town's only barber and he doubled as the undertaker. There was another man who assisted with the undertaking business, but Amos didn't know much about him.

About the only thing Nessa and the other teachers said about Margie Meyer was that she was boy crazy. If Lily hadn't known it, she would have figured it out. Margie peppered her side of the conversation with questions about the boys. Had Miss Lily talked with any boys yet? Had she talked with Jed Culpepper? Is there any way Miss Lily could make Jed sit by her? If not Jed, how about Ken White? In a pinch, Ben would do, but he's so serious, you know.

Lily thanked Margie for her time and went back to the buggy.

"Get me out of here, my head's spinning. It was almost impossible to carry on a conversation with that girl."

She told Amos about it and they chuckled, amused by the transparent single-minded focus of a thirteen year old girl. As they drove down the main street again headed to the Culpepper ranch, Sheriff Jim Larkin happened to step out. He stopped and waited for Amos to pass before he crossed the street.

"Sheriff," Amos called out as he motioned for Jim to come over. "I need some information. Lily wants to visit her students before Monday, and I don't know all of them. We need you to tell us where they live."

"Sure thing, give me a name."

"Lettie Stewart," Lily said.

"Oh, right. The Stewart place is out on the old silver mine road. It's a log cabin. Looking at it, you can tell where they added on a room. You can't miss it." The sheriff paused. "Do me a favor, keep a close eye on that little girl. Her daddy can get mean. I know he's hurt his wife before, but she's afraid to say much in the way of a complaint. If you have any suspicions that he's hurting Lettie, please let me know."

"I'll do that, Sheriff. What does he do for a living?"

"He lost his job at the Poker Palace Saloon. Now he just drinks. His poor wife has started taking in laundry and doing alterations, but they're just barely getting by. Amos, I'm glad you're going with Miss Lily. I wouldn't want her out there on her own."

They went down the list of names and Jim told them where to find the ones Amos wasn't familiar with. He even knew that the Simmonses lived near this side of the Low Quarter in a little pale yellow house. They decided to go to one more in-town home, then they'd stop for lunch at Mary's Restaurant.

By late afternoon they'd visited all the students except for the ones in their church and Billy Simmons.

"All right, Mr. Cameron," Lily said, "one trip to the Low Quarter and we're done for the day. Are we going to go home and saddle up?"

"No, I'm afraid not, Lily. It's too late. I'm not willing to get us out on that desolate trail and possibly run into trouble. It'll be dark long before we get back. No."

"Please? I'd really like to get them done today."

"No, sweet. I'm sorry. It won't be safe."

"Will you take me tomorrow afternoon?"

"I can't. John and I are making the benches for the school-yard. Angus is supplying the lumber. I can take you Saturday or Sunday afternoon."

Lily looked deflated. "I'll be talking to the church ones on Sunday afternoon. Not sure how long it'll take."

"I can take you Saturday. If something happens and I can't, you can always spend your lunch talking with him on Monday. He'd probably enjoy that."

"Mmm," she mumbled, unhappy with the situation.

There wasn't much chat until they were nearly to Lily's house. "What are we having for supper?" Amos asked.

"What? Oh. I didn't plan ahead, but there's plenty of food."

"If you'd rather not cook, we can always go to my house to eat." He gave her a salacious look and raised an eyebrow. "But I still expect you to find a way to thank me for driving you around today. You promised, you know."

That brought her out of her moodiness and she laughed. "If I remember correctly, I didn't exactly promise that. I believe you said you expected it."

"Did I? Well, I don't recall you challenging me, so it might as well be a promise."

Supper was easy; she fixed them a hearty breakfast meal of bread toasted in butter, ham, and eggs. Lily carried on light conversation throughout, although her mind was focused on how she planned to thank him later. She was going to try something new for them, and it would definitely be a step further.

When Amos was ready to leave at the end of the evening, albeit reluctantly, Lily asked him if he could come extra early in the morning for breakfast. She wasn't ready just yet to stop their intimate sessions and cuddle times after their meals.

CHAPTER 6

a t her table the next morning, Amos mentioned that although he only planned to work half a day, he might be a little late since it would be his first day back.

"That won't be a problem," she said. "I have some stew meat that needs to be cooked. It'll be easy to reheat if we need to. You should invite John for lunch since he's going to build the benches with you. That's the least I can do to show my appreciation."

Amos looked up and smirked. "I'll do that. After all, you can't show him appreciation the way you showed me appreciation last night."

She grinned in a look she hoped was brazen. "I could tell you liked that. I like those noises you make. The moans and sounds that aren't quite words. Makes me, I don't know, it makes me want to do things to hear you make more sounds like that."

Amos laughed. "Are you aware you make sounds, too? But I know what you mean. Last night I felt like you took me to the edge of Heaven. The feel of your hand on my bare cock, it was like velvet on fire."

"My hand couldn't be better than your own. I didn't know what I was doing."

"My cock sure knew what you were doing. You saw how fast you got a reaction. I tried to last longer, but you had me so worked up I lost control. I couldn't help it, not for the life of me." He paused. "It was so good I couldn't stop thinking about it. I had to go home and do it again."

Amos helped her clear the table. He started to pour hot water in the dishpan in the sink.

"I can do those later, after you leave. Let's go to the couch."

He followed her and before long they were both making noises. She started to unbutton the placket flap on his britches.

"Lily, honey, you'd better not do that. I can't very well go to work with a wet spot on my clothes."

"If I open them up wide enough to get my mouth down there, there won't be a wet spot," she said as she continued to unbutton. The look on his face made her stop. "Uh oh. I've gone too far. I thought that was a thing some women do. I'm sorry. Please don't think ill of me."

"Oh sweet Lord, Lily, I don't think ill of you, and you haven't gone too far. I'm just surprised to hear you say that. Surprised to hear that you want to do it." He snorted just a little. "I'd be thrilled for you to do that. Are you sure?"

She smiled and let her answer be the continued unbuttoning of the six buttons. With the flap loose, she found the opening in his undergarment and freed his hardness, happy to see it for the first time. Lily lowered her head and kissed the tip, then ran her tongue across it. She felt Amos pull her hair away and realized he wanted to see better, and that encouraged her. She ran her tongue around it, flicking it at the mushroom head. She kissed and licked down to the base and back up. When she sucked it into her mouth, the sound he made spurred her on. Lily bobbed her head up and down as she took in more each time until she could take no more of his length.

The teasing and flicking of her tongue kept up, especially around the head and along the underside where she found a slight ridge.

"I'm so close, baby, almost there." She felt a slight pull on her hair and wondered if it was intentional on his part. "Just a little more. Suck a little harder," he whispered.

She did, and she shifted her head slightly to get the most direct angle. Lily sucked and concentrated her tongue action on the underside of the mushroom head where it met the ridge.

"Aah!" Amos called out as she felt his seed inside her mouth. She swallowed, and had to swallow again to get it all down.

Lily kept licking, gently, as Amos' breath returned to normal. It was as though she was washing him with her tongue.

"Sweet Lily girl, that felt incredible. But I don't have time to take care of you and return that favor. I need to leave soon."

She smiled. "I meant to give you a sweet release, not an obligation. Besides, I wanted to make sure you'll be thinking of me all morning."

Amos slowly nodded his head and stroked her hair. Then he gave her the tenderest kiss she could imagine.

When he left, she watched as his horse took him down the road to the mill on the other side of town. It was still early.

Why won't that man ask me to marry him? Do I need to tell him I've fallen in love with him? Hell, I'm a modern woman. Maybe I should take charge and ask him to marry me.

LILY POURED hot water into her dishpan and added a bar of soap. She swirled it around, then replaced it back on its holder. As she washed the dishes, she thought about what she had just done and how happy it seemed to make Amos. That was a bold move for a woman to make. Would other women have done something like that? she wondered. She was bold, all right. But was she bold enough to pop the question to her man? After all, she came all the way out west to marry a relative stranger. That was bold.

That's right! I am bold. I'm strong. I can ride, I can shoot, and I can take care of myself, even though Amos apparently wants to think I'm a helpless woman. But I'm not helpless, no, sir. And I believe I can show him. I know I can.

Her decision made, Lily rushed to finish the kitchen so she could change clothes and make herself presentable. She remembered the meat she needed to cook and cursed. She browned it quickly, roughly cut an onion and some carrots, then added them and some water. Seasoning it the way she wanted it, she let it sit on the hot stove burner while she went to the water closet one more time. When she returned, it had begun to boil, and she moved the covered cast iron Dutch oven to the farthest burner so it wouldn't get direct heat.

The dress she put on was plain, she thought, and suitable for a schoolmarm. She was almost out the door when she remembered there could be snakes on the trail, so she got her father's gun and put it in her pocket.

In the barn she saddled Atlas. Spying a machete hanging with other tools, she grabbed it and secured it to the saddle. *I might have to cut through some overgrown brush or vines.* They left the barn and Lily closed the door. The stirrup seemed awfully high without Amos there to give her a boost, but she finally made it up in the saddle. A big smile crossed her face; she was eager for this adventure.

Then they were off. It was exhilarating to be out, free, doing what she wanted to do. She urged Atlas into a fast trot for a few minutes just to feel the wind on her face.

This is how we were meant to live: free. Free to do as we wish, free to feel the wind, free to do what we need to do without having to check in with someone, like those poor city men back in Lincoln. They're condemned to a life lived inside four walls, with bosses telling them what to do and when to do it. Then when they come home, they're little more than yes-men to their wives. And the women have it even worse—why, most of the ones I know don't even shop for their own food and supplies. The men do it on their way home. Their emasculated men. No, give me my real man any day. My Amos. He's right at home outdoors, rugged, forthright, and self-sufficient. He has a job that's mostly outside and his bosses live the same way, so they understand what it is to be real men. And as of this moment, I'm a real woman. A woman deserving of a real man.

When she got to the place where the trail to the Low Quarter veered off, she felt a renewed sense of elation. About a hundred yards in, she thought it wasn't so bad. Everyone who talked about this road must have traveled it when it was much worse. It was rutty and uneven, but as long as she let Atlas go at his own pace, he was fine. She wasn't worried. She had time.

In another hundred yards, the trail narrowed and she could see how a wide wagon might have a problem. Some of the overgrowth was just scrubby bushes that a wagon might roll on over without much trouble, but there were some thick vines and low tree branches that would have to be cut for a wagon to get through. Lily was grateful she was on horseback.

She came to a rickety bridge over a dip that looked like it might become a stream in rainy weather. The bridge didn't have a stable look to it, but it held when they crossed it. The trail narrowed and widened and became unlevel and then smooth again for the next mile or so. Lily didn't have a good sense of the distance she'd come, or how long she'd been riding, for that matter. Soon she came to another bridge and it appeared to be in similar shape.

I can handle this. It isn't as bad as Amos made it out to be. At least that's what she thought until she came to a wide dip where a bridge had washed out. There were boards lying on the bed of the dry creek. They were off to the side of the place where the bridge had been, and Lily suspected someone moved them over to allow horses to go directly across without having to choose their steps carefully.

Lily surveyed the dry creek bed they needed to cross and saw that the sides were steeper than the other creeks they'd crossed. A bridge was sorely needed in this particular spot. A wagon probably wouldn't be able to negotiate the gap. It might have been able to take the sharp slope of the sides, but only if the gap was wider. She didn't think a wagon could do it because it wouldn't be completely down one side before the horses would have to make their way up the other side.

But a horse and rider could do it. She held on and gently urged Atlas forward. He didn't struggle but he did have to exert himself to make it up the other side. She felt a sense of triumph when they leveled off again.

Before long they came across another rickety bridge. It crossed a much deeper streambed that had water slowly flowing downstream. It wasn't much water, probably only three or four inches in the deepest spots, but to Lily, it looked forbidding. She chided herself, reasoning that it only looked bad because it was a little deeper than the others had been. Just because the last bridge had collapsed, didn't mean this one was going to. She held her breath as Atlas selected his steps and they made it across.

There were no more bridges and it wasn't long before a house appeared, then another. The houses were mostly clustered together, and the fields were on the other side of the houses. That seemed odd to Lily, but sure enough, it looked like the houses were nearer to her and the alfalfa fields were mostly on the other side of them, instead of houses being together with the field that was owned by the same person who owned the house. She figured that must be where the most fertile soil was. There were fruit trees here and there, and some of the houses had gardens.

She saw a pale yellow house and made her way to it. The door was opened by a little boy with an inquisitive look.

"Are you Billy?"

"Yes, ma'am, I am. Billy Simmons."

"Well, Billy, I'm Lily Holt, and I'm your new schoolteacher. I wanted to visit with all my students before Monday so we'll all know each other already. You can call me Miss Lily."

"Well, Miss Lily, my momma's not home right now, but since you're the teacher, you can come in." He opened the door all the way.

Lily got a look inside. It was sparsely furnished, but it looked clean and orderly. What furniture there was, was old and threadbare. So were Billy's clothes. They were faded and worn, but clean.

"Since your mother's away, maybe it would be best if we talked out here. We can sit on this step if you like."

Billy seemed to consider her words, then spoke deliberately. "I reckon that would be fine." He came outside and they sat on a step.

"I wanted to get to know you a little bit. I hope you'll tell me a little about yourself and what you like about school. And of course, what you don't like."

Billy nodded slowly and seriously. "Well, I'm not partial to tests. I'd say that's the main thing I don't like. And homework. I like recess best. Playing with the other boys. There aren't many boys to play with, out here. Well, not any to play with. One boy's older but he quit going to school and he works all the time. It's just me now."

Lily noticed that Billy's speech was a little slower than her own. She could tell it wasn't because of any defect; he was simply deliberate with his words.

"I see. I'd like to help out with the testing situation, but I'm afraid I don't see a way around them. Why do you think you never liked them? Are they hard for you?"

Again, Billy pondered his answer. "I reckon I was just always nervous to take 'em. My momma helps me study, so I mostly know the answers. I just don't want to disappoint her."

"That's good of your mother to help you study. Not all students are lucky enough to have a parent like that."

"My momma's the best. It's the truth."

"Is there a school subject you like?"

"That one's easy. Readin'. When I was little, my momma read to me all the time. Then when I learned to read, we'd take turns readin' to each other. But we cain't do that anymore. After Pa died, Momma had to sell all our books to buy food. She had to sell a lot of her stuff to buy food." He looked away, and it struck Lily that he didn't seem to look away in sadness or shame. Rather, it seemed he was resigned to their situation; that he'd gained wisdom from unsettling times, even at his tender age.

Lily gave him a conspiratorial smile. "I can't help the tests, but I do have a plan that will help with the books. It'll help the whole community with free access to books. I won't tell you the plan now because I want to tell all my students at the same time. Until then, you and I can keep it our little secret. Can you do that?"

His eyes widened a little. "I sure can, Miss Lily. I won't tell a soul. Not even Momma. Cross my heart." He made an X sign over his heart and held up his hand as though taking an oath.

"Good. Now about those other things you told me: I'm so sorry to hear about that, Billy, both that your father died and that your mother had to sell things to get by."

"Momma said it was the Lord's will to take Pa when he did. Something ate at him and made him miserable. And that made him start drinking." He paused and looked off in the distance again. "He was mean when he drank. Momma says the Lord was lookin' out for us, to take Pa so young. She says no matter how hard it gets, we'll get by. We always do. We have each other."

"How do you get to school? Do you walk?"

"I've only had to walk in the mornings a few times. We used to have our own horse, but Momma had to sell it. She sold it to our neighbor on the condition that she could borrow it to take me to school. Sometimes she can come get me in the afternoon and sometimes she can't. I walk home by myself if she's not here. It's not that bad."

Lily talked with Billy for a few more minutes before she decided to head home.

"I sure am pleased to meet you, Miss Lily. I wish Momma could have been here. You be careful going home."

She was enchanted with the boy. She was even more enamored when he didn't laugh at her for having trouble mounting her horse again. He came over and held the stirrup firmly so it wouldn't move. "Try it again, Miss Lily, you can do it. There, you almost made it that time. Try again, just a little higher next time. That's all right, it's all right, now try again. Take a deep breath and push off just a little harder. There you go, that's it!" He was sincerely pleased that she made it successfully onto the saddle, as though it was his victory, too. Lily wanted to hug the child.

The exuberance she had previously felt over her successful adventure was tempered by the thought of the Simmons' hardship. As she started homeward, she couldn't help but think about how hard Billy's mother must work to keep them above water. She didn't know how long the father had been gone, nor did she know how long Mrs. Simmons had been struggling with financial matters. *Financial matters* seemed like a hifalutin phrase when she was talking about scraping up enough money just to have food to eat. She respected the diligence and hard work ethic Mrs. Simmons must possess.

The gut-wrenching sound of boards breaking brought her

out of her thoughts, and almost instantly she heard other popping sounds she couldn't readily identify. She heard Atlas give a long, high-pitched squeal, and then she saw the bottom of the deep gulley rise to meet them.

AMOS AND JOHN left the sawmill, grateful to Angus for volunteering to deliver the wood to the schoolyard for the benches. He promised them the lumber would be there ready for them by the time they finished lunch. Otherwise, they'd have had to go home, hitch up a team to the buckboard, and go back to the sawmill.

"Amos, when are you going to make an honest woman out of Lily?" John asked, mainly to make conversation as they rode side by side.

Amos grinned, remembering that morning. "I'll have you know she's still an honest woman, but I know what you mean. Soon, I think. I've been giving it a lot of thought for a few days now, but I just haven't asked her yet."

"Well, why the hell not? You know she'll say yes. Anybody who's seen you two together knows she'll say yes."

"I know she'll say yes."

"Well, what are you waiting for?"

Amos's expression sobered a little bit. "I'm waiting for a time when I can kiss her and not hear a nagging voice deep down inside saying it should be Will kissing her instead of me."

"You're a damn fool, Amos. You and Will were best friends almost all your lives. That day you're talking about may not come for years, maybe not ever."

"You think so?"

"I do. Any man would feel like that. But you can't put off the rest of your lives waiting for that to happen, because it might not. Marrying her might even make that day come sooner."

"I suppose it could. I do want to marry her, mighty bad, in fact."

John chuckled. "Sounds like you might be having trouble *keeping* her an honest woman."

"Friend, you've no idea the battle I fight to keep her virtue intact. I'm afraid the time might come when I lose the battle and compromise the schoolmarm."

"There's no reason for anyone to know, Amos."

"That was Lily's argument, too."

"Well, she's wiser than you are, then. Marry that woman, and soon, so your conscience can rest easy. Damn fool. You should already be married."

"All right, all right. I'll ask her."

At Lily's house, Amos knocked instead of barging in. "Lily, we're here and we're hungry," he called out. There was no response so he knocked again. Again, no answer.

John whispered, "Maybe she's in the water closet. Let's give her a minute or two more."

Amos nodded but he was becoming worried. When he knocked again to no avail, they went in. He hurried through the little house but there was no sign of Lily.

"I'll go check the barn," John said as he ran out the back door. He was back quickly, his breathing a little heavy from the exertion of running. "She's not there and one of the horses is gone, too."

"Lily, what have you done?" Amos asked no one specifically as he made his way to the stove. He lifted the lid of the stewpot and saw condensation. When he stuck his finger in, it was warm but certainly not hot. She knew they were coming for lunch. It should have been hot. He opened the door of the stove and his suspicion was confirmed. There were only dying coals there. "Damn it, she's been gone for hours, and I'll bet I know where she's gone. Come on. We're heading to the Low Quarter."

John's expression was one of shocking disbelief, but he followed. Amos saw him pat his holster to make sure he had his gun. It instinctively made him check his own.

Once underway, John asked if Amos hadn't warned Lily about the Low Quarter.

"Oh, I warned her. Even Nessa and the sheriff told her she shouldn't go by herself. I told her I'd take her tomorrow or Sunday, but apparently she couldn't wait."

"What are you going to do about it?" John asked. "I know what I'd do."

"I'm going to make her wish she'd minded me, that's for sure. At least that's what I plan to do."

"Meaning?"

"She should have returned by now. All she wanted to do was introduce herself and spend a few minutes talking with a student there."

"Well," John reasoned, "we don't know what time she left. Maybe it wasn't as early as you think."

"Why would she even go if she knew we'd be here for lunch?"

"That's an excellent question."

They rode side by side when the trail allowed it, single file at those other times. A knot formed in Amos' gut and it got tighter the farther they got. They had only short distance visibility since the path meandered and it occasionally had branches or scrub brush jutting into the path. Amos prayed with each bend in the trail that they'd find Lily.

He wasn't sure if he saw her or heard her first, but they found her, crying and limping home.

"Lily!" He jumped down and ran to her, possibly holding her tighter than he ever had.

She kept sobbing and he had a hard time understanding. "I had to shoot him, Amos, I had to shoot Atlas. He broke both front legs. I had to shoot him."

"What happened, honey? How did this happen?"

"The last bridge on this trail. Some boards broke when he stepped on them. I heard his bones break. I had to shoot him, Amos. I didn't have any choice."

John heard it all. "You get her on home and doctored up, Amos. I'll go check and see what all we need to do. I'll meet you back at Lily's house."

"Thanks, John."

Amos held Lily away from him so he could check her for wounds. Her arms were bloody in several places and her sleeves were in tatters. She had small scrapes on her head and bruises were already appearing on her forehead and jaw near her ear. Her dress was soaking wet or muddy in places. He noticed that her dress and even her petticoat had several large rips. He started to lift her skirts, and she asked what he was doing.

"I saw you limping. I'm checking to see how badly you're injured."

"Oh," was all she said, but that might have been because she was still crying.

"You've got a lot of cuts and some look deep. A couple might even be deep enough for Dr. Larkin to put in some stitches."

"No, please, just take me home and tend to me there. If you still think I need the doctor, I'll go."

"All right. Let me get you up on my horse. It's probably going to hurt you some."

He got up and settled behind her, one arm around her waist. He prayed a silent *Thank you* that she was alive. Then he prayed for the strength not to throttle her, because he wanted to.

Her crying subsided into sniffling and an occasional sob before she could get it under control again.

"Did your visit with Billy go all right?"

"Yes. He may be my favorite in the class. He and his mother are having a hard time just surviving. Amos?"

"Yes?"

"I wish I hadn't gone. I know you didn't want me to, and I should have listened to you. But it seemed so right at the time. Then on the way back—" The sobbing started in earnest again. "I had to shoot him, Amos."

"I know, honey. It breaks your heart. That's one of the hardest things a man could ever have to do. Or a woman. You're lucky he didn't land on top of you. We're both lucky. I can't imagine losing you."

"I'll replace him, I promise I will."

"You don't have to replace him, honey. He was your horse."

"Oh. Right. I keep thinking he was Will's, I guess."

"What was making you limp? I didn't get a chance to see it clearly."

"He threw me off and I think I landed first on one knee, sideways. I can't remember exactly. Before I knew it I was sprawled out beside him at the bottom of the ditch. I had a hard time getting up because my skirt was under him and while I was trying, I saw his legs. My gun was in my pocket. I had to shoot before I was even able to get up. I couldn't let him lie there in pain."

"I can feel the gun against my leg. I'm glad you thought to take it with you."

"Amos, I'm sorry I didn't listen to you. I understand now."

"We can talk about it later, honey. Right now I just want to get you home and tend to those wounds."

They were silent the rest of the way except for the times when Lily wept.

When they got to her house, he rode around to the back.

"Why are we going in the back door?"

"Because you can't wear that dress inside or you'll get dirt and mud everywhere. I didn't want to pull it off you on the front porch."

"Oh."

Amos loosely tethered his horse to the rail he'd recently finished, then he lifted Lily down. She stood still as he unbuttoned her dress and pulled it over her head. When he saw the mud on her petticoat, he told her it had to come off, too. He pulled it down and she stepped out of it.

Once inside, he told her to have a seat at the kitchen table. He put some more wood in the stove and stoked the embers to light it. While he was at it, he put a pot of water on what would soon be the hottest burner.

Lily heard him opening cabinets. "What are you looking for?"

"I know Will has some liquor in here somewhere."

"Corner cabinet on the left."

"Got it."

He poured some into a small glass and handed it to her. "Sip that. I'll go gather supplies."

Amos found the iodine, bandages, and carbolic acid. When he set the acid on the table, he said, "I'm glad I didn't laugh at you for buying this. I didn't dream we'd be using it this soon."

"Let me get some more whiskey down me. That stuff hurts."

"Yes, ma'am. Good idea."

He put the time to good use. He poured some sugar into a bowl and dropped in iodine, stirring to spread it evenly after each drop. He washed his hands and brought several clean rags and towels to the table.

Amos knelt in front of Lily and unbuckled and removed her shoes. He took great care removing her stockings because they were embedded in her wounds here and there. Her breath caught each time a stocking stuck to a cut and he had to pull it away.

"Drink some more, Lily. I think you're going to need it."

She abandoned the sips and took swallows, screwing up her face and shaking a little with each one. When the glass was empty, she refilled it and downed that one, too. Lily was much better at it on the third glass.

When she was about to pour more, he stopped her. "That's enough for now, honey. I don't want to make you sick, just numb."

Amos checked the water and it was hot enough. He poured it into two large bowls. He put a soap bar in one of them, then took them both to the table.

"All right, let's see what we're dealing with here. I'll start at the top."

He took the pins out of her hair and let down what hadn't already escaped. There was only one scrape in her hair and it only needed to be cleaned; it wasn't too bad. Some light bruising made her face look worse than it was. She only had light scrapes and they, too, only needed to be cleaned. He washed away the mud splatters.

Amos walked behind her and told her to lean forward a little so he could check her back for scrapes and bruises. He looked down the neckline of her shift but didn't see any injuries. "I need to check your front, too."

She lifted her chin so her head wouldn't be in his way.

"This is definitely not the way I pictured seeing your breasts for the first time. It was a lot more pleasant in my imagination."

Lily smiled just a little, despite her obvious pain. Amos suspected the whiskey was taking effect.

As he looked down her shift, he didn't see anything obvious, but her breasts blocked his view of part of her midriff. He gently pressed his hand against her. "Does this hurt? Or this?" He didn't get responses until he pressed on her right side. "Ow. I landed on that side. I think it was a big rock, mostly buried."

"All right. I need to see it. I need to lift up your shift. Raise up just a little so I can pull it out from under you." She did, and he pulled it up to reveal her side. He ran his fingers over the bruise and Lily made a sound as she curled her body away from his touch.

"That tickles."

"All right. I think it's just a regular bruise. I'm pretty sure it would look a little different if you'd ruptured an organ and it was bleeding inside. I may get Doc Larkin to come by later, just to be sure. Now, I need to wash all this dirt and mud off your arms and legs so I can treat the cuts."

He started with her neck and upper chest where dirt had come in through her neckline. Then he tackled her arms, rinsing the dirt off the cloth several times before he took a fresh cloth and gave them a final rinse. He went to her legs next and started at her upper thighs. *How hard did she have to struggle for dirt to have gotten that high up under her skirt?* As he cleaned downward, he took stock of the injuries that looked the most threatening. He still wasn't sure the doctor didn't need to stitch up one of them, maybe two. He made the definite decision to get Dr. Larkin to come by later.

When she was washed clean of the dirt and mud, he went back to tend the wounds on her arms. The lighter scratches didn't need any treatment other than the cleansing he'd already done. On the ones that were slightly deeper, he dabbed carbolic acid. She hissed and tried to shrink from his touch, but he persisted. One cut was deep enough to require that drops of carbolic acid be used to irrigate it. Her hissing turned to a groan of pain.

"I know, honey, but it has to be done."

"I know. It just hurts so much."

He looked at the bandages. "Do you have any petroleum jelly? And scissors?"

"Yes. Petroleum jelly is in the water closet in one of the cabinets. Look on the far right with the bath oils and powders. My dress shears are part of my sewing kit in a covered basket.

It's in the cabinet to the left of the one with the petroleum jelly."

"Good. I'll be right back."

When he returned, he smiled at her. "You give accurate directions, my sweet. I hope if I put the petroleum jelly around the outside of the gashes, it'll help keep the bandages from sticking where the blood dries while they heal."

Lily nodded. First Amos put the petroleum jelly around all the cuts he planned to cover with a bandage. He cut a few pieces of the bandaging strips into sizes to correspond to the wounds. Using the spoon as both a measure and an application device, he put a little of the iodine and sugar mixture into each one, then covered them with two or three layers of the cotton bandage. When the entire arm was treated, he wound a long strip around her upper and lower arm to hold the individual dressings in place and secured it. He did the same thing with the other arm.

He settled down lower for better access to her legs. "You gave these legs quite a beating, Lily. This is probably going to hurt more than your arms."

She nodded. "They do hurt more." Her gaze went to the window, but Amos doubted if she was focused on anything outside. "My skirts got caught under Atlas and my legs were bare. It was hard to pull them out from under him and I struggled so much, I made the rips worse. I've never felt so frustrated and helpless. I was just about to rip them off when they pulled free."

She started to cry again. Amos knew it was the reminder about the horse.

He dabbed at a few cuts with the carbolic acid. Lily tensed her legs and he could tell she was trying not to holler.

"I'm going to have to irrigate these deeper ones. Brace yourself, honey."

The worst gash was on her knee; he figured it was the knee

that hit the ground first. Some of the dirt had come out when he washed her legs with soapy water, but he could still see dirt in it. "I think this, more than any of the others, may need to be sewn up. If it wasn't on the bend of the knee, we might chance it, but it'll probably take longer to heal as it is. Unless you're able to keep your legs totally straight, you'll probably keep reopening it. The other one isn't quite as bad, but I can tell you did a lot of scrambling on your knees. Get ready. Here we go."

He held a clean rag on her leg just under the gash to catch the runoff. When he slowly poured the carbolic acid in, she cried out. "Oh, Lord, that hurts so much!" Fresh tears pooled in her eyes.

"Lily, honey, it hurts me to see you in pain. And it breaks my heart that you're suffering the agony of having to put a horse out of its misery. I'd give anything to take that away. But the fact is that today, in this circumstance, you should be grateful for the pain and agony. Because if I didn't think you've already been punished enough, I'd have blistered your ass so badly you wouldn't sit comfortably for days."

He saw the surprise in her eyes, then went back to his task.

"Oh, Amos, you won't do that," she said dismissively. "You wouldn't do that to me."

He looked up at her again with a look that he hoped said *Oh, yes I will*, but he didn't say anything aloud. *This isn't the time for that particular discussion. And it's certainly not the time for that argument.*

Amos made a mental note to be sure and have the discussion before they married. It wouldn't be fair for her to enter into their marriage without being aware of what might happen if she ignored his word in the future.

When he finished dressing her injuries, he began cleaning the mess he'd made while treating her. When they heard a horse approaching, Lily livened up considerably. "Amos! My robe. It's hanging on the back of my bedroom door." He quickly retrieved it and ended up having to help her stand. He held the robe while she put her arms in the sleeves and he tied the belt for her.

"I'm a lot more achy and sore now than I was."

"You took a bad spill into a deep ditch, Lily. Then you had to exert an awful lot of effort to get up and out of it. I imagine you'll be even worse tomorrow."

When John knocked, they both told him to come in.

"How's the patient doing?"

"I'm sore and all cut up, it seems. But Amos has been taking good care of me."

"I'm glad to hear it. Is there anything I can do before we settle down and talk about the next steps?"

"Well, yes," Amos said. "While I finish cleaning the table off, you can check the stew on the stove and see if it's hot enough to eat."

"I can do that," he said as he lifted the lid. "It is definitely hot enough. Want me to go ahead and get bowls and spoons?"

"Go right ahead. Just play like you live here." Amos remembered being amused when Lily said those very words to him. He winked at her. Apparently, she remembered because she winked back and grinned.

"Play like," John said, almost under his breath. It sounded like he was amused, too.

"I'm sorry I didn't make cornbread, but there's light bread wrapped up in a towel on the counter," Lily said. "I'll cut some slices if you bring me the loaf and a bread knife."

"That's not necessary," John said. "I'll play like I can slice bread, too."

"THIS WON'T BE nice table talk, but I need to tell you what I found. Do you want me to wait until after we eat?" John asked.

"No," Lily said. "We aren't sticklers for polite table conversation. I need to hear it. Go ahead."

"All right. I found the horse and, Lily, you were right to take the action you did. Those were bad breaks. I tried to get the saddle for you, but I couldn't because of the way he landed, and I didn't have any rope with me. Amos, people don't need to see that. We need to get out there first thing in the morning, at first light, and move the horse away from the bridge and out of the gulley. It empties into a ravine about forty yards from where he is now. The horses can drag him. Once we get him within a few feet of the edge, I think we can throw a rope over a tree and the horses can get him right to the edge without being in danger. Once he's that close, you and I together can push him over. I'm pretty sure."

"All right. So far that's plenty of rope and axes we need. Anything else?"

"I fastened the machete to the saddle. It might be handy to have," Lily said.

"I saw it, it's still there."

"What do we need to take to fix the bridge?" Amos asked.

John drew in a deep breath. "I didn't like what I saw, Amos. Not at all. There were four bridges, or there should be. One bridge was washed out completely. The remaining ones need to be reinforced. I wouldn't want my loved ones traveling that trail like that. I know it's a lot of work, but I propose we build a new bridge where the other one's been washed out, replace boards on Lily's bridge and add more supports, and shore up the others so they'll be safe. You should see the construction, Amos. Whoever built the things didn't care one whit about safety. Either that or they were just incompetent."

"Is it really that bad out there?"

"It is. You and I can't get all that done in one day. We're going to have to enlist some help."

"We'll need it, for sure," Amos said.

"I know where to get it. I'm heading back to the sawmill and I'll round up some help while I figure out how much wood we'll need. I'll pick up bolts and nuts, screws, screwdrivers, drills, brackets, hammers and nails, and whatever else I can think of."

"Oh, my, that's so much," Lily said. "Amos, I still feel like I need to atone for the trouble I've caused. Will you let me pay for the materials?"

"No, honey, the condition of the bridges isn't your doing. I'm sure the town will foot the bill. You'll have to find another way to atone."

"This sure is good stew, Lily, even with light bread," John said. "But I'm afraid I only have time for one bowl. I'm going to have to excuse myself and get to the mill."

"All right. I'll go out with you. I want to fetch Doc Larkin."

"It's on my way, I'll stop and send him," John said. "You can stay here with the patient."

Amos thanked him, but declined. He told him he'd best get on over to the mill.

As he passed the table, Lily took his arm and patted his hand. "John, I'll probably never be able to thank you enough for all you've done to help us. To help me. I'm going to try, but I don't think I will."

"Nonsense. That's what friends do." He patted her hand.

Amos stood. "I'm going to ride out with John. I'll do the dishes when I get back. You rest."

"I think I can do them. There aren't that many."

He leveled a look at her. "I think you should mind what I say. Don't do any work while I'm gone. I'll only be a few minutes. You understand?"

"Yes, I understand. I might lie down." She resigned herself to do what he said.

"Good choice." He blew her a kiss. "I'll be right back."

He came back in just a few minutes with Dr. Elliott Larkin and his wife, Sadie.

"She must be lying down in the back. Come on back here," Amos said.

"Lily, honey? The doctor's here with Sadie."

"Hello, Lily, I hear you had a fight with the bottom of a gulley."

"That sounds accurate. It's safe to say the gulley won."

"Well, let me have a look. Sadie, would you help her with her shift so I can see her side?"

Amos left them and went to the kitchen to clean. By the time he had it tidy and wiped the table one last time, Elliott and Sadie emerged.

"You should have become a doctor, Amos. I agree with your assessment. I only sewed up her knees, and the rest looked fine. The active bleeding has stopped, so you can fix her some willow bark tea for the pain. I brought some bark. If you don't know how to brew it, Sadie can show you. Lily's going to be fine soon. She'll be sore, but encourage her to move and walk around. I told her to try her best to keep her legs as straight as she can for a couple of days, but a little bending won't hurt. That bruise on her side is going to be tender but it's not serious. Get some arnica cream for the bruise and general muscle soreness. I didn't have any extra, but Clint has it at the mercantile."

"Thanks, Doc. Willow bark tea and arnica cream. I'll go get some cream now," he said as he put down the dishrag and dried his hands on his britches.

Sadie piped up. "I'll stay here with her while you're gone, and I'll go ahead and make some tea." She stood on tiptoe and kissed Elliott on the cheek. "I'll be on home when he gets back."

Amos and Elliott walked out together.

CHAPTER 7

*A*mos saw a familiar horse standing outside the mercantile so he went inside in search of John.

"Hey, how's Lily doing?"

"She's going to be fine. Doc just left and he only sewed up her knees. I'm here now to get some arnica cream for her."

"Good. I was worried about her. Good news at the mill, too. We got some volunteers to help out. Then a few more signed on when Angus said the town would pay them time-and-a-half for labor. Angus and Henry are coming, too. I told them the situation. Plans right now are to take a couple of wagons with supplies. Everything we think we'll need to build that one that washed out will go on one wagon, together with the supports for the bridge she fell from. The rest will go on the other one. The lighter wagon will stay on this end of the road and shore up those bridges that need it. The other wagon can't go farther than the washed out bridge, so it'll stay there. You, me, and Angus will ride on to the bridge she fell from."

"Angus?"

"Angus. We thought he could help most with pushing the horse into the ravine."

Amos chuckled. "Hell, he could probably pick up the damn thing and carry it to the ravine."

John agreed. "Anyway, after the horse is taken care of, we'll check the bridge and see exactly what we need for replacing the broken boards and reinforcing it. Then we'll ride back to the wagon and get what we need. Probably have to tie the boards to the horses and drag 'em."

"Good plan. I'll be glad to get them fixed, especially the one where she fell. It's a wonder she wasn't killed. If we don't take care of them now, who knows? The next person to cross it could end up dead." He paused a few seconds. "We just won't tell Lily that by not minding me, she probably saved lives."

John laughed at that. "Well, I'm here to buy every bolt, nut, screw and nail they have on hand, at least most of them. Clint said he'll buy back what we don't use. Oh, I nearly forgot—we'll meet at that field at the head of the trail at daybreak."

"I'll be there."

AMOS RETURNED to find that Sadie had made a big jar of willow bark tea so he wouldn't have to make any for the next day or two, and he was suitably grateful.

"I already brought her a cup with a little honey in it. She can have another cup now if she wants it, but I'd wait to give her any more until bedtime. Then another two cups would be fine."

"I wonder if she'll be feeling well enough for church on Sunday. She wanted to talk to all the children before school starts. I think there were three she wanted to talk to. For that matter, I hope she's able to teach school Monday."

"Elliott said he wanted her up and around, so if she's all right otherwise, there's no reason why she can't go. You might have to lift her in and out of the buggy so she doesn't have to bend her legs much."

"I can do that. We can either sit on the front pew or the end of one so she can stretch out her legs while she sits. All right, then. I'll try to get her there."

Sadie said her goodbyes and left, leaving Amos in the bedroom with Lily.

"How are you feeling?"

"Foolish."

He grinned. "I meant physically."

"The stitches hurt when he did them, but it's not so bad now. My side hurts when I move around very much."

"Oh, that's what this cream is for. We need to lift up your shift so I can rub it on."

"All right." She pushed the sheet down and off her. "We discovered this is easier if you lift me and I pull up the shift."

It wasn't lost on Amos that he was about to see her bloomers again and a lot of bare skin, and she didn't seem at all unnerved about it. She'd probably been all right with Elliott, too, but he was a doctor and Sadie was right there helping; that was different. Very different. He thought of how free and giving of her body she was when they kissed. He knew from Will that she had never been serious with any other men. Was it possible she would have been this at ease with them? No, he didn't think so. At least he didn't want to think so.

I want you to marry me, Lily. Be my wife, my lover. This isn't the time to ask, though, not when you're hurt and healing. But as soon as you're better...

When her shift was lifted enough to expose the bruise, it kept falling. Finally, she rolled up the hem in the front until it was just under her breasts, and she lay back down.

Amos removed the lid from the tin of arnica cream and set it down. He scooped some out with one finger and dotted it around the bruise.

"That's cold and it tickles," she said, flinching just a little.

"Sorry. It'll warm as I rub it in. Does it hurt when I touch it like this?"

"Not really. It's a little tender if you rub too firmly, but I wouldn't say it hurts."

"Good. We don't want that," he said. He continued to massage the cream into her skin until he heard a sigh come from her. "That's probably enough for your side. Are any other muscles getting sore?"

"Yes. My shoulders and upper back. The upper arms, too. I put them through a bitter struggle trying to pull myself up and out of that ditch. They weren't very achy before, but they are now."

"All right," he said as he held out his hand to help her sit up. "Scoot this way and turn your back to me so I can get to it."

He took a little of the cream and massaged it into one arm, then the other, applying it above the bandages. He tried to get to her shoulders and back through her neckline and armholes, but it didn't work.

"Amos, just pull the shift off, over my head. I don't mind if you see me."

"All right." He tried to say it as evenly as he could, but his heart had begun to beat a little faster and his mouth felt awfully dry. He put the tin down and grasped the shift, carefully pulling it over her head when she lifted her arms.

Most men were either breast men or ass men, or maybe leg men, but not Amos. He appreciated every part of a woman. How could someone appreciate only one part of the sunset, or just the corner of a beautiful painting, or a small section of a powerful waterfall? He couldn't do it. Amos thought beauty was in the whole of a thing. And each enchanting part of a woman's body held its own beauty. How could he choose one part?

He looked at her back now, at the shape of her shoulder blades and the ridge of her spine that drew his eyes until it disappeared under fabric. It was beautiful. Her skin was flawless, smooth, and it invited his touch. How he wanted to kiss it!

Amos dipped his fingers into the jar, then rubbed his hands together to warm the cream. He felt her skin quiver when he first touched her shoulders. Maybe his touch startled her. He massaged the cream into her neck first, that delicate, slender neck that begged to be kissed. He moved down to her shoulders and watched as his big, strong hands covered and kneaded them. He was careful to keep the movement of his fingers fluid so he didn't press too hard in any one place.

He saw Lily's head droop forward and he knew even without seeing her face that her eyes were closed. She let her head roll to the left and right and back again, stretching her neck muscles. It seemed like even more of an invitation to smother her neck in kisses.

Amos got more cream and warmed it on his hands again. As it warmed, he wondered how this evening was going to end. It would be so natural to make love to her tonight, to make her his, but everything about that was wrong. *She's in discomfort from injuries she just received today in a serious accident. Her emotions are fragile after having to shoot Atlas. We aren't married. We aren't at my house, in my bedroom. No, it can't happen tonight.*

He massaged downward from her shoulders, all around her shoulder blades, being careful not to push on them with any real pressure. Instead, he gently rubbed little circles on them. He pressed harder on either side of her spine all the way down to her waist, then he hesitated a moment before he let his fingers roam inside the waistband of her bloomers, continuing the massage of the skin directly beside her backbone.

She didn't register any surprise or shock or apprehension. Instead, she moaned, "Oh, yes," in a low, breathy whisper.

Amos thought that must be what she would sound like when they did finally unite as one. The sight of her body, the feel of his hands on her skin, the sensual sound of her voice, the thoughts swimming in his mind, all these things had made him hard as a rock. *I'm going to need the strength of giants before this night is over*, he thought.

He got some more cream and went over her shoulders and back again, all the while trying to ignore his own physical response to her. It wasn't working. Finally, he stopped massaging and put the lid back on the arnica tin. He stood and turned briefly, to place it on the far side of her bedside table where there was room. When he turned back to her, she faced him. The sight of her took his breath away. And his speech.

Lily grinned at him, her eyes twinkling, and pointed at the large protrusion in his now-tight britches. "Please tell me this isn't the time you chose to finally know me in the biblical sense, not when I'm all achy and cut up and my arms and legs are wrapped up like a mummy."

That was exactly what he needed to lighten the mood of the situation, and his mood, specifically. He laughed and said, "No, we're in the wrong house for that."

"Oh, well," she said with a feigned wide-eyed eagerness, "I think I can walk over there if you'd like."

"I don't think so, honey. It won't be tonight. That mummy thing just isn't doing it for me."

"No? Something is; you can't hide that. I could take care of it with my mouth again, but you'll have to bring it to me. Might get awkward. I don't think I can contort myself into position to do it like before."

Amos chuckled at the imagery. "Maybe we'd better just rustle up some supper instead. Where's your nightgown?"

"In that top drawer," she said, nodding her head in that direction.

Amos retrieved it and slid it over her head when she held up her arms. He knew she kept her robe on a hook on the bedroom door. He got it and helped her into it for the second time that day.

Amos didn't let her do any heavy lifting in the kitchen, but he did let her do the lighter things. Together they threw together a decent meal. It was nothing fancy, but it was hearty and filling.

"I wish I still had some of that apology pie. It was one fine pie."

"After today, I may have to make a dozen pies. Two dozen, even."

"No, you don't. You said you regret your decision to go and I believe you. The fates punished you much more harshly than I would have."

He half expected her to voice some kind of protest again, but she didn't. *Good.*

"They don't have to be apology pies, you know. You could make a celebration pie. Or a holiday pie. Or a Thursday pie. The list is endless," he said.

"Do you really want me to make you a pie?"

"No, of course not. I just wanted something sweet. It's not important."

"Would you settle for some buttery toast and jelly? Or honey?"

"That might hit the spot."

"I'll make it if you'll clear the table."

"Deal."

When the last dish was placed on the drainer, she turned and put her hand on his arm. "Will you sit on the couch with me?"

He hesitated. "I'm meeting the men at dawn, so that means I'll be over here to fix our breakfast way before that, while it's still dark."

"I don't mean to get anything started like you're thinking. I just want to feel you sitting next to me. I need to feel your arms around me. Please. Just for a few minutes."

"All right, honey, of course." He was both humbled and

elated that she needed him, and that she wasn't afraid to tell him outright.

Amos led her to the couch and tucked her at his side and under his protective arm. Ever so gently, he rubbed her shoulder and upper arm. It was no longer than a few minutes when he noticed her breathing was easy and rhythmic. She'd fallen asleep in his arms, but she woke when he tried to pick her up to carry her to bed.

"Amos?"

"What is it, honey?"

"Don't leave me alone tonight. I'll sleep better knowing you're here. There's a bed in the other bedroom you can use."

Against his better judgment, he agreed. The truth was that he wanted to stay. He needed the assurance that she was all right.

"I'll stay. I need to take care of some things outside, then I'll come back in. You go on to sleep." He gave her a gentle kiss and a nudge in the direction of her room. "Sleep well, Lily. I'll wake you for breakfast before you know it."

TRUE TO HIS WORD, he stayed overnight in the bed in the room next to hers. He fell asleep with images of her body on his mind. Occasionally, thoughts of her harrowing ordeal pushed forward, but he managed to suppress them. *Her breasts, her perfect breasts, so high and firm. What will they feel like when I touch them? When I cup them, and squeeze them, and suck them?*

Amos rose early and started a fire in the stove. He put water on to boil, made coffee, and heated a cup of willow bark tea for Lily. Breakfast was quick; he scrambled a half dozen eggs and covered them to keep them hot while he woke her.

He walked back to her bedroom, a lamp in one hand and her tea in the other. The lamp bathed the room in a warm glow and Amos couldn't take his eyes off her. He leaned over and kissed her cheek. "Good morning, sunshine."

"I don't see any sunshine."

"That's why it'll have to be you. Here, I heated some of Sadie's tea for you. How do you feel this morning?"

"Sleepy. I can't report any more than that until I stand and walk around some." She removed the covers. "I need to go to the water closet. And I'll take this." She took the teacup. "And this." She picked up the lamp. "Oh, and good morning," she said as she walked out of the room. "I'll meet you in the kitchen."

Amos grinned and shook his head. He did notice that other than trying to keep her legs straight as she walked, she didn't appear to be in any undue pain.

He brought their eggs to the table. Their bowls matched, but his held twice as much egg as hers. She didn't question it.

"Thank you for cooking my breakfast."

"You're more than welcome. Did you sleep well?"

"I did. I don't think I even woke up in the night."

"Good. You seem to be moving around well enough."

"The cuts and scrapes don't hurt, but Elliott was right. And you, too. I'm stiff and achy. More so than last night."

"That's what the willow bark tea's for. I can rub some more arnica cream on you, too. It'll help loosen those muscles."

"All right, but you know what happened last night. You can't go meet those men with your, um, with that thing pointing skyward, looking like it's trying to escape."

Amos laughed at that characterization but admitted she was right. "It'll go back down before I get there."

When they were finished with breakfast, he took the big pot of hot water and poured some into the dishpan. He thought it was too heavy for her to deal with yet. He added fresh water to the pot and put it on the back burner of the stove to have for later.

As he rubbed the arnica cream on her body, he forced

himself to talk instead of relishing the sight and feel of her. "What do you plan to do today?"

"Elliott said to move around, so I'll be up and about, doing normal things. I just might do them a little more slowly and with straight legs. It feels so odd to do that, but it feels worse when I forget and bend one of them."

"Good. If I were you, though, I think I'd crawl back under these covers and go back to sleep. Don't get up until you feel like it. Pamper yourself some."

"I will definitely go back to sleep."

He helped her put her nightgown back on. "I need to get going, Lily. Need to get Samson saddled and loaded with my tools. I have no idea when I'll be back. John rounded up several men to work, but I didn't see the whole scope of what has to be done. I could be early or I could be late."

"As long as you come back to me safely, I'll be fine."

He felt a tug on his heartstrings with that. Amos put his arms around her for a gentle hug. "I'll come back to you, honey. No power on this planet can keep me away."

CHAPTER 8

*Y*es. Tonight. I'll do it tonight. If she continues to feel better and things feel right, I'll propose tonight. She may not be healed yet, but I can't wait much longer. I have to know she'll marry me. Well, I'm pretty sure she will. I want it settled, though. I hope I don't have to do much convincing to get her to marry me soon. The sooner, the better. It's not enough to have her in my arms now. I need her in my bed.

Samson moved at a quick pace, but not too fast. A hint of brightness was just beginning to paint the eastern sky. It was a brisk morning and Amos was relieved they'd have good weather for the work they had to complete. Almost all of the men were already there or were within sight. No stragglers to hold them up, so they wasted no time. When the men were all within earshot, John explained the plan to them. He divided them into three teams: the ones who would brace and reinforce the nearest bridges, the ones who would rebuild the bridge that washed out, and the ones who would first take care of moving Atlas and would then repair and reinforce that bridge, which was the last one before Low Quarter. That last team was John, Amos, and Angus.

The instructions were clear, and each man knew his job and in which order the teams had to travel. There wasn't a place anywhere along the trail where there was room for a wagon to pass another one. That meant that most likely, they'd have to take the wagons all the way to Low Quarter to turn around at the end of the day.

Even though John had requested and coordinated this workday, Angus assumed the leadership role. It wasn't that he wanted the role; it was given to him in an unspoken fashion by the men. They all worked for him, all except Henry, who was his business partner. Even Henry respected Angus' ability to bring people together to get results in a way that bolstered everyone. They all knew him to be a good and generous man. It didn't hurt that he had a quick wit that drew people to him. Even his physical presence commanded attention, if not respect. He was a mountain of a man at six feet and eight inches tall, topped by bright red hair and beard, with an unnatural strength that was legend in Big Rock.

When they arrived at the first bridge, Angus jumped down to inspect it. He saw what John had seen, a potential problem with the structural supports. It appeared they had begun to lean, just ever so slightly, but he didn't think the load-bearing capacity had been compromised yet. He deemed it safe for the heavy wagon to cross.

"Team one, two of ye take the supplies ye'll need off the wagon and stay here and work on it. We'll go on to the next bridge with the other two on the team." Angus walked back to the last wagon and helped them unload the supports and hardware, a post-hole digger and shovels, and some miscellaneous items.

When he reached the bridge again, he jumped down into the gap and pushed against the bridge to see if the leaning had created any give. He pushed with his considerable muscle power and was able to make it budge a little bit.

"I thought so. Men, don't just add supports to it as it stands now. Looks like ye need to use a horse to pull the bridge back to where it's level and straight again. Let's do a job that'll last that we can be proud of."

Angus returned to his horse and the column continued to the next bridge. The process was repeated, and it appeared this bridge needed less attention than the previous one. It only needed more support columns. For good measure, they decided to add a couple more crosspieces under the bridge, spanning the width, screwed to the underside of each board on the bridge surface.

The remaining two teams with the biggest jobs ahead of them resumed their trek. At the next stop, the bridge that was no more, Angus surprised the others when he pulled out a piece of paper and began drawing a schematic of the finished bridge. The men gathered around to listen as he explained. When John, Amos, and Angus rode away toward the last bridge site, they left behind a group of men with a singular mission who knew exactly what to do to build the best little bridge for miles around.

"Amos," Angus said after they'd ridden in silence for a few minutes, "when do ye plan to marry that lass?"

"People surely do seem curious about that," Amos said, casting a sidewise glance at John, who shrugged in return.

"Aye. We all ken it'll happen, we just want to know when."

"And how, exactly, do you all ken it'll happen? I don't remember making any announcement."

"We've got eyes and we're an insightful lot. What are ye waitin' for? A sign from the Almighty?"

Amos saw John's shoulders shake with suppressed laughter. He decided to go ahead and tell his friends the decision he'd just made that morning. "Something like that, I guess. Will had been a friend for so many years, part of me felt disloyal to him."

Angus looked at him. "Doona be an eejit, Amos. We were all

there that day. We heard him tell ye to marry the lass. He even tried to make ye promise to wed her."

Amos nodded slowly. "I know, I know. But I spent so much time listening to him tell me about the plans they had and his dreams of a future with her. I know how much she meant to him. It wasn't possible to just forget all that and make a move with her as though Will had never been involved. I'm going to do it. Everybody knows I'm going to do it. Hell, she probably knows I'm going to ask her. It's just a matter of when. It would probably be best to wait until she's healed before popping the question, though."

"Aye, good man. If ye doona mind a personal question, I have to ask one. Did the lass suffer any repercussions for no' listening to ye?"

"I was going to, but she was hurting so bad both physically and emotionally. I felt she'd been punished enough. She was so overwrought about having to shoot Atlas, she was inconsolable. I couldn't add to that. I told her so, too. Told her that she should be grateful for her pain, that if I didn't think she'd suffered enough, I'd have blistered her backside already."

"How did she respond to that?" Angus asked.

"Something to the effect of 'You can't do that. You wouldn't do that.' I was treating a deep gash at the time and we didn't talk about it anymore."

"I have a little bit o' experience here. If ye think ye'll ever resort to that in the marriage, the lass should ken about it before ye wed."

"I agree. I'd already planned to make sure we discuss it before taking vows," Amos said.

"Ye're another lucky man, Amos. Lily's a bonny lass, a smart lass; I like her ideas for the school. Nessa's told me about their visits. Looks like yer only problem is going to be a little willfulness, and I would no' even think of it as a problem."

"No?" Amos asked.

"It'll keep things alive and interesting."

They were at the bridge almost before they knew it. The three dismounted and surveyed the situation.

"Lily was right; this is a lot deeper than the others."

"Aye. I reckon we'd best get down there." Angus stepped over a few feet to ensure he didn't land too near the dead horse and he jumped.

Amos threw a few coils of rope on the ground below, then he and John half-slid and half-stepped down the slope. Something drew Amos' eye and he leaned down to pick it up. A piece of fabric had stuck to a sharp rock. "Oh, good Lord. This is a piece of the dress Lily wore yesterday. Being down here and seeing this, it makes it so real. I can imagine how hard she had to struggle and fight to make her way out, still probably hysterical from having to shoot Atlas." He put the green scrap in his pocket and said a short, silent prayer of thanks that she made it out alive.

They turned their attention to the horse. Although all three were grown up men able to face almost any task, none wanted to deal with a maggot-infested horse carcass swarming with flies. It was obvious other animals had left their marks, too.

"Well, let's see if we can get that saddle and bridle off him," Angus said. He tested his strength on different parts of the animal to see if he could move it enough for them to remove the items. Amos removed the bridle while Angus held Atlas' head off the ground. It was harder than it looked because rigor mortis had set in and the horse's body didn't bend. Angus might have been able to lift the horse's back end, too, but he couldn't get a solid grip.

They were fortunate that Atlas landed on his right side; Amos could unfasten the girth cinches fairly easily. The problem was sliding the cinches and the right stirrup out from under the horse.

"We could try a lever and fulcrum, using one of those

broken boards and a big rock, but the boards are probably rotten. Otherwise, I doubt if they would have cracked in the first place. We're going to have to get a couple of horses down here, anyway. Let's go ahead and use them to move the horse enough to get it off the saddle."

As Amos stood to the side of the horse, he realized the indentations in the mud above Atlas' rump were Lily's knee prints. One had about half an inch of water flowing over it, but the other was dry. As was the blood that hadn't soaked into the dirt. Lily's blood.

The next hurdle was to get the horses down into the gulley. They found a spot downstream where the side slopes were at a gentler angle. The horses didn't seem to mind too much; they even stopped to drink the flowing, shallow water. They bristled at the sight of the dead horse, but the men calmed them enough to get them still. After a false start or two, they got two ropes tied to Atlas and the men bent down to go under the bridge. On the other side, they tied the ropes to the horses' saddles. John and Angus led their horses far enough to move Atlas off the saddle and Amos was able to free it and the padded blanket. He threw the saddle, blanket, and bridle on the ground above the gulley. When he turned back around and looked down, he saw another piece of green fabric embedded in the mud. *She said her skirts were caught under the horse.*

They continued pulling Atlas' body under the bridge and toward the ravine and were able to get within several feet of the edge without making the horses skittish. At that point, they untied the ropes from the live horses, threw them over a strong tree limb that hung over the gulley, and then they tied them to the horses' saddles again.

"Ye two guide the horses and let me stay with this one. I may need to shift him as he moves to the edge," Angus said. He reminded them that they had to be careful not to let the horses go far enough to tip Atlas over the edge. He was tied to the live horses and would yank them.

When Atlas was just at the edge, Angus called for them to halt. He cut the ropes as close to Atlas' body as he could so they wouldn't lose much length on the rope. John and Amos each reeled in a rope and coiled it, then hung it on their horses before they joined Angus at the edge of the ravine.

"All right, men, this is what we came here for," Amos said.

They scrunched down and tried to anchor themselves as much as they could by stretching out a leg and digging their boots into the dirt and mud for leverage. Then they pushed. The body moved, but not much. The other two men heard a loud grunt of effort from Angus, and suddenly Atlas was at the bottom of the deep ravine and the men were lying in the dirt and the mud, breathing heavily.

In a few minutes they brushed themselves off the best they could and returned to the bridge, turning their attention to the next task. John suggested they check the rest of the boards for rot to see if they needed to replace more than just the two broken ones. With that taken care of, they were almost ready to head back to the crew that was working on the bridge that had washed away. Amos couldn't figure a good way to fasten the extra saddle to his own horse, so Angus took it from him. "It's no' verra far. I'll carry the damn thing. It can ride back to the mill on the wagon and ye can get it Monday."

"Well, it can ride on the wagon until our paths diverge. I can carry it in my own hand that far, and get the saddle home this evening."

"No. I saw ye looking at Lily's blood on the ground. I saw it, too. I've ne'er seen that look in yer eye before. Go home, Amos. Go to Lily's. Wrap your arms around her and doona let go. Tell her what's on yer mind and in yer heart."

"Are you sure? You want me to go on home now?"

"Aye. We've enough men to work here without ye. And tell the lass I said hello and to get better soon."

"All right, I'll do that. Thanks, Angus."

~

LILY DIDN'T WAKE up again until late morning. Her first thought was the memory of how sweet Amos had been that morning when he made her breakfast and tea. She was grateful he'd slept in the next room instead of going home. She was also a little bit surprised by it since he was so concerned about removing himself from too much temptation. *Maybe that just shows how much he cares about me, that his concern for my well-being and peace of mind overrode his resolve.*

She stretched and twisted as she lay there, assessing her pain and achiness levels. *Not too bad*, she thought. *A little bit of arnica cream should help, and so will some willow bark tea.*

The first order of business every morning was to light a fire in the stove and put on water to boil and coffee to brew. That was unless the need to use the water closet made it the first order of business. She didn't bother with a robe since she was the only person there. Besides, Amos had seen almost all of her last night. Lily warmed at the memory of how aroused he'd become as he rubbed the cream on her. It made her feel sort of powerful in a way.

Stove lit, water on a burner, coffee percolator on a burner, check, check, and check. She was about to go to the water closet when she spied the jar of willow bark tea. It didn't taste good enough to sip it as though it were an imported tea, so she took a glass out of the cupboard and reached for the sugar bowl and a spoon. She shook the jar so the little bits of sediment that settled to the bottom would spread, then she poured some into her glass. After dissolving a hefty spoonful of sugar in it, she chugged until none was left. It made her shudder a little bit. Even that much sugar couldn't disguise the bitterness.

In the water closet, she had a difficult time. It was hard to sit without bending the knees. She finally bent her legs as far as she dared without pulling the skin too tight and let herself fall down onto the seat. Then she stretched her legs out in front of her, realizing how silly she must have looked, and she chuckled to herself. *Thank goodness this is a solo activity.*

She decided on an easy breakfast of toasted bread and jelly. "Actually," she said aloud to herself, "this is my *second* breakfast of the day."

As she ate, she thought of so many things. Well, she thought of only one thing: Amos. But she thought of several different things related to him.

He was so gentle with me last night. So loving and tender. Yes, loving. If he doesn't already love me, he's well on his way. I think he does. Hell, I know he loves me. I know I love him. I've fallen hopelessly in love with this man. My man. My real man. When will he ask me to marry him? Maybe tonight? It can't be far off. I don't think he's the kind of man who wants to wait much longer before we can be fully intimate. I wouldn't mind jumping the gun on that particular issue, but my real man's a man of honor and integrity. I respect that so much and admire him for it. I can trust him to do the right thing, even when I might be willing to slide. Or backslide, as it were.

He's loyal, perhaps to a fault. It was his loyalty to Will that kept him from pursuing a relationship with me, even though Will practically decreed that it should be. How can I fault him for that? He loved Will as much or more than a brother. Not only did he feel disloyal to Will for desiring me, he probably realized that every time he looked at me, I'd be a reminder that his best friend was gone. It's hard to fill a void like that. I have to remember that his grief is so much greater than mine. One good thing, though, is that John has appeared and it looks like he and Amos are becoming fast friends, too. I hope so. Now we just need to get John married. I wonder if he's on the list for a mail order bride yet.

What if Amos doesn't tell me he loves me anytime soon? How long should I wait before I make the first move and just tell him I love him? It's fun thinking of the ways he might respond to that. Surely, he'll feel freer and more at ease, then, and tell me the same. After I tell him that, should I go ahead and ask him to marry me? Is that taking it too far? He is a real man, after all, and they seem to like being in control. Although, he hasn't minded my sexual advances. That might be different, though. Yes, I'm sure it is different. After all, one is right-now and the other is a lifetime commitment. I wonder if there's anything I could say to hurry a proposal from him. Probably nothing that isn't obvious and I don't want to be that way. Real men, you know. They don't want to be told what to do. Or be manipulated. They're resolved and assertive. Self-confident. They make up their own minds and expect their households and those in their care to abide by their wishes.

Yes, you ninny, I realize I failed miserably at that yesterday, but I paid dearly for it. He accepted my apology. I can live with this. If he's the lord of the manor, then I'll be his lady. If he's the king of the castle, then I'll be his queen. I'm not used to being told what to do, either, but I can just get used to it. I can do this. I know I can. Amos is a fair man and an understanding one. He won't make our lives miserable with rigidity. I know he wants a happy, comfortable home life where we'll flourish. I'll submit to his leadership, just like the scriptures dictate. I'll obey, just like the scriptures and the vows require.

Damn right I will. I'll do it because I'm a real woman. Real women are self-confident, too. We're strong. Strong enough to say "I love you" first and strong enough to propose marriage to the men we love. Strong enough to surrender ourselves to their authority and protection. That's right. It takes guts to have that kind of trust. Yesterday, I dishonored both of those things. The only directive he'd given me was to go out only with him until I was familiar with the town, and that was for the purpose of keeping me safe. I defied his authority by disobeying and as a result, he wasn't able to keep me safe.

This umbrella of authority and protection, with its rules and structure, is the place where all of us in the household will thrive. It works best when we embrace the roles nature has given us. My duty is to honor and obey. My role is to support Amos, to lift him when he's down, be his friend and confidante, share with him my thoughts and opinions so he can make informed decisions for our family, and keep our home a warm and happy refuge from the ill winds that blow and would threaten our domestic peace, harmony, and delight. The charge I look forward to most eagerly is the one in which I yield my body to him for our shared ecstasies. I want to fulfill his desires with such a fervor that in his quiet moments he can think of nothing else, save for fulfilling mine to the same end.

The sound of a horse galloping past brought her out of her thoughts and back to the kitchen table. Were those really her thoughts?

"Whoa, now that must be what they call an epiphany," she said aloud to the empty room. "I don't think I've ever had those thoughts consciously, at least most of them. Well, truth is, I may have consciously thought about the sex part a few times."

Was that a daydream? A voice from Heaven? Maybe it was her mind summing up the lessons she'd learned yesterday after her ordeal and Amos' response to it. *That must be it*, she thought.

Lily ladled hot water until she filled a large pitcher and took it to the water closet for a sponge bath in the lavatory. She threw her gown and bloomers on the floor in the corner. Her face was first, then she washed downward, avoiding her cuts. As she saw her reflection in the mirror, she thought of Amos seeing her nude like this. He'd seen her last night, at least most of her. He'd rubbed her naked shoulders and back and side, and although he didn't touch them, he saw her breasts. He liked what he saw; that was obvious. She smiled at the memory of his erection. Shortly after that he went out to tend the animals. *They probably weren't all he tended to*, she thought. Yes, it was most satisfying to have that effect on the man you love.

The man I love. I love saying that! I can't really call him my lover yet. I can't call him my husband—I can't even call him my fiancé yet, either. For now, he'll just have to be the man I love. With luck, by the end of tonight, perhaps he will be my fiancé.

Amos, my real man. Tall and handsome, rugged and brawny. He's broad-shouldered, red-blooded, and as masculine as a man can get. Seductive as hell, with kisses that make me forget my name. Forceful and bold, with a herculean—

"Hercules! Oh, poor Hercules. Last night he spent the night alone for the first time in who knows how many years." She ran into the bedroom as fast as she could without bending her knees, and couldn't quickly decide what to wear, so she just grabbed her robe and stuffed her feet into her shoes. She didn't even bother to lace them, then she realized she probably couldn't reach them to do that, anyway. Next she went to the kitchen to grab a carrot, then started down the hall to the back door. The back door entrance had six steps. She turned around to go out the front door. It only had two.

As she walked slowly and awkwardly because of her knees, she kept talking aloud about Hercules. "I meant to tell you already about what happened to Atlas so you wouldn't wonder and worry. I wanted to love up on you so much and let you know everything was going to be fine. I'm sorry, Hercules, but I was hurting so much. I hope you won't think it's too late for me to come and offer some consolation."

There were tears in her eyes, partly from her having had to kill Hercules' companion, and partly for the separation anxiety Hercules probably suffered. She knew horses and riders often develop a relationship where the rider believes they can communicate in a primitive way. Surely, horses can develop ties to each other and communicate. Lily didn't really expect Hercules to comprehend her words, just her sympathy and empathy.

She opened the barn door and stood there confused for a moment. There were no horses in there. *Maybe Amos put him in his barn so he wouldn't be alone*, she thought. She walked across the yard and grew agitated when she saw something on the door. It was a lock. A damn lock. She jiggled it for the longest time trying to find a way to get it open, then she banged her fist against the door as though Amos were inside. Or as though the horses could open it. She mumbled all the while, until her mood came out with her words.

"Amos, you son of a bitch! You lousy, stinkin' son of a bitch. You locked my horse away from me!" This time her voice was raised to such a level that she didn't hear his horse stop just behind her.

"Lily, honey, I didn't hear most of that tirade. Would you mind repeating it?"

She whirled around. "How can you just stand there like that? You know good and well what you did. You had no right! Hercules is my horse. You had no right to take him away and lock him up! I have to see him! I need to see him. Now, open the door." She stood aside to give him access.

"Well, let's talk about this, honey. The way I see it, I did have the right to do it. I absolutely had the right, and I felt I had the duty, given what happened yesterday. I'm still living up to my obligation to protect you and the property, and that includes the livestock. I couldn't take the chance that you'd try to go somewhere and risk getting hurt again."

She crossed her arms and glared. "Unlock. The. Door."

"In a minute. Lily, hear me out. Out there by the bridge, I nearly broke down. I found torn pieces of your dress." He pulled them out of his pocket and held out his hand to show her. "One was on the side slope, the other one was under the horse. I remembered you telling me how you struggled so hard to get your dress out from under him. There were imprints of your knees in the dirt and mud, with marks from your legs all around them, every which way. I could see how you must have struggled. It was like a gut-punch when I saw your blood dried in the bottom of the knee mark. Your blood. Lily, honey, you must have been so frightened. At that moment, all I wanted to do was put my arms around you."

"Pretty words, but I want you to open this door. I need to get to Hercules."

"They're more than pretty words. I just opened my heart to you. You might at least try to listen to me."

"I want this door open, and I want you away from me. The sooner, the better. If you open the door, I'll put a lead on him and take him home, and you won't have to bother with us anymore. You've dispatched your duties admirably."

The last sentence was punctuated by her finger jabbing into his chest.

"Stop that, Lily. I'm warning you."

"Stop what, dealing with crises the best I can?" It wasn't just anger behind the tears that fell. It was frustration and pain and hurt feelings. "I remembered that Hercules was out here by himself. After what I did to his companion, I had to talk to him. And brush him down and show him some tenderness. I need to explain. And apologize. And tell him I'll do my best to keep him healthy and safe. I know that sounds silly and stupid, but I have to do it." She wrung her hands and balled them into tight little fists and then wrung them again, absent-mindedly showing her anger and frustration, then she wrapped her arms in front. Her voice was pitiful as she sobbed and said, "Please, Amos, let me see Hercules."

He stepped up and put his arms around her. "Lily, I do understand that, and it's not silly or stupid. You experienced a horrible thing yesterday, horrible and painful. You need to do whatever helps you get past it, silly or not. It hurts me to see you so distraught like this. I'd give anything to be able to take it away."

She pulled away and the anger was back. "Take it away? It's your fault I'm distraught!" She started hitting his chest again. This time it was all anger and it made her lash out. "I apologized for yesterday, sincerely apologized. I thought you knew I was sincere and forgave me. But this," she pointed at the lock on the barn door, "is wrong. You had no right. I apologized and said I wouldn't do anything like that again, and I won't. Even if you had the right to lock him away from me, you didn't have a reason. I wasn't going anywhere. He's my property. Will left him to me."

"I had to be sure, Lily, I told you that. It would have killed my soul if you got hurt more."

"Look," she said, reaching the end of her self-control. She leaned forward slightly, pointed her finger at Amos' face, and shouted, "You unlock this door right now, damn it, and I'll put a lead on him and take him home. I know how to do it now, so I don't need you to tend to him. We don't need you to tend to either one of us!"

Amos looked at her for just a moment, then he moved. She thought he would unlock the door, but he didn't. Instead, he went to her left side and put his left arm behind her back, his left foot in front of her. It forced her to lean over a bit. With his right hand, he lifted the tail of her robe and tucked it under his left arm to expose her bare skin from just below her waist on down. Then his right arm flew, hitting his fleshy target, over and over.

"Amos, stop this! Ow! You can't do this to me. Stop! We're outside! Ow, that hurts. Ow. Ow. Ow. Please, that's enough!" She put her hand back to protect herself.

He paused. "Get your hand out of the way, Lily, it could get hurt."

She didn't move it. "Move your hand or I'll take off my belt. I don't think you want that."

"I don't want *this*!" But she moved her hand. "Just get it over with."

He gave her a few more licks, lowered her robe, and helped her straighten up slowly. Lily was still angry. She wasn't contrite, she wasn't ashamed, and she wasn't mortified. She was livid.

He stood there, arms akimbo, apparently waiting for her say something.

Well, all right, but it won't be what you want to hear.

"Will you *please* unlock the door now?"

He fished the key out of his pocket and opened the door. She pulled a rope bridle off the wall and put it on Hercules while she kissed and cooed and whispered to him. In almost no time, she led him out of Amos' barn.

"I'll come over and cook supper for us tonight," he said.

"I won't eat it. And I didn't invite you. Stay home." She didn't even look at him when she said it.

WELL, that sure as hell didn't go as I planned.

Amos felt annoyed and bewildered. And crushed that his plans were thwarted. It was time for a new plan.

An idea came to him. He went in the house and washed off the morning's dirt and mud and put on clean clothes. On the way back out, he picked up Lily's pie pan and stood at the back door to make sure she wasn't anywhere in sight. He hurriedly took his back stairs two steps at a time and put the pie pan in one of his saddlebags. Amos was off as soon as his backside hit the saddle.

When he arrived at the restaurant, he was pleased that the

parking area was almost empty. He dismounted, pulled the pie pan out of the saddlebag, and headed inside.

Mary greeted him with a big, friendly smile and said, "Hello, Amos. Sit anywhere, I'll be right with you."

"I don't have time to sit, Mary. I have a pie emergency."

She had turned to head into the kitchen, but she pivoted and said, "You have a what?"

"A pie emergency. I have to make an apple pie, and I need to be quick about it."

"Well, Amos, I've got a whole apple pie right there on the counter. You can buy the whole pie and take it. I just need you to return the pie plate."

"No, I have to make it myself, or it won't count."

"Count for what, hon?"

"An apology pie," he said. "I have to apologize to someone and when she had to apologize to me once, she started with an apple pie. I need to do the same thing."

"Now we wouldn't be talking about that sweet Miss Lily, would we?"

He got a sheepish look on his face. "Yes, ma'am."

"Are you two getting married?" she asked with her arms folded across her chest.

He leaned over and whispered, "That might depend on this pie."

"Well, come on back, then. Let me get Henry to cover while we're baking. You do know that people are betting on whether or not you'll marry her, don't you? And when you'll propose. And when you'll tie the knot."

"How are my odds looking?"

"Good that you'll marry her, but you're too damn slow getting around to it. Some people already had you married by now. They aren't too happy."

"What dates do you have?"

She grinned. "I haven't placed my bet yet. Let's go make that pie, and have a nice little chat while we do it."

❧

LILY LED Hercules into his stall in the barn as she unsuccessfully tried to stop crying.

"I feel so foolish, Hercules. So much for my epiphany this morning." She removed the rope lead and hung it on a hook. She'd return it to Amos' barn sometime while he was not home. "I really thought Amos was the one. My real man. I wanted him to be my real man. I still do, Hercules. But I guess I'll just have to get over him. It's going to be hard with him living right next door. I can't move away because I signed that contract to be the teacher, so I'm stuck here."

She picked up a horse brush and gently brushed him, following the brush with her other hand to feel how smooth he was.

"He doesn't trust me, Hercules. I apologized and he accepted my apology, but he didn't believe me when I said I wasn't going to do anything like that again. He didn't trust me. You have to have trust in a relationship, Hercules. It won't work without it. And I have to trust he won't hit me again! You should have seen what he did. He spanked me! It was embarrassing and it hurt. It still hurts, but at least it's not on fire anymore. What am I going to do, Herc? How do you fall out of love?"

She stopped brushing and walked around to the horse's face and gently petted him. When she reached into her pocket for the carrot, she would have sworn he nodded his face as if to say *thank you*.

"The truth is I don't want to fall out of love with him. He's exactly the man I always wanted, the kind I always dreamed of, except for that trust thing. Well, and the spanking thing. In every other way he's my perfect real man. Go figure, trust and spanking. One hurts my feelings and the other hurts my back-side. Yes, I know spanking's not a new thing. I even know a couple of wives back in Lincoln who get them. I just don't want to be one of those women. You know, it's odd, now that I think of it; they do seem to be happy with their marriages. It probably happens even more out here in the west, I don't know. I just don't think that's for me, though, not at all. Maybe I'll ask Nessa about it. But I'll tell you this, when I was a girl and dreamed of being married and living happily ever after, I never once included *that* in my dream.

"That thing about trust. It's possible that might work itself out in time. Maybe he hasn't known me long enough to know if I'm trustworthy or not. I might concede to that. Would I have been convinced if I were in his shoes? I don't know for sure. He might have been wise not to trust me implicitly. We won't tell him that, though. I wouldn't have done anything wrong, but I suppose he couldn't know that.

"Here, let me get my big boy some hay. I never did tell you about Atlas, boy. I guess you figured out he isn't here. He hurt both his legs, Herc, and the breaks were severe. I couldn't let him suffer. So, I fixed it and sent him to that big pasture in the sky. You'll see him again one day."

The last thing she did before going back inside was to draw water for Hercules' trough. Inside, she put more wood in the stove to heat the water and the coffee she'd made earlier.

Lily cleared the table and sat waiting for the coffee to get hot again. Her thoughts from earlier flooded back.

Well, so much for being a queen. Queens are trusted. And I'm pretty sure they aren't spanked. The question I have to ask myself is whether I can live with the specter of a spanking looming on the hori-zon. I'm a grown woman, damn it. And even if I had done something to earn one, just for the sake of argument, does he have the right to give it to me? Most people wouldn't think it appropriate for him to see as much of me as he did today without us being married. Of course, he's been tending to my wounds and he saw a lot of my body then. People would probably approve of that, or at least let it be an exception. But we aren't married, so should he feel free to exert that kind of authority? Well, we are in a relationship, and up until an hour or so ago, I was praying it would end in marriage. Would that lend the same authority as being married? Some might think so. Damn. I don't know what to think. Why can't romance be simpler? No, that's not right; it is simple. It's very simple. I'm a grown woman, a real woman. And I'm not about to give any man control of my life. Or my backside!

She stood and thought it might have been a little bit easier getting up this time. Maybe she worked some of the stiffness out when she was tending to Hercules. She poured a cup of coffee and decided to have some more willow bark tea, too. Instead of sitting down to drink, she took the tea with her down the hall to her bedroom to find a dress to wear. Here it was, the middle of the afternoon, and she was wearing a robe over nothing.

Lily took a big swig of the tea and set down the glass. She rummaged for bloomers and a clean shift and put them on. At least she tried to. She couldn't figure out how to put on bloomers without bending her legs too much, so she put them back in the drawer. She'd be fine without them. Once in her shift, she looked through her dresses. Amos threw away the one she wore yesterday. She didn't have so many that losing one wouldn't be noticed. There was an older one that wasn't really one of her favorites, so she decided to put it on. She hoped she'd remember after school tomorrow to go to the mercantile and see if they had any dresses her size in stock.

She downed the rest of the tea and headed to the kitchen. The water was hot so she ladled some out into a pitcher again to put in the dishpan. There were only a few dirty dishes, so she washed them.

Now she'd enjoy the coffee while she looked at some of her

notes. She reviewed her plans for the first day and tried to think of ways to make the subjects and the learning process more enjoyable. Despite the coffee, her eyelids were getting heavy. The couch looked comfy. Yes, planning for the first day of school could wait.

~

A KNOCK at the door woke her. She considered not answering since it was almost certainly Amos, but just in case it wasn't, she went to the door and opened it. Sure enough, it was.

"I'm not ready to talk to you," she said as she pushed the door to close it.

His hand stopped the door before it shut. "I came to apologize. I made pie."

A grin crossed her face and she was glad it was hidden from him behind the door. She composed herself. "Thank you, but I don't want to talk right now." She pushed the door again to close it but felt resistance. She pushed harder but Amos stuck his booted foot in the opening and nudged it open more.

He raised his voice enough to make a point. "*I rolled out a damn pie crust for you.* You don't have to talk, but you could at least listen."

Lily opened the door. "Did you really make that pie?"

"I did. I didn't use canned filling, either. Everything was from scratch."

"I didn't think you knew how to do that."

"I didn't. I went to Mary for help and she made one next to me and showed me what to do."

"Oh, my. You went to a lot of trouble for that."

"Yes, ma'am, I did." He paused. "But you're worth it."

She softened to the point she felt her tension easing and opened the door all the way. "Come on in."

"Thank you. Do you want to sit down and let me get everything?"

"I think moving helps. I'll get us something to drink and you can get plates and forks. How about that?"

"Sounds good."

They quietly got the items, smiling nervously whenever their eyes met.

"Do you need help to sit down? Help staying steady?" Amos asked, his concern apparently sincere.

"No, but thank you. It's awkward and not very attractive, but I can do it."

"All right." He went around to the other side of the table.

"Now let's see how good this apology is," Lily said, and her smile was genuine. She could feel herself warming to his company.

"I'm kind of curious myself."

They were both pleasantly surprised. "So how's my apology so far?"

"It's off to an excellent start," Lily said.

"I'm glad. So, here goes. Lily, I overreacted, and I am sorry. I went too far. I won't make any excuses for it, I was just wrong. You were right. I should have trusted you. And you were right that I shouldn't have kept Hercules from you. I wish I could give you a good reason why I did. It was a bad choice. I'd give anything if I hadn't made it. What I agonize most about is that I hurt your feelings and caused you such anguish, especially since it's on top of the pain and stress from yesterday. If even once I had stopped and tried to put myself in your shoes, I'd have realized you'd want to check on Hercules. But I didn't. I didn't even try to look at things from your side. That was a big mistake on my part. I hope you can forgive me, Lily."

"It may take another piece of pie," she said. Amos hurried to cut them each another piece. He cut his eyes up at her and grinned as he put another piece on her plate.

"Well, it's good that you aren't going to keep me guessing here."

Lily laughed. She considered her options and decided to go out on a limb. "You did more to hurt me than you think. I had a plan to carry out."

"I had a plan, too. I'm sorry they both didn't come to fruition. What was your plan?"

"If you hadn't told me you love me by the end of the day, I was going to tell you."

She wondered for just a brief moment if Amos was going to cry, but he didn't. He jumped up, pulled out her chair, and lifted her up into his arms. Lily looked into his eyes, needing him to kiss her. He pulled her hair back and out of the way.

"It sounds like we had much the same plan. I was going to tell you how much I love you, too. So let me do that now. Lily, I love you."

"I love you, too, Amos."

The kiss was joyous. Joyous with a big dollop of relief and a hint of a fresh start. Maybe a little giddiness.

"I love you, Amos," Lily said when their lips finally parted.

"I love you, too, honey."

There were a few more kisses before Amos pulled her to the couch.

"I'm glad we're back on kissing terms," she said.

"And touching terms," he added.

"And now we're on *I love you* terms, too. That's even better."

They resumed their familiar spots on the couch and settled into a comfortable embrace, with Amos being reasonably careful not to aggravate Lily's soreness. Their hands at first were tentative in their explorations even though they'd been this far before. There was a newness about them, as if saying those three little words put them on a new level and they weren't quite sure what it meant for them.

Before long Lily all but ceased conscious thought and

147

disappeared into a world where there were only the two of them and their desires. She didn't realize he had unbuttoned her dress bodice until she felt his hand squeeze her breast through her shift. It wasn't long before he was inside her shift, caressing her bare breast and teasing a nipple into pebbled hardness. He rubbed and gently pinched and lightly tweaked it until she begged him for more and pushed herself harder into his hand.

"Soon, love, soon. I want more, too. I want to suck this into my mouth and torment your nipple with my tongue while I tease the other one with my hand. I'll keep doing it until you're soaking wet for me and aching for release, then I'll kiss my way down and do much the same thing on that sweet, sweet spot below. It'll be so sensitive, every touch of my hand, every blow and breath, every flick of my tongue, every lick, every suck will have you writhing and squirming, trying to achieve your own satisfaction. When you think you can't take any more, I'll show you that you can. And when I'm ready, I'll enter you and take us both to that place of ecstasy. Soon."

"I want it now, Amos, I want you. Inside me. Not soon. Now."

He pulled back a few inches away from her. "Maybe we should cool this down. We're getting pretty intense, at least I am." He leaned back and sighed, then leaned up again. "You know what? The plan I had for today included more than telling you I love you."

"So did my plan," she said.

Amos grinned. "I'm pretty sure I don't have to tell you how much I enjoy being with you. So much so, that I'd like to spend the—"

"Amos, will you marry me?"

He was surprised she butted in, but it was a most interesting interruption. "Well, now, I may have to think about that for a while. Did you want an answer tonight?"

They both laughed. Lily playfully hit his chest a couple of times and he captured her hand. "That's a big decision, a life-time commitment. I should weigh it from every angle. Don't want to go into anything lightly. At least ponder over it while we eat a bite."

She rolled her eyes. "Well, I believe there are a couple slices of apology left. We can have those."

"That sounds good. Speaking of apology, you never actually gave me a response. Will you forgive me?"

She got serious. "I certainly didn't want to earlier. I had a hard time understanding why you didn't trust me and felt you had to hide Hercules. After a long talk with myself, I realized you really haven't known me very long, maybe not long enough to know for sure if you could trust me. I knew I wasn't going to do anything wrong, then I remembered that just yesterday I wasn't too trustworthy. Why should I expect you to trust me after that? You accepted my apology. So, since I realize trust can grow and I know it will, and since you apolo-gized for it and won't be spanking me again, then I can forgive you."

"Wait, Lily. I need to be clear here. I'm not apologizing for the spanking. You deserved it. I stand by that. I'm apologizing for not trusting you and locking Hercules away where you couldn't get to him."

With a little difficulty, Lily stood and looked at him accus-ingly as she buttoned her bodice. "But you said you overre-acted! You said you were sorry."

"For locking Hercules in my barn, not for busting your backside. I was right to do it and I'll do it again if you act like that."

"No! No, you won't! I'll not have it, and I'll not marry a man who'd do that to me. I'm not a child. I take back that proposal. I won't marry you now. Not now, not ever, as long as there's a possibility you'll strike me in any way. It's not right. Just leave."

Amos jumped up and went to her, but she tore away from his hold. "I said leave. Go." Her eyes teared up.

"We love each other, Lily. We can work this out; it's what people in love do. We can talk it out. Tell me why you feel that way, and I'll tell you why I feel the way I do. I know we can reach an understanding."

"An understanding? What I understand is that it's my back-side on the line and you have nothing to lose."

"No? What about losing the only woman I ever loved? You think that's nothing?"

"Then you shouldn't treat your grown woman like a child. It's unacceptable. Here's what I think. I think you'll never lay a hand on me again. Now get out."

"You love me, Lily."

"I'll get over it. Just get out, Amos. I can't look at you. I don't want to see you anymore."

"This isn't over, Lily."

"It's over, Amos. I won't live with a man who'll treat me like that." Her tears fell in earnest and she turned her back to him. She heard the door slam shut, followed by heavy footsteps hurrying away.

Lily leaned over, her forearm on the wall and her head on that arm. She beat the wall with her other hand. "What have I done?" And one more time that day, she sobbed.

Amos stormed off the porch and headed to his house.

Great job, there, Amos. I could have had it all, almost did. Bungled that one up, but good. Should have explained my side better. Made her understand. Well, hell, how could I? She wouldn't listen. I should have made her listen. There has to be a way. Stubborn woman. That one issue, that one thing. Does she think I want to wallop her every day? Surely not. It likely won't happen often, maybe never. It's up to her. Hardheaded, stubborn woman. No. No, she's not. She's a wonderful woman. She's kind and funny and loving and giving and sweet Lord, so responsive to my kiss, to my touch. It's just this one thing. This one little issue that shouldn't be. She won't find a man around these parts who doesn't have the same attitude. She might as well go back to Lincoln to the city men she can control.

Amos had reached his door, but he didn't open it. He wouldn't. He had something important to do.

She already told me what she wants. She wants a real man. Right now it's what she needs most. I'm a real man. Hers. And she's mine, damn it. She's mine and she's not getting away from me. I just need to remind her how a real man handles things. Be a man, Amos. Be that real man she wants. Be the real man you are.

Amos turned around and headed back to Lily's. His feet didn't even touch the front steps; he jumped down to the ground, walking resolutely back to his woman. His pace increased as he got closer to her house. By the time he was two-thirds there, he was running. He bounded up her steps and across her porch in a split second and threw open the door. He burst inside and she looked up from where she'd been crying against the wall.

He took her by the shoulders, shook them a little to get her attention, and backed her against the same wall.

Her eyes, still wet with tears, grew big and round. Amos knew she'd never seen him this forceful.

"You listen to me, Lily, because this is how it's going to be between us. Do you understand?"

She hesitated, but nodded.

"Good. We love each other, and that love's going to grow every day. You're going to marry me, and soon. Damn soon. We'll share our bed, our love, and our lives. You'll have my babies and our family will grow up strong and happy."

Lily nodded again.

"You're going to marry me and you'll vow to obey, just like

I'll vow to cherish. Hell, I cherish you now. I expect you to keep your vow, and if you don't, you know what you can expect. Not because I don't cherish you anymore, but because I do. That's completely up to you. If you don't want it to happen, then all you have to do is keep that vow. Because, lady, if you do something like you did yesterday, I'm going to tear your ass up. That's what a real man does, Lily. He takes care of the ones he loves. I love you and I'm not letting you go. You will marry me. I know what I want, and I want you by my side. Now, do you understand what I'm saying?"

She nodded. Amos let go of her shoulder with one hand and cradled the back of her head with it. It was a powerful, forceful kiss.

He ended the kiss, and rested his forehead on hers for a moment. "Let's start this over. Lily, will you marry me?"

"Yes. Yes, I'll marry you."

He kissed her again, hard. "Good. Because I really wasn't going to give you a choice in the matter."

"So… I have to marry you? Like it or not?"

"That sums it up."

"I can live with that," she said slowly.

THEY ATE a light supper and tidied the kitchen.

"Lily, I need to unwrap your dressings and check the wounds. If you ladle out a bowl of hot water, I'll go get the supplies we need."

"All right."

He returned with the carbolic acid, iodine, and dressings. Next he retrieved the sugar bowl, a spoon, and a smaller bowl. Lily returned with some clean washcloths and towels, and sat. He started with her arms and removed the bandages, unwinding slowly. Amos was particularly gratified that the petroleum jelly had kept the dressings from sticking. They were both pleased with her progress and agreed that most of them didn't need to be bandaged again. He cleaned them all and redressed the larger ones, all on her forearms.

Next he lifted her skirt—she wore no petticoat—and placed it up high on her legs so he could reach the wounds on her thighs. He had to push her shift up a little, too. He began to unwind the long bandage on her right leg and nudged her legs apart enough to allow his hand in to get to the wounds. He took a sharp breath and fell back on his heels. "Lily, you aren't wearing bloomers."

"I tried, but they're hard to put on without bending my legs. I gave up. Can't you just ignore it?"

Amos looked up and gave her an odd look. "No. I'm a man, Lily. We can't ignore such things."

She shrugged. "Just do the best you can."

He did, but the best he could do took a lot longer than expected. He kept getting distracted. She kept getting quietly amused.

Her wounds were definitely improving. There were some on her legs that didn't need any more attention, so he washed them all and retreated and wrapped only the larger, deeper ones.

"Will you rub the arnica cream on me again?"

"Are you still sore?"

"Yes."

"Of course, I will. But good Lord, you'll be naked, Lily."

"I'll try to cover up. Then you can put a long flannel nightgown on me so you won't be tempted."

"Honey, I'll be tempted no matter how you're dressed."

He helped her remove her dress and shift, turning his head until she covered herself. He rubbed the cream first on her side, then on her shoulders and back. He had the same reaction as before, and neither of them was surprised by it.

"Will you let me take care of that for you?" she asked.

"Oh, Lily, it's getting harder and harder to restrain myself. That would make it almost impossible for me."

"You know it's all right with me if we do. We're engaged, and we'll be married soon."

"I know, but we're in the wrong house. Besides, I need you to be all healed up before we do that."

"I need to be healed? Why couldn't you just be gentle?"

"Lily, once we're on fuckin' terms, the first time we're together, I reckon I'll be able to give you about a minute-and-a-half, maybe two, of gentle. After that, I doubt if I'll be able to contain myself. If I feel then the way I feel right now, a sledge-hammer couldn't pound you any harder than I will."

CHAPTER 9

The plan was to meet at Lily's early Sunday morning to prepare breakfast together, then Amos would go back home and they'd both get ready for church. He'd pick her up at 10:30 and they'd go together.

When he arrived, he brought eggs and bacon from his house since her supply was running low. He threw them on the table and picked up Lily, kissing her as he spun her around. They were both laughing when he stopped. "I will never get tired of kissing you," he said.

"I don't believe I will, either. You know what your kisses do to me."

"As do you, my sweet girl. I just happened to stop in time this morning so I could prevent that."

"All right, but let me make sure nothing's changed from last night," Lily said with a smirk. "You still love me, right?"

"With all my heart, I do."

"And I still have to marry you whether I like it or not?"

"You do, you most certainly do. If you try to get away," Amos whispered as he pulled her close again and tenderly kissed her forehead, "I will track you down and tan your hide, and you'll still have to come back and marry me."

"You must want me… fiercely."

"Fiercely. Good word for it. *I want you fiercely*. We could interpret that a couple of ways. Both would be accurate."

"Yes. All because you're a real man, and that's how real men are," she said slyly, then changed the subject. "Is it all right with you if we keep our engagement secret for a few more days?"

"It's fine, but why?"

"I want all the excitement going on to be about school starting and the children's enthusiasm. The focus should be on them and I don't want to overshadow that."

"That's the nicest sentiment, Lily. Considerate, even selfless. I think I may have just fallen in love with you all over again. We real men are like that, you know."

Breakfast was fairly quick and Amos helped her clean up their mess. Before he left he carried two big pots of boiling water to the bathtub and gave her one last passionate kiss. "I know you can't soak with your bandages, but I'll put the chair here. Maybe you can sit in the tub if you can bend your knees enough to just have your bottom and your feet underwater." He paused before his next sentence, not sure if he should even offer. "Do you need for me to help you bathe?"

Lily smiled at him a little indulgently. "I'm afraid we might not make it to church if you did that. It may take me longer than usual, but I'll manage. Thank you, though."

WHEN HE CAME BACK to get her, he thought she looked beautiful and he told her so. Her hair was up high on her head, but not in a severe style like some women wore. It looked soft and touchable. Shorter loose wavy tendrils escaped the pins and framed her face. There were only faint traces of skinned places or bruises on her face, and they would likely be overlooked. Her dress was perfect, and perfectly feminine. It had an easy neckline, not too busy with detail. There was an elegance to it. It couldn't be called form-fitting. It was loose enough to be comfortable, and it only hinted at her figure without being dowdy. Indeed, the only form-fitting parts were the shoulders, sleeve cuffs, and a wide belted waist that made it clear a shapely woman wore the dress.

"I've never seen you look more beautiful, Lily."

"Thank you," she said and smiled graciously. She made an on-the-spot decision to wear this dress for their wedding. "But I do need your help with something."

"Of course, what is it?"

She handed him her bloomers. "Woman, what are you doing to me? With this fresh on my mind, I'll never be able to concentrate on the sermon."

Lily giggled as he bent down to let her step into the leg holes. He pulled them up while trying to hold the skirts out with his elbows. She saw him and took hold of the skirts, pulling them up as he got her bloomers up. He tied the bow and let her skirts fall, smoothing them out.

"Now I need help with the stockings, too. And buckling my shoes."

"Well, this is a new experience, helping a woman put her undies *on*."

"Perhaps we should talk about how many women you've helped divest themselves of their undies?"

"Or perhaps we shouldn't talk about that. Come on, let's go. We can still get there early. You might be able to talk to one or two of the children before service and save time later. The McBrides are usually early because they come so far. He's built up a huge ranch south of town. Nice people."

Lily checked her reticule for paper and a pencil to jot down notes. They were there. "I'm ready now."

Amos lifted her up onto the buggy after having some fair amount of difficulty. Lifting a woman up onto a buggy when she can bend her knees is no problem. Lifting her up there when she has to keep her legs straight is another matter altogether. They discovered if he gripped her around her mid-thigh and she steadied herself with a hand on his shoulder, he could put her directly on the floorboards. By the time they figured it out, they were both giggling like small children getting away with some mischief.

They pulled into the churchyard just in time to see the McBrides go inside.

"You're in luck, that's them. Rosemary's parents are Derek and Molly."

They stifled giggles when he had to get her down much the same way he lifted her up. Amos did it as quickly as he could in the hope they wouldn't be seen with his hands in an inappropriate place on her body. At least it seemed inappropriate in the churchyard.

Lily giggled a little more as she tried to hurry without bending her knees. She knew how silly it must look. Inside, Amos led her to Derek and Molly and introduced her. He let her introduce herself to Rosemary.

"Rosemary, I came a little early to see you. I was hoping you'd spend a few minutes with me so we can get to know each other a little better. I thought it might make the first day of school go more smoothly. Are you willing to chat with me before the service starts? Just a few short minutes."

Rosemary felt proud that the new teacher would come early just to talk to her. "I would be honored, Miss Lily," she said with the utmost gravity.

"Wonderful! Let's go to those chairs back in the corner, out of the way."

Amos noticed that the chairs they used had no arms. That meant Lily would likely need help standing when the time came. He placed his Bible on the end of a pew in the back to save places for them, then hovered not too far from Lily and Rosemary.

They were through talking in just a few minutes. Rosemary jumped up to walk away and rushed back to Lily to whisper to her, "That's Elizabeth Woods. You should probably talk to her, too."

"Yes, I would like to do that."

"I'll get her." With that, Rosemary was off. She grabbed Elizabeth's arm and led her to Lily.

"You must be Elizabeth Woods. I've been looking forward to meeting you."

Elizabeth greeted Lily and sat down. Their conversation lasted a little longer. Elizabeth was only ten years old, but seemed much more mature than that. She still wanted to be a doctor when she grew up. The child handled herself so well and seemed so confident that Lily felt sure she would succeed in her goal.

They heard the pianist play the call to worship so they wrapped things up. As Elizabeth walked away, Amos walked up and helped Lily rise. She asked him to point out April Sullivan and he did. She was the only student left to be interviewed.

They enjoyed the music portion of the service. When Reverend Copperfield came to the pulpit, the room got very quiet. He had a reputation for spreading the word with solid reasoning and explanation, real life examples, and humor. He announced that since everyone's focus was on the start of school, he'd preach to the children. He added that the grownups should still listen because it applied to them, too. He chose the fifth commandment, *Honor thy father and mother*. He talked about how it was the only commandment with promise, and in his own opinion, that was reason enough to abide by it. He talked about how to honor them, then he flipped the coin and talked about the responsibilities of parents, including that verse that he detested when he was young, the one about sparing the rod and spoiling the child. He brought that part of the message full circle when he pointed out what he always thought of as a loophole—that a child can be spared from the rod. Yes, he discovered the secret. But it wasn't really a secret, it was right there in the Book. It all went back to the commandment. If you want to be spared the rod, then honor thy father and mother.

He added another thing, a very timely point. It wasn't in the scriptures, he said, but there were parallels and it was good advice. Parents aren't the only ones who should be honored. There's no scriptural promise attached to it, obviously, but they should also honor their schoolteacher. He shared that when he was young, the schoolteacher hung a big ugly paddle on the wall, within her easy reach. He seemed to recall that it did help him with his honoring. He needed that help since his parents were of the old-fashioned variety and believed that if their child got a lickin' at school, he'd get twice as many and twice as hard when he got home. So, by Jove, he honored that teacher.

The pastor wrapped up the message and dismissed the service. Lily made her way straight toward April Sullivan and introduced herself to April and her parents. She spent a few minutes with the girl and found out everything she needed to know. On their way out, there were a few good-natured comments about honoring the teacher and the need for her to get a paddle for the wall, and she expected that. Lily laughed with them.

They loitered in the churchyard visiting with other people until they were just about the last ones there. It wasn't because they necessarily wanted to visit, they just didn't want anyone to see him lifting her up into the wagon.

The schoolhouse was across the road from the church, and Lily's eyes widened with excitement at something she had totally missed on their way into church. There were five big, long, sturdy benches scattered about.

"Amos! The benches. Somebody built our benches!"

He took delight in hers. "Angus and the men stopped and built them on their way home Saturday after they repaired the bridges on the Low Quarter trail. He said there were so many men working on them, it hardly took any time at all."

"One of the first things we'll do as a class is write thank you notes to Angus and the men. Oh, Amos, these and the bookshelves are going to make so much difference."

Lily got quiet then, thinking of the things she wanted to do on the first day. She wanted it to be a good day for each student, a good impression that would make them eager to come back the next day, and the next. One of the children wanted to be a blacksmith. One, a doctor. The town's blacksmith, Emmett Burke, and Dr. Larkin both attended church. If she didn't run into them sooner, she'd approach them next Sunday about talking to her class. That thought brought her back to the message that morning.

Of all the different parts of the sermon and all the points made by the pastor, the thing Lily remembered most was that all a child had to do to avoid a punishment was to honor and obey. It was the same thing Amos had pointed out about wives, and even she had come to the same conclusion. Somehow it seemed more profound and doable coming from Reverend Copperfield.

I can do this. I know how to do the right thing. Maybe it won't be so bad after all.

"Lily, have you given any thought to classroom misbehavior?"

"What do you mean?"

"How will you handle it when a student acts up or disobeys? The pastor talked about the paddle on the wall at his school.

There was one on the wall at my school, too, and my teacher wasn't afraid to use it."

"I won't punish the children like that. No paddles needed."

"I don't think I'd let them know that, human behavior being what is. If they know you won't take them to task, some of them will take advantage. I can almost guarantee it."

"Surely, I can handle it in other ways. Missed recess, detention after school, extra homework assignments, things like that. You don't think that's enough?"

"For the young ones, probably. And the girls. But boys are different. Trust me, I was one. I suggest you get your bluff in on them early. They don't have to know you won't use a paddle. Don't let them know."

"All right. I'll think about that."

"I can make a paddle for you." He looked over at her and grinned. "It won't hurt to hang one up in there. Not in a prominent place as a constant threat, but where it's only occasionally seen, as a subtle reminder."

Lily nodded. "I'll think about that, too. That might be the happy middle-of-the-road solution. I'd rather they learn things just for the joy of learning rather than under the threat of physical harm. I want school to be a refuge for them. A safe place, you know?"

Amos considered that. "The joy of learning. I can remember that joy." He took her hand and squeezed it. "I wish I'd had a teacher like you."

"I do, too. Will might have written his own essays."

Amos cackled. "It is clear you never met Will."

This is good. We're talking about Will without feeling guilty.

LILY SPENT the afternoon preparing for school. She kept smiling to herself and shaking her head, amused at just how excited she was for the first day. And no matter what anyone said, she was right to act on her hunch that she should visit with each student beforehand.

Physically, she was improving. She was still a little achy, but not so much that she couldn't press on. Still stiff-legged, but she was able to bend just a little more than the previous day. Lily thought maybe she could use that to her advantage with the students. It might engage them more if she had to ask them to help her with small tasks she couldn't manage.

Once again she went over the schedule in her notebook. The days were outlined in fifteen-minute increments, and she fine-tuned them once again. Monday wouldn't be so critical as far as learning new material; she wanted to spend time in review so she could get a sense of where each child was scholastically. She had planned a couple of fun exercises to get the students involved.

Lily filled a big box with supplies she had at home that she needed to take to class. She'd been surprised to find not one dictionary in the whole schoolroom. Clint and Shirley at the mercantile could order one for her, and in the meantime, she'd take her own copy to use. She was familiar with the textbooks she'd found piled on the floor. It might be good to order more, but she'd wait to see if they were truly needed or if she just wanted them.

As she went through her closet, she remembered she needed to purchase a new dress. Possibly two or three, since her time would now be tight and she'd have less of it to do laundry, or even to take it to the laundry. She picked one of her favorites to wear the next day and set it out, along with a fresh shift, petticoat, bloomers, and stockings.

Supper was almost ready when Amos knocked and came on in. Lily ran to him, threw her arms around him, and planted a big kiss.

"Now that's the way to greet a man," he said. "If you want to do that every time I come in the door, it's all right with me."

"I'm getting more and more excited about school tomorrow. But first, tell me again. I have to marry you, right? I don't have a choice?"

Amos grinned at her. "I'll drag you to the altar kicking and screaming if I have to."

"I don't think you'll have to, but it's kind of nice to know you would. Wait. No. That doesn't sound right. It's nice to know you want me that much. Yes. That's definitely better." She paused. "Well, I don't know, I kind of like the idea of you dragging me to the altar. It would be such a caveman thing to do."

"Is that a good thing? Caveman style?"

"It probably wasn't in real life, but yes, there's a certain romance to it. A man staking his claim on the woman he wants. You know," she grinned at him, "not taking no for an answer. Like a *real man*."

"Does that make me a real man caveman, or a real caveman?"

"Real man caveman, I think."

He saw the big box on the floor. "Do you want to take these to the school this evening? We can go after supper."

"No, I want to neck on the couch after supper and take us halfway to Heaven. You should know that by now."

"What was I thinking? We can take the wagon in the morning. I'll have to be at the mill before school starts, so you'll get there early. Very early."

"That'll be perfect. It'll give me plenty of time to get things set up before the children arrive."

～

AMOS KNOCKED ON THE DOOR, then opened it and entered as he always did. Normally, Lily ran to kiss him, but she wasn't in the kitchen or parlor this morning. "Lily? Honey?"

A shriek came from the bedroom in the back of the house, and Lily came running out clad only in her shift, carrying her bloomers. "I overslept!" she said as she pressed them into his hand. "Biscuits are in the oven and the coffee's ready. I haven't even taken the time to pour myself a cup. And I need help with these again today."

He grinned. "It would be my pleasure to help with these," he said as he knelt. "And I mean that truly. A pleasure. Heartfelt, and felt in other places, too."

She grinned at him. "I meant to have everything ready by the time you got here. I'm going to make us late."

"Calm down, sweetie, they won't care if I'm late. You'll still be on time for school, so everything's all right. And I might not be late for work anyway. There. You now have on bloomers. All is well. Except for this."

Amos pulled her into his arms so quickly, she gasped, then she giggled. "I've come to expect a kiss when I come in the door. And yes, you still have to marry me, like it or not."

Lily relaxed then, and welcomed him as she normally did. "I needed that kiss," she said. "Now I have to rush again," she said as she turned around and headed back down the hall. "I'll save the shoes and stockings for last."

"I'll put this box in the wagon and take care of the biscuits."

When he came back in from outside, he poured two cups of coffee. Then he took the biscuits out of the oven and buttered them while they were hot. By the time Lily came back in, everything was ready. Everything except Lily, who wore a robe over her shift.

"I didn't want to chance getting my dress dirty while I eat," she explained.

"Are you excited about your day?" he asked when they were

seated.

She beamed. "More than you can imagine. I only wish I had arranged for the newspaperman to come take a photograph of us on the first day of school. I'm sure the children would have enjoyed seeing themselves in the paper when it comes out on Thursday."

"I can stop by Caleb Carter's house after I drop you off. If he can't make it today, surely he'll be able to come in the next day or two. Still in plenty of time to have a photograph in the paper Thursday."

"Oh, Amos, that would be perfect. What would I do without you?"

"Well, fortunately we don't have to find out." His smirk came out then. "You can thank me tonight."

With breakfast over, Amos stood to clear the table while Lily headed back to continue dressing.

"What did you pack for your lunch?" he asked.

"Lunch! Amos, I forgot lunch!"

"Don't worry, I'll throw some things in a sack. I'll see you don't go hungry."

On the ride to the school, Amos surprised her with a gift. "I didn't think you had anything like this, and I thought it might come in handy. It's made so you can wear it as a pin or on a ribbon or a chain around your neck. Or with a fob and chain like a man's pocket watch."

Lily opened the box and was touched by his thoughtfulness. It was a feminine-looking, silver and pewter filigree brooch with a hinged section that held a timepiece. She turned it over and read the inscription. "To Lily from Amos, with all my love." She looked up at him. "When did you ever have time to get this? I know it wasn't at the mercantile. Was it?"

"No. I saw it in Rawlins not too long ago. I took care of the purchase by wire and had it shipped it to me."

"Amos, it's beautiful. And incredibly thoughtful. You know

166

I'll think of you whenever I check the time."

"That was my plan."

Lily laughed at that. "How will I thank you for this?"

"Well, that's two things you need to thank me for tonight."

"Oh, I'll be thanking you for this for many days to come. Maybe weeks."

He smugly puffed out his chest. "That was my plan, too."

LILY WAS EARLY ENOUGH that she had plenty of time to prepare a few things. The first thing she did was pin her new watch to her dress. She wrote her name on the blackboard, put the schoolbooks on the new shelves, and placed a slate, chalk, and an eraser at each seat. She looked in the heavy bag Amos had packed for her lunch and smiled when she saw the contents. "That sweet man. I definitely won't go hungry with all that."

When the children began to arrive, they greeted her with eagerness. Again, she was glad she had spoken to each of them beforehand. Some of the younger ones even hugged her. There was none of the first day awkwardness she had sometimes experienced as a child.

The first thing she did that captured the attention—and interest—of the students was to pair them off, an older one with a younger one. Lily explained that since she was new and they already knew each other, it put her at a disadvantage, and she didn't want to be in that boat alone. She would prove to them they didn't know each other as well as they thought they did. They would all learn something new about each other. She wrote a few oddball questions on the board and had them interview each other. Each pair then stood at the front when it was their turn and introduced each other. There were enough funny answers to keep it lively, and they all enjoyed the introductions.

One of the questions had been, "What made you happy in the last twenty-four hours?"

Billy and Margie introduced each other. Billy's answer to that question had been that on the way to school, he and his mother noticed that somebody had built a new bridge on the road to his house, and it looked like the other bridges had been worked on, too. When their introductions were complete, Lily explained about the bridges.

"Well, Billy, I happen to know about the situation with the bridges. I had an accident on my way home from your house when some boards broke on the last bridge, the one nearest your house. I fell—that's where I got all these scrapes and cuts, and I have to tell you, I've been very sore." She wasn't going to tell them about Atlas. "I told my story to some men who work at the sawmill, and they decided to rebuild or repair all four of the bridges on that road. They didn't want anyone else getting hurt. I'll be fine, but you may have noticed I have to walk sort of funny. Have you ever tried to walk without bending your knees?" The class giggled.

"I'm mighty sorry you got hurt, Miss Lily. Mighty sorry. But I sure am glad to have a new bridge out there. My momma never liked having to walk down into that stream and up the other side where that ol' bridge washed out."

"I can imagine that," Lily agreed.

Just as she was about to launch into announcements about some of the new things in store for them, a man she didn't recognize quietly entered the back of the room. A couple of the older children were seated where they could see the entrance.

"Mr. Carter," Ken said, "are you going to write about the new teacher in the paper?"

"I am, Ken. And I'm here right now to take a class picture to go along with the article."

Lily was happy to see the big eyes and excitement that followed that comment.

"Miss Lily, will you come outside and help me pick a spot? I have a good one in mind, but we need to move a bench to it."

"Certainly," she said as she walked toward him. "Girls, make sure your hair is in place and your collars are straight." When she reached the door, she turned and produced giggles among them when she whispered loudly, "And make sure the boys look good, too."

They moved a bench so the building would be the back-drop. Caleb arranged the students so that all the girls sat on the bench, the two younger boys knelt in front, and the other three boys stood behind the bench. He had Lily sit on the bench, too.

After the photo was taken and the children were back inside, Lily helped him move the bench back to its original location. They arranged for Caleb to develop the photo that day, and he'd return at the close of the school day Tuesday to interview her and make sure he had all the children's names listed correctly. The students were still abuzz when she went back inside.

Lily then went on with her announcements. She mentioned that Miss Nessa would be back to teach them music, and they expected to have the sessions about once a week. When she mentioned that on some days they would go to the community hall to use the piano, there was applause.

"You've all noticed the benches outside and those massive bookshelves in the back of the room. Aren't they nice?"

There was agreement.

"I see that some of your lunches are in the way of your work areas or at your feet, where you kick them, so I just decided the bottom shelf on the right is now dedicated to storing your lunches. That'll get them out of your way while we're working. So go ahead now and take your lunches back there."

Everyone except Billy Simmons took a lunch to the shelves. He sat quietly and seemed happy to watch the others. *Good thing Amos packed so much for me.*

She continued when they returned to their seats. "Now some of you probably know Mr. Angus Kelly; he's Miss Nessa's husband. He and his business partner, Mr. Henry Tucker, are the ones we have to thank for the benches and the shelves. They provided the lumber, and they and some of their workers did the labor. We need to thank them, don't you think?" They all nodded. She wrote the men's names on the board. "Your very first assignment is to write a letter of thanks to them. Some of you aren't old enough to have studied the parts of a business letter, but some of you have, and I know who you are." That drew both groans and giggles. "You younger ones, just write the thank you the way you think it should be. What you say is much more important than getting it in the format of a letter. Think about how you might use the benches and the shelves, about how helpful it'll be to have them. I want you to first write your message on your slate. When you have it the way you want, you'll write it on this paper I'm handing out. I'll hand out pencils, too."

"Are you going to grade these?" Elizabeth asked.

"Not for a grade, no. But I will read them, and they'll help give me an idea about everyone's penmanship, grammar, spelling, punctuation, and that sort of thing. So please, do your best on them. Billy, you might want to thank them for their work on the bridges, too."

He nodded thoughtfully, already deciding what he was going to say.

∽

"ALL RIGHT, everyone, it's time for lunch now. It's a beautiful day outside and since there are benches to sit on, you might enjoy eating outside. It's recess whenever you finish eating, and I'll ring the bell when it's time to come back in. Enjoy!"

The students rushed to retrieve their lunches and went

outside, except for Billy. He sat at his table, quietly drawing on his slate. Lily proceeded with the plan she'd come up with since noticing he had no lunch.

"Are you not eating, Billy?"

"No, ma'am, not today. But Momma's selling some more things today and we'll have food tonight. And food for my lunches for a few days. I'll be fine."

"Yes, yes, of course, I'm sure you will be. But," she said, as though an idea just came to her, "that makes you the perfect person to help me decide something. Pull up a chair beside me while I get my things out."

Billy did, and he looked at all the food she unloaded from her tow sack that Amos had packed. "I have a recipe for a dessert that includes either apples or pears. It also has cheese in it. I want someone to help me decide which has the best flavor, the apples or the pears. I'd like for the dish to be the best it can be, you know."

"All right, I can do that. I'll give you my honest opinion."

"Good. Let's start with the apple and cheese. Do you like your apples and pears sliced?"

"No, ma'am, I prefer mine whole. Cuttin' 'em up is for girls. I eat mine like a man."

"All right. Here's the apple, now let me slice some cheese to go with it."

Lily handed him the apple and spread her sack so the end of it was within his reach. She put the cheese slices on it. Billy made comments as he ate. "This isn't the sweetest apple I've eaten, but the cheese helps that some."

"Yes, I think the contrasting flavor of the cheese makes the apple flavor seem sweeter in comparison." He nodded his head in serious agreement.

Lily ate her lunch, too, biscuits with a ham slice, cheese slices, and her willow bark tea to drink. Amos had also packed a pint jar of water, and she got it out for Billy.

"I reckon I'm ready for the pear now," he said.

"Yes, but first, I believe we need to get the taste of the apple out of your mouth. It might influence how you like the pear. Here, eat this biscuit. That should do it. Follow that with some water, and we should be ready for the pear."

"All right."

Billy practically sucked down the biscuit with the small slice of ham in it, then drank some water. While he did that, Lily sliced some more cheese for him to eat with his pear. When he was done, he put the lid back on the water jar and pushed it back toward Lily. He picked up the apple and pear cores. "Do you want me to throw these out in the woods out back behind the cemetery? That's what we've always done before."

"Yes, that would be fine. Would you mind taking mine, too?"

"I'd be happy to, ma'am. Now," he said, giving his words great weight, "let me tell you my opinion. I believe you should go with the pears this time. I liked the taste better. The apple was good with the cheese, but I believe you'll have to add more sugar to get it as good as the pears would be."

"Thank you, Billy, you just helped me make up my mind. Pears it will be. You might as well go on out and play now. It sounds like some of the others have finished their lunches and are ready to play."

"Yes, ma'am."

AFTER LUNCH, Lily told them about the plans for a lending library for the whole town that they'd have right there in their school, and that delighted them. They were even more delighted to learn that they would be the librarians. When asked where the books would come from, she said she'd have Mr. Carter put all the information in the article he was writing for the paper. She would ask for people to donate books and periodicals they were no longer interested in keeping. Another avenue they would explore would be publishing companies. Miss Nessa, in addition to teaching her music classes, would spearhead the effort to write to publishers and ask them to donate some of their books. The third way they'd get books would be to ask the board that oversaw the school to purchase books outright.

As she was speaking, Lily noticed Ken White and Jed Culpepper whispering. Actually, they were doing only a little whispering. Mainly, they were communicating with small gestures and looks, as though they had developed their own sign language. She gave them a sharp look without interrupting her discussion of the library, and they behaved for a while. It wasn't too long before they were doing it again. They were quiet about it—only being disruptive to the classmates who could see them. This time, she asked them to please pay attention. There was something just a little unsettling about the look the boys exchanged. It was a very brief look of smug satisfaction.

Lily decided to have an activity that would wake everyone up; it was after lunch and she'd just made a long announcement. Eyelids were getting heavy on some of them.

"All right, everyone. We're going to have an exercise that everyone can participate in, but it's mainly for the young ones. Everyone remembers the alphabet, right?" They all grinned and nodded, and then she addressed the three youngest children. "Did you ever put a list of words in alphabetical order?"

Rosemary's eyes widened. Billy spoke up. "Miss Lily, Lettie and I have, but I don't think Rosemary did. Last year was her first year."

"All right, that's fine. You three can work together as a team. Now I want everyone to be supportive and encouraging if they should struggle. If everything goes well and we go through two or three rounds of this exercise successfully," she paused for emphasis, "we'll add five minutes to recess this afternoon."

Cheers went up.

"Everyone get your slates. Everyone except these three younger ones, because you three have a special job. The rest of you, I want you to print your last name clearly on the slate so we can all read it. Billy, on your slate, I want you to write the alphabet. You three can use it as a reference. You two girls don't need to do anything yet."

When the writing was completed, she had everyone except the younger three stand in a line across the front of the classroom, in no particular order. "I want you three to alphabetize them by their last name. Discuss it among yourselves. Lettie, you use your slate to write down the names in order. When you think you have a correct list, I want Rosemary to move the people and have them stand in the correct order according to Lettie's list. Then we'll have everyone check it and we'll see if we all agree. Understand?"

Heads nodded. "All right then. Everyone except these three, line up and hold your slate in front of you so we can read it. Now, you three can get to work. Discuss it among yourselves. Agree on your selections."

As Lily expected, the students responded well. This was a new type of activity for them. She didn't bother to tell them she designed it to build teamwork and cooperation. It was better to just let them think it was fun.

She stayed just close enough to hear the young ones do their work, and she heard Billy help Rosemary. "Sometimes it's hard to just look at the names and remember the ABCs at the same time. I have to say the ABCs in my head until I get to the letter I want. Let's do it this way. Do you see any names that start with an *A*?"

"No. Not a *B*, either. Oh! Culpepper! There's a *C* name," Rosemary said.

"Then it has to be the first name on the list."

Lettie wrote it on her slate. They let Rosemary go through the rest of them and only pitched in when there were multiple names that started with the same letter. When they completed the list, Rosemary was excited to move the big boys and girls where they belonged.

Lily asked the older ones to verify the order, and it was correct. Before she could give them the next instructions, a couple of the older children asked if they could do that again.

"Yes, but first, I want Billy, Lettie, and Rosemary to come up front and figure out where they fit in."

They did it correctly. For the second round, Billy joined the group at the front, and the girls alphabetized first names. For the third, Rosemary alphabetized middle names all by herself.

"Well, I think that deserves an extra five minutes of recess, don't you?"

Applause broke out and Lily heard a few of the older ones tell the three young ones they did a good job, particularly Rosemary. The child beamed at the praise. Lily was pleased.

After recess, Lily made one last announcement that excited the children. "I know that some of you have decided what you'd like to do when you grow up. Ben, for example, wants to be a lawyer. Elizabeth wants to be a doctor. Ken, possibly a blacksmith."

Rosemary's hand shot up, but she didn't wait to be called on before she blurted, "I want to be a teacher, just like you and Miss Nessa."

"I'm sure you'll be a fine one, too. Miss Nessa and I can help you learn about what you need to do and study to be a teacher. But Miss Nessa and I don't know anything about being a lawyer, or a doctor, or a blacksmith, so I thought I could ask real ones to come and talk to us for a few minutes about what it's like to be a lawyer or a doctor and what kind of education and training it requires. I've already spoken with Mr. Ross

Bailey, our attorney here in town, and he's agreed to come visit with us in a few weeks. I hope to have other professional people and tradesmen come in every few weeks. So, Ben, be thinking of all the questions you'd like to ask Mr. Bailey. I think he's looking forward to coming."

When the school day drew to a close later that afternoon, Lily was pleased with her class. She wondered if the day had gone as well in their opinions as it had in hers. There hadn't been any awkward or tense moments for anyone. Indeed, all the students seemed to enjoy the day. She knew that might not last since she'd have to start teaching in earnest the next morning, but the day had gone exactly as she'd planned. Everyone left with an eagerness to come back, and they all had things to look forward to in the school year. Lettie and Rosemary even hugged her as they said goodbye.

Lily was preparing and organizing for Tuesday morning when she heard footsteps coming up the steps and into the entry foyer of the building. She smiled. She knew Amos' walk.

"You're early, aren't you?" She rose to greet him.

"A little bit. I wanted to see how your day went." Amos grabbed her and pulled her out of view from the door and windows. She didn't have to be told what he wanted; she threw her arms around him, tiptoed, and pressed her body hard against his for the duration of the kiss. It was a long duration.

"I do like the way we say hello," she said. "But it seems indecent here in the schoolroom in the middle of the day."

"Mmm, yes, indecent." He kept nuzzling her cheek and neck, his hands roving and cupping her body in places. He drew the next words out, waiting a second or two before speaking the next. "Wicked. Unseemly. Salacious. Sexy. Devilish."

She joined in, whispering, "Scandalous. Wanton. Steamy." His cheek was against hers and she felt his smile.

His words were whispers in her ear. "Libidinous. Erotic. Lascivious. Prurient. Lewd. Sexy."

"You already said sexy."

"It deserves a double mention. You're sexy as hell, you know."

"I think you are, too. And amorous. Carnal. Lusty. Licentious. Impure. Hot-blooded. Aroused."

"Oh hell, I am definitely aroused right now. We might need to stop before we get caught like this."

She leaned her head against his chest and nodded, then she pulled away. "We can continue this list while I'm thanking you tonight. I have two things to thank you for, remember."

"Remember? That thought's kept me going all day."

She grinned and pointed at his bulging britches. "I'll be able to get it that way again. I'm pretty sure."

"Darlin', you can get it that way when you aren't even in the room. All I have to do is think about you."

"Maybe tonight while I'm thanking you, you can tell me exactly what you're thinking about that makes that happen." She pointed again.

"You want me to talk dirty? Tell you my private, obscene, decadent, torrid, depraved, and hotter-than-a-pistol fantasies of you?"

"Depraved?" Lily looked at him with a coy, one-eyebrow-raised look. "Are your thoughts that dirty?"

"Some are pretty raunchy. Downright filthy, even. You may be so frightened you'll run."

"But… what if I don't run? What if I want to do the things in your thoughts? Act out your fantasies?"

"Lily." Amos looked down and shook his head. "You're killing me here. Just hearing you say things like that… I won't be fit to go to the restaurant any time soon."

"Nobody's in here with us now. I could take care of it for you. We could lock the door."

"No. No, we can't. It would be hard to explain if someone were to try to get in, or even explain it if they saw me come in and then close the door." He pushed her an arm's length away. "Do you need help gathering your things?"

"No, I just need to stuff a few things in my satchel and I'll be ready. Are you as surprised as I am at how many synonyms we came up with for that?"

"I'd bet I can come up with some more tonight. I'm expecting the best inspiration I ever had."

"Now tell me all about the first day of school," Amos said after Mary had taken their orders and brought their drinks.

She couldn't have stopped the big grin from popping across her face if she wanted to. "I think it went well. Very well. I had them write thank you letters to Angus and Henry and the other men for the library shelves and benches. Billy thanked them for fixing the bridges on the way to the Low Quarter, too. Will you take them to Angus and Henry in the morning when you go in?"

"Of course, I will. I want to look at them first, though," he said, chuckling a little.

"I need to look at them more closely and take some notes. I told the students I wasn't going to grade the letters, but I would look at them to see what they know of letter writing and punctuation and such."

"What did they think about the library idea?"

"Amos, they seemed thrilled. I think they liked the idea of learning how to be librarians as much as they liked the thought of having books to read." Lily giggled a little bit and leaned forward. "I can't tell you how excited they were when they found out Caleb was there to take a class photo for the paper." She paused to take a drink. "He's coming back over to the school house tomorrow after class to talk to me about all the new plans and make sure he has all the children's names matched to the photo."

"Who knows? Maybe by the time they grow up, we'll have a real library in a real library building and one of them might well be the librarian."

"I suppose that could happen, couldn't it?"

"I don't see why not. The town's growing by leaps and bounds."

"Is there any new development in the works now?"

"There is. Philip Hickam came in today and talked to Henry and Angus about building a slaughterhouse west of town. When it's done, the local ranchers won't have to ship their cattle by rail to Laramie anymore. The Becker twins—they work at the mill, too—worked summers at a slaughterhouse when they were teenagers. Then when they got out of school, they worked there full time. They got into the discussion and their knowledge kept us focused. Once it's completed, it's going to bring the need for butchers and meatpackers. Pave the way for a meat market in town. We'll have to build insulated wagons that can keep meat cold so we can transport it to Rawlins for train shipment. They've already got cold train cars available. Then all this butchering and packing requires the need to have an icehouse in town. There are a couple of mountains close by that hardly ever thaw out at the top, and we'll need men to go there and cut ice and bring it back. That's a lot of construction, which means a lot of business for the sawmill. I think Angus and Philip are going to talk to Emmett Burke and his uncle, Gann Douglas, about investing in the new businesses."

"Amos, that's huge! That's going to mean several more people moving here to work the businesses. And some of those people moving here might be families with school-aged children."

"That's exactly right. And existing businesses will need to expand to meet increased needs. We're sending out lumberjack teams every day for a while. A lot of construction's going to be going on."

"Then this is a big opportunity. Will they only be asking for high dollar investors? Will they accept smaller investments?"

"I don't know, but I can find out. Do you want to invest?"

"I have that money in the account Will left me. It's not a mint, but I would think the return would be better than the bank's interest rate. What do you think?"

"You're right about the increased return. Are you sure you want to put Will's money into it? I have confidence in just about anything Philip does, but any investment carries risk. I'm not sure it's a good idea to put all your eggs in that basket."

"I worry about that, too. What about a third to a half of the balance? That would still leave us with a comfortable amount."

"Leave *you* with a comfortable amount. He left that to you."

"That's very true, so I *could* do with it as I please." One eyebrow raised as she said that slowly, then she went back to her non-teasing expression. "But you're my fiancé, about to be my husband, and," she looked around the room, then whispered, "I love you. I not only want your input, I want your blessing."

He grinned at her and leaned forward to be heard when he lowered his voice. "This damn secret. I want to kiss you so much right now, I can almost taste your lips."

Her teasing expression returned. "You'll just have to wait until tonight."

He shook his head doubtfully while he looked down at his food. "You know, you've got a lot of thanking to do tonight. That's a heady responsibility. Quite the burden on your shoulders. Hell, you'd better start eating faster so we can get out of here."

"Yes, you're right, of course. Besides, I'll need all my

strength to perform to your satisfaction."

"Speaking of me being your fiancé, have you decided when I'll be your husband? I want it soon, you know."

"I do know. I do, too. When would you like to marry me?"

"A couple of weeks ago. You know that."

She grinned at him. "When would your second choice be?"

"There was another couple who were married not too long ago. They were in a hurry, too, and decided to get married right after the Sunday church service." He shrugged. "Their friends were already there. The preacher just announced it in the morning service and invited everyone to stay for the wedding if they wanted to. I can't remember if they served any refreshments or not. We wouldn't really need to. Everybody's going to want to go home, anyway. As for the when, let's marry this Sunday."

"That's soon!"

"It is, and at the same time, it's not soon enough for me. We don't have to do much to get your things to my house. One trip with the wagon will more than cover it. We don't even have to do that beforehand. It's not like you're moving very far."

Lily sat there and weighed his words a few moments. A slow smile spread across her face. "You're talking me into it. As for refreshments, we can have the best of both worlds. We could have Mary bake several dozen cookies and wrap them in either some thin cotton or gauze, tied with ribbon. Two or three cookies per bundle. They could be little favors for people to pick up out of a pretty basket as they leave. We wouldn't have to worry about drinks. Or any clean-up. And it would get them to leave quickly."

"Perfect." He lowered his voice. "Cause once we say *I do*, we'll be on fuckin' terms. I'll want to leave there as quick as lightning."

She leaned in toward him again. "I'm looking forward to that every bit as much as you are, maybe more."

Amos chuckled. "I appreciate your eagerness, but I doubt if it's possible to look forward to it more than I do."

"Oh, I think it might be possible. Remember, I haven't felt that… release before."

"Oh, the pressure," he said, closing his eyes and rubbing his forehead. "I hope you realize that not all women experience that their first time. Maybe not their first few times."

"I've heard that. I wonder if maybe they weren't quite as eager as I am. Because, my dear almost-husband, I'm going to give it my very best effort."

He grinned again. "I will, too, baby. I will, too."

When they finished and went out to the buggy, Amos picked her up and set her on the floorboards. "I forgot to ask you how you're feeling. I was afraid it would be such a busy day, you'd be hurting a fair amount."

"No, I'm not. I realized this afternoon I was feeling much better and was able to bend my legs more. I drank the willow bark tea at lunch, and that may have helped. Or, maybe I was just too excited to notice any pain. Who knows?"

The mention of the tea and lunch reminded her about Billy, and she told him what she did to feed him.

"You didn't get to meet his mother over the weekend, did you?"

"No, she was out working in their field. He told me all about her, though. That boy is so sweet. He seems wise beyond his years somehow. I can tell the bond between him and his mother is a strong one. He seems to understand how important that is and values it more than your average eight-year-old would.

"Uh oh. Sounds like the teacher has a pet."

"That's entirely possible. I'm going to have to be very careful that it isn't obvious to anyone else."

"Tell me about the rest of the day."

"It was all good. Well, no, well, yes. Yes, it was fine."

"Indecisive?"

Lily gave a rueful little laugh. "No, but I think you might have been right about getting my bluff in right off. I hope I haven't missed my chance."

"Tell me what happened."

She told him, and she also told him about the look between the two boys and how she interpreted it.

"No, it's not too late. You can still get your bluff in. Just leave it to me."

"What?"

"Just trust me on this. *I'm* going to get your bluff in on them. Tomorrow."

"I have no idea what you mean."

"That's all right. When the time comes, you'll know. Just play along."

When they got to Lily's house, Amos helped her down and carried her satchel and empty lunch sack inside. "You need to check their letters and plan for tomorrow, don't you?"

"Yes. I won't need much time to prep. I've gone through it several times already. But I do want to spend plenty of time looking at their work on those letters."

"All right, good, that'll work. I'll go on out and tend to the horses, then I need to head to the house for a few minutes. I'll be back over here after that."

"You'd better be," she said as she pulled him to her by his collar. "I've got some serious gratitude to demonstrate." She gave him a quick kiss and let go of his shirt.

"A bold and brazen woman when it comes to sensual desires. I like that."

"The sooner you tend those horses and check on the house, the sooner I can be grateful."

A big grin was Amos' response. Then he ran out the front door and she heard him jump in the buggy and *hyah* the horses.

Lily looked at her satchel on the table, then looked over at the couch. *Bold and brazen woman, indeed. That man won't know what hit him.*

She started unbuttoning her dress and headed down the hall at a speedy clip. She undressed faster than she ever had before and threw her clothes in the basket she used for dirty laundry.

The water was cold as she stood naked in front of her lavatory and placed a rubber stopper in the drain. She found her scented bath soap bottles and dropped in a capful of the gardenia scented one. The wet cloth was refreshingly brisk as she washed her face and neck. Lily dropped the cloth back in the water and wrung it out. She washed her chest and breasts next and thought how her nipples would look just like they do now, hard little buds from the cold water, when Amos finally lavished attention on them with his mouth and his hands. An uncontrollable shiver went through her and she wondered if she should tell him that he could arouse her when he wasn't in the room, too.

She scrubbed her underarms and made a note to rub a dab of baking soda on them once she was dry. She'd just be careful not to drop any of it anywhere else on her in case she was successful in getting him to take them both to further heights tonight. Baking soda probably wasn't the best flavor for inflaming the passions.

Oh, I need to think of some more synonyms for flaming passion.

When she was once again fresh and clean all over, she started to walk away when she got a good look at her hair. *He'll like it down better.* Out came the pins and the comb she had in it. Lily brushed through it several times before she was happy with how it looked. She must have twisted the bun just right that morning because her hair fell in loose, flowing waves nearly down to the middle of her back. Even she thought it looked pretty and inviting, and she was usually more critical of her hair.

Lily looked around the closet until she found a small atomizer of gardenia-scented perfume. With a very light touch, she squeezed the rubber bulb and a tiny amount came out on her wrist. She quickly rubbed her wrists together and then rubbed each wrist behind her ear and over her hair a few times. The next stop was the kitchen for the baking soda, then she was off to the bedroom again.

Lily opened the drawer and reached for a fresh nightgown, then thought better of it and closed the drawer. She decided to wear her robe over her bare skin. *That man definitely won't know what hit him.*

She slid into some slippers and went back to the kitchen, then she stoked a fire in the stove and put on some water to heat for tea. She put the loose tea in the teapot, got out two cups and spoons, put some cream and sugar on the table, and sat down with the letters of thanks to the men.

Lily studied each letter and made copious notes and comments to share with each student individually. As she made notes, she began to formulate the groups she could teach together when they had their writing sessions and language discussions.

Some of the letters surprised her, particularly Lettie's. She was such a shy thing, and perhaps foolishly, Lily expected her work to be shy, too. She figured it would be average. To her surprise, it was charming, if that was a word that could apply to a thank you letter. Lettie was only eight, but her work was that of someone older. The format wasn't correct at all, but she hadn't been taught the parts of a letter yet, so Lily dismissed that. It was the wording and phraseology, written as though she had a gift for syntax and even rhythm. Why, she knew of adults who never attained this level of harmony of the language arts.

What surprised her even more was the drawing Lettie included on the bottom of the page. It was readily identifiable as the exterior of the school building, complete with bell, steps, handrails, the new benches, and even trees and shrubbery. She thought back to when they did the letters and realized Lettie had had to do it from memory alone. That was remarkable. Lettie definitely had artistic talent and an artist's eye.

Billy's thank you didn't surprise her. It was exactly what she expected from the young man. It seemed well thought out, deliberate, and organized. The vocabulary seemed advanced for his age, then she remembered how much he and his mother loved to read. That was where he most likely acquired those words.

Margie's letter was more or less in the correct format, but the margins were sloppy. All the component sections of a letter were there, but they weren't lined up well. Instead of dividing a long word and going to the next line, she wrote the squeezed word so that it snaked either up or down in the right margin. There were two places where she used a caret to indicate a word to be inserted, and the word itself was so squished above the other words as to be illegible. Lily remembered when she talked to Margie the first time and how it made her head spin. The poor child wrote the same way she spoke.

Overall, Lily was most pleased with the letters, and she hoped Angus and Henry and the other men would understand how much they truly appreciated all the work and the gift of the materials to make the items. She would make Amos understand that she wasn't the only one who saw the benefit of the shelves and benches; the children did, too. She wanted Amos to make sure Angus and Henry understood.

The water in the big pot on the stove was boiling, and she ladled some into the teapot. She put all the schoolwork back in her satchel. She had studied tomorrow's schedule enough. Unsure of when Amos would be back, she went to her bedroom to select clothes for tomorrow and set them out over the back of an upholstered chair in the corner.

Lily headed back to the kitchen and found the sack her lunch had been in. All that was left inside were the papers the biscuits had been wrapped in, the knife she used to cut cheese slices, the jars that held her willow bark tea and the water Billy drank. She washed the knife and jars and set them aside to drain dry. An apple and a pear went into the sack and she was reminded of Billy again. He was definitely going to be the teacher's pet if she didn't watch it. And now, possibly Lettie, too. That child clearly had some depth to her, more than was obvious upon just meeting her.

The tea had steeped long enough. Lily poured a cup, doctored it just the way she liked, then carried it to the couch. When she realized it had gotten almost dark, she jumped up and lit a lamp on the kitchen table. She lit the one in the parlor and turned it almost as low as it would go. She did the same thing in the bedroom and the water closet. Then she went back and turned up the one in the water closet. Sometimes light was helpful in there.

She looked around for anything else she needed to do, then sat down to enjoy her tea and think of synonyms for *titillating impropriety*. She was going to be ready for him tonight.

When she heard his footsteps on the front porch, she jumped up to greet him. This time, he didn't even knock, he just came on in. Lily liked that. When Amos saw her hair down around her shoulders and nearly covering her breasts, he made a sound like a low growl. She pressed her body against his, her arms around him as far as they would go.

"I'm glad you're here."

Amos kissed her and she felt his hands cup her buttocks and pull her even tighter against him. "Lord have mercy, Lily, you're naked under this robe." He pulled his head back and looked at her with a combination of smoldering heat and minor annoyance.

"I think you might underestimate how grateful I am," Lily

NORA NOLAN

said in her sultriest voice, then she leaned in and up to nibble
his neck. Amos closed his eyes and moaned, giving in to the
sensation. She unbuttoned his top shirt button and kissed a
little lower. Then the next button, and the next, trailing a hot
path with her lips and tongue. When all the buttons were
undone, she parted the sides of the shirt and put her hands on
his chest and rubbed. Massaged. Caressed. Then she ran her
hands all over his chest and belly and sides, randomly kissing
and licking and sucking while her hands explored.

"That feels so good, baby. I can't even begin to tell you..."
His voice was deep and husky.

"Good. That's what I was going for," she said as she slowly
dropped to her knees and reached for the buttons on his
britches.

"Sweet Lily," he said almost under his breath, almost too
quietly for her to hear. She felt the swelling flesh on the other
side of the fabric she held in her hands. Then she felt his hands
in her hair. He stroked it and pulled it away from her head by
running his fingers through it and lifting it up and out. He did
that two or three times before entwining her hair in his fingers,
pulling it just a little every once in a while. Just enough to make
her look up at him.

Lily wondered if looking down at her affected him the same
way looking up at him affected her. It wouldn't be the same
way, she reasoned. They were in distinctly different roles. But
she wondered if he felt it, whatever it was, as deeply as she did.
She was at his feet, on her knees, in the very core aspect of a
dutiful, yielding, biddable woman in love with her in-control
powerhouse of a *real man*.

She freed his hardness and took his sac in her left hand. Lily
felt a tug on her hair and looked up again to find his eyes fixed
on her. She kept her eyes on his as she opened her mouth
wider and licked around the smooth head, letting her lips
touch him ever so briefly. His moans grew as her mouth

188

worked some kind of sorcery on his body. It amused her that at this very instant, she was the one in control, regardless of her submissive posture.

She began to use firmer touches and stronger licks and sucks and saw him close his eyes. She untied the belt of her robe and let it fall to the floor. She cleverly put her hands back on him, on the inside of his thighs and the base of his length. Lily was looking at it, imagining what it would feel like inside her when she heard his voice.

"Sweet Lord, Lily, what are you doing?"

"Right now I'm imagining this thing sliding into me and my muscles trying to grasp it so I can hold it inside me longer."

"Oh, ye... oh! Come on, come on, baby, I'm almost there. Suck it, sweetie, suck it harder."

Lily felt him pull her hair, and it was more than a tug. He established a better grip and pulled her face onto him. Her gag reflex kicked in and he let her loose some, just for a moment, before he did it again. His moans turned into bellows and he let go of her hair as he spent in her mouth. The sounds he made went from the loud bellow to sighs to softer moans that held a hint of wonder.

"Baby, I need to sit. You made me weak in the knees." He sat in the middle of the couch and patted his thighs. "Now, you come here to me."

She nearly froze and looked at him in confusion. "You want to spank me?"

He laughed softly. "No, sweetie. Well," he said, thinking about it, "that might be fun, but it's not what I want right now. Come straddle me."

She did, and leaned against him. "Oh, Amos, I love how this feels, skin to skin, my breasts against your chest."

"It feels wonderful, babe. I've fantasized about this very thing."

"Mmm. Tell me about this fantasy."

"No."

"No? Why not?"

"Because if I'm talking, I can't do this." She was at just the right height that he didn't have to lean over very far to take a nipple in his mouth and suck nearly half her breast into his mouth.

Lily threw her head back and cried out. "Amos! That felt... I felt... I felt that all the way down between my legs. Like lightning shot through me."

"Good. That's what I was going for," he said, echoing her words from earlier. He flicked her hard, tight nipple with his tongue and teased it with his teeth. He flicked her other nipple with his fingertips and nails, then gently rolled and soothed it before he pinched it almost too hard for her. Almost.

"Yes. Yes, Amos, yes. That feels like magic, like you cast a spell over me. This feels too intense to be a normal sensation."

"It is normal, sweetie, get used to it."

"Amos," she leaned over and breathlessly whispered close to his ear, "make love to me, please."

He stopped and looked around the room as if searching for the words to say. "It's only six more days until we're married."

"I know, only six days. We might as well go ahead. Even if I were to conceive our child tonight, no one would ever know. Only six days."

"We shouldn't, Lily. Besides, we're in the wrong house."

Lily hit her head against his shoulder two or three times. "But I want to know what it feels like to reach, you know—"

"Your climax?"

"Yes."

"What if I can make that happen without taking your maidenhead?"

He saw her skeptical look. "All right."

A slow, sexy smirk formed on his face. "Lie back and spread your legs for me."

*a*mos arrived early the next morning to make sure she hadn't overslept again. She hadn't, and after she welcomed him in her usual "grateful" manner, she accused him of arriving early so he would find her undressed.

"I will neither confirm nor deny that to be the case. I merely wanted to make sure you were up on time." He shook his head slowly and assumed an innocent countenance. "The fact that I might catch you naked, and nearly did, was pure serendipity."

"Remind me not to play poker with you. I almost believed that."

Amos laughed. "I'll go work on breakfast. You can go ahead and get dressed."

He found coffee on the burner, but when he licked his finger to test the pot, it was still cool. There was water on to boil and biscuits in the oven. He sliced some bacon and whisked a few eggs with a fork. He made enough to feed them both for lunch. When she finally came back in, everything was on the table. Amos could tell her robe was over her dress.

"You'll be proud of me. I got my bloomers and stockings on all by myself."

"I'm glad you're healing, but I'm kind of disappointed I didn't get to help with that."

"Shall I wait tomorrow and let you do it for me?"

He got an optimistic puppy dog look on his face. "Would you?"

Lily laughed as she sat down and took a sip of coffee. He'd already added cream and sugar.

"Thank you for finishing breakfast."

"You're welcome. I hope you like it because you're having it again for lunch, only cold."

"It'll be fine, thank you. Really thank you, for everything you do for me."

Amos only shrugged.

"If you will, I want you to take those thank you letters to Angus and Henry first thing this morning. I want them to know how grateful we are—the students, too—for the materials and the work they did. They were as excited as I was."

"I will do that. Sometime today, either late morning or early afternoon, I'll be there to take care of appropriately scaring those boys into behaving."

"I know, I know, you won't tell me yet. I'll go along when it happens."

"I don't want you to give it away or anything. It might be a good little piece of theater."

～

THEY ARRIVED at the school quite early, and Amos went inside with her.

"Amos, you aren't going to get me all worked up again, are you? I don't know how well I can handle that right here before school. Besides, someone else might arrive early, too."

"No, I promise no more than a goodbye peck on the cheek. But there's a chill in the air still and I thought I'd check to see if you need the stove lit. I neglected to check if there was wood in there."

"I checked yesterday and it had some wood ready to be lit. I didn't think we needed it, but it's cooler this morning. It might be a good idea to get a small fire going. By the way, who provides the wood? In most schools, the parents of the children do."

"It's probably the same here, but I'm not sure. We can find out. I'll be happy to bring some any time you're running low." He picked up the box of matches and some kindling and before long, the fire was going. He kissed her on the cheek. "I'll go on to work now, but I'll see you later."

Lily walked him to the door and left it slightly ajar. She wanted the children to be able to come in, but she wanted to try to keep the warmth in if she could. Back at her desk, she opened her notebooks and reviewed the notes she'd made. Today would be the day to test her; she'd have to learn how to teach various levels in one room. She'd already figured out how she'd have some groups reading in their books or working on an assignment while she worked with another group.

She was engrossed in her plans when she heard footsteps and looked up. It was Billy Simmons and a woman she presumed was his mother. Lily stood and walked over to greet her.

The woman turned to Billy. "Son, you go back out and play for a few minutes while I speak with your teacher."

"All right, Momma." He put his lunch on the bottom shelf and ran back outside.

"Miss Lily, I'm Sophie Simmons, Billy's mother." She extended her hand and Lily shook it, noting the woman's bright eyes and pretty face.

"It's nice to meet you, but you're welcome to call me Lily when there are no children around."

"All right, if you'll call me Sophie." Lily thought Sophie's smile was lovely and it matched her sparkling eyes.

"What can I do for you, Sophie? Did you want to speak with me?"

"Yes, I did. Billy told me what you did with your lunch yesterday. I don't normally like to accept anything we don't pay for or work for, but not when it comes to food for Billy. And I particularly want to thank you for doing it in a way that didn't embarrass him. He has lunch today and will for a few days."

"It was my pleasure. Teachers aren't supposed to have favorites, but..." she left the sentence unfinished, but she smiled and knew Sophie would understand. "Um, Sophie, if you don't mind my asking a personal question, how long, I mean, how do you plan—"

"To feed us when this money runs out?" Sophie smiled and Lily knew she hadn't overstepped. "It's all right, I don't mind answering questions. I don't exactly know yet. Maybe I'll find something else to sell, although I'm running out of things that anyone would want."

"Have you thought about moving away from the Low Quarter and looking for a position here in town? It must be hard living out there and working in the fields."

"We would love to move here, but I can't afford to buy a home. I've talked to neighbors in the Quarter about buying our place, but the one who responded is only willing to pay pennies on the dollar for what it's worth. Unless I can sell our place, I can't even afford to live in the boarding house. I know it's the least expensive option."

The boarding house!

"Sophie, you can cook and clean house, can't you? Would you be willing to do that for a living? Do you have any other experience?"

"Willing? Of course. It's honest work. Before I married, I was a bookkeeper in Rawlins. I worked for an accountant and kept the books for some of his clients. Then I met Lewis." Lily saw Sophie's manner change just a little bit. "He misled me about his success in life, and I didn't find out until we were married and Billy was on the way. That's when Lewis starting drinking. Ultimately, that's what killed him."

"Billy told me his father was gone. I'm sorry for your loss."

"Don't be sorry. It was the best thing for us."

"Billy said that, too. He said his father could be mean when he drank."

"Yes. He was." Sophie nodded slowly and looked down. "When Lewis passed, I prayed thanks to God that my seven-year-old son would never again have to try to protect his mother."

Lily couldn't find a trace of bitterness in her tone. "Sophie, I'm so sorry you and Billy went through that. You know," she said, smiling, "I see a certain wisdom in Billy that's advanced for his age. Now I understand why. I believe he came out of that experience with more empathy than other children have. The way he talks about you, it's clear he loves you very much."

"Yes, he does. I know that for sure. Since you brought up working, I have to ask. Do you know of any positions in town that might be open? I could make the trip into town every day until I saved enough to move. I try to come in with Billy, anyway."

"It's very possible I might know of something, but I'd rather not say exactly what it is until I verify it. Realistically, how soon would you and Billy be able to move if a place came available that you didn't have to pay for?"

Sophie tilted her head and got a questioning look. "Is there such a place? If money were no problem, we'd be able to move immediately. We have very few things left."

"That's perfect. I'm going to make a point of finding someone to talk to about this today. If all goes as I expect it to, you'll hear back in a day or two."

"Oh my, Lily, you have me excited now. I hope all the pieces fall into place."

"I do, too, Sophie. More than you can imagine."

~

As she was about to call the older children to the front for their lesson, the door opened and Angus Kelly walked in carrying a leather case, the kind salesmen sometimes used to hold their samples. Amos was behind him, but he stayed in the foyer, a great big grin on his face.

This must be it. He didn't mention Angus before.

"Miss Lily," Angus said, and all the children looked at him. "May I address yer class for a few minutes?"

"Of course. Class, you all probably remember Mr. Kelly. He's Miss Nessa's husband."

They nodded and a few of the older ones said hello to him. Angus set the sample case on Lily's desk.

"Aye, they remember me." Angus said individual hellos to the ones who were children of men he worked with at the sawmill. Lily could tell they were proud he knew their names. "Henry Tucker and I were verra pleased to get these letters o' thanks from ye. I've had a soft spot in me heart for the school since Miss Nessa started teaching here. Me men and I were happy to do the work when we learned there was a need fer it. We're mighty glad ye like the outcome. Now," he picked up the stack of thank you letters, "I want to single out Lettie." He focused on her and started walking to her seat.

Lily saw the look of panic on Lettie's face and noticed how she shrank back in the seat. Angus must have seen it, too, she thought, because he smiled broadly at the child and dropped to his knees beside her so he'd be at eye level and wouldn't appear so imposing. "Lettie, this is some fine artwork, verra fine. I took some art classes when I went to college. I can tell ye already ken some things that have to be taught to other artists, like perspective and shading. Do ye ken what those things are?"

Lettie's eyes got wide and she shook her head no.

"That just proves ye have a natural talent. Ye must enjoy drawing."

Her eyes were just as wide and she nodded yes this time.

"Aye, I thought so. I'd sure like to see ye develop that talent ye have. Miss Lily," he said as he twisted so he could see her better, "ye do no' teach any kind of art in school, do ye?"

"No, Mr. Kelly, I'm afraid not. Besides, I would be the last person qualified to teach that subject."

"Well, would ye consider lettin' me come fer about an hour every few weeks and show the class a few o' the basics? Anyone can be taught to draw, even ye, Miss Lily."

A chorus of "Please, please" arose from the children, and Lettie's pleading eyes touched her the most. She held up her hands in surrender. "Yes, Mr. Kelly. We'll make that work. You may come."

The children clapped and cheered, but Angus turned back to Lettie. "Lettie, I'm going to build a frame for yer letter and hang it in me office. I want to show off the talent we have in this school." Lettie beamed, and Lily wondered where the skittish, cowering child went.

Angus went back to stand by the sample case on Lily's desk. "I ken about the lending library," he said as he pulled out a used textbook, "and if ye'll accept a book that's been written in and worn, I'd like to donate an old art book from me college days."

Lily gladly accepted it.

"I've asked Miss Nessa to find a few books on art, everything from basic drawing techniques to how to appreciate the old masters, and we're going to donate 'em, too." That drew more applause. "Now, one last thing about art. In honor of Miss Lettie, I would like to donate a few things to the class. Not necessarily the library, but the class. I know ye will no' be using these in class, but I thought there might be some of ye who would enjoy drawing, or tryin' to. Maybe ye could take something home overnight to try out, or use them at recess on a rainy day. So, thanks to Lettie, I'd like to give ye some of me own art supplies. Here are several sketchpads. As you can see, some of me own sketches are still in 'em. I'd like for ye to do that, too, leave yer work for others to see. But I'll understand if ye decide not to. Here are three or four boxes of charcoal pencils. Some more lead drawing pencils, some rubber erasers —ye can see how I used 'em—they come in mighty handy. These are colored pencils. Now I recommend that ye start out with just plain ol' pencils until ye get comfortable drawing. Oh, here are some rulers and drawing guides. And I promise ye all, right now, that I'll keep the school in art supplies as long as yer interested in it. Now, raise yer hands if ye want to learn to draw."

Everyone raised their hands. Some waved so high, they rose out of their seats, even Lettie. Angus gave them a big grin as he nodded his appreciation.

"Now, let me see, I covered Lettie's talent, the new books for the library, coming in every few weeks for a lesson, donating some supplies, so, yes, I believe that's it, except for this. He pulled a paddle out of the sample case and turned to address Lily directly. The children grew somber and the room went silent. Lily did a masterful job of not giggling.

"Miss Lily, we made this according to yer special instructions," he said loudly as he reverently stroked the strip of wood. "We used that certain cut o' wood ye wanted and drilled these holes precisely as ye instructed for maximum effect and minimum wind resistance. I've made a few of these in me days, and this 'un handles better 'n anything I've ever seen. It delivers with much more force. Oh, and we finished it with that special wax coating ye wanted that gives extra sting, too. I tried it on me own thigh and, well, let me tell ye, I thought I'd fallen into a dozen beehives. I can still feel the sting." He finished by rubbing his right thigh as he handed it to Lily.

"Thank you, Mr. Kelly, this is just what I asked for. I appreciate your attention to detail. I believe you're an artist with wood just as you are with drawing on paper. This is perfect. My hope, of course, is that I'll never have to use it. But it'll be good to have it, just in case. Thank you again."

"Yer welcome, of course. Ye can see I put a hole in the handle with a hangin' string. I've got a hammer and a nail if ye ken where ye want it. I'll be happy to hang if fer ye."

"I'm not sure where I want it yet."

"In that case," Angus said with a grin, "I'll leave ye the nail but I'm taking me hammer with me. It's me favorite one. I guess I'll be takin' me leave now."

"Class, let's thank Mr. Kelly for the art supplies and the books and the promise to teach us some drawing lessons."

They thanked him, but it wasn't with the enthusiasm they'd shown earlier. The paddle had put somewhat of a damper on the excitement.

"Oh, Mr. Kelly," Lily said, "would you wait for me outside, please? I'd like to speak with you."

"Aye."

"Ben, I might be a few minutes. Would you please lead the class in an alphabetizing exercise like we did yesterday?"

"Yes, ma'am," he said as he jumped up from his desk. She noticed the children brightened.

LILY NODDED AT AMOS. "How did I do?"

"You were perfect."

She took a little bow, then turned to Angus.

"Angus, that really was nice of you to give us all those supplies and the art books."

"Happy to, Lily. That little Lettie really does show some natural talent."

"You did her a world of good with your praise. But I want to tell you about something else, unrelated."

"Oh?"

"Yes. Has John Garrett mentioned anything to you about how things are going at the boarding house?"

"If ye mean how Miz Helen is declining, aye, he told me. We need to take action pretty quick, I'd say. I was going to call a meeting to discuss our options."

"I may have the perfect solution, and we could solve two serious problems at one time."

"Ye got me curious, lass, tell me more."

"Well, I have," Lily remembered what had happened and faltered a bit as she blushed, "as you know, a student in the Low Quarter. He came to school yesterday without a lunch because his mother had no money to buy food. I shared mine with him. She sold something yesterday to Clint at the mercantile so they can eat for a few days. She came in this morning to thank me for feeding Billy and we had a nice long chat. Angus, since her husband died, she's had a hard time of it. She's tried to sell her place so she could move to town, but the only taker is offering a pittance instead of what it might be worth. It's not enough for her to get a place in town.

"I got a peek inside their home. It was a very modest place, but it was neat as a pin. She's a good housekeeper, and she says she's a good cook, too. She's such a nice young woman, I hope we can help her. She's smart, too, she said she worked as a bookkeeper when she met Billy's father. He'd lied to her and led her to believe he'd be able to support them, then he started drinking, and she said that led to his early death. There's something about her that I immediately liked."

"And ye think she'd be the perfect person to hire to help out at the boarding house."

"I do. And they'll need a room, of course."

"Rooms, plural. They should each have their own room." He turned his attention to Amos. "We could take two of the units on the brides' side and put a door in, adjoining them. We could do that with the two units that are closest to the water closets, put another door in the wall between the room and the WC, and that would give them their own enclosed suite with their own facilities."

Amos agreed that should work. "It's not the same as having your own house, but it should work fine."

"She'll be thrilled with it, I'm sure," Lily said. "I'll be thrilled for Billy. He told me he doesn't have any friends to play with in the Low Quarter. It nearly broke my heart. He'll have plenty of children to play with here."

"How soon do ye think they could move?"

Lily grinned. "Immediately. But, Angus, I think she has no money at all right now, since she bought food with the last of it."

"Aye. We'll offer her a bonus if she can move immediately. How about that?"

"It's perfect."

"Do you need to interview her or anything?" Amos asked.

"No. Lily's instincts about people are pretty sharp. And as she said, this will solve two big problems at one time. Nobody is going to object. I just need to tell people now and get going on the work. We can get two doors installed in one day. Today's Tuesday. We could have it ready for them to move in on Thursday. I can send a man out there with a wagon to move 'em Thursday morning."

"I think that man should be John. You know, since he lives at the boarding house, he could tell her what to expect, help her feel welcome."

"Aye, good idea."

"What are you up to, Lily?" Amos asked.

"I'm not up to anything," she responded.

"Lily?"

"Well, she's such a pretty woman. Friendly, easy to talk to, and John needs a wife."

Angus chuckled.

"Lily, I don't think you should play matchmaker."

"If we send John to fetch her, I won't have to. I can almost guarantee it."

Both men shook their heads in amusement, but Angus agreed to send John.

"I'll go talk to the sheriff and then head to Harriet's. She can go wi' me to tell Miz Helen what we're doing. Word will get out about what's going on; we'll no' have to spread the word ourselves."

"When can you let Sophie know that you want to hire her?"

"We should do that soon, I suppose, especially if we think we can get her moved on Thursday. She'll need time to pack, even if she doesn't have much."

"I still have my boxes and crates from when I arrived. She might be able to use them."

"Aye, we'll get them to her. Can ye go this afternoon after school?"

"We might not have to unless you just want to take her the boxes. Most days, well, some days, she comes to walk home with Billy. She sold her horse. In the mornings she borrows it to bring him in, but it's not always possible in the afternoons."

"All right, we'll be here this afternoon at the close of the school day." Angus looked at Lily and grinned. "That is, John and I will be here. If she's here, we'll talk to her then. If not, we'll give young Billy a ride home and take the boxes. Well, I reckon we need to take the boxes whether or not she's here. Does Amos know where they are?"

"They're in the barn," he said.

"Lily, if she is no' here when school lets out, would ye like to go wi' us?"

"I'd like to, but I can't. Caleb Carter is coming to interview me for an article in the paper on Thursday."

"Well, lass, thank ye for bringing this to me. You're right. It's a perfect solution to both problems."

Amos chimed in. "And a perfect solution for John, too. Just wait until he hears you've found him a wife."

"I have an interesting idea. Don't let him know I said anything. Let him meet her, and then see what he says about her." She held up her hands. "Without any interference from me."

"Is this going to be a wager between ye two?" Angus asked.

"Yes," they both said at the same time. Then she added, "I just have to think about my terms."

"Yes," Amos agreed. "We can discuss that later."

Angus chuckled, recognizing what kind of bet this was going to be. It was going to be none of his business.

THE REST of the school day went fine, and fast. Lily wrote homework assignments for the older students on the blackboard. When she dismissed them and opened the door, outside were Caleb, Sophie, Angus, John, Amos, and Molly McBride, who was there to collect her daughter Rosemary. Caleb sat on the front steps, off to the side, so he wouldn't be trampled by the children running out. Sophie sat on one of the benches with Angus on one side of her and John on the other. Amos stood close by. Molly was in her buggy.

Judging by the expression on Sophie's face, Lily felt sure it was going well. Sophie was pretty anyway, but her smile was captivating. It lit up her face and made her eyes sparkle more. And, yes, John couldn't take his eyes off her.

The last student out of the building was Billy. He reached his mother just about the same time Caleb stood and started to speak.

Lily gently cut him off. "Watch this," she whispered and nodded in their direction.

They couldn't hear words, but they heard Billy's whoop and holler, and they saw him run into his mother's arms. John and Amos both looked like they might shed tears. From where they were, they couldn't see Angus' face, but Lily suspected his eyes were misty, too.

Lily beckoned Caleb in to sit with her at her desk.

"May I ask what that was all about? It was clearly good news."

"Yes, of course. Angus has just offered Sophie Simmons a job at the boarding house. They'll live there and Sophie will cook and take care of the place."

"Well, that's good news. I heard Miz Helen isn't doing well."

"She's not. And Sophie has been trying to sell her place in the Low Quarter and move to town but hasn't been able to. So, this solves two problems."

Amos peered into the door and greeted Caleb. "Lily, I'm going to go show John where the boxes are, then I'll be back to take you home."

"You don't have to do that. I can walk."

"I know," he said. "I want to."

"All right, then. I'll see you in a few minutes."

Caleb got right down to business when Amos left. He showed Lily the photograph of the class, and she was immensely pleased. She grinned all through the identification of each child. "This is wonderful, Caleb. The children will treasure it. They're already excited about being in the paper."

"I'll bring a big stack over here so each of them can take one home. If their parents want more than that, they'll have to pay for them." He smiled, but he meant it.

"That's generous enough," Lily said.

They continued the interview, and Lily told him all about the new lending library. She mentioned the shelves and the benches that had been built and donated by the sawmill. She told him about the music sessions Nessa would teach, and she shared with him the results of recent studies from abroad that seemed to show that students who learned music performed better at mathematics and did better on tests overall in other subjects. Lily explained that some of her students already knew the path they wanted to take in their lives. One wanted to be a lawyer, another a doctor, another a blacksmith, one a teacher, and a couple wanted to be ranchers like their fathers. To help them focus on what they needed to do to attain their goals, she was going to invite guest speakers to come in and tell about what it was like to do the work they did, and the education and training required for it. She'd already asked Mr. Ross Bailey to visit, and he readily agreed. Soon she'd be asking others. Perhaps even a newspaper editor. Oh, and as of today, Angus Kelly was going to come in every few weeks and teach some basics pertaining to art and drawing.

"Art and music? Aren't you afraid some parents might think that's frivolous?"

She laughed and smiled at him. "Are you going to be the one to tell that to Angus Kelly?" Caleb laughed, too. "I don't believe it's frivolous at all. We drum facts and figures into their heads all day, and that's a good thing. They absolutely need to learn the facts and figures. They also need to understand how to apply that knowledge to real-life situations. Sometimes that requires a little creativity. In some cases, the arts reinforce those facts and figures. Let's go back to music, for example. You've got whole notes, half notes, quarter notes, eighth notes —fractions! You have to know that to count beats in a bar. Music is very mathematical."

"Miss Lily, this may be the most interesting article I've written. I heard from a couple of parents that their children came home yesterday eager to go back to school today. That had never happened before. I'm sure this is enough for now. It might even be enough for a two-part article, to be completed next week. We'll see. Thank you for your time. If I have any questions as I write the piece, I'll be back for clarification. I hope that's all right."

"Of course, it is. I'm happy to do whatever I can to help."

Caleb left and as Lily cleaned up for the day, she reflected back on what a stellar day it had been. She was up early, shared breakfast and a little intimacy with the man she loved, she met the mother of her favorite student and they got along well, she enjoyed "a little theater" as Amos had called it when he and Angus visited, she suggested a solution to a couple of problems and it worked out better than she hoped, her school was going to be featured in a newspaper article, and the day wasn't over yet. She still had more time to spend with the man she loved.

"WE STILL NEED to figure out the terms of our wager," Lily said to Amos as he drove the wagon home.

"What are you thinking about?"

"If I win, and John shows interest in Sophie, we make love."

"That'll work fine if it doesn't happen until after Sunday."

"Amos, it won't be anything special after Sunday."

He gave her an odd look.

"Oh, you know what I mean. We'll be making love anyway after Sunday."

"I know what you mean, but really, it's only five days now. You can wait that long."

"But I don't want to."

"How about if I do what I did last night? Twice?"

"Twice. That does sound pretty good. I think I can live with that. What if I lose? What do I have to do? Maybe kiss you all over and end up at that part of you I've grown so fond of?"

"Oh, sweetie, that does sound tempting, but I'm thinking of something else."

She waited for him to finish. "Well, don't stop with that. What are you thinking? What do I have to do?"

He smirked. "You, my sweet Lily, have to take a spanking from me. Exactly as I want to deliver it. You don't get to say no to anything."

"That's too much! I don't think that's equal in nature to what I get if I win."

"All right. How many orgasms do you want? Three? Four? I can do that." He laughed at his wording. "Actually, you can do that and I can make it happen."

"I need to reconsider my choice. Maybe I need to choose something to cause you pain instead of you having to do something to give me pleasure."

"What if I told you you'll probably win? This afternoon, John wanted to drive Sophie and Billy by himself. He told Angus he could go on home."

"I knew it." Lily was elated. "In that case, we'll call it at four releases. You can spread them over a couple of nights."

"No, all in one night."

"I'm not sure I can take that, Amos. You saw what one did to me."

He nodded smugly, and a smile crept into his smirk. "I saw. You can take it. I'll make you take it. I'll make you want it in spite of yourself."

Lily wondered fleetingly if a person could be pleasured to death.

~

THAT EVENING, after the messiness from supper was cleaned and Amos removed the built up ashes in the stove and put in fresh wood to be ready for the next fire, they sat on the couch. They didn't jump into the necking part immediately as they usually did. They both seemed to the other to be a little pensive.

"I think I like this best of all," Lily said, "just sitting with you, leaning against you like this, your arms around me. I don't think I've ever felt so at peace and so safe."

"I was just thinking along those same lines. This is home. This is what home should feel like."

"So, we've been wrong all these years. Home isn't wherever you hang your hat. It's wherever you're in your lover's arms."

"I think there may be truth in that. If I were to lose everything I own, I'd still be fine as long as you were with me. We could start over and rebuild. It would still feel like home with you by my side."

"It would, wouldn't it?" Lily pondered that a moment. "You know something? I've come to look forward to the end of each day, just so I can spend time with you."

He nodded. "And the beginning of each day, too. I look forward to breakfast with you. Starting my day out right with you."

"Just think, after Sunday, we'll wake up next to each other. That will truly be starting the day out right."

Amos agreed. "Speaking of days, anything special happening at school tomorrow?"

"There is, actually. Nessa's going to come in the afternoon for our first lesson in music basics. The children are all looking forward to it."

"Do you know if any of them are musically inclined? Or if they sing well?"

"I don't know. Surely, Nessa would have mentioned it if

there were. They may all be like me, and doomed to forever be in a chorus instead of performing solo."

"I've heard you sing at church. I think you have a nice voice," Amos said.

"I'm all right when there are others around me singing, but that's about it. I enjoy it; I just don't do it that well all the time."

"I'm kind of the same way. Although there have been times when I've been out fishing or riding and I knew there was nobody else for miles, and I just let loose and belted it out. It's a wonder my horse didn't bolt and run."

Lily chuckled at that. "What about you? Does your day hold anything exciting tomorrow?"

He looked like he didn't want to answer. "I don't know about exciting, but I'm scheduled to be on the team to go out and fell trees."

"Oh," she said. "Well, we both knew this day would come eventually. I'm not sure I could ever have been prepared for it. Amos Cameron, you promise me you'll exercise every caution out there. You men look out for each other. For once, I don't want you thinking about me all day. You concentrate on work and safety, you hear me? Because at the end of the day tomorrow, I want to be at home in your arms again. Just like we are right now."

His voice softened and his arm tightened around her. "I promise you that, Lily. Not just me, all the men have safety on their minds now. It cost a man his life to remind us how dangerous the work is. We don't take that lightly. Listen to me. We will be safe out there. And I will come home to you at the end of the day. We'll be at home in each other's arms, just like we are right now."

"I love you, Amos."

"I love you, too, sweetie." He kissed her cheek, then her neck. "Of course," Amos went on, "home's more than just being in each other's arms. It's also the best place for scurrilous activities. Feverish ones. Sensuous."

Lily recognized he was going back to the little game they started the day before of words that pertained to sex. "Sizzling. Tempestuous," she said as she closed her eyes to concentrate on the feel of his mouth on her.

He nuzzled her neck some more. "Torrid. Impassioned."

"Seductive. Frisky."

Amos chuckled and pulled his lips away from her neck. "That one makes me sound like a pup."

Undeterred, she continued. "All right, then. Stimulating. Concupiscent."

He pulled away again. "That's one I don't usually think about. You get extra points." He went back to her neck and stroked her breast, too. "Lecherous. Debauched."

"Titillating. Enticing." She moaned a little at the sensations he delivered with his mouth and his hand.

"Bawdy. Nasty. Obscene."

"Whoa. You're using some dark words here."

"Yes, ma'am. What can I say? Men just think that way."

"All of them?"

"Probably not soft and small city men. No, that's not true. Probably them, too."

"Really?"

"Sweetie, we're men. It's what we do. We think about sex. Almost all the time. You have to figure that with thinking about it that much, it's going to go rough and raw sometimes. Vulgar. Depraved."

"Is that what men want?"

"Most men are happy with whatever they get. Nice and sweet or downright nasty. It's all good."

"You did tell me once you had dirty fantasies."

"Sure did. And unless I'm wrong, I believe you said you'd act them out with me. Do you regret saying that now?"

"Well, not yet. We can revisit this topic after Sunday."

"I wouldn't want to frighten you. I promise I won't go too dark too soon." He grinned at her. "Let's get these clothes off you. I want to practice what it'll take to give you four releases in one night. It's entirely possible we'll have to raise that number. Maybe double it."

Lily laughed. "I can't even imagine that many. I hate to kill a mood, but can you check my wounds? We skipped it yesterday."

CHAPTER 11

*A*mos quietly entered Lily's house while it was still dark. He set his own lantern down and lit the lamps in her kitchen and parlor. Then he got a fire going in her stove and put a pot of coffee and a big pan of water on the burners. On his way back to her bedroom, he stopped in the water closet to light a lamp in there.

She didn't awaken when he brought in the light, or even when he set it down and gently sat on the bed. For a few moments he just watched her sleep.

"Wake up, sleepyhead, I have to be at the mill shortly after dawn this morning. You told me you wanted an early breakfast with me."

"Mmm, I do." He saw her smile before she opened her eyes. When she did open them, she reached up and touched his lips. "Just think, in five more mornings, I get to wake up next to you."

"I was just thinking that very thing before I woke you up. I've heard it's bad luck to wish your life away, but I don't care. I wish it was Monday morning right now, and we were in our bed at our house waking up together."

"That's exactly what I thought about last night before I fell asleep. Funny how my first and last thoughts of the day are about you."

"It's not funny at all," Amos said. "I do the same thing."

"Well," she said with a chuckle, "I guess if you aren't going to shuck your clothes and climb in with me, I might as well get up."

"The water should be getting warm now. I'll bring some into the water closet for you and pour it in the sink. Or did you want to take a full bath?"

"No, I'll just wash up in the sink."

"All right. I'll bring your coffee, too."

"Thank you. I'll be in there shortly."

By the time Lily gathered her clean underthings and robe and went to the water closet, Amos was leaving it, hot coffee and hot water in place as he'd promised. He went back into the kitchen to prepare breakfast while she washed. She thought he must be the most considerate man who ever lived. And he was hers.

Breakfast was a simple affair again, with toasted buttered bread and scrambled eggs. Amos even made them both scrambled egg sandwiches to take with them for lunch. He used the last of the eggs and told Lily, hoping at least one of them would remember they needed to stop at the mercantile on the way home that afternoon.

Across the table from him, Lily reached out and took his hand. "Amos, please be careful out there today. I can't lose you."

"You won't, sweetie. I have to come home safely so we can go over to Emmett's blacksmith shop and check out his wedding bands."

She brightened. "That's right, we do need to do that. Right before we stop to buy eggs."

"See? You have nothing to worry about. Just have faith. And when you think about me today, think about how good it'll feel when you see me this afternoon, and how much we'll enjoy looking at wedding bands. And maybe think about how you can show me how glad you are that I came home safely."

"Well, you must be right. You men do think about sex almost all the time."

"Any man would confirm that. But don't go asking any, all right?"

Lily giggled, briefly thinking of going up to someone like Mr. Bailey, or Clint at the mercantile, and asking how often they thought of sex, and specifically, what scenarios they thought about.

THE DAY GOT off to a good start. Once again, Billy was early, and he was accompanied by his mother.

"Good morning, Sophie," Lily said. "I can't tell you how glad I am that everything worked out perfectly all the way around yesterday. It'll be nice having you in town. You know I'm new, too, and I'm still trying to make friends."

"I can't thank you enough for making this happen for us. Billy's as thrilled as I am. I asked Angus Kelly if maybe he wanted me to start out on a trial basis, and he said no. He said he trusts your instincts. I was impressed by that. He must think highly of you."

"Maybe not me personally, but he has liked the ideas I've had about the school. You'll find Angus is a good man. I trust him and his instincts, too." Lily decided to go out on a limb. She was awfully curious since she had a good bit riding on the answer. "Did John Garrett take you and Billy home yesterday?"

Sophie's expression changed just ever so slightly, but it was enough for Lily to deduce that John had made a favorable impression. "He did. He seems like a nice man."

"I think so, and Amos does, too. When I first got to town

and learned my fiancé had died, Amos was saddled with the responsibility of taking care of me and finishing the work on the house that was left to me. John had been one of Will's friends, too, and he helped Amos finish the work. That's how I've gotten to know him."

Sophie nodded. "Yes, he told me about that. That was such a sad turn of events for you. I hear Amos is a wonderful man, too, though. And that you two seem to be getting along well."

That scoundrel John told her about Amos and me. Well, shoot. It probably isn't as big a secret as I hoped we could keep it. Might as well tell her.

"He is. We haven't told anyone yet, but," she leaned in toward Sophie and spoke more softly, "we plan to marry Sunday after the regular service. The pastor will announce it that morning and invite everyone to stay a few minutes longer."

Sophie's eyes grew with excitement. "Billy and I will be able to see it." Then she got a shy but slightly mischievous look on her face. "John's already asked if he could escort us to the services."

"Things sound promising with you and John. I sure do hope it works out."

"Well, it's so soon yet. It would be silly, foolish even, to think of possibilities at this point. We only met yesterday."

"It was about that quick for Amos and me. Well, for me, anyway. Amos struggled for a long time with guilt over having feelings for me, since I was his best friend's fiancée."

"John hinted at that. But I think it speaks well of Amos that he felt that way. Shows he's an honorable man."

Lily nodded. "I thought the same thing."

Another student walked in and Sophie said her goodbye.

"Sophie, when things settle down, we'd love to have you and John and Billy over for dinner sometime."

"I look forward to that."

~

THE MORNING PASSED QUICKLY. Lily rarely had a chance to think about Amos, only doing so when she looked at her time-piece brooch, and she tried not to let any worry creep in. She tried her best to focus on wedding bands and think about how they might be intimate that night.

Lunchtime and recess were spent in preparation for the afternoon sessions and the next morning; she wanted to keep her evening as free as possible. Today would be a short day for her; Nessa was taking up the last hour of the school day with an introductory music lesson. The students were looking forward to it, and Lily could use the extra time prepping for the remainder of the week.

Nessa arrived a few minutes early, so they gave the children a quick outhouse and drink-of-water break while she wrote things on the board. Nessa and Lily were both surprised to find the children back in their seats a full two minutes before the allotted time was up. "Looks like they really were looking forward to this," Nessa whispered.

She'd already told Nessa she was going to sit on the front steps so she could work without distracting the children. As she walked outside, she heard Nessa explain to the children that she had borrowed hymnals from the church, and they'd have to share with a partner and be very careful with the books.

Lily sat on one of the middle steps. Nessa's voice was in the background, so she could hear what was going on without the classroom sounds being a distraction to her. She looked around, at the new benches, at the new church house across the road, at the parsonage next door to the schoolhouse, and although she couldn't see the cemetery, she knew it was behind the school. Down the block was the new community hall. She realized she was growing fond of her new hometown.

She settled in and looked at her lesson plans for the next day. She had an idea to make the times tables memorization a little more enjoyable for the younger ones and wrote it down, so she could flesh it out later. She found herself shifting back and forth from listening to Nessa, to tuning them out and concentrating on her own work. Nessa was going to use the Doxology from the hymnbook as an example while she went over some basics like beat, rhythm, clefs and notes. As she was listening to them sing the short, familiar song of praise, she heard a horse galloping toward her.

She didn't recognize him, and he didn't even look her way. Just about the time he was on the road in front of the schoolhouse, he started yelling the pastor's name. He was headed to the parsonage.

"Copperfield! Reverend Copperfield! They want you at the doc's office. Reverend Copperfield!" the man yelled.

The pastor emerged, putting his jacket on. "Lester, do I have time to hook up a horse to my buggy?"

"They didn't say," the man said. "Hop on. I'll take you."

"Who's hurt?"

"Don't know," Lester said. "I just happened to be outside when one of the lumberjacks flagged me down and asked me if I'd come get you."

Lily jumped up in fear. "Lumberjacks?" she shouted. "A lumberjack was hurt?"

"Yes, ma'am." It was all he said before he urged the horse into a gallop again, the pastor holding on behind him.

"No, no, no, no, no, it can't be, not again. Not Amos! No, no!" The words started out low, almost under her breath, but her volume rose to a loud wail as her feet moved almost of their own will. "Please God, don't let it be Amos. Please not my Amos."

She'd never run so fast, and damnation to anyone who thought it unseemly for a woman to run. The tears fell from

217

her eyes and she felt them fly off her cheeks from the wind as she ran. She even felt one hit her ear. With her voice back to a normal speaking tone, she ran around the corner just in time to see the stranger's horse with the pastor on it turn the last corner. She wanted to be on that horse just to get there a few seconds sooner. She had to find out how Amos was. Her hair was falling from the pins, but she couldn't be bothered with anything that trivial now.

The street seemed so long. She was vaguely aware of people stopping to watch her, but she was undeterred. Lily tried to run even faster as she continued praying and willing Amos to be all right. "Don't let it be Amos. Don't let it be Amos. Please don't let Amos be dead. No, no, this can't be happening again. Not to Amos. You're coming back home to me tonight!"

Lily finally rounded the corner and the first thing she saw was Amos, about fifteen feet in front of her. She let out a hysterical cry of relief and elation, followed by several repetitions of his name. She tried to slow down her pace but couldn't completely. Amos put one foot out and back to brace himself just in time for her to run into his arms. She wept uncontrollably, her cheek against his chest and her hands pounding him. "I thought you were dead, Amos. I thought it was you. I couldn't bear it. I thought you were dead."

He held her tight and tried to soothe her. "I'm just fine, sweetie, I'm fine. It was Bart Green who got hurt. He'll be all right. It wasn't even tree related. He tripped and fell down a hill and broke his left arm in a couple of places when he tried to break his fall. He's got even worse cuts than you had, and he's mighty banged up and bloody, but he'll heal." Soon she stopped pounding his chest and put her arms around him.

"They came to get Reverend Copperfield. The man didn't know a name, and I just knew it was you. I thought you were dead. I figured it must have been terrible."

"I guess it was, to Bart. I think they got the pastor because they're good friends. Fishing buddies. He'll probably stay with the Copperfields until he's getting around better. Um, Lily?"

"Yes?" she asked, her eyes still closed and arms still around him as though she'd never let him go.

"I think it's fair to say we aren't a secret anymore."

She lowered her arms and turned just a fraction so she could see. There were people all along the side of the road, watching them with big smiles. She turned her head some more and was surprised to see Nessa and her students, and they were beaming, too.

She turned back to Amos and dropped her head to his chest again, this time in embarrassment. Amos grinned and shrugged at the crowd, then put his arms back around her. The crowd laughed and applauded, but they began to disperse. She heard Nessa tell the children they needed to get back to school, now that they knew everyone was safe and everything was all right.

She and Amos stood there a while longer so she could calm down and collect herself. He made her laugh when he tried to get her hair back up. "That's better," he said, "but it isn't as good as when you fix it."

"As long as nothing's sticking out horribly and I don't look like a clown."

He pulled her close again for a second while he chided her. "I would never let you go around looking like that."

She smiled up at him. They headed back to the schoolhouse.

"Miss Lily, are you and Mr. Amos gettin' hitched?"

They were back in the schoolhouse getting Lily's reticule and satchel and lunch sack.

"Well, we haven't told anyone. I'm very pleased that you all, my wonderful students, will be the first to get the official news. Yes, we're getting married Sunday after the morning services.

As a matter of fact, we're on our way to look at wedding rings now."

They clapped and whooped, and Lily heard a couple of them say something like "told ya so."

Lily thanked Nessa for closing out the day for her, and she and Amos left.

∼

"SOMETHING TELLS me you two aren't in here looking for horseshoes," Emmett said as he reached under the counter and brought out his tray of wedding bands.

"Oh," Lily said with just a tiny bit of consternation in her amusement. "Does everybody know?"

"They do now. You just missed Harriet. She rushed in to tell me what she'd seen in the street between you two."

She took hold of Amos' arm and turned a little inward toward him. "This is embarrassing."

"Don't be embarrassed. Harriet was thrilled. I haven't seen her this happy in a long time. A lot of people are going to be happy about this."

Amos chuckled. "I wonder who had Sunday in the pool over at Mary's."

"Not me, I'm afraid. I had Friday, the day after tomorrow."

Lily picked up one of the rings. "These are beautiful, Emmett."

"Thank you. They're definitely one of a kind."

She slipped it on. "Look at that, Amos, it fits perfectly!" She got excited. "Is there one like it for a man?"

"Sure is, right here," Emmett said as he handed it to Amos. "I can adjust it for you tomorrow if the fit needs some work."

"It's just a little too small," Amos said.

Emmett handed him a bunch of rings connected with string. "Try these and see what size you need."

"This one," Amos said as he handed it back to him.

"Good. It's only a half-size difference. I can enlarge it and you won't even be able to tell. If it had been two or three whole sizes too small, I'd have made a new ring."

Amos looked at Lily for confirmation. "Are these the ones you want, sweetie?"

She nodded with a great big grin. "I do."

"Hey, you'd better save that kind of talk for Sunday," Emmett said, grinning.

Lily looked at Emmett, then back at Amos. "Amos, maybe we should get married on Friday. We can't take a honeymoon since school just started, but that would give us a little extra time. What do you think about getting married at the school, at the end of the day? I'd like for my students to be there; they're such a big part of my life now. Do you think the preacher would do that?"

"Sure he would," Emmett interrupted. "He loves things like this."

"I'll marry you anywhere you want, sweetie, and the sooner, the better."

As they were leaving, Lily said to Emmett, "I guess you need to be thinking of what you'll do with your winnings."

"Well, no, you should," he said with a huge grin and a shrug. "I'd already decided to donate it to the school if I win."

"Oh, thank you, Emmett. We'll put it toward books and supplies for the new library. Oh! I almost forgot. I'm asking business owners and tradesmen if they'd come to our school and give a little talk about what their job is like and what it takes to get started. There's a boy in our class who thinks he might want to be a blacksmith. Do you think you might come visit us and share a little about what the work entails and what kind of training you went through to get where you are?"

Emmett considered that. "I could, but it would be more

effective if you brought the class here and they could see it firsthand. Would that be possible?"

"I don't see why not. The children would love it. It would be best to do it in a few weeks, though, so I can space out the visits. I'll come see you later and we can work out the details. And, thank you, Emmett. You don't know how much I appreciate this."

~

REVEREND COPPERFIELD WAS AMUSED by their odd wedding venue and wholeheartedly agreed to officiate in such a place. After all, it used to be the church building before the new church was built across the road. Charlotte, the reverend's wife, agreed that he shouldn't mind officiating there. He'd performed many wedding ceremonies before in that very building.

When Amos and Lily stepped outside the parsonage, they knew without looking at a watch that it must be time for school to be let out. The yard was littered with people waiting for their children to be excused. Among them were Sophie Simmons, who just happened to be in a wagon with John Garrett.

"Amos, I'd like to wait a few minutes before we head home. I want to thank Nessa again for taking over the class for me when I thought you'd been the one to get hurt."

"Of course, sweetie." He barely cracked a smile when he added, "But we both know the real reason is so you can get a reading on the situation with John and Sophie."

Lily giggled. "Maybe that, too."

"Maybe, my ass," Amos said, "that's the main reason." Lily could tell by his mannerisms and voice he was launching into his real-man-dominant-alpha, dirty, flirty side that made her weak in the knees and wet in the bloomers. He'd only begun doing that recently, but she recognized the tone of his voice. She loved when he talked dirty and mentioned the dark things he'd do to her. Heaven help her if he ever did them in reality; she'd be mortified. But she loved to listen to that talk. That deep voice, almost a whisper that sounded gravelly and hard, but smooth and hot as molten lava at the same time. When she heard that voice whispered near her ear, any semblance of propriety and moral behavior went out the door. "You better tell the whole truth to me, girlie, or I'll have your ass and turn it bright red whether you win this bet or not."

She couldn't do more than shoot him an amused smirk because they were now too close to John and Sophie, and they'd be overheard. That was all right, though. The look on his face let her know he wanted to continue the conversation later, too.

"Miss Lily," John said, "aren't you on the wrong side of that schoolhouse door?"

She smiled at him and nodded. "Nessa's covering for me right now. She's been teaching a music lesson this afternoon. How did it go today with connecting those rooms into one unit for Sophie and Billy?"

"They did more than that, Lily!" Sophie said with wide eyes and much excitement. "Angus and John decided to include a third unit so we could have our own sitting room. He put up a wall on the end of my room so Billy can get to the water closet without having to walk through my bedroom. It was a complete surprise! My room's a little smaller, but it'll be worth it. Why don't you two come by and see it?"

Lily looked at Amos, and he replied, "Sure, we'd love to see it." When they got close enough to the wagon so he could be heard with a lowered voice, Amos added something else. "Listen, we don't want the children to know yet, but we're moving up the wedding to Friday afternoon, here at the schoolhouse. We want you both there."

Lily nodded enthusiastically. "Yes, and we need to tell Angus and Nessa. Henry and Opal, too."

John spoke up. "Henry and Opal left for Omaha today. Something about her brother being injured."

"Sorry to hear that," Amos said. "Sweetie, who else do we need to invite?"

"I'm too excited to think straight right now. Maybe I can think of others to invite tomorrow."

"John, what's the latest word on Bart Green?"

"Doc's still got him. I think he wanted to keep him in his surgery tonight, and tomorrow he can go to the Copperfields' to convalesce."

"And you're moving tomorrow," Lily said as she looked at Sophie. "It's going to be a big day. Do you need Billy to help, or will he be at school?"

"Oh, he'll be at school. I don't want him to miss. John and I can lift everything I have. It'll only take two trips, maybe even one if we can get things piled up. There's not much room in the boarding house, and it already has beds that are nicer than mine, so we won't need to move them. I won't need them anymore."

"Sophie, if you need to store anything that won't fit into your boarding house rooms, we can put it all in my house for now." She shrugged. "I'll be moving into Amos' house. There's no need to leave anything behind just because you don't have room for it in that small space."

"You know, I was going to ask what you plan to do with your house after you two marry," John said.

"Oh, we haven't even had a chance to talk about it yet," Lily said as she looked at Amos. "And there's no rush. We have plenty of time to decide."

The schoolhouse door burst open and children came running out.

Amos told John and Sophie they'd be along to the boarding

house to see the changes in just a few minutes. Lily was already making her way to the school. The children, energized by being released from school, greeted Lily loudly on their way out the door and home. A couple of the older ones congratulated her again.

When all the youngsters emptied from the room, Lily threw her arms around Nessa. "Thank you so much for all you do."

Nessa hugged her and patted her on the back. "It was my pleasure. I'm just so happy Amos is all right."

"I appreciate that," he said from behind them.

Lily broke the hug, but she held Nessa by her shoulders. "We've had a change in plans that you need to know about. You and Angus. The wedding is no longer on Sunday. We've decided to get married right here at the school, at the end of the day on Friday. The pastor's already agreed. We want you both there."

Nessa hugged her again, tightly and briefly. "It might be a little presumptuous for me to mention it, but you know me, so..." Nessa held up her hands in a shrugging gesture. "Would it be all right if I sang a song at your wedding? I've done that sometimes for other weddings. Actually, Bethie Hickam and I have been singing at events since we were kids, back east. She and her husband are out of town now, though."

Lily wondered why Nessa's offer to sing made her cry. Maybe she was still overwrought over being so worried about Amos, and that was just another sweet thing making her cup— and her eyes—runneth over. "I would dearly love that." It came out in a broken, teary whisper. Amos and Nessa both seemed touched by her intense emotion.

Nessa hesitated to offer any more help. "Would you like for me to help teach tomorrow or Friday? Give you some extra time to get ready? Or substitute for you on Monday so you can have another day to yourselves?"

Lily composed herself. "No, that's awfully sweet of you, but we plan to keep it simple. The only thing we talked about doing was having Mary make cookies and wrapping two or three in some pretty fabric tied with ribbon for people to take home as favors. We didn't want to serve refreshments. But we can go over to Mary's in a few minutes and get that taken care of. As for Monday, it's sweet of you to offer. But so much has happened in so short a time for us, we just want to settle down into, well, just settle down." She looked at Amos. "I think we'd both like to see some normalcy and routine in our lives."

"All right, I can understand that. But about those cookies," Nessa said. "You leave it to me. I'll arrange everything. I'll have them here, all pretty as can be, and it'll look lovely. It can be part of our wedding gift to you both."

"Oh, Nessa, you've done so much, I can't let you do all that, too."

"Hogwash. I'm doing it." Nessa tossed her hand as if to dismiss the conversation. "Oh, let's iron out all the details about the timing."

They decided the ceremony should start a half hour before the end of the school day. It only took them a few minutes to come up with a detailed schedule of what would happen from the end of the afternoon recess until the end of the school day.

AMOS AND LILY JOINED SOPHIE, Billy, and John at the boarding house, where Lily still chuckled about the name Harriet gave it, the *Bride & Board*.

Billy's face shone with excitement. "Just think, Miss Lily, when I leave school tomorrow to go home, I'll be comin' to a different home. Right here in town!" He took her hand and pulled her. "This is my room. It's bigger than the one I have now in the Quarter. And look here." He pulled her a few more feet. "Our outhouse is inside the house. Inside! And it flushes!"

His excitement was so real, so raw, she wanted to put her arms around him and squeeze. So she did. "I'm so happy for you, Billy. This looks like it'll be a wonderful home for you and your mother."

Billy pulled away and his countenance sobered; once again, he seemed like the child Lily had grown to care about so much. "I reckon it will be wonderful, Miss Lily. I reckon so. We'll be startin' out fresh, won't we?"

"You will. Just think—you have a whole new set of memories to make."

Billy nodded slowly and a grin formed. "And they're all gonna be happy ones, too."

"Pretty soon we'll start receiving books for the library and you and your mother can read to each other again. I know that'll make some happy memories."

"I'm looking forward to that." He nodded sagely.

AMOS LIFTED LILY onto the wagon when they left the Bride & Board. "Would you like to go to Mary's to eat, or do you want to go on home?"

She looked at him and sighed, then put her hand on his arm. "It's been quite the day. I feel like my emotions have been in the lowest valley all the way to the highest mountaintop. I can eat bread and butter for supper and be happy, as long as I can be at home in your arms."

His voice was as soft as his eyes. "Home, then." A moment later he added, "Home in each other's arms, that is. Oh, wait. I forgot we're out of eggs. To the mercantile first, then home."

When they got to the house, he parked in front and jumped down to lift her to the ground. "Hey, it looks like you're bending your knees a little more."

"I am. Today was much better than yesterday. I'm definitely

on the mend. I guess all that running helped. The big bruise is lightening up and all the cuts are healing nicely. They haven't gone away, but they aren't giving me any problems. You know, I was hoping to be all healed up by the time we married, but it seems so trivial now. It's not going to bother you that I still have little cuts and a big bruise, is it?"

Amos laughed. "Well, hell, it hasn't bothered me so far. You go on in and I'll get the horses tucked in bed. I'll be in to help with supper." He handed her the box of eggs.

Lily grinned at him and stood right where she was until the wagon was out of her sight behind the house. Once she was inside, she decided to slip out of her dress so she wouldn't get it soiled with supper preparation; it was still clean and she could wear it again. Off came her shoes and stockings, and she slipped on her robe and house shoes. As she was washing her hands in the water closet, her reflection in the mirror reminded her it might be nice to take her hair down for Amos again. He liked it down. It was down and brushed, wavy and full before she went on in to the kitchen.

She wanted tea, so she put the water on to boil before she readied the teapot. The tea would calm her, she thought. There was a nagging *something* that Lily couldn't identify. It wasn't related to the logging incident in the woods, and it wasn't related to the impending wedding. She was pretty sure of that. But somewhere in the back of her mind, there was a worry that hadn't fully formed.

To keep the meal easy, Lily decided to slice some ham and fry it and boil potatoes to go with it. Bread and butter still sounded good to her since she'd mentioned it earlier. As she stood at the sink scrubbing the potatoes, she tried to figure out what was vexing her in the back of her mind. It wasn't about school; that was going well. It wasn't about Amos; he'd convinced her he was fine and the work teams were being very cautious in the woods. It would come to her later, she was sure.

Lily put on a big pot of potatoes, thinking she might have the leftovers for breakfast with some onions and cheese, or maybe take them for her lunch. Or both, since it was a big pot full. She set the table with cups for tea and glasses of water. The water for the tea was hot, and she ladled some into her teapot to let it steep.

Before long, Amos came in and washed his hands and asked how he could help.

"I guess you can get that skillet and fry the ham."

It took him all of twenty seconds to put the skillet directly over a hot burner and throw in the ham. "Give me something a little harder to do next time. That was too easy."

"I guess if you see anything that needs to be done, then you should be about tending to it. I can't even think straight."

"My sweetie," he said as he pulled her to him, leaned against the countertop, put her head against his chest, and stretched his arms around her. She put her arms around him, too. "Just think. Two days from this very minute, we'll already have been married for a couple of hours. I look forward to that. What do you think we'll be doing exactly forty-eight hours from now?"

He felt her smile against his chest. "I'm not sure about the specific activity at that very minute, but I'll bet we won't have any clothes on," she said.

"For two people who have never been married before, I think we have a pretty good handle on it."

She chuckled. "Maybe you do. I just want to do that thing married people do."

"You mean know each other Biblically? Cleave together? Make the beast with two backs?"

Lily tilted her head up. "You've read Shakespeare? That was from Othello, wasn't it?"

"It was. I did. I," Amos paused, "regrettably went through a phase where I got into poetry and Shakespeare for a while. We studied it in college and I..." he dropped his head a couple of times, not sure he wanted to finish the sentence. "I enjoyed it. I discovered I liked a few poets and I read a lot of their work."

"Why is that regrettable? I love poetry and Shakespeare. Well, other poets more than Shakespeare, really. Why do you regret it?"

"I guess I really don't regret it. Like I said, I enjoyed it. For a while I tried memorizing a few special ones. I thought they might help me get the ladies."

"Did it work?"

"Not once."

Lily giggled. "Why do you seem so reluctant to tell me this?"

"I was afraid you'd think poetry wasn't something a real man would waste time with."

"Are you serious?" Lily laughed, her voice low and with a hint of wonder. "You just elevated yourself to a whole new level of *real man-ishness*. Poetry speaks to our souls on such an intimate level. You're such a self-assured, vital, and self-aware real man that you're comfortable exploring the subtle mysteries of life expressed in beautiful words and thoughts and rhythm. I find that quality in you very… seductive."

"Seductive, huh? And here I thought I just liked rhyming words."

Lily grinned up at him and slapped his chest playfully. "Go ahead. Sling some poetry at me. Maybe I can figure out why it didn't help you with the ladies."

"I only tried that once with a poem. When it didn't work, I chickened out on trying poetry again. It's been so long, I don't think I can remember whole poems anymore. I can probably remember a few of my favorite lines, though."

"I'm listening. I want to know if you like the same ones I like."

"All right. I like Poe. My favorite of his is *Annabel Lee*. There's a line in it I always loved, but only now, with you, am I feeling it deep down. I know exactly what he meant."

"It's one of my favorites, too. Let me guess which line. *But we loved with a love that was more than love—I and my Annabel Lee.*"

"That's the one. It says what's in my heart, and it says it better than I ever could."

"Me, too, Amos. Aren't we the romantics?" Lily asked. "What else do you like?"

"Oh, let's see... Robert Burns. *My Luve is Like a Red, Red Rose.* I remember a few lines. I'll have to say it with the right accent. We should get Angus to recite if for us; that would be better. He's part Scottish, you know. Here goes. *As fair art thou, my bonnie lass, So deep in luve am I; And I will luve thee still, my dear, Till a' the seas gang dry.*"

Lily sighed. "*Till a' the seas gang dry.* It's beautiful. The words are so simple, but powerful. That was perfect, Amos. Angus couldn't have done it any better."

"Oh, there's Elizabeth Barrett Browning, too, that sonnet where she counts the ways she loves him. I forgot most of it, but the best line is the last one, anyway. *...and, if God choose, I shall but love thee better after death.* That's deep emotion, don't you think? She loves him so much she hopes God will let her love him for all eternity." He paused a beat. "I love you that much, Lily."

"I love you that much, too. Amos, are you sure you want to wait two more days for us to be intimate? Because poetry is finally going to get you your way with a woman, in a spectacular fashion."

"I can recite them again Friday."

Lily moaned and slapped his chest again.

"Wait," he said. "Want to hear one more? It's a bit racier, but I know the whole thing."

With a little grin, she rolled her eyes. "I suppose so. If we aren't going to make rapturous love, at least we can talk about it."

"All right. I know all of this one.

"OUR HEARTBEATS RACE *in love's embrace,*
　　Her sweet tongue licks fire all o'er me.
　　See her love-wet skin
　　Where she holds me within,
　　But not the face before me.

OUR BREATHS ALIGNED, *our limbs entwined,*
　　Our need explodes a savage pace.
　　Her breasts bucking wild
　　Have me beguiled,
　　But I cannot see her face.

WERE *dreams but real and I could feel*
　　Each lusty pleasure mentioned here,
　　I'd hold fast to the charms
　　Of the one in my arms,
　　Whose face I would know so dear."

"AMOS," Lily said as she leaned back to see him better. "That reminds me so much of what I said to you about Will's letters. I never heard that one before, and I thought I studied all the poets. Who wrote that?"

He grinned at her. "I did, that night you said what you did about Will's letters. It was the night we first kissed."

"And you went home and wrote a poem." She put both her hands on his chest and lovingly caressed it. "There's something almost magical about that. To me, anyway."

"It was a powerful picture you painted with those words

you said. I felt them, deep down. I think it's what got me past worrying about you being Will's woman. You hadn't been able to see his face or picture yourself with him, so even though you were to marry him, you hadn't been able to see yourself as part of a couple with him. I put myself in that position and wrote it down. That's what helped me move on more than anything else."

"I think it's beautiful, and all the more so because it's what was in your heart."

Amos shook his head. "It won't go down in history as having been written well. I tried for iambic pentameter but I had so much trouble, I settled for just finding words that were close to how I felt. We won't even talk about structure consistency. That's about as good as it'll get."

"Iambic pentameter? I'm impressed you even remember that."

He laughed and shrugged." I forgot all the other terms. I only remember that one because it's fun to say. I can't remember exactly what it means."

"Maybe you'll recite it for me again on Friday? While I'm undressing you? I think that would be a good time."

"It would be a fine time. I'll do that. Actually, I wrote two more verses. They'll have more meaning after we're married, I think."

When the potatoes were done, they put everything on the table and helped themselves.

"I just decided I'm going to purchase some poetry books for the library," Lily said. "We all need more poetry in our lives."

"I don't remember learning much about it in school in my younger years. Does it fit into your curriculum anywhere?"

Lily smiled. "I decided a few minutes ago that it will, whether it's supposed to or not. It'll be later in the year, though. I want to get a few books on poetry first."

"I have one. You're welcome to it, but I'm not donating it to the library."

Lily grinned at him and changed the subject. "Tomorrow's going to be a big day at school. Caleb said he'd bring each student their own copy of the paper with the class picture in it. They're excited."

"It's going to be a big day all around, then. We might be able to wrap up our bet tomorrow night since John's helping Sophie move. If all goes as you think it will, I'll have to give you a most satisfying evening." He gave her a lusty and anticipatory look, complete with smirk.

"Indeed you will. And I fully trust it'll happen. But, you know," she said as she slowly shook her head in mock seriousness, "something unexpected could happen and make me wrong about this whole thing. I could end up with my backside in dire peril." She gave him a look that belied her words. She knew she'd win the bet. "You never told me why that's what you wanted if you win. Why would you want to do that?"

Amos softened his eyes, but retained the smirk. "Some women enjoy it. You might, too, under certain conditions." He took on a mock serious look, too. "We owe it to ourselves to see if you do. I'd feel awful if I withheld such pleasure from you."

She just shook her head and laughed. "Good thing I'm going to win. They'll get along better than any of us expect."

Then her eyes widened when she realized the import of those words.

"What is it, Lil?"

"Something's been bothering me, nagging at the back of my mind, and I just realized what it is. They will have a good day tomorrow."

"Well, that's a good thing, isn't it?"

"Yes, it is, she'll be moving into the boarding house."

"Again. That's good, right?"

"Yes and no. Remember when John asked me about the house? I don't think he was just making conversation. I think he wants to buy it. Or rent it, I don't know. If he does, it'll be because they're getting married. And if they marry, they'll move into a house that's more suited to a family than the boarding house."

"Oh, I see. So she won't be living at the Bride & Board anymore, and it'll be harder for her to perform her duties there."

"Exactly. I imagine John and Billy would need her at home in the mornings, instead of her leaving home early every morning to fix breakfast for a houseful of people. Then she'd be cooking supper at the boarding house every evening just when it's important for her to be home with her family, cooking their supper. Oh, Amos," Lily fretted. "We're going to have to find someone else to take Sophie's place at the boarding house."

"We don't have to do that, sweetie. The town can find someone who's suitable. It's not really your responsibility to find someone to fill that vacancy."

"That's true, it's not my responsibility, but I feel responsible. I mean," she stopped and laughed a bit, "Sophie hasn't even moved in and begun to work, and they already seem smitten. I hoped that would happen, but I never dreamed it would happen this fast. Angus was so happy I found a solution for two different problems, and, well, I hate for him to be disappointed."

"If he's disappointed in anybody, sweetie, it would have to be John."

"I don't want that, either."

"Besides, Angus is an old softy. He'd like for them to fall in love and find happiness, too. Oh, and one other thing, it's not just Angus—he's only the main voice and go-getter of that town committee. There are plenty of men in that group to help find someone else to hire."

"I don't fully understand how that group works. I know they bought the boarding house for the town and paid for the bridge improvements. Angus pretty much speaks for them even before he's talked to the rest of them. I think Emmett's the same way. Exactly what kind of committee are they? Were they voted in? Are they the town council?"

Amos snickered. "No, nothing official like that. They just... showed up. It seems to be a system that works. Big Rock's a good little town, and we do our best to take care of our own."

"That's definitely true. It's part of the charm of this place. But it looks like at some point when the town's grown up enough, it may have to take a look at the committee or council or board or whatever you want to call it, and think about making it more official."

$\mathcal{L}$ ily arrived at the schoolhouse early Thursday, having had an early evening the night before. She and Amos had spent the evening together on the couch again, but they spent most of the time talking instead of necking. They'd talked about little things and big things, silly things and serious things, and various things in between. Mostly, they enjoyed sitting there in each other's arms. Sometimes they didn't talk at all.

The class kept her mind occupied, at least most of the time. Those times when she checked her brooch watch, she was reminded of Amos and her thoughts immediately went to the things that would happen Friday afternoon when they got home. The plan was to move a few of her things over that night, just enough so they could go a day or two without having to leave the house. She hoped they'd rarely even leave the bed.

Around midmorning, Caleb Carter quietly opened the door and stepped in. Lily saw him and waved him on inside and up to the front.

"Class, I believe Mr. Carter has something for each of you."

237

"Yes, I do. I want you all to have your own copy of this." He handed the stack of papers to Lily, then took the top one and held it up. "You see, your picture is on the front page. And all of your names are listed here in the paper." That excited them. "There's a big article to go along with the picture, and it's so big, it had to be continued," he opened the paper to show them, "on this page. Miss Lily, before you read this, there's something in here you might not even know. I told Shirley over at the mercantile about the library donations, and she volunteered the store to be a donation station so people could drop off their books when they come in for supplies. She thought that might make it easier for people to help out."

"That's wonderful! I'll be sure and thank her next time I'm in there."

"I hoped that would be all right with you," Caleb said. "I was hoping I didn't overstep. I need to get back and sell some papers. You all have a good day now."

Lily and the class thanked him as he walked out. She looked at the article again.

"Before I hand these out, let's use it as a reading exercise. Who would like to come up here and read first?" Three or four hands shot up and she chose Margie. When the girl reached the desk, Lily showed her how much to read. When Margie was through, she let the child pick the next reader. The article was long enough for five children to share the reading duties.

The afternoon ended up passing more quickly, or so it seemed. The children seemed livelier, but not in a misbehaving way; they seemed eager to get home and show their families their pictures in the paper. Lily was eager to get home, too. Every time she noticed Billy, she was reminded of the bet she had with Amos about John and Sophie, and that was only one of the things on her mind.

She was getting married in one day. One more day, and she'd be Mrs. Amos Cameron. She was more than eager for that. Another thing on her mind was the boarding house. Of course, Amos was correct when he said it wasn't her place to find someone to replace Sophie. Besides, she was just borrowing problems right now. Not only was it not her place, but things might not happen as fast as Lily expected them to. Yes, she was definitely borrowing problems.

Lily was glad when it came time to dismiss the children. Billy was especially restive; she could tell he could barely keep in his seat. He was excited about going to a new home, and Lily was excited for him.

She dismissed the students a few minutes early and she'd never seen such excited, happy faces. Lily smiled to herself as she tidied up the room and readied it for session the next morning. *Tomorrow afternoon, we'll be married right here in this room.* She knew the children would feel special, being included in such a special event; at least she hoped they would. They had already become important to her, special, far more than she had expected would happen in just a few days. They already seemed like her second family.

She tidied the room, straightened the chairs, and sat down to look over her lesson notes for the next day one last time. No matter how she tried to concentrate on school things, thoughts of the next day crept in. *I want to surprise the children, but how can I let other people know they're welcome to come if they want to? Should I wear the dress I chose all day while I teach, or should I bring it and change in the cloakroom just before the ceremony? I'll just have to fix my hair in the morning and touch it up when the time comes. Maybe Nessa can help with that. Nessa. Should I ask her to stand up with me, like a matron of honor? I wonder who Amos would pick if we did that, Angus or John? Probably John. I'll bet he always expected his best man would be Will. Is there a way we could honor Will tomorrow, or is this not the time for that?*

Lily gave up trying to look at schoolwork. She left her notes and notebooks where she wanted them on her desk, took one last look around the room, and locked the schoolhouse door behind herself.

On the walk home, she decided to stop at the Bride & Board and see how the move went. Between wanting to gage the grown-up relationship and wanting to see Billy in his new home, she figured she had plenty of reason to stop.

The door to their new suite was open and she heard laughter coming from inside. She stepped in the doorway. "I hope I'm not interrupting," she said to announce herself.

"Miss Lily!" Billy said, the joy apparent on his face.

Sophie hugged Lily and ushered her inside. The furniture that had looked so meager and sparse in the Low Quarter house looked comfy and inviting in this smaller room.

"Come see my room, Miss Lily," Billy said as he took her hand. Sophie started to say something to him, but Lily grinned and shook her head. She let Sophie know she wanted to see his room, and that he wasn't a bother.

"This is one fine room, Billy. It looks so organized and tidy in here. Why, you've got everything you could possibly need in here. You have a bed and a side table next to it, a chest for clothes, and this—this is a fine little bookshelf. I like how you have all your toys arranged on it."

"See there, Miss Lily? That empty spot? I'm saving that for when I have books again."

It was hard for her to respond without tears. "I hope that time comes soon, Billy." As she walked quietly back into the room they were using for a parlor, Lily realized how Billy could teach her so many lessons in this life—actually, he already had. He'd shown her the simple things. They were simple, but they were the things that mattered. *Don't fret over what you don't have. Love and protect your family. Enjoy them. Be happy and do what you can to make life better. No problem's so big that you and your loved ones can't handle them together. Have faith.*

As she rounded the corner, she was certain she caught John

and Sophie pulling apart from a kiss. They didn't try to hide anything. If they had been kissing, it seemed like something they were already comfortable doing.

"It looks like you two got a lot done today," she said.

"We did," John said with a glance at Sophie. "It went better than we expected."

Lily caught that look. It was more than a look from a friend who'd helped someone move. That was a lover's look. Even though it was quick, she recognized it.

"Um, Lily, did you mean it when you said I could store some things at your house temporarily since you're moving into Amos' house?" Sophie asked.

Lily's smile spread across her face. "Of course, you can." *It's going to be your house soon enough, anyway*.

"Oh, thank you. That's a relief. We have a few boxes still on the wagon with kitchen things and items we can't use here very well. It'll be nice not to have the boxes in our way. And I had no idea what I was going to do with a couple of the bigger furniture pieces."

"Why don't we take it on to the house now? I'm on my way home anyway. You might as well stay for supper. It won't be anything special and we may not all eat the same things, but we have plenty of food," Lily said with a laugh.

"Only if I can help cook," Sophie said.

"It's a deal," Lily said.

BY THE TIME John and Billy had the wagon unloaded, Amos arrived, pleasantly surprised to find they had company. He went inside and greeted Sophie before he kissed Lily. "Looks like the move took place pretty smoothly," he said to Sophie.

"Couldn't have gone better. He had that wagon piled pretty high, but we got it all in one trip. Good thing you men rebuilt that bridge that collapsed and shored up the other ones."

"It's amazing how things seem to happen at the right time, isn't it?" Amos said with a smile and a thoughtful nod. "Almost like some mastermind is orchestrating things to work together for good."

"Yes," Sophie answered, "that's one of my favorite scriptures. It was a tough lesson learning that good things can come out of the most tragic and sad events in our lives. At the time, you can't see it, but later, you understand. Oh, well." She remembered their experience of Will's passing. "I don't have to tell you both about that. You're a walking example."

"I suppose we are, at that," Lily said. "You three wash up," she said to the men, "supper's ready."

Table conversation was light and lively, with a few false starts when someone was about to say something about the impending wedding, but remembered that Billy was there.

"Momma, can I have some more 'taters and cornbread?" Billy asked.

Lily and Sophie both answered yes. One spooned more fried potatoes out of the bowl, and the other cut another wedge of cornbread out of the cast iron skillet that was still warm to the touch.

As she watched him dig into the potatoes, Lily made a decision. "Billy, do you remember the day we first met when I came to your house?" He nodded, his eyebrows raised for emphasis since he couldn't talk with his mouth full. "Do you remember when I told you about the library, but I said it would have to be our secret until I made the announcement at school?" He nodded again the same way. "Well, I'd like to share another secret with you, so we can talk about it here at the table. But I need for you to not say anything to the other boys and girls until I say something about it tomorrow in class. Will you do that?"

Billy swallowed part of the big mouthful, put down his fork, and looked at her curiously as he nodded. When his mouth was clear, he answered, "I sure will, Miss Lily."

"Thank you. Remember I told the class that Mr. Amos and I are going to be married on Sunday? Well, we've changed our plans a little bit. Instead of Sunday, we're going to have the wedding ceremony tomorrow afternoon, at the school, at the end of the school day. When we decided to move up the date instead of waiting until Sunday, I knew I wanted to have the wedding with all my students in attendance. Do you think the children will enjoy being at the wedding?"

"I'll say they will! I've never even been to a wedding. I bet some of them haven't, either."

"You're probably right about that. And I hope you're right that they'll appreciate being there."

"Is anybody else gonna be there?"

"Yes, John and your mom will be there, and other friends. Anybody who wants to is welcome to come, but we didn't get much chance to put the word out to everybody. I think Miss Nessa was going to tell a few people."

Amos laughed. "All she has to do is tell Harriet, then the whole town will know."

"Amos!" Lily chided with a giggle, inclining her head toward Billy.

"Billy, you don't have to repeat what I just said."

Billy had a big grin on his face, happy to be in on a grownup conversation. "I promise I won't say a thing."

It was a comfortable and happy meal as they chatted about the wedding and a myriad of other things. As the meal wound down, John spoke up. "I know you'll be going home to a new house tomorrow, Lily, just like Billy did today. Is there anything I can help you move over there this evening so you won't have to go back and forth over the weekend?"

"There were some things I wanted to get moved tonight, but

I haven't had a chance to throw them all in a bag or a box. I guess we can just do it la—"

"Nonsense!" Sophie said. "You and Amos go back there right now and gather everything you wanted to move over there. Billy and I can clean up this kitchen, and John can help until you have everything ready to go." At Lily's hesitant look, Sophie wiggled the fingers of both hands back and forth in a *shoo* gesture. "Go on. We've got this."

By the time John and Sophie and Billy left, the kitchen was clean and everything they'd wanted to move was moved, including all the perishable foods. The only things that remained of Lily's personal items were the things she'd need the next day.

They settled into their customary and comfortable positions on the couch: Amos on the far end and Lily beside him, his arm around her as she leaned against him.

"Well, you clearly won the bet, my dear. I believe I owe you a memorable evening."

"Yes, you do. I'm almost positive I saw them break apart from a kiss earlier at the boarding house. They seem to be getting more at ease with each other."

"I'm almost positive they've already been as 'at ease' with each other as a couple can get."

"What?" Lily jerked her head around to look at him. "What makes you say that? Did John say something?"

"Not about them specifically. But he did ask me again if you had plans to sell this house. I told him you were selective about who you wanted as neighbors and you'd only sell to a friend. He said he hopes he's your friend. I didn't tell him you already told me you'd sell to him. You called it, sweetie. You saw the signs before I did."

"What signs did you see?" Lily asked.

"He touched her a lot. She did the same. And when I first got here and he stood beside her, he had his arm around her.

That alone would be a giveaway that they were together, but it was more than that. His hand was low on her hip, and tight. A man doesn't do that unless he's sure about himself. That's pretty intimate and personal. It was his whole demeanor with her."

"I suppose they had a good opportunity out there at her house in the Low Quarter. Worked out pretty conveniently for them—they didn't even have to move the bed afterward. She left both of them with the house."

Amos laughed, shaking his head. "That sly son of a gun. He planned it this way. No wonder he kept insisting he didn't need any help to get them moved. Got to hand it to him. They haven't had much opportunity to be alone. I'm happy for them, aren't you? This is good for all three of them."

"Tell me, Mr. Cameron, why is it all right for them to make love outside of marriage, but not for us?"

"Because, soon-to-be Mrs. Cameron, she's an experienced widow and you're the virginal schoolmarm whom everyone around here holds in high regard since she has so much influence over their young. It would not do for your reputation to be tarnished."

"Is there really that much difference between outright making love and what we've been doing? I daresay we've done a thing or two that some married couples have never done."

"You're probably right. But we can honestly say your maidenhead is intact. That's all people would need to hear. Yes, it's a glaring hole in the moral code, and I feel certain it's a loophole that's been used by couples since time immemorial. I don't make the rules, Lil."

"It's a good thing my socially sanctioned deflowering is only a day away, or I'd be arguing this point."

"Discussing. I believe you mean discussing the point. Arguing isn't good. You'll always lose."

"Always? I don't think so. By the law of averages, I'd have to win some."

Amos laughed. "But by the law of Amos," he said as he took hold of her and lifted her face down across his knees, the upper part of her body over the wide arm of the couch, "you'll end up like this. Does this feel like any way to win an argument?"

"Amos!" Lily said, not sure whether she should laugh or not. She did. "Let me back up."

"I will. Just making a point." She heard the fun in his voice as she felt his hand rubbing her backside. "Have I ever told you just what a fine ass you have? It is superb. So soft." She felt him pull up her skirt and petticoat, and he rubbed her again with only the thin fabric of her bloomers between them. He caressed. He kneaded.

Lily wondered why he didn't go ahead and bare her all the way. After all, there wasn't one square inch of her he hadn't seen and touched already. He rubbed and squeezed. He ran his hands down her bare thighs to the tops of her stockings, then stroked her stocking-covered legs. His touch varied, making her want more stroking. He worked his way back up her legs to her bottom again and palmed each globe.

"Beautiful, perfect handfuls, with just the right amount of jiggle. I do love that jiggle. Perfect cheeks. Cheeky cheeks. Saucy, pert little ass cheeks just begging to be smacked." With that, he delivered a minor stinger to her right buttock. Lily made a little gasping cry, but it was more of surprise than any kind of pain. It hadn't been that hard.

She didn't protest and Amos rubbed the stricken cheek. "Even through these bloomers, I saw that jiggle and it makes me want to see more." He struck the other side, the one nearest him. "Mmm, just look at that." He rubbed again.

Lily was in a quandary. What he was doing felt good. Very good. She was glad for loose bloomers, or else he might know how aroused she was becoming. She knew she was aroused because of the touching and caressing, not because of the smacks to her backside. Why, they weren't even real smacks; he was only playing. That wasn't the part that was exciting to her. It wasn't. It was not. *It couldn't be.* Was lying over his lap part of it? Not being able to see what was happening? Not being able to see what he saw? Being vulnerable and at his mercy? *No, no, no, and no. That could not possibly be exciting me.*

He swatted again, a few more times, and each time, he complimented her backside. They were compliments, sort of. He made them sound very dirty, though. Very lewd.

Lily was embarrassed and confused when she heard herself moan and realized she was making little movements against Amos' lap. She wanted out of this position, something that gave her some degree of control. "All right, you win. I won't argue. I'll be sure to discuss." She pushed up from the arm of the couch. But Amos put his hand between her shoulder blades and kept her down.

"Not just yet, sweetie, I'm enjoying this too much." With his right hand, he untied her bloomers and pulled them down. When he met resistance from her body weighing them down, he pulled harder until they were free and dangling from her ankle. "Now, I can see that jiggle better." He swatted again. It stung for a moment, but Lily couldn't honestly say it hurt. He swatted the other side.

She couldn't help it. She wiggled her backside upward in search of his soothing, rubbing hand. Amos chuckled. "My sweetie does like this after all. You want some more, little girl?"

She wanted to answer *yes*, but she couldn't bring herself to do it. Instead she went with "Amos, let me up! I won this bet, not you, you know."

Amos relented and pulled her up onto his lap. "That was a fun one. The bet one would have been different. At least to start with. Admit it. You enjoyed that."

His smirk was hard to look at. It seemed like his eyes smirked, too, if that's possible.

"I have no idea what you're talking about," she said as calmly as she could.

Amos thrust his hand up her disheveled skirt, between her legs, and his smirk intensified, if *that* was possible. "You may not know what I'm talking about, but your body does."

She closed her eyes and leaned in to hide her face in his chest. His low, amused chuckle rumbled through his chest and she felt it as much as she heard it. "Would you like to collect on that bet now? I think you're already in need of a good climax."

"Maybe we should just wait until tomorrow."

"Whoa, is this my Lily speaking? What happened to wanting to argue about premarital and marital relations? Where's my girl who's been wanting to fuck all this time?"

"I know, I know, I get it. I'm right here. I'm just a little... flustered right now. Is it all right if we just sit together? You know, at home in each other's arms?"

"I'll never say no to that, sweetie. Besides, we've got the rest of our lives to play."

FRIDAY MORNING CAME ALL TOO SOON and not soon enough. Lily took a bath and luxuriated in the feeling of the water, wishing she could bathe again right before the wedding so she could be fresh for Amos. *Maybe I'll suggest we bathe together when we get home.* As she used items, she put them in the last bag of her things to be taken over to her new home. She was grateful Amos had offered to cook breakfast at his house so she wouldn't have that bother. He would come get her and her bag —and anything else she might have forgotten—in plenty of time to eat and make it to school.

Lily decided to wear an everyday dress and take her nice

one to change into before the ceremony. She painstakingly fixed her hair and after a little more time than she wanted to spend, had it looking the way she wanted. She started to spritz herself with her favorite gardenia perfume but decided to put it in her pocket and apply it later. Stockings and shoes were next, and she was ready. She went through the house again, checking all the closets and cabinets and drawers to make sure she had everything. She carried the carpetbag and her pretty dress on a hanger and set them on the couch. One last trip to the water closet and she was ready. When she stepped out on the porch, she looked up to see that Amos was halfway there. His timing was perfect.

As they were finishing breakfast, Lily looked up to see one of her favorite expressions on Amos' face. It was the one she thought of as his sweet boy look, happy and hoping she would be, too.

"I don't know if you've considered that silly wedding custom about something old, new, borrowed, and blue, but I knew you wouldn't have anything new with you today." He pulled a paper and ribbon-wrapped package from his pocket. "So I had Emmett make something for you. I hope you like it."

Surprised, Lily took the package and untied the ribbon. There were two layers of wrapped paper, each folded over the object several times. She finally removed the paper to reveal a beautiful silver hair comb. The design Emmett made across the bar part was the same design as the one on their wedding bands. When she realized that, her hand went to her heart and she mouthed a long, drawn-out *Oh*. The teeth of the comb were perfectly aligned zigzags, made that way to hold in her hair better. "Amos, this is the most perfect gift. This is the second time you've given me the perfect thing. You spoil me! You're the most thoughtful man. I don't imagine I'll ever be as good at selecting a perfect gift for you."

"Lily, love," his voice softened, "today you're going to give me the sweetest gift a man can receive. Nothing I can give you will ever match that."

～

ALTHOUGH THE MORNING PASSED UNEVENTFULLY, Lily had the oddest feeling of disconnection. She felt as though she was detached and floating somewhere above, watching her body go through the motions of teaching class. She only came back together—connected again—a time or two when Billy caught her eye and just for a moment gave her that deliciously smug, knowing look of having a shared secret.

She was just about to let them out for recess when Nessa came in and stood in the back. Lily had planned to tell the children about the wedding after the break, but she decided to do it right then.

"I have an announcement before we dismiss for recess. Remember Wednesday when I told you that Mr. Amos and I are getting married on Sunday? Well, our plans have changed. We're going to be married… today." She saw raised eyebrows on some of them, and some darted their eyes around to see how the others reacted. Lily continued. "We're getting married this afternoon, right here in the schoolhouse." There were gasps and smiles. "It'll be the last thing before we dismiss. I wanted you all to be at my wedding." This time there was clapping and whistles from the boys.

Nessa stepped up beside Lily. "It's going to be exciting, boys and girls. It hasn't started yet, but you should be aware that sometime after lunch, you might hear people outside who are here to help get the place ready for a big wedding. There will probably be more people than there are chairs, so we'll need you all to sit close to make more room on the benches for others to sit. There will probably be people outside who won't be able to get in."

"That many?" Lily asked.

Nessa nodded. "I think the whole town wants to celebrate with you two. You know, their hearts went out to you the day you arrived. And now, they want to share the happy day." She paused for effect. "I hope it's all right with you all. I know it's probably not the best thing for us to do, but it's possible, just possible, that we won't be doing as much schoolwork this afternoon as we should. At least not the really serious lessons."

Jed spoke up first. "It's all right with us!" The rest of them echoed the same message.

"Good," Nessa said, almost shouting over them. "Recess!" They were outside in no time.

Lily looked at Nessa and shook her head. "I can't believe all this. I feel so unprepared."

"All you have to worry about is getting dressed on time. I've taken care of everything else. Everything. Well, I had help, of course. Mary had a half dozen women making cookies at their homes so there will be plenty. I went to Mrs. Canfield's to get some pretty ribbon and fabric for the cookies, I got to talking with her. She went wild with ideas and took me back to her storage room. She has two big arches appropriate for people to stand or walk under. She's going to decorate it with some beautiful white ribbons. When I told her about wanting some-thing thin to wrap the cookies in and some pretty ribbon to tie them, her eyes lit up. She said she had the perfect thing and it's just been taking up space. Come to find out it was sent to her by mistake and the company told her to keep it instead of ship-ping it back when they corrected their mistake. It's really pretty, Lily. It's a thin, white cotton batiste dotted Swiss. Not really the kind of fabric suitable for wearing around here. She says she's made some undies out of it, but that's it. And the ribbons look so pretty with it. She and Mary both had some big baskets and she decorated them, too. Mary's got white table-cloths for the tables we're setting up out here. Not too many of them. They're bringing chairs from the community hall for the overflow guests." She put her arm around Lily. "It's going to be beautiful."

"I'll never be able to thank everyone for all they've done! Especially you."

"That look on your face says it all. I need no more thanks than that. What? No, don't cry! You don't want swollen red eyes for your wedding. Caleb's coming to take a wedding photo of you and Amos."

They had to change the subject so Lily wouldn't cry.

"ALL RIGHT, boys and girls, it's getting close to time for the afternoon recess," Nessa said. She'd been in and out a couple of times for quick errands, but mostly she'd stayed at the school to help Lily get through the afternoon. "That means that our school day is, well, it's over. We're going to have an extra-long recess. I know, I know, hold your excitement a minute. When recess is over, it'll be about time for the wedding ceremony. Now, listen closely. I want you to stay outside because we have some getting ready to do inside. People are out there now, some working with the decoration and cookies, and some are early guests. I want you to stay out of their way, do you understand? All right. Yes, I said cookies. They're for people to take home and enjoy after the wedding. You'll have to wait until then, and you can each have your own little cookie bag. Please don't get dirty at recess. And when we come back in, remember what I said earlier about sitting close together so others can squeeze in. Now, go play!"

Nessa turned to Lily. "Why don't you go hit the outhouse and I'll be waiting for you in the cloakroom. Or as I'm calling it today, the Bride's Room. I brought another dress to change into, too."

"Good idea. I'll be right back."

While Lily was gone, Nessa tacked up a pretty paper sign with elegant script on the cloakroom door. It said *Bride's Room*.

Lily was pleased at the gesture when she returned. "Angus wrote that, didn't he? He's so artistic."

"Yes, he is," Nessa said. She wanted to speak up so badly, but she couldn't tell Lily she'd be receiving something else with his artwork soon. It wouldn't be right. Harriet always wanted these things to be a surprise to the bride and groom. Although in this case, she suspected the groom already had an inkling.

The ladies got changed and Nessa helped get Lily's hair back to its proper state. They both admired the pretty comb Emmett made.

"I'm glad Amos gave you something new, because Mrs. Canfield sent something blue, and I'm going to let you borrow my pearls to wear." She reached inside the neck of her own dress and pulled the necklace over her head. It looked perfect with Lily's dress. "I figured you could provide your own something old." She pulled the lacy blue garter out of her pocket and showed it to Lily. "It's a good thing it's only a decoration for Amos to appreciate, because this flimsy thing would never hold up a stocking." They both laughed at that while Nessa dropped to her knees. "Hold up your skirt while I tie this on your leg. Your legs are more slender, it's going to have to go higher on your th—"

Nessa squealed and landed on her rump. "Lily! You aren't wearing bloomers!"

Lily chuckled. "I thought Amos might appreciate it."

Nessa was already laughing almost uncontrollably. "I daresay he will. I call that being as ready for the wedding night as you can get. It looks like you planned to get a head start."

Lily laughed. "I suppose I am. You have no idea how I've waited for this." She lowered her voice, glad to have the ear of a woman she trusted. "I think we've done about everything else but... the final act. I practically begged him, but he wouldn't deflower the schoolmarm out of wedlock. Think back to your own wedding day. Do you have any advice for a new bride who knows *some* of the ropes already?"

Nessa finished tying a pretty bow with the garter ribbons and stood up and dusted off, smoothing her skirt. "I do. You remind me of me a little bit. We married in Rawlins, almost as soon as I got off the train. He was going to give me some time to get used to him, in case I was hesitant to marry a man I'd only laid eyes on that very day. I told him no, if I was going to be married, I wanted to be a wife in every way. I wanted a consecrated union from the start." She snickered at the memory. "To this day, I haven't seen Angus move as fast as he did to get us to the preacher's house."

Lily laughed with her. "I can only imagine what that was like."

"It was exhilarating. New. Such a heady experience. Yes, I do have advice for you. Lose any inhibitions you have; this is neither the time nor the place for them. Go wild. Be bold. Make some fantastic memories you'll treasure later. Try anything." She looked at Lily for emphasis. "Anything."

"What are you telling me? What do you mean by anything?"

"Angus is a man of... diverse carnal desires. Perhaps things others might not enjoy so much. Or at all. I made it my priority to satisfy those desires. Not only that, it wasn't long before I desired them, too. As a result, he's never hesitated a moment to satisfy any desires I might have. He'd give me the moon if he could. We've been married this long and that side of our relationship is as fresh and as thrilling as it was that first day."

"Bold," Lily said thoughtfully, but still with a smile. "No inhibitions. That would suit Amos well, I'm sure. He... well, never mind. I shouldn't say."

"Hogwash. I just told you something very personal. Spill."

"He seems to like my backside. Likes to watch it jiggle when he…"

Nessa folded her arms across her chest and looked impatient, even if it was a lighthearted conversation. "When he spanks it or when he fucks it?"

Lily's eyes widened. *Oh good grief. Maybe I need to joyfully embrace the spanking so he won't want to do that other thing.* "Well, the spanking one."

Nessa's grin was far wider than was called for, Lily thought.

"Yes, I'm familiar with that practice."

"He spanks you for fun?"

"A few have been real ones, but yes, we enjoy it. Angus can be very creative."

"Nessa," Lily said as she stepped closer to her, "he's spanked you for real before?"

"Oh Lordy, yes. It's not unusual for that to happen in a marriage, you know. I think it's fairly common. It happened in my family. I just accepted that was how it was. Expected it, even. Your family wasn't like that?"

"Not that I know of. If Mother was ever punished, it was all kept private. I had no idea that happened to grown women. I was fit to be tied when Amos did that to me. I almost said no to the marriage when he did."

"Oh, that would have been a pity. At this point, I'd probably break an engagement if the man wouldn't do it."

They both laughed at that.

"I hear voices. I better go on out there and see what's going on. You stay here. Charlotte Copperfield will come in and take over and let you know what to do and when."

"All right."

"You're a beautiful bride, Lily. Remember, no inhibitions. Be bold. This is the greatest adventure you'll ever have."

There was a quick hug and Lily was alone again. *Well, that was enlightening. Maybe that response I had last night wasn't shameful after all. Maybe I could get used to the loss of control and just let myself relax and enjoy it, and let him enjoy it. Even play along with it. At any rate, it sure beats that other thing she mentioned.* Lily shuddered involuntarily.

THEIR EYES WERE LOCKED on each other as she slowly walked down the makeshift aisle to the front of the schoolroom where Amos and Reverend Copperfield stood. In her hands she clasped the snow white Bible tied with a wide strip of bleached white muslin that had been stiffened with sugar water and ironed so it would hold its shape. There were a few fall wild blooms tastefully tucked among the loops of the bow. It had been a gift from the Copperfields.

She'd never seen Amos look more handsome. She didn't even know he owned a suit. And the soft, warm smile on his face was the sweetest. There was love in his eyes. She couldn't describe them any other way, but that they were full of love for her. Lily tried her hardest to memorize the way he looked so she could recall this moment the rest of her life.

She'd taken several steps before she realized the men were standing under a huge arch that had been decorated with puffy strips of stiffened sheer white dotted Swiss with pine and cedar boughs affixed here and there. Her smile widened when she realized she'd been so fixated on Amos that she hadn't even noticed such a breathtaking archway and the fresh scent of the greenery in the room. She'd have to be sure and tell him that later.

When she reached the front, she stood facing her groom as the pastor subtly indicated. *It's time. This is it. This is happening. The pastor welcomed everyone, Nessa sang a beautiful solo, and it's time for our vows.* Lily had been afraid she'd be nervous, but she wasn't. She was sure Amos wasn't, either. He looked so sure and composed, like there was no place he'd rather be than right here, vowing to love and cherish her no matter what happened to befall them in their life together. She was vaguely aware of the people packed in the room, standing in the back and along the walls and spilling out the door and down the steps.

In all her life, she'd never dreamed she'd have such a perfect wedding. And such a perfect *real man* to marry.

The room was quiet as the pastor spoke of love and commitment, and the enduring nature of one of God's greatest blessings, the covenant of marriage. He likened it to the evergreen trees, always alive and fresh, steadfastly growing each day, sharing their beauty and scent whether they be covered with snow or bent low with stormy winds or standing tall and reaching toward the sun. When they'd completed the vows and the placing of the rings on each other's fingers, the pastor paused and closed his officiant's manual. "Lily," he said, "Amos wants to read something to you, as something to incorporate into your vows." The pastor took a step back so the young couple would be the focus of everyone's attention. He nodded at Amos, who took a smallish book out of his breast pocket and opened it. He looked up at his bride as he spoke her name, then began to read, his voice clear and strong.

"LILY,

How do I love thee? Let me count the ways.
I love thee to the depth and breadth and height
My soul can reach, when feeling out of sight
For the ends of being and ideal grace.
I love thee to the level of every day's
Most quiet need, by sun and candlelight.
I love thee freely, as men strive for right.
I love thee purely, as they turn from praise.
I love thee with the passion put to use

In my old griefs, and with my childhood's faith.
I love thee with a love I seemed to lose
With my lost saints. I love thee with the breath,
Smiles, tears, of all my life; and, if God choose, I shall
but love thee better after death.

AMOS HANDED the book to the pastor, then he took both of Lily's hands in his. When he began reciting the last line, she joined him and they spoke in unison. "*And, if God choose, I shall but love thee better after death.*"

Reverend Copperfield stepped back into his original position. Lily saw that his eyes were as misty as her own. "I now pronounce you man and wife. You may kiss your lovely bride, Amos."

There were a few giggles when the kiss lasted longer than expected. "Ladies and gentlemen, I present Mr. and Mrs. Amos Cameron."

Amos put his arm around her and turned her toward the congregation. People cheered and clapped as the happy couple stood there with broad smiles they couldn't have concealed if they wanted to, even though a tear found its way down Lily's cheek.

The pastor was the first one to step in front of them and shake their hands, and everyone else followed suit. At one point Lily commented that she had no idea there were so many people who lived in the town. The pastor, who had taken his place near Lily so he could shake everyone's hand, quipped that he wished he could get them all to Sunday services. "Maybe you two should get married every Sunday."

Lily knew most of the people in line, but Amos introduced her to the ones she didn't know. Some people only shook hands and briefly wished them well, others had longer messages. The Kellys were among the first in line, and some other men from the sawmill. Lily spotted more familiar faces in line. Harriet and Arthur Simmons were coming up, followed by Billy, Sophie, and John. Behind them were the McBrides, and more of the schoolchildren with their parents.

Harriet kissed Amos on the cheek and moved forward enough that she could monopolize both of them. "I just can't tell you both how happy I am for the two of you. When I think of how far you've both come since Lily arrived, why, it just delights my heart and soul. When Emmett told me you two were getting hitched today, I wanted to shout it from the rafters. I had to tell everybody I came across and share the wonderful news."

Both Lily and Amos could see Billy, half hidden behind Arthur. The boy had to clasp his hand over his mouth to keep from laughing out loud at Harriet's words. He clearly remembered Amos' comment at the supper table the evening before. John and Sophie had to look away to maintain composure, and Lily and Amos both managed admirably not to laugh in Harriet's face.

"When you have just a few spare minutes, just a few, maybe five or ten minutes, Arthur and I have a gift we'd like to give you. Now, it's nothing much, just a little something we give to all the mail order couples. We just like to share what we consider our own little secret to having a happy marriage. Would it be possible for you two to drop by our house on your way home from work Monday evening? I promise, we'll push you back out the door in less than ten minutes. Maybe even five."

Amos spoke up and said they'd be happy to do that. Lily added her thoughts. "A gift isn't really necessary, but if you give it to all the couples, then, thank you for the thought."

Harriet leaned over to Lily's ear and whispered, "You'll want to thank me later."

The handshake line moved quickly after the Harriet bottleneck. Lily remembered to thank all the women who helped bake or decorate for helping make her special day so memorable. Mrs. Canfield came through the line and introduced herself to the couple. Lily couldn't help herself—she threw her arms around the woman and offered profuse thanks. Mrs. Canfield acted charmed by the gesture.

When the couple was finally able to make their own exit, Lily was surprised at the scene before her outside. Another archway, identical to the one inside, was at the top of the steps. She thought it would have given anyone the impression that when they stepped through it, they were entering a special place for a special event. Near the bottom of the steps on the lawn, four tables were set up, two end to end on either side, funneling people in and out of the building. On the tables were pretty beribboned baskets that held little dotted Swiss sacks of three or four cookies, tied with the same ribbon that was on the baskets. Most of the guests were gone, and there were still several cookie bags remaining.

Caleb stopped them and insisted they stand under the arch so he could take a photograph. Most wedding photographs she'd seen had the somber husband sitting in a chair and the somber wife standing behind him with her hand on his shoulder. Not theirs! His arm was around her and their joy would surely be obvious, Lily thought. She hoped so. Caleb was confident he had a good shot the first time, so it went fairly quickly.

"I've been telling everyone to take a bag of cookies. I think the children each took two bags, but I told them to do that," Mary said. "They enjoyed the wedding so much."

Lily thanked her for her part in the cookie production and for acting as hostess over the cookie tables. "Honey, it was my absolute pleasure. Now you two have been detained long enough." She picked up five or six cookie bags and shoved them into Amos' hands. "I had Angus bring your buggy up front." She nodded vaguely behind them. Lily and Amos turned to look and saw that someone had tied dotted Swiss bows to each horse's harness and to both entrances to the buggy.

"I can't believe they decorated so much!" Lily said.

"We all had fun doing it," Mary said. "It was practically a whole-town project. Now go on, git. Don't come out until Monday. I took the liberty of sending Henry to your place with plenty of food. You won't have to cook much for a day or two."

Lily ran around the table and hugged Mary. "Thank you. And I never thanked you for helping him make that apple pie. Thank you for that, too."

THE SHORT RIDE home was filled with little kisses and lewd comments in low voices and chuckles and giggles. Amos pulled the buggy near the front porch steps and jumped down. "Stay there a minute," he said. He grabbed the carpetbag, another bag of her things, and the cookies and ran them into the house, leaving the door open when he came out.

"Now, Mrs. Cameron, I'd like to carry my bride over the threshold."

Lily stood and expected him to set her on the ground and let her walk up the steps on her own, but he surprised her. He put one hand behind her knees and pulled and caught her upper body with his other arm when she toppled backward. "Whoa!" she shouted, startled. "That was quite the move. I thought I was going to fall."

"I hoped it would work out. I would have felt awful if I'd dropped you."

When she saw he was grinning, she did, too.

"I knew I wouldn't drop you. You're just a tiny little thing."

"I'm not tiny, Amos. I'm about the same size as all the other women around here."

"Compared to me, you're tiny."

They were at the front door and he stopped. Lily rose up, Amos leaned his head down, and they kissed before going through the door. Inside, they kissed again and he set her on her feet without breaking the kiss. His hands were all over her, already searching for the buttons of her dress.

"My husband, what would you think about a nice, hot, soapy, sudsy bath? We can undress each other and then I can lather you all over, and you can lather me—"

"I've imagined that very thing."

"So have I," she said. "Do you want to tend to the horses while I start a fire and put the water on to boil?"

"Yes, ma'am. But I hate to be away from you even for that short time."

"Maybe you can make the time pass faster. Imagine all the things you want us to do this weekend."

He snorted. "Lady, I've been doing that for weeks already." He cupped one of her buttocks as though the gesture replaced a parting kiss, and he was back out the front door.

Lily hurriedly put wood and some kindling in the stove and lit it, satisfied that the fire wouldn't fizzle. There were two pots of water on two burners, and she added another big pot. She picked up her bags and hurried back to the bedroom, deter-mined to find clean sheets and make the bed. What she saw in the bedroom took her aback. Amos had already put clean sheets on the bed. The covers were turned down invitingly. *That sweet, thoughtful man. I'm going to have to be extra nice to him.*

She noticed other little details. The pot-bellied stove had plenty of wood and kindling stacked next to it. There was a pitcher of water and two drinking glasses on the dresser. On a table in one corner was another pitcher of water sitting inside a pretty basin-type bowl. There were a few towels and wash-cloths and a little bar of soap fanned out beside the bowl. A little jar of some kind of oil sat on one of the bedside tables; she presumed that would be his side of the bed. And she wondered what he'd do with the oil. In two corners, the two near the head of the bed, there were overstuffed chairs with ottomans and Lily knew immediately that could soon become one of her favorite places in the house. She imagined herself sitting there reading, or writing, or checking schoolwork, or just gazing out the window.

Lily put away the items that were in the bags Amos had carried in and put the bags in the back of the closet. She didn't know what else to do. She couldn't take off her clothes because they were going to undress each other. Shoes. *I can go ahead and take off my shoes.*

In her stockinged feet, she headed to the bathroom and opened the cupboard doors until she found her bath items. *A bubbly bath would be nice. A scented one.* She found most of her items on the shelf, but she had to dig through an unpacked box for the rest of her things. She found what she was looking for: a nice bath brush she'd once splurged on. The top of the handle had a little carved outline of a bathtub and the silhouette of a woman in the tub, facing the other way, holding the brush over her shoulder as she apparently washed her back. It wasn't a fancy carving or even a fancy brush, just plain wood. It was the carved image that charmed her. It was almost cartoonish. She set out some bubbling soap and some scented bath oils. She'd let Amos pick the one he liked best. After she poured some of the soap into the tub, she opened the water spigot and the cool water poured in.

When she used the toilet, she remembered just a few days prior when she couldn't bend her legs and thought again how ridiculous she must have looked, lining herself up and letting herself fall to the seat, her legs spread, sprawled out in front of her. The thought made her giggle. *Thank goodness I don't have to do that anymore.* She turned the tub water off before she left the room.

The water was heating but needed more time, so she

poured glasses of cold water for both of them. She hadn't spent much time in this house, so she explored the cabinets in the kitchen. When she came across a bottle of whiskey, she got it out just in case Amos might like some.

She heard the back door open and ran around the corner to see Amos down the hall. He was taking off his muddy boots, using the toe of the other foot to push them off. When he saw her, he grinned and walked toward her. She ran into his arms.

"I started to undress, but since I mentioned undressing each other, I decided not to."

"Good. This'll be like unwrapping a present."

"Amos, you've seen me naked, you know. I haven't seen you naked yet. I'm looking forward to that."

"You want to undress me first?" he asked.

"I do. We can do that while the water's getting hot enough."

They stepped into the water closet, where he stood still. "I'm ready. Make me naked."

She dropped to her knees to remove his socks.

"My woman on her knees serving me. I like this. A lot."

She looked up at him and grinned with a wanton look in her eye. "Wouldn't it be better if I were on my knees after we were naked?"

He laughed. "Well, you got me there. It would be better, yes, it would."

While she was still on her knees, she removed his belt and unbuttoned his pants placket, looking up at him occasionally. She loved looking at him like this.

She stood and started on his shirt. There was no talk, only appreciative moans from both of them. Lily didn't just take off his shirt. She caressed and kissed his chest upward to his shoulders, letting the shirt fall naturally when her hands reached his shoulders. Instead of removing his pants next, she circled him, kissing and stroking his chest, belly, and back. His britches were next, then it was his turn to undress her.

"I wanted to do this all sexy-like and romantic, slow and teasing, building up tension. But damn, the tension's already getting to me. I want to rip this dress off, tear everything else off you, too."

She grinned. "If it weren't my favorite dress, I'd say rip away."

"I know. It's my favorite, too. I'll just have to put up with this torture."

"I'm not sure how to take that—it's torture for you to undress me."

He chuckled. "I know you know better than that. Here. Lift your arms." He pulled the dress over her head and tossed it into the hamper basket. He untied the petticoats and let them fall to the floor. She was down to shift and stockings since she'd foregone her bloomers. He bent and kissed her neck and she shivered and breathed an *oh*. As he nibbled along her neck, he gathered up her shift and when he stood straight again, he pulled it up and over her head.

"Well, that's two surprises. You went all day without bloomers?" She nodded. "Wicked woman. Decadent. And I love it."

He walked around her, touching, squeezing, patting as he went. "I wondered where your something blue was. That's the fanciest garter I ever saw."

"It's useless as a garter. Purely decoration."

"Nice. I'd leave it on, but we're about to get in the tub."

Soon they were both bare and they fully embraced, skin to skin, top to bottom. The kisses became more and more passionate, hands searching and stroking more urgently.

"This feels so wonderful," she said when she broke the kiss. "But the water's probably hot enough now and I wanted to be fresh when we, you know, consummate this union."

"All right, sweetie. Do you want to leave your hair up for the bath?"

"Yes."

"All right, that might be best. I want to take it down myself after the bath, though."

When the bath was nice and hot, bubbly, and scented with Lily's favorite gardenia oil, Amos helped her in and then stepped in behind her. Once seated, he pulled her back against him, put his arms around her, and let them settle on her breasts. He cupped his hands in the water and poured handfuls of sudsy, soapy water all over her front, going back to her breasts between handfuls.

"I could do this all day. I like how these feel, all slick and wet."

"Well, if you're going to take a long time, I might as well get started washing you." With that, she reached behind her back and took his hardness in one hand and his sac in the other.

"Oh, sweetie, with you doing that, I definitely won't be staying in here a long time. You'll have me ready to shoot in no time. You have no idea how close I am this very minute."

Lily reached over the side of the tub for a washcloth and the soap bar. "Then would you like to wash me?"

"Oh, yes, ma'am, I would. All over, as a matter of fact."

They both got quiet as he set about washing her, and it was clear to her he was taking his time. "Maybe this would be a good time to recite your poem for me again. And add those last two verses."

"All right, I can do that."

"OUR HEARTBEATS RACE *in love's embrace,*
   Her sweet tongue licks fire all o'er me.
   I see her love-wet skin
   Where she holds me within,
   But not the face before me.

                              .   .   .

OUR BREATHS ALIGNED, *our limbs entwined,*
    Our need explodes a savage pace.
    Her breasts bucking wild
    Have me beguiled,
    But I cannot see her face.

WERE *dreams but real and I could feel*
    Each lusty pleasure mentioned here,
    I'd hold fast to the charms
    Of the one in my arms,
    Whose face I would know so dear.

HEAV'N HEARD MY PLEA, *and you came to me,*
    Blood and bone and soft flesh anew.
    Now this is our bliss:
    We can cuddle and kiss
    When I wake up next to you.

SOFT AS A SIGH *and as hard as goodbye,*
    You sparked fire in this mortal man.
    But one thing I knew,
    This one thing true:
    You've been mine since time began."

"AMOS, I love it even more. It will be a joy to wake up together. What did that last line mean, about being yours since time began?"

"You mentioned once something about Will's passing might have happened just because you and I were meant to be together. I got to thinking. If that's the case, then everything that's ever happened had a role in us being together."

She was quiet a moment. "Amos, I love you so much. I want to finish this bath and get to bed so you really can make me yours."

～

"Do you feel like you're officially mine now? All consummated and consecrated and sanctified and a bunch more words I can't think of when I'm inside you like this?"

He was on top of her, but much of his weight rested on his elbow. She wanted him to be still, just so she could feel him inside her. He brushed some of her hair off her face and kissed where it was.

"Complete. That's a good word. Like part of me's always been missing, but with you inside me, I'm complete now."

She tightened and loosened and tightened her internal muscles, over and over, trying to hold and feel him better. Amos kissed her, a sweet and loving kiss, and began moving inside her, ever so slowly.

"I can feel each movement you're making," he whispered, "and you're about to drive me insane. I don't know how much longer I can be gentle."

Lily smiled, her eyes still closed. "Mmm…"

Amos shifted so his mouth could reach her nipples. He sucked and nipped and licked while she moaned longer and a little louder. Before going to her other breast, he kissed a trail up to her neck and kissed and sucked on that sensitive spot. He shifted all his weight to his left arm so he could tease her little pearl with the other hand. Lily's moans and whispers of his name became louder and more urgent.

"Amos, please, that's enough gentle. I think I need that sledgehammer now."

He was happy to oblige.

SHE LAY in the crook of Amos' arm with her head resting on his shoulder and the top of his arm. She had his other hand in hers, playing with it, rubbing it, kissing it a time or two, and massaging all around the fleshy part of his palm.

"You know, I think I'd grade it an A plus, plus."

"Well, sweetie, in all fairness, you've never been with another man. You don't have anything to compare it to. I might be a B or a C compared to someone else."

Lily laughed. "Fair enough, but I was talking about the poem."

Amos laughed even louder. "Oh hell, the poem's a C plus, B minus at best. But that sex, I'll have you know, was a fine A plus, plus. I," he insisted, "was an A plus, plus."

"You just got through saying you might be a B or a C compared to someone else."

He shrugged. "I was being modest. I was undoubtedly A plus, plus material."

"How was I?"

"So incredibly hot, you made me an A plus, plus."

He leaned over to kiss her and that soon led to more, and then more. The long evening stretched into a long night. They didn't even stop to eat anything until almost dawn. After a nice, leisurely breakfast and another long, shared bath, Lily dragged him back to bed. He didn't protest too much.

"SWEETIE, I have to. I need to go tend the horses. They need some exercise. Come with me," he said as he pulled on a pair of britches and his boots.

"Oh, all right." Lily grabbed a robe and slipped her feet into some shoes without buckling them. "Since John's spending so much time with Sophie, I'll help you build a fence. I've never done that before, but I'm teachable."

"Thank you. I'll take you up on that offer," he said with a big grin. "While we're out, we can decide where it'll go. Are you thinking about a fence around the whole property, or one just in the back for the horses?"

"We'll need one for the horses, either way. I don't want them grazing on the flower beds and vegetables I want to plant in the spring."

"I was thinking along those same lines. Should we build just on our property, or go ahead and include yours, too?"

"Well, pretty soon it's going to be John's, and he might like to go ahead and share a larger space. I'd say for now we enclose both into one big space, and later we can put a divider fence between them if we need one."

"You seem pretty sure John and Sophie will end up in that house."

"I don't have a single doubt."

In the barn, Lily went straight to Hercules and fed him one of the three apples she had in her pocket; she tossed the other two to Amos. While Hercules chewed, she started sweet-talking him while she rubbed him.

Amos watched her as he tended the other two horses and occasionally talked to them. He watched as she got near Hercules' ear and whispered, albeit loudly. The horse would move his head up and down or shake it sideways and whinny back at her. Sometimes he turned his head around to look at her and would nuzzle her cheek or shoulder.

"Looks like you're charming all the males around here, not just me."

"Hercules and I have a good thing going. He understands me," she quipped.

"Maybe I need to have a long talk with him, then."

"He won't divulge my secrets."

"You have secrets?"

She laughed. "Not that kind. Just the ways of women in general," she added with an exaggerated look of confidentiality. "We have to keep our mystery, you know."

"I don't know, I think I'm getting to know you pretty well."

"And you're doing it in a fine manner, too. What's that you say, Hercules?" She got close to his mouth and stroked his face as she pretended to listen to him. She turned to face Amos. "He promised to tell me the secrets of real men. And he also wants to know if we intend to muck these stalls anytime soon, or just move them over to the cleaner ones."

Amos shook his head and grinned. "Real men don't have secrets. That's what makes us real men. And, yes, I should probably muck, either way."

"We. We can muck. I want to help."

"You never have before. I won't hold you to that when you find out how unpleasant it is. Let's let them out to stretch a little and graze."

"Is that all right without a fence?"

"They'll be fine for a while. I'll get 'em some fresh water in the trough. They'll likely stick around until they run out of grasses and weeds to eat. I doubt if they'll be tempted to walk away anytime soon. We can check on them periodically until we get ready to go back in. You bring that wheelbarrow over here and I'll run get the other shovel in your barn."

He came back and handed the shovel to Lily.

"I mentioned it, but we never talked about it. Can we have a kitchen garden next spring? All this manure and hay sure would be good for the soil. I want to put in some flower gardens, too."

"Of course, we can. I didn't realize you had gardens before. I thought you were more of a city girl than that."

"We didn't have our own. But a neighbor and good friend had one, and I always enjoyed helping her. She taught me a few things, like using manure and hay and eggshells in the soil. Other kitchen waste, too."

"Now see, there's a secret about you I didn't know."

"Well, neither does Hercules, so don't feel bad." Lily started to shovel and didn't get far before letting out a string of "Ew we ew ew." She stepped back into the cleaner floor of the middle of the barn and said, "I'm going to have to get boots and britches so I can keep helping you with this. Would you mind that?"

Amos looked up from his shoveling to see her stark naked, except for her shoes. After she dropped the robe on some hay bales, she picked the shovel back up and got to work. He watched her for a few moments before he said anything. "It probably would be smart to wear them when we're out here with the horses or building fences, but I'd rather you didn't go into town dressed like that."

She kept shoveling. "Oh, no, I wouldn't want to do that, either. It might not seem right for the schoolteacher to be dressed like that."

He chuckled. "But it's all right for her to be undressed?"

She shrugged. "Inside her own barn, why not? I just know I can't do this with a robe or a dress on without getting it filthy." She went back to the task at hand.

Amos watched her lean over and push the shovel, then slide it back and pick it up to dump it in the barrow. More specifically, he watched how her breasts bounced and swayed, how her shoulder and back muscles flexed with certain moves and her thigh muscles and buttocks flexed with other moves. He knew he wasn't going to be able to work like this, not with her naked alongside him and him with a raging erection.

"Lord have mercy, woman, I can't work with you looking like that."

She straightened up and looked at him and the fullness in

his britches, looked down at herself, then looked at him again. "Oh, right," she said with feigned annoyance. "I'll take care of it." She dropped her shovel and pulled him out of the stall into the cleaner area before dropping to her knees in front of him. There were no protests from him, and she looked up at him when she had his buttons undone. His eyes showed no amusement, only heat and desire. He made no sound other a sharp intake of breath when she freed him and took his hardness in her mouth and his sac in her hand.

Lily realized she was being rougher with her attentions. Her mouth was still soft, of course, but she was being much less teasing and gentle with the actions of her mouth and hands. Sometimes not gentle at all. She felt the scratchy, rough-hewn wood and hay stalks under her legs. Was she being brusque because the surroundings were rugged? Was the primitive setting, complete with animals, making her act like one? Whatever the reason for it, she embraced the raw, brutish need that came over her, and her treatment of him changed accordingly. She squeezed tighter on his sac, rolling his rocks with vigor. Her mouth grew insistent and determined, not waiting to hear his moans and sighs and then giving him more of what he reacted to. Her hand at the base of his staff squeezed. She pulled, and pulled on his sac at the same time, but not that hard. Amos let out a little cry that might have been protest, and it urged her on.

Suddenly, she felt her head pulled and realized Amos had hold of her hair. He had it pulled upward and back just short of pain. "You want to play rough, little girl? I'll show you rough." His hand pushed her head forward and held it there. His hardness filled her mouth and she wondered if he was going to push it all the way inside her mouth and choke her. "Don't stop. Give me more tongue. Flick it up and down, and all around the top. Good girl."

Good girl. She felt her own wetness on her thighs. *Good girl.*

Why does that make me this hot? I had doubts about myself before, doubts about my subservience in intimate situations, but those doubts have flown for good. Because I'm his girl. Not his wife or partner, but his girl. Right now, I'm his property. His submissive possession. He's in control and he wants to remind me. Funny, this isn't like other times being on my knees. This time I don't feel I'm controlling anything. His hand in my hair is making that clear. Lily found herself not a little apprehensive about what Amos defined as rough. But at that moment her nipples would have cut glass, and every nerve in her body seemed on alert and ready to fire. She was covered in gooseflesh that had nothing to do with cold. *Can Amos see the state I'm in? Will he know I want him to assume authority over me? That I need for him to? That I need his power and dominance? At this moment, I would beg for it.*

"Now suck. You know what I like. Do it. Do it the way I like it."

She did; at least she started doing what he liked. She heard moans that spurred her on; she was proud of herself for giving him that pleasure. Without conscious thought, she did something new, something that seemed so right in this crude setting with these raw and depraved impulses governing her actions. Lily pulled her mouth away from him and licked the top of his inner thighs. She kissed and nipped with her teeth at sensitive areas, eliciting a grunt or two from him. She hadn't done this before. Lily didn't consider what he might think or even if he'd enjoy it; at this point she was acting completely on instinct, and perhaps subconscious curiosity.

She repositioned enough that she could move her head farther between his legs. Stroking his length with one hand, she explored that area behind his sac with the other one. Later she would recall that the day before, as Amos was touching her all over, she thought if she was that hypersensitive there, he must be, too. Now she was lost in a haze of sensual discovery, feeling, tasting, sensing the way his body reacted. Lily's wet finger slid along his cleft and reached his pucker, then she gently circled it, absorbing the feel of the wrinkled skin there. She nipped and kissed just far enough so she could reach it with her tongue.

The sharp tug of her hair pulled her head back. Her eyes shot up to meet his and they showed a storm she'd never seen before, as if he'd made his own sensual discovery. "As nice as that feels, it's not what I told you to do. You'll regret that in a few minutes. Now you'd better suck me the way I said to, or you'll find yourself in even more trouble. You understand me?"

She nodded.

"I want to hear you say it. Do you understand me? Do you understand what's going to happen to you?" He squeezed harder on her hair, not to move her head, but just to pull her hair tighter. Their eyes were still connected.

"Yes, sir, I understand." She couldn't help it. She felt her fluids streak down her thighs. *Yes! Be forceful. Dominate me. Make me!*

He loosened his hold on her hair. "Get to it, then."

She made a move to put her mouth on him again, but his hand in her hair stopped her. "I gave you an order. I told you to get to it. I think you should acknowledge that you heard me and that you'll obey me."

Her head was angled back a little, awkwardly, as she kept her eyes on him and spoke. "Yes, sir. I'll get to it as you wish, sir."

"Good girl."

Good girl. I know I'm melting because I can feel it running down my legs. Yes, I want to be your good girl.

As she lavished her sweet ministrations on him, she couldn't help but wonder what was to come. She was certain she'd earned a whipping, but would it be playful, or would it be as serious as he was acting? Still, it wasn't an actual punishment, so surely he wouldn't make it that bad. He'd playfully swatted her bottom several times since they got home from the wedding. Several times. Something told her other men probably didn't do it that often to their wives. Every once in a while, perhaps, but not as often as Amos did. After all, he'd told her over and over how beautiful her ass was and how much he loved to watch it move. Just how much and how long would he be able to watch it move this time?

Still wondering how hard he'd spank her, she decided to do her absolute best with her mouth and hands. Maybe if she performed well and satisfied him the best she could, she could mitigate the upcoming punishment. Maybe. She did all the things she'd done before that she knew gave him pleasure. Something about knowing she had the punishment coming aroused her far more than she'd expected it to. Not knowing how harsh it would be raised that arousal to a feverish level. She stopped hoping it would be a light one. *What's brought on this primal urge? Why am I craving something that repulsed me just days ago? No, it's worse. What I want from Amos is much worse. What I hunger for is far more base and depraved than that.*

And why is he playing along so well?

Lily instinctively knew this thing she was going through would only happen when they were being sexually intimate, and not every time at that. It wouldn't spill over into their everyday lives, and there would still be plenty of the kind of relations they'd been having up until now, namely, normal. Even their normal was extraordinary. But this, this was the kind of epic play they could fall into occasionally when they wanted to shake things up.

Amos held her head firmly by her hair as he thrust into her mouth. It caught her off guard and she gagged. He pulled out to let her get a breath, then he did it again, and he held her there a little longer before he released her. He bent down nearly to her eye level and said, "You weren't concentrating on the task I gave you. It's time for you to pay, and now, it'll have to hurt worse than I previously planned. You clearly need to learn a lesson in obedience."

She couldn't think of what to say. He took hold of her arm and pulled her up, and he wasn't patient about it. "Yes, sir, I know I deserve it." She almost blurted out the words.

He pushed her forward, almost into the wall of Hercules' stall. "See that knot in the wood?"

"Yes, sir."

"Plaster your nose to it until I have things ready."

The knot was about eight or ten inches below the height of her nose, so she had to assume an uncomfortable and most awkward and embarrassing stance to accomplish what he wanted. She couldn't see him, but she could feel his eyes on her. It only added to her humiliation, and she knew that was his goal. *He's almost too good at this game.*

In less than two minutes, he was at her side, roughly grabbing her arm again and pulling. She saw what he'd done. There were three hay bales, two side-by-side, and a third one on top of one of the two. There were horse blankets covering most of the horizontal surfaces. Without words, he pushed over the two-stack and indicated she should put her hands on the lower bale. She knew how she must look from behind and was even more shamed when he pushed her legs apart.

"I didn't wear a belt out here, but I found a strip of leather that used to be part of a saddle. It should do, don't you think?"

"Yes, sir."

An evil-sounding low laugh came from Amos. "And you're going to let me know just how much you appreciate this lesson, aren't you?"

"Yes, sir. Um, sir?"

"Yes?"

"How am I going to do that, sir, exactly?"

"You're going to thank me when I stop. And you're going to beg me for more. And I'm going to give you more." He walked in front of her and lifted her head with his finger under her chin. "And you're going to be very convincing."

"Yes, sir," she whispered, worry and fear creeping into her headspace.

Amos went around behind her and stood there, rubbing her backside and up and down the inside of her thighs. She heard another laugh much like that earlier evil one escape him. "I don't know that I've ever seen you wetter. I can foresee more of these sessions in your future, little girl. And you won't like some of them."

Little girl. I'd rather be his good girl. Little girl has its charm, I suppose. Just not as much.

"Yes, sir, I understand. I trust you'll teach me the lessons I need to learn, however I have to learn them."

That laugh again. "Good girl."

Lily smiled in spite of her situation. *There it is.*

His hand slashed through the air and cracked against her skin. She took a deep breath and steeled herself for the next one. It came with the same force, as did the next volley of five or six licks. He rubbed and stood back to see the color settle into her sweet backside. He stepped back in place and delivered a few more, ending with a couple on the tops of her thighs.

Lily's hindquarters stung. She hadn't cried yet, although her eyes were full and would probably spill over soon. She'd yelped a few times and squirmed.

He walked around and lifted her face with his finger again. "Are you ready for the leather now?"

Her breath wasn't steady. "Yes, sir, please."

He smiled and nodded and Lily wondered if her sweet Amos had been taken over by some demon. She closed her eyes and waited. He scooted her legs apart again.

When the strap hit, she screeched. He delivered four in quick succession before stopping. Her tears finally fell. He didn't move to deliver any more, and she realized she was supposed to ask for more. "Please, sir, I don't think I've learned my lesson yet. I'm afraid I might still disobey. Please, more." She had enough gumption to add, "And harder, please."

They weren't harder and there weren't many more, but the last two were on each inner thigh, and the two before that were on the tops of her thighs. Her legs trembled uncontrollably.

Lily heard something hit the floor and she knew it was the thin leather strap. She felt his hands gently rubbing her skin, tracing the marks he'd left. His touch was light and comforting, so different from his actions only moments before. As he rubbed, he occasionally let a hand stray into her slit. She was almost overwhelmed by all the sensory input. Amos took a couple of steps away and returned with a bottle of liquid she knew was horse liniment. He rubbed it into her welts, a few cooling, soothing drops at a time. Again, he delved down lower, and again, his touch awakened all the unmet need she'd built up earlier. She knew he could see how this had affected her, even she could tell her parts were swollen and, well, wet. She couldn't hide it, and she didn't want to. She wanted Amos to see what he did to her.

Apparently, he not only saw, but he was affected, too. She felt his hands pull at her hips and then she felt him thrust inside her to the hilt. He was relentless, merciless, and she held on to the lower hay bale for dear life. *Sledgehammer, indeed.*

As she felt those little waves of heat spread across her lower belly that signaled her peak was nearing, she raised her head and widened her eyes at another sensation she felt. His thumb, inserted into her own little puckered rosette, carried with it the cool slickness of the liniment. The fullness of his thumb in her, the cool sting of the liquid, and the mighty force of his thrusts catapulted her into a shattering, violent release that drew a scream from her. She felt him join her in a shared ecstasy, and only then, as they were coming down, did she realize she'd screamed his name.

Before he even had a chance to catch his breath, Amos pulled her up and into his arms. She wasn't sure when he'd had a chance to sit down, but she found herself on his lap with a blanket and his arms around her, holding her tightly.

His breath still wasn't normal, but he didn't wait. "Sweetie, are you all right? Did I hurt you?"

Lily nodded. She needed to say the words, but she couldn't just yet with him looking right into her eyes. It was too embarrassing. She leaned on his shoulder and whispered in his ear, "Yes, you did. Just like I wanted you to. You took command. You made me do things, shameful and humiliating things, and I loved it. You made me beg you to punish me. You've shown me a side of me, of my desires, that I never knew existed. I thank you for that." She let her head rest on his shoulder.

"Sit up, sweetie, so we can talk."

She shook her head. "I don't think I can."

He chuckled. "You mean after what we just did, you can't even talk about it?"

"It's too shameful. What does it say about me that I would crave that kind of treatment from you?"

"It says you're the best wife who ever lived. For years I've had some fantasies like that. I told you once that some of them were dark. Now you have a little hint of how dark. It gets darker. And to be able to let that side of me out with a woman I love and trust, I've got to be the luckiest man alive."

Lily sat up and looked at him. "Really? You don't think I'm bent or broken or anything?"

"Of course not. I hope you don't think I am, either. I told you you've been mine since time began. We were destined to find each other. Must be written in the stars somewhere. Oh, and if I ever take you into something so dark you don't want to do it, tell me."

"I promise." She let out a contented sigh. "I guess we can muck the stalls now."

"I'm not sure I can. You made me weak. Let's just put them in the other stalls. I'll clean them out later."

"I'll help you."

"I don't know, sweetie. Look what just happened when you tried to help."

They both giggled a little bit. She liked hearing that sound from him. Any other man might sound silly. "Then I guess we'd better check on the horses. They might be half way to Rawlins by now."

CHAPTER 13

*M*onday started out well. The newlyweds were still on an emotional high from a deepened sense of intimacy and a higher level of trust and commitment. School went quickly for Lily, and work was busy for Amos and included all the expected bawdy comments from his coworkers. It was all in fun and it tickled him, knowing that he'd done something over the weekend that most of them would never do except in the far, dark corners of their imaginations. He'd not only seized an opportunity to act out some sordid fantasies, but together they'd set the expectation to explore that side of their natures even further in the future. The most he would say to his buddies was that he'd found the perfect woman to marry and he was one lucky son of a gun.

School was already out, and Lily sat at her desk grading papers. They had promised Harriet they'd stop by her house on their way home today, so since school let out before Amos would be able to leave work, she was going to use the time to grade papers, review assignments, and do some prep work for the next day. If Harriet indeed only kept them a few minutes, they planned to stop at Mary's Restaurant for supper.

Her papers were graded, the non-graded practice exercises were reviewed and weaknesses identified, and she was as ready for the next day as she could be. Lily walked over to the shelves in the back of the room that would be the library and browsed through the books that had come in today, donated by the McBrides. There were *The Owl and the Pussycat* by Edward Lear, *The Return of the Native* by Thomas Hardy, *Black Beauty* by Anna Sewell, two Jules Verne books, three Mark Twain books, three books by Louisa May Alcott, one by Henry David Thoreau, and three biographies; one of Charlotte Brontë, one of George Washington, and one of William Shakespeare. Lily was thrilled with the books and had already written a thank you note to Molly McBride. If donations continued to pour in like this, the class could have a lesson on library books and librarian duties within a week or two. They could have a special session to glue a card pocket into the inside cover of each book and insert a card to record the check-in and return dates. She had already purchased a notebook to record the person's name, the name of the book, the date checked out, the date due, and the librarian's initials at check-out and check-in. Caleb hadn't had books to donate, but he donated the card-stock to use for the cards and card pockets. All she needed was a little file box for the cards, and she thought she'd seen one in the mercantile. Maybe she could get Amos to stop there before they headed home.

Amos. A big smile spread across her face as she recalled their activities the previous weekend. *If anyone had told me six months ago—six months? Try just days ago. Who would have dreamed I would change so much between that day Amos gave me the real spanking out by the barn, and the day before yesterday? Is it even possible to change attitudes so drastically?* There was absolutely nothing erotic about that real spanking, at least not to her. At least not to her that day. Looking back on it now, she could see how there was a lascivious aspect to it, a vulgar detail or two others would probably find depraved, but she now found to be deliciously demeaning. What would the townspeople think if they knew the schoolmarm, to whom they'd entrusted their children, had an occasional desire to be shamed and debased by her big, strong, he-man husband? How would they react if they knew she was so blindly spellbound by her forceful, rugged husband that she sometimes hungered for his touch to be cruel and his hands to deliver an exquisite pain? That she felt so safe in his care that she wanted him to assert his rule, roughly if he wished, and force her to do his will and subject her to the most wicked and unnatural corrections and acts of perverted penance he could devise? The thought made her shiver involuntarily, and that made her realize just how aroused she'd become. This was so new, all these sensations and desires, and she was so inexperienced. She'd never even heard of impulses like this before. What if this was just a phase they were going through? What if the time came when she no longer had these desires? *Does Amos think about these things? I'll have to ask him.*

Lily looked at her watch-brooch and saw that it was about time for her husband. She straightened the books on the shelf and walked around the room, making sure everything was tidy and ready for class the next morning. It had been a warm day and they hadn't needed a fire in the stove, so she didn't have to check it. The bottom shelf on the other side was cleared of any of the students' lunches, so no one had left theirs. That was about all the time she could kill inside. She picked up her reticule, pulled out the keys and locked the schoolroom door behind herself. She'd enjoy one of the new benches while she waited.

She sat so she could see the mercantile across the street. Occasionally, she'd see someone and wave, or they would see her first and holler a greeting. *I love this little town. Where would I be if they hadn't embraced me when I came and vowed to take care of me in remembrance of Will? They're good people. Good friends.* She shifted on the seat and turned her knees the other way.

"Hello, Sheriff, Amy," Lily said as she waved. They smiled at her and waved back. *I wonder if Sheriff Jim and Amy get adventurous in their love life. They don't have any children so they wouldn't have to keep quiet. The sheriff, umhum, I suspect he could get a little wild. Don't know about Amy. She looks more prim and proper. Or maybe that's what they would have us think. Yes. Definitely. Just look at the sheriff. He's a real man, for certain. If he's in the mood for some scurrilous activities, I wouldn't be surprised if he makes her go along with it. Or, maybe she likes it. Is she hiding a big secret, too?*

She heard Amos shout a greeting from the other direction, so she stood, grabbed her bag and walked to meet him, a big smile plastered across her face. He jumped down so he could lift her up beside him, then he hopped back up. "You still want to go to Mary's when we leave Harriet's house?" he asked.

"Sure, if you do. I didn't plan a meal, but if you want to go on home, I'm sure we can rustle up something."

"No, no, I want to go to the restaurant, too. We won't have to cook or clean up." He gave her a lazy grin. "More time to fuck."

She grinned back at him and continued the conversation in a hushed tone. "I got through the day just fine, but when everyone left and a single thought of you crept in my head, it was all over. I've been thinking about Saturday ever since!" Her wide-eyed look of innocent surprise made him laugh.

"It came to my mind, too. It came, it parked, and it stayed there the whole damn day. A couple of times I had to turn away from people so they wouldn't see. I felt like a teenager again."

"Amos," she leaned in close to him, "do you think Jim and Amy Larkin fuck and play like we do?"

His expression changed and he leaned back away from her. "What the hell, Lily, what would make you ask that?"

She shrugged. "It's a natural question. I was thinking of you, then I was thinking of Saturday, and then I saw Jim and Amy walk over to the mercantile. And I wondered if they ever had Saturdays like that. It was a perfectly natural thought progression."

"Well, it sounds logical when you explain it like that. You and I can talk about that subject anytime you want to, but I won't have you talking to anyone else about it, you hear me? It wouldn't be proper for the schoolteacher to be taking part in this kind of conversation."

"Of course. Yes, you're right. I won't. But if you had to guess, do you think they'd be that bold?"

"I don't know. Married couples can keep a lot of things private. Push comes to shove, I'd have to say, yes, they're every bit as depraved as we are."

"Really? I wanted us to be the most depraved couple in town."

"I'd call that a lofty goal to aspire to."

"Step down off that high horse," she said, one eyebrow raised. "You'd like it as much as I would."

"We can discuss our friends and neighbors later," Amos said as he pulled the wagon to a stop. "We're here now." He added in a whisper, "Please don't find any reasons to linger here. I'm hungry."

"Come on in!" Harriet called out. "Arthur's timing us so I don't keep you any longer than I promised."

"When my lovely bride gets to talking, she can lose all track of time," Arthur said with a wink at his wife.

"Now come sit down, right here. That's your gift on the table; go ahead and open it."

"Oh," Lily said. "It's a beautiful box."

"We think so, too," Harriet said.

"Uh oh," Amos said. "I believe I recognize that crafts-manship."

Arthur looked at them and grinned.

"As I said, Arthur and I give this same thing to all our young couples. We've been happily married all these years, and we found the secret to our happiness right at the beginning. Some people look at us like we're loons, but I'm not exaggerating a bit. One day I was about to let my stubborn pride tear us apart until he finally had enough. And I felt his wrath." She nodded at the hunk of pretty paper in Lily's hands. "Open it. What you'll see represents the thing, or even the philosophy, that saved our marriage."

Lily got the paper removed and saw their gift. She looked up at Amos with a shocked expression.

Amos laughed and pulled it out of the box, turning it over in his hands. "Angus Kelly made that paddle, I can tell. Nobody else I know could do reversed script as well as this. The man's an artist."

He'd fashioned the paddle so that when it was applied to the skin, one side of the paddle would leave an imprint of the cursive word *Obey*. The other side of the paddle would leave the name *Lily* emblazoned on her backside.

"Harriet, I don't know what to say, and truly, those aren't words I get to say very often," Lily said.

"I'm sure we don't have to give you any instructions with that. The bottom line is, use it." Harriet cackled as she leaned over just enough to slap her own thigh. "I said bottom line. Bottom line!" By the time she straightened back up, the other three were laughing with her. "Anyway, whether it's for serious infractions, or just for the fun of it, use it. Play with it. Do both. But, Lily, let me tell you what I've come to realize, my own secret, you might say. Come on. We'll step outside and Amos can bring the box when he comes out in a couple of minutes. Men, please give us just a little bit of time."

"Bottom line, indeed," Harriet whispered mostly under her

breath, still amused at her own unintended use of the expression.

Outside, Lily heard the men's muffled voices inside and wondered what they could be talking about. But she was more curious about what Harriet was about to say.

"These men out here in the west, they're the best men you'll find in this whole world. But not a one of them wants to take orders from anyone else, particularly his own wife. They *will* be in control. I never found that to be much the case back east."

"That's what attracted me first to Will, then to Amos. I call them *real men*. I like it that he's one to assume authority and take a dominant role. At the same time, it's a protective role. You know, the king of the castle."

"I do know. It sounds like you two might be just a little like Arthur and me. Remember, if you want to be deliriously happy, satisfied in every way from the porch to the bedroom, submit yourself to him willingly. You might think you'd lose a piece of yourself when you do that, but it's just the opposite."

Lily smiled at Harriet, a hint of playfulness in her eyes. "I learned that very lesson just this past week."

"Sounds like we should have given this gift to you days ago. Did I understand you correctly?"

"You did. Harriet, he told me we should keep it between ourselves, but I feel like you might be a kindred spirit here."

"I would like to be, dear, anytime you want to chat. Amos might make an exception in this case. That's exactly why we give this particular little gift to all the newlyweds. Now, let me share this with you. Arthur keeps me on a short leash. I might be punished for any little thing, and in ways that might shock you. Here's another thing I learned: I never tell him no." She lowered her voice again. "It's the little things. For example, I present myself to him for punishment in ways that would horrify other women. When he assumes the mantle of authority or gets that stern tone, it just does something to me, I can't describe it. I melt a little bit. I'm compelled to give myself over to his dominance, demonstrably so, so it's clear to him without words that I'm surrendering to him completely. The first time you do that, you realize how hard it is. It takes faith and trust and pure guts, but you'll never be the same again. And I can sometimes reach my peak during corporal punishment. It's not uncommon for me to instigate something myself, the need is that great. Oh, I can hear their footsteps coming this way. Don't forget—find creative ways to keep your king happy. Let's find a time we can get together and talk more."

"I'd like that, Harriet."

"Miz Harriet," Amos said as he joined them outside. "Thank you again for the gift. Sometime I'll have to ask you how all the other couples reacted to it. And believe me, I'll give Angus a talkin-to for not telling me about it ahead of time."

Harriet laughed. "He knows not to spill the beans. Did you and Arthur have a nice chat?"

"We did indeed. I think we're going to continue it one evening next week."

"Wonderful! Lily, you heard that. It means you and I need to meet up at that time and talk more, too."

"I can't wait to hear all you have to share," Lily said. Harriet gave her a conspiratorial smile, as though something wicked and delicious lay before them.

Amos set the paddle box in the wagon and lifted Lily up to the driver's bench. They all four waved as Amos urged the horses into motion. As they neared the restaurant, Lily asked him if he still wanted to stop for supper.

"Hell, no. I want to get you home and get you naked and write all over your ass with that thing."

"Yes, sir."

THEIR DAYS SETTLED into a routine normalcy, although Lily wondered sometimes if their intimate pursuits would be considered normal. Most of the time, their lovemaking was what she thought of as normal for newlyweds. There were long, sweet, loving sessions. There were shorter, funny ones. There were fiery, perfervid sessions, and heated, almost angry sessions. And there were all those impromptu ones when he'd bend her over a table or over hay bales. And then there were those other times, too. She was pretty sure those other times wouldn't be considered normal for most people. But oh, how they thrilled her.

School went well, better than Lily could ever have dreamed when she imagined her first year of teaching. She grew to love her students, every one of them, and in her heart, she considered them her second family. Just like family, there were aspects to each one's personality she didn't appreciate, but she loved them, nonetheless.

Nessa was proving to be invaluable. She loved teaching the music lessons and working on the library project, and the students enjoyed them, too, without exception. She said she loved doing the work so much, she wasn't going to accept any salary for it. The board tried to pay her, but she wouldn't accept it. She waved it off and told them, "If you don't officially hire me, then you can't officially fire me." Lily appreciated her for more than that, too. They'd become fast friends.

Ross Bailey, the attorney, came to talk to the class, and he was surprisingly entertaining. He told about some cases his large firm worked on back east that had gained notoriety at the time because of the blatant stupidity of the clients. She liked this humorous side of Mr. Bailey, and was especially pleased when Bailey told Ben that when he was ready for a part-time or a summer job, to come to him. Ben was delighted. So was Lily. It cemented in her mind that it had been a good idea to invite guests to talk to the students; next, she needed to confirm the date for their visit to Emmett's blacksmith shop.

Lettie Stewart seemed to be withdrawing, and that worried Lily. She'd come out of her shell that day when Angus praised her artwork and donated the art supplies to the school, and from that day forward, the child blossomed. Lily thought she saw signs of regression now. She planned to talk to Lettie about it when the opportunity presented itself.

AMOS AND LILY fell into the habit of inviting Sophie, John, and Billy for dinner almost weekly. When Sophie cooked for the boarders, she'd make an extra pie or cake or plate of cookies, whatever the boarders were having, to take for dessert. Tonight, it was a lemon pound cake.

As usual, there was no shortage of conversation over dinner. The biggest topic that night was the newest impending big building projects, the slaughterhouse and the icehouse just outside of town, and the butcher shop in town. Once those plans were nailed down, the sawmill was going to be especially busy, and the men knew they might be in for longer hours until things calmed down for a while.

Lily asked if they knew whether Philip was still looking for investors, and John said he thought so. Lily turned to look back at Amos, and he smiled and nodded.

There was a lull in the conversation. Billy had already eaten seconds on the pork roast and potatoes, and was eating more slowly now on the food that remained on his plate. He moved a few whole corn kernels around with his fork.

"You know, back before my daddy got mean and sick from the drinking, he took me fishing down at the river a few times. He told me he learned a trick about fishing from the time when he lived with the Indians. He was just joshing me. He never lived with any Indians." He looked up around the table and the grownups were all focused on him. He didn't usually say much at supper except to ask for more food. "He said the secret to catching a lot o' panfish is to put one or two kernels o' corn on the hook with your cricket. I don't know where he learned it, but we caught some fish that way. Crappie and bluegill bream mostly. Sometimes we just used corn if we ran out of crickets. It worked. Almost every time."

Amos glanced at John and back at Billy. "You just put corn on your bare hook?"

"Yes, sir, we sure did. Turns out, fish like corn."

Amos and John looked at each other again. "I've got line and plenty of hooks. Let's take Billy fishing in the morning. I even know a good place—Will and I found it when we first moved here. We only fished a couple of times before we starting building and," he shrugged, "just never went back. There's even a good stand of cane on the way we can cut for poles."

"You have any wood bobbers? I really liked watchin' the bobbers float on the water."

"I do, I believe. Red ones. And if I can't find them, I'll make some," Amos said.

When excitement over that topic died down, Billy mildly surprised the grownups again. "Miss Lily, have you noticed that Lettie's been sad a lot lately?"

"I have, as a matter of fact." She put down her fork. "Do you know what's bothering her?"

"Yes, ma'am, it's her daddy. He's on a drinking binge again. Lettie said when he gets like this they just try to stay away from him. She said her momma's got a black eye and bruises and cuts on her face."

"Do you know if he's ever tried to hurt Lettie?" John asked.

"He has. She didn't tell me exactly what he did, but I watched her start out walking for home. She was limping a little bit."

"Remember what Jim said about them that day when we asked for directions?" Amos asked. "He said he suspected abuse there, but he'd never been able to confirm it. We need to go to the sheriff and tell him. I should probably do that instead of going fishing in the morning."

"No, Amos, you boys need this fishing trip. I can tell you're all three eager to go. I can go see the sheriff in the morning. I know as much about it as you do."

"All right, if you're sure."

~

WHEN THEIR GUESTS HAD GONE, Amos said he needed to go turn the horses out for a while and muck the stalls while there was still daylight. He also needed to find his fishing gear; he knew it wasn't in the house.

Lily saw an opportunity to take some of Harriet's advice from their second conversation. "I'll come help. Maybe the work will go faster that way."

"That's not necessary, sweetie, if you want to stay in."

"Oh, ho ho," she said with a knowing nod, "it's necessary. Besides, Hercules told me how bored they get out there. We should put on a show for them. I'm going, whether you like it or not."

"Ah, I see. I believe I understand the situation better now. 'Whether I like it or not.' Those were poorly chosen words, little girl. You'll come to regret them. I'm wearing my belt this time." He headed down the hall to the back door. "Follow." When they reached the end of the hall, he turned to her and said, "Leave your bloomers and petticoat here. You won't be needing them."

"Yes, sir."

Once inside the barn, after the horses were led outside, Lily asked him if he wanted her to help him look for the fishing supplies. He replied tersely, "I want you to take off your dress and shift. You can leave your shoes and stockings on."

"Yes, sir."

He positioned some hay bales as they'd been before, then he placed a couple of horse blankets over them to protect her skin. When he looked up, she was naked save for her stockings and shoes. "Clasp your hands behind your head. Good. Turn around; let me see your ass."

He walked over to her and clutched her buttocks, one in each hand. "This ass is mine, isn't it?"

"Yes, sir."

"And it is a fine one, too. A work of art. Spread your legs some." He squeezed her cheeks and pulled them, up and down, apart, back together. Letting go of one of them and pulling the other cheek out, he ran his fingers from her little pearl to the top of her cleft. He did it a second time, but this time he lingered and teased her little brown pucker. He licked her neck and whispered in her ear, "And who does this belong to?"

"It belongs to you, sir." She tried not to make the sounds of protest that wanted to come out of her mouth.

"Yes, it does. I'm taking ownership of it tonight, and when I get through, it's going to look a hell of a lot different. You go stand in that corner and keep your arms where they are. Don't take your nose out of the corner until I tell you to turn around. Understand?"

"Yes, sir." Her voice was soft and quivery.

"Good. Go on."

He found the fishing gear and a couple of other things he'd hidden away just for this occasion and put them nearby but out of sight. "Turn around, girlie."

She did, and the sight of her almost took his breath. The position she was in, standing ramrod straight with her chest thrust forward, was deceptively proud-looking. It was the look in her eyes that undid him. They reflected so many emotions;

pride, eagerness, doubt, excitement, fear, they were all there. So was the trust.

A couple of hours later, the horses were properly tended to in nice fresh stalls. Amos had let her help clean them after all. He knew she was most uncomfortable after what he put her through; and that worked into his plan perfectly. He picked up her clothes, the fishing supplies, and another box.

"You may stand up now. We're going back to the house."

"Yes, sir."

He held the barn door open for her.

"Well, wait, Amos, I need my clothes."

"Nah, you don't. I'll just make you take them off again when we get inside."

"But someone might see! I can't be seen naked, with, with this thing—"

"Lily, if you don't want me to take off my belt and hold your arm while I lead you in a slow march to the house, striping your legs as we go, then you should mind me. It's almost dark. Even if somebody were to pass by, they wouldn't see you."

Lily wanted to argue about how dark it was, but it didn't seem prudent. She crossed her arms over her breasts and took off running.

When Amos came in, she was still in the hallway, leaning against the wall, catching her breath.

"Lily, girl, that may have been the hottest yet." He set down the items in his hands and cupped his crotch. "Look what happened from just watching you run to the house."

"Again? I don't see how you can do that."

He laughed. "It's all you, sweetie. You've got my body thinking it's a damn teenager again."

"You had that much sex when you were a teenager? You never told me that."

"I didn't say I had sex. Actually, I did have sex a few times, but mostly I got hard-ons. Every teenage boy does. I guess you could say I did have a lot of sex, but it was almost always with myself." He kissed her softly on her forehead. "You go lie down while I get a cloth and some arnica cream."

"All right."

Lily's head was comfortably cradled in her arms and her eyes were closed. When she felt the bed sag from his weight, she opened them and spread her legs more because she knew he would ask her to.

"That's my good girl." Those words still stirred something inside her. "You were incredible tonight, sweet. You just keep amazing me more and more each time."

"So were you." She half-turned over so she could look directly at him, but he pushed her back in place.

"I can't get you cleaned up if you keep moving."

"All right. I was just going to say how I love you so much for helping me... explore this side of me."

"I could say the same thing. I worry about you, though. My being a demanding and overly harsh master SOB doesn't hurt me any. I like punishing you up to a point. And, sweet mercy, Lord knows I love to turn this fine ass red and then look at it, knowing I made it that way because you yielded yourself to me. And that's true whether we're playing or not. But, Lily, sometimes I want to stop, or hold back, so the strokes aren't so hard. It kills me to do this to you." He finished with the cloth between her legs and opened the arnica cream.

"I want it, Amos, I really do. I'll admit, when each stroke hits, it's a burst of pain, but that dies down and leaves the good pain."

He snorted as he tenderly rubbed the cream over her stripes and bruises. "Good pain."

"I don't know how else to explain it. It's like I disappear into this place inside me, and I'm only aware of the pain. It makes me feel more alive."

"More alive than just regular alive? Is that something like loving with a love that's more than love?"

Lily's eyes widened and she couldn't stop the grin. In that moment, she knew what she was giving him for his birthday in a few weeks.

JOHN AND BILLY arrived at dawn Saturday morning. When she saw Billy riding on John's horse, Lily suggested that they saddle Hercules and let Billy ride him. That idea was met with great enthusiasm from the boy. He hadn't ridden a horse since Sophie'd had to sell theirs.

The trip to the river was savored by all of them. The fall morning air was almost too cold to be comfortable, but they knew the sun would warm them and take the edge off the chill before long. When they weren't talking, they could hear the field and forest noises of animals setting about their business of the day. It was one of life's quiet pleasures to hear the woods wake up.

They were quick to find and cut the perfect canes for each of them. Before much longer, their rigs were ready, complete with whole kernel corn joining the crickets and worms John and Billy had collected while it was still dark. Billy was the first to throw his line out. "All right now, little fishy, you know you want a feast like that."

Amos stepped a few feet downstream and offered his line to the deeper water out in the middle. John stayed near Billy but cast his line away from Billy's. Within the first hour, they'd threaded eight fish on the stringer. Both men gave Billy the credit and thanked him for sharing the trick with the corn. He beamed.

"At this rate, we'll have enough to feed the whole boarding house for supper."

"Well, you'll have to build a fire outside to fry 'em. Momma loves fish, but she doesn't like the way the house smells after you cook it. We always cook fish outside."

"Well, shoot, how about you and I cook the fish? I'm a pretty good fish fryer. Your momma could just cook something to go with the fish."

"I reckon that would be fine. She'll probably make corn dodgers and fried potatoes. That's what she usually cooks with fish."

"Man, that's going to be one mighty fine supper," John said. He looked over at Billy and decided there wouldn't a better time than this one. "Billy, you may have noticed that I think real highly of your momma."

"I did. It's not real hard to figure out."

Amos, who wasn't completely out of earshot, turned his head so they wouldn't see him laugh.

"I suppose you're right about that. I can't hide how I feel. I love your momma, Billy. And I'd like to have your permission, and your blessing, to ask her to marry me. I'd like for the three of us to make a home, be a family."

Billy nodded very slowly. "I've been wondering when you'd speak up. When was the last time you got drunk?"

"Me? Drunk?" John was caught a little off-guard. "I can't rightly remember. I don't believe I've been drunk since I was a much younger man."

"Do you drink at all?"

"I sometimes have a drink with friends, when I visit them, or when we go to the saloon after work. But I don't get drunk. I don't usually have more than a couple of drinks. I don't even keep a bottle in my room at the boarding house."

"Well, that's good. What do you act like when you're drinking? Do you get mean?"

Amos couldn't help reacting to that one, but he tried to pass it off as a cough. He knew what was coming.

"No, not mean. Not mean at all. I, um. Well, I, uh… I sing." The last two words were very quiet ones.

Billy turned to look at him. "You sing? Are you a good singer?"

John and Amos both answered. "No."

"Does that mean you'd be a happy drunk?"

"I guess it does. Now, I wouldn't sing after just one drink. Not even after two drinks. Maybe three. Probably after four. But these last few years, I hardly ever drink at all, and that means I don't hold my liquor very well. Matter of fact," John straightened up, wanting to assure Billy of his sincerity, "if you asked me not to drink at all any more, I would gladly give it up, for you and your mother."

"That's a fine offer, John, but I won't hold you to that. If you can handle it and won't get mean, there's no reason why you can't take a drink now and then."

"I appreciate that. Thank you. I promise you'll never have an issue with me that's caused by drinking. Other than, you know, the singing, I've never had a drinking problem."

Billy nodded but didn't look at John. He pulled in his line and set the pole neatly on the ground, taking care with the hook. He put his hands on his hips and looked straight across at the far side of the river. His words were quiet, dignified, and even more deliberate than his normal speech. "Don't you ever hit my momma."

"Hit her? No, Billy, I'm not that kind of a man. I wouldn't hit any woman, and especially not your mother. I love her."

"My daddy said he loved her, too. Didn't stop him."

John's heart went out to this little boy who was more wounded by what happened to his mother than by the damage done to him. Amos wasn't laughing anymore, either.

"What about spanking?" John asked.

"Well, I'm not real fond of it, I'd have to say. But I haven't gotten one in years. Momma says I behave just fine."

"No, not for you. You may not have had a chance to learn this, but most husbands, well, most of them won't allow their wives to act up. They won't put up with that behavior. So when the wife does something she shouldn't, the husband spanks her, much the same as he would a child."

"That won't be a problem. Momma won't act like that. She never has. She knows how to behave."

"But what if—"

Billy took up a position directly in front of John, with a resolute look on his face. "Look. If you ever think my momma needs a lickin', you just find me. I'll take it for her."

That surprised both John and Amos, and their respect for the boy solidified.

John began to nod. "I promise you, Billy, I will never lay a hand on your momma in anger. I'll never hit her, slap her, punch her or physically hurt her in any way, not even a spanking. Or you, either. You have my solemn promise and vow on that." John put out his hand for Billy to shake.

Billy looked at the hand, and back at John again. He spat in his palm and held up his hand to be shaken.

John wasn't so old that he didn't remember the solemn gravity of a spit-shake from his childhood. It carried with it the implied threat of damnation, plagues, life-long poverty, and painful, itchy, oozy sores on the private parts of the one who breaks the promise.

He spit on his palm and they shook.

WHEN AMOS TOLD Lily what had transpired on the fishing trip, she was thrilled. She wasn't surprised by Billy's protection of his mother. It just deepened the feelings she already had regarding him.

"You know this means we'll have to start looking for a live-in replacement for Sophie sooner than we thought."

"You know you aren't responsible for that, don't you?"

"I know. But that doesn't change anything."

~

THE NEXT MORNING brought bad news. When the church service began, Reverend Copperfield made the announcement that one of the town's most beloved citizens and their friend, Helen Bonner, had passed away in the night.

Lily leaned over and whispered, "Way sooner than I thought."

There was also some wonderful news, but this news wasn't announced from the pulpit. John had proposed to Sophie and she accepted. Lily's conviction that they needed to find someone urgently to manage and cook at the Bride & Board made that specific need her primary prayer all morning and throughout the day. That is when she and Amos weren't otherwise occupied enjoying each other's company. And each other's body.

~

THE NEXT TIME she saw John was when she ran into him and Sophie at the mercantile. She was leaving as they arrived, and all she said to them was, "We need to get together and figure out how you're going to get my house. Do you want to buy it outright? Rent it? Contract for deed? It'll be yours; we just need to get the details worked out. I've got this feeling that we need to do it soon. Very soon."

John wasn't surprised. Most people would have thought that was odd. It wasn't odd to them; it was just Lily.

❧

ABOUT A WEEK AND A HALF LATER, Sheriff Jim Larkin appeared at the door of the schoolhouse and motioned for her to come outside. She called on Ben to take over the lesson she was teaching to the younger ones.

"Lily, Lettie's daddy's dead. Her mother's hurt; the doc's got her right now. I need to take Lettie to be with her mother."

"Is she going to make it?"

"Yes, but he roughed her up pretty bad. She breathed a lot of smoke, too."

"Smoke?"

He nodded. "Stewart beat her up and knocked her out. Locked her up in a room and set the house on fire. She came to and it was dark in the room, then she smelled the smoke. She struggled something awful to get out, and finally did. Alice knew where she and Lettie had hidden his gun, and the first thing she did when she got outside was get her hands on it. She was barely able to move, but she went around to the other side of the house, and he was there. You can imagine the rest."

"So it was self-defense?"

He nodded. "That's what my report's going to say."

Lily had an inkling he was holding back, but the look on his face had a finality to it.

"I'll go in and bring Lettie out here. The poor thing. If the house burned, they're going to need new clothes more than anything else, and immediately. I'll organize that."

"Thank you. Amy's going to want to help. I'm sure the doc will put them up until Alice has healed enough, but I have no idea where they'll go after that."

The idea hit her quickly. "I do! Jim, she's going to need a way to support herself and Lettie. I imagine she knows how to cook and clean. They could move right into Helen and Tim Bonner's quarters in the boarding house. You know it's a nice

302

big apartment attached to the Bride & Board, with a separate entrance. It'll be perfect."

"What about Sophie?"

"She and John Garrett are getting married. She can still work if necessary, but she won't be living there. She might not have as much time to work as she has now because she'll have her own household to take care of. They've been in a quandary over the best way to handle it. That's why Alice is the perfect choice to run the Bride & Board. Sophie can help out and teach Alice how to do the books. Sophie could probably work there part-time indefinitely."

"That sounds like a good arrangement. The board won't mind. I'll go ahead and mention it to her. I don't want her lying there, feeling bad, and having to worry about how to support herself on top of that."

"You're right. I'm glad we can ease her worries. I'll be right out with Lettie."

In less than a minute, Lily was back outside with Lettie beside her.

"Lettie," Jim said, softening his tone considerably. "Let's sit down here on this bench. I need to tell you something important. There you go. Lettie, I'm afraid your daddy's dead." He gave her a moment to let that sink in. Her expression didn't change.

"Lettie," Lily said, "do you understand what the sheriff said?"

The girl fixed her gaze on Jim. "Did Momma shoot him?"

Before he could formulate his answer, she spoke up again. "I was going to shoot him, but Momma wouldn't let me. She said nobody my age should have to live with havin' killed somebody."

"She's right about that, Lettie," Jim said. "I'm a grown man and I'm the sheriff, so I've had to kill people before. It's not an easy thing. You don't get over it."

"Maybe the people you had to shoot weren't as bad as

Daddy. He needed killin'. I wouldn't want to kill anybody else, 'cause that would be bad. But Daddy, he needed it."

Neither of the grownups knew the best way to respond to that.

"Lettie, I need to take you over to Dr. Larkin's house. Do you know him?"

She shook her head. "I never went to the doctor."

"Well, I know him real well. He's my brother, and right now, he's taking care of your mother."

Panic visibly washed over the child. "She's hurt? How bad? Is she gonna be all right?"

"Don't worry, honey, she's going to be just fine. But she's been beat up pretty bad, and she breathed some smoke that's making it harder for her to breathe right now."

"Smoke? There was a fire?"

"I'm afraid there was, Lettie. The house burned. You won't be able to live there anymore. I'm afraid all your things burned up."

"We didn't have much. Can I go see Momma now?"

"You sure can. She's asking about you."

Jim mounted his horse and pulled Lettie up to sit in front of him. Lily took her hand. "Lettie, I need to pick up some things after school, then I'll come over to the doc's place to visit with you and your mother. Would that be all right?"

Lettie nodded. "That would be nice, Miss Lily."

Lily went back in the schoolhouse and diplomatically explained to the young ones that Lettie's father had passed away and her mother was injured but would be fine. When she was pressed for details, she told them the sheriff hadn't told her everything and he hadn't finished his investigation and final report yet. That pacified them.

When she called for a recess, Billy made his way to her desk. He asked her very quietly, "Did Miz Stewart shoot Lettie's daddy?"

Lily wasn't going to lie to the boy. "Yes, she did. He was a bad man and he was hurting them."

"Is she going to be in trouble with the law?"

"The sheriff said she won't. He said she shot in self-defense."

"Good. Lettie told me last week she was about to shoot him when her momma stopped her."

"I wish you had told me, Billy. I might have been able to get the sheriff to intervene."

"I couldn't, Miss Lily. Lettie made me swear I wouldn't tell anybody. Lettie's my friend. I had to keep my promise to my friend. I tried to get her to tell you, but she wouldn't do it."

She put her hand on his shoulder. "You did the right thing, Billy. I'm glad she has you for a friend. She might need one even more in the next few days."

"I'll be there whenever she needs me," Billy said before heading on out for recess.

After school, Lily hurried over to the mercantile. Shirley Keller had heard that Stewart was dead and his widow was at Dr. Larkin's, but she hadn't heard there had been a fire. When she found out that Lettie and Alice had nothing but the clothes on their backs, she flew into action. She went through the folded stacks of clothes and pulled out undergarments for both Alice and Lettie. She'd seen Alice recently, and she was pretty sure she could gage her size. They weren't as sure about Lettie's bloomers, so they chose a few that had tie closures instead of button closures. They'd be more flexible. Not knowing exactly how Alice was injured, they selected a couple of dresses that were on the plain side, without any fussy details. Lily had noticed that Lettie mainly wore full dresses with an apron-type pinafore. They found a couple that filled the bill and then selected another more fitted type of dress. Next came the socks and stockings, and that was all Lily could think of that they needed. Shirley whispered, "One more thing," and went down the next aisle to pick up a nice new dolly. It was one of their better ones, and Lily was a little ashamed she hadn't thought of it. The child probably would get comfort from a doll she could cuddle.

Shirley tallied the items and wrote *Ladies' Aide Society* at the top of the ticket. "I'll start the notification chain going. Pretty soon we'll have donations of money and goods and Alice and Lettie will have more than they ever had before."

Lily was in a hurry to get on her way, but she paused long enough to say, "I love the people in this town."

She was eager to get to the doctor's place, but she was even more eager to get to the Bride & Board and see if Sophie had heard the news. It was entirely possible she hadn't. Lily thought it was a good sign when she found Sophie out front, sweeping the porch and entranceway.

"Sophie, a terrible thing has happened."

"Lily, that's not what your face is saying." She looked confused.

"I know, I know. It's terrible, I mean, in that a man died, but it's all good for everyone else."

Sophie stopped sweeping. She held the broom in one hand and the other one rested on her hip. "Who died? Do I know him? I don't really know that many men in town."

"Probably not. He was Ed Stewart. He's the father of one of my students, Lettie Stewart."

"Oh, well, Billy talks about her. I never met them, but I know who Lettie is."

"Stewart was abusive to them both. Apparently, he tried to kill Alice this morning, then trapped her inside the house and set it on fire. She fortunately came to and managed to escape the fire. She had a gun, and as she walked around the burning house, she found him. I don't have any more details than that. But Sophie, Alice is going to need a job. I suggested to the sheriff that the town should hire her to move here, into Miz

Helen's quarters, and take over the management and cooking duties."

Sophie's eyes grew wide and she dropped the broom to throw her arms around Lily, who laughed with her.

"Let's not get ahead of ourselves. The sheriff was going to propose it to her this afternoon. But I can't imagine she would say no. I can't see that she has any other choices. She's been trying to take in laundry to get by, but they live so far out, it wasn't bringing in enough to support them. This is a good thing for everyone as far as I can tell. Except for Stewart, of course, and Alice and Lettie for having to go through this tough time."

"Bad for Stewart, yes, but I've been in that position. It's not bad for the wife and child. They feel mostly relief right now. Like they've finally escaped a prison without bars. When you go see them, you'll see I'm right. They won't be in mourning. So you won't have to act sad, either."

Lily thanked her for that insight and headed on over to the Larkins' house. She hoped when she left there, she'd have wonderful news to tell Sophie, John, Amos, and of course, Billy.

As it happened, she did.

FRIDAY EVENING FOUND SOPHIE, Billy, and John having supper at the Cameron home again. It was a happy occasion and they all felt excitement over upcoming events.

Sophie told them about when she had gone to visit Alice at the doctor's house, and they'd bonded immediately. She'd hoped they would; it made sense since they'd both married men who turned out to be alcoholic abusers and they had children the same age who were best friends. Sophie had explained to Alice that she was getting married soon and would be moving out of the Bride & Board, but she'd continue to work there until Alice was fully healed and trained in all the management aspects. She expected at some point to begin working less and less until it was all in Alice's hands. But she emphasized that if she was ever needed, if Alice were sick or there was a special occasion to prepare for, she'd be there in a jiffy. There was another helpful thing that had transpired just this week; the town hired two of the miners who were residents of the Bride & Board to assume the roles of caretakers. The men, who both wanted to save money to build their own places, were happy with the arrangement. They would cut and chop firewood, tend to repairs and odd jobs, keep the paint looking fresh, and help with anything Alice and Sophie needed muscle for.

The subject changed to the upcoming wedding of John and Sophie. They wanted a small, quiet ceremony with only their dearest friends in attendance. That would be only the Camerons, Nessa and Angus Kelly—Nessa would sing—Alice and Lettie Stewart, and a small handful of men who worked with John at the sawmill. John asked for a calendar and Lily fetched the one she used for school activities that she kept in her book satchel.

"Let's get this wedding date nailed down," John said, "the sooner, the better. Hon, is there any reason we can't get hitched on Friday, the 21st? That's one week from tonight."

"We're both ready, and Billy's itching to get moved into his new house, so I don't know why not."

"All right," he practically shouted. "Oh look, that next Friday, the 28th, is Amos' birthday."

"Really?" Sophie asked, appearing quite excited. When she saw his confirmation nod, she said, "This is perfect. I'll have my own kitchen again. Let me cook your birthday dinner. We'll have you over to our house for a change. Oh, I'm so excited!"

"Billy," Amos said as leaned toward the boy. "Next Friday

night, why don't you spend the night here with us, and let your mom and John have a night to themselves?"

"Oh, boy! Can I, Momma?"

"Yes," John said, and the adults tittered a little.

"Yes, Billy, if you promise you'll behave."

"I will, Momma. I always do."

"He'll be fine," Amos said. "Tell you what, Billy, if the weather cooperates, we'll go fishing early Saturday morning."

"I'm so scattered tonight," Sophie said, "I forgot, or we forgot, to let you know that I got a visit from Mr. Williamson at the bank today. They had an inquiry about available property from a farmer wanting to move to the Low Quarter. We talked about price and came to an amount I'm happy with. He said if the man has the money to pay full price, he can buy it from me directly. If he doesn't, the bank will buy it, then they'll raise the price enough to make it worth their while, and let the man pay some of it down, then he'll have a mortgage to pay to them. When that comes through, together with John's money, it'll be more than enough for us to pay you the full amount for our house, and we won't have to make those monthly payments that we talked about."

"Are you both sure you want to do that?" Amos asked them. "I'd rather you keep a good amount set aside for a rainy day. We aren't in any kind of hurry for the money."

"I did the math myself," John said. "We'll have plenty saved for that rainy day. Neither of us wants to start out our lives together in debt if we don't have to."

Amos shrugged agreeably and pointed to his wife. "She has the final say here. It's Lily's house, so it's Lily's money."

Lily grinned at them, then looked at Amos. "Don't sellers often give a discount if the buyer can pay the full price?"

"I believe they do." Amos smiled back, then looked at their guests.

"Then I need to lower the price. But we can do that later.

I'm ready for pie," Lily said.

~

THE FOLLOWING WEEK was another fine one. Lettie was back in school looking like a whole new child, and it wasn't because of her new clothes. She had an easy smile with twinkling eyes, and her whole carriage and bearing were relaxed. *This is the Lettie she was supposed to have been this whole time. It's such a tragedy she was miserable for the first eight years of her life. She was right about her dad—he did need killin'.*

When Nessa came in for their weekly music lesson, she had some big news for them.

"There's going to be a big Christmas party and dance in December for the whole town, at the community hall. It'll be a party for the whole family. There will be food, games, prizes, dancing, and fun for everyone." The children were already getting excited. "Wait, wait," Nessa said, "you haven't heard the best part yet. They're going to let us present a short concert to start things off. We'll sing three or four of our best songs and the whole town can hear how wonderful you sound. It's going to take a lot of practice to get ready, so we'll really have to buckle down and get serious."

"Miss Nessa," Lily offered, "if you need to sneak in an extra practice here and there, we can make that happen."

"Yes! I was hesitant to ask, but, yes, we'll need it."

The week seemed to fly by to Lily; before she knew it, it was Friday night and everyone who'd been invited to the wedding was at the church. Sophie looked lovely in a new dress and John looked handsome, she thought. Even Billy looked all spruced up in new clothes. They were typical school clothes, not a suit or anything like that, but they were new and Billy looked happy to have them. He stood a little straighter.

The few spectators took seats and Nessa began to sing. On

the chorus of the third verse, John and Reverend Copperfield took their places at the front. When they all saw John's face break out in a huge smile, they turned to see what he was smiling about. It was Billy, walking his mother down the aisle. A quiet, collective "*Aww*" rose from the guests.

When they reached the front, he kissed her on the cheek and gave her hand to John. It was probably supposed to be a whisper, but eight-year-old boys are seldom good at whispering. He said to John, "You remember what you promised me. We shook on it."

It was a surprise to Sophie, as it was to everyone. There were a few amused looks.

"I promise, Billy. I won't forget," John's whisper was much better, but everyone was close enough to hear it anyway. Billy took a seat beside Lettie and her mother.

The whole group almost lost their composure when Reverend Copperfield pulled one of his little antics. When all the vows were completed, right before he pronounced them man and wife, he added a new vow for John.

"And do you, John, vow before the Lord God Almighty and all those gathered here today, to honor and hold sacred the promise you made to Billy, until the end of your days?"

John nodded slowly. "I do."

"Then I pronounce you man and wife. You may kiss your bride."

THE NEXT WEEK also passed in a blur. Lily and Amos liked having neighbors, but they realized with the proximity, they wouldn't be able to have any more play sessions in the barn. They would just have to get inventive inside the house. It was a small price to pay.

John and Amos marked the layout for the fence they

planned to build. They decided to make it one big pasture area instead of two. They could always add new divider fencing later if it was needed. They planned to get started on Saturday, and Billy looked forward to helping. He found he liked spending time with the men.

At Amos' birthday dinner, the Garretts gave him a double batch of cookies and a small bottle of whiskey. He opened it and offered the adults a drink, but only John took him up on it. When Amos asked him if he wanted a refill, he declined. Billy smiled at him and John winked back.

Lily brought him a present to open, too. It was a new hunting knife Emmett had designed. It was loosely modeled after a latter version of the famed Bowie knife, but Emmett had made his own modifications. The three inches of blade at the point were sharpened on both side edges, giving it a machete quality for better and deeper thrust penetration into the animal carcass. The hilt was a little wider for better hand protection, and it was elegantly balanced when held up on a fingertip at the hilt mid-point. Amos and John were both impressed. Billy wanted one, too.

Not long after that, Amos and Lily said goodbye and headed home with Amos carrying the cookies, knife, and half-empty whiskey bottle.

"I am surely to goodness glad that we built these houses so far apart. Now that we have neighbors and I'm married to a woman who gets mighty loud at times, it's good we don't have to worry about them hearing us. They'd probably come running, asking what the hell I'm doing to you."

Lily laughed and Amos was reminded again how much he loved to hear that sound. "I suppose you could always gag me if necessary," she answered.

"Oh, sweetie, what an idea. Let's try that some time."

"Yes, sir. Whatever you'd like, sir."

"Damn, sweetie, look. I'm getting hard again, just talking

about it."

"Well, it *is* your birthday."

"And don't you forget it."

Once inside, Amos set the items on the table. He grabbed a cookie and picked the knife up to admire it again, while Lily lit a few lamps through the house.

"Sweetie, this is a perfect hunting knife. You did a great job with this gift. Thank you again."

"Well, that's your public gift. I have another one for you, but it's definitely a private gift."

He put the knife down. "You have my attention."

"You should get comfortable on the couch. I'll go get it."

"Yes, ma'am."

In a moment she came back to find him in the middle of the couch, comfortably leaning against the backrest with his fingers interlaced behind his head. His long legs were spread out in front of him. She set the box down and picked up a piece of paper.

"So I get to open it now?"

"Not just yet. First, I want to read the poem I wrote for you."

"You wrote a poem for me?"

"I did."

He grinned. "I can't wait to hear it. Wait. Take off your clothes."

"What?"

"Clothes. Off." He dipped his head toward her, then toward the floor, indicating she should take them off and drop them on the floor.

"You want to hear the poem while I'm naked?"

"Yes, please."

She shrugged and said again, "Well, it *is* your birthday." Lily stood and started to strip.

"Slower. Tease me."

She did, and she enjoyed it. His comments and encouragement and burgeoning erection indicated he was enjoying it, too. Lily picked up the paper and sat down seductively on the coffee table.

"Do you have to read it? I committed yours to memory, you know," he teased.

"I did, too. I just wanted to make sure I got it right."

"Put it down, then. Here, give it to me. I'll put it right there on the back of the couch in case you need to look at it." He put his hands behind his head and laced them together, assuming his comfortable position again.

Lily smirked. "All right, th—"

"Straddle me."

"Are you going to let me recite this thing?"

"Oh, little girl," Amos said with a lewd grin, "you wouldn't be about to complain or pout, would you?"

"Oh, no, sir, I'll be your good girl and straddle you."

"Well, come on, then. Don't forget I'm the birthday boy."

Lily did as she was told. Before she spoke, she gave him a kiss and stroked his shoulders and chest, managing to undo two of his shirt buttons.

"I sure like how this poem's starting out."

She whispered the title in his ear, then straightened back up and began reciting. He tried to keep his hands off her, but largely failed.

"*FOR AMOS, my real man,*

I HAD to come west to find my real man,
  And find him I did, 'though not according to plan.
  My lumberjack's strong, with a powerful frame,
  Great big hands and a touch that sets me aflame.

. . .

His voice in my ear and his hand on my breast,
  His lips at my neck and I'm a woman possessed.
  Possessed by this man who owns me complete,
  Our heat fed by lust, teased with torments so sweet.

The sting of the switch, the bite of the strap,
  When it suits his desires, I'm over his lap
  Where he rubs and he probes and paddles me red.
  His little girl would be wise to do what he said.

I cry and I scream but no mercy he shows.
  He knows my limits, my fears; that's as far as he goes.
  But within those limits there's much to explore
  In minds and bodies, and in our souls to their core.

With each revelation, each secret revealed,
  We understand it all better; he leads and I yield.
  I yield to my confidante, playful lover, best friend,
  Is it fuck in the barn today? Or plug my rear end?

The sweetest of times since he made me his bride:
  When we lie skin to skin, and I hold him inside.
  Dry tinder and kindling, I beg to ignite,
  Reduced to colors and senses and lightning and light.

The storms in his eyes match the need in my own.
  His urgent thrusts hurl me upward, right into that zone
  Where the light in me shatters as we spiral high
  And I swear I could steal the stars from the sky."

. . .

FOR A MOMENT he didn't say anything and Lily couldn't read his expression. "Amos?"

"I'm amazed that you captured what's in my heart, too, and on my mind. You can take the knife back. That poem was the best thing you could have given me."

"You're just saying that because I'm naked. It's not that good."

"To me, it is. I want to frame it, but it wouldn't do for anyone else to see it."

Lily chuckled. "Indeed, it would not!"

"I'll fold it up and keep it in my wallet."

"Please make sure it's not where it could fall out easily. I'd hate for Clint Keller to pick it up and suffer a stroke."

"Do you think the Garretts are asleep yet?"

"I don't know." She was still straddling him, so she knelt up, reaching the fullest height she could in that position so she could see out the window on that wall of the house. "It doesn't look like any lights are on, so I imagine they're all in the land of nod."

"Good." He lifted her up off him and stood her on the floor. "Follow me."

"What are we doing?"

"Since you recited that poem, I've got this hankering to fuck in the barn and plug up your rear end."

"Please let me put the dress back on, or put on my robe. We can't chance them waking and seeing me! Especially Billy."

"Your robe is fine." She headed to the bedroom to fetch it from the hook on the back of the door. He heard her laugh even before she came back into the hallway.

"We got so sidetracked by the poem, we forgot about your gift."

Amos laughed at himself. "Hard to believe I did that,

considering it's supposed to be another something nobody else can see.

They sat side by side on the couch. He opened the box to find two more gifts wrapped in pretty paper. He unwrapped the larger one to find what he recognized as a finely crafted leather Scottish tawse. Angus had described it to them once when he was in a mood to share.

"Where did you get this?"

"Axel Archer at the saddlery made it."

His eyes turned dark and brooding. "You went to him and described what you wanted?"

Lily laughed and waved her hand. "Oh, Heavens, no. Harriet showed me hers and I decided we need one. It was Arthur who went to Axel's shop. Apparently, Axel's accustomed to making specialty items for them."

Amos held it up, raised his arm, and applied it to an invisible target. "Nice heft. I can see why it's popular."

"Harriet said it doubles the sting, at least. We'll have to try it out easy at first. Now open that little one."

Amos let out a whistle and a little chuckle, holding it up so they could both see them more closely. "Nipple clamps?" She nodded.

"Wait," he said, "that's part of the same design that's on our wedding rings. Emmett made these, didn't he? Do you think he knew they were for us?"

"I suppose it's possible. Harriet did say that when Arthur drew what he wanted, Emmett proposed a modification. He said his design allowed them to be adjustable, but would still stay on when loosely tugged. That way they wouldn't keep falling off when set to a lesser tension. I thought that sounded like the voice of experience."

"Outside, woman. We've got some toys to try."

"Yes, sir, we do. These nipples aren't going to clamp themselves."

EPILOGUE

*R*osemary McBride stole the show at the Christmas party concert. Nessa had cleverly written music for the nursery rhyme *This is the House that Jack Built.* She choreographed it to be a funny part-sung, part-spoken skit, and she built in time for some of the antics between some lines. Rosemary was given the base line "This is the house that Jack built." The premise of her part was that as the song progressed, she was to appear to have trouble remembering her line. To complicate things—or to appear to—she was to hold up drawings of the house that illustrated each line. Lettie had made all the drawings. They were affixed together at the top so pages could be flipped over. Some children were given specific lines that were always performed solo. Margie Meyer, the perpetually boy-crazy student, was given the line "This is the man all tattered and torn that kissed the maiden all forlorn." She was to assume a dreamy-eyed countenance and hold her hands clasped over her heart in a swoon. Margie had it down to perfection. Most of the lines had hand motions for the rest of the singers.

As the song progressed, various other singers were to run

over to Rosemary and pretend to whisper the line in her ear or offer frenzied help with the illustrations, then they would run back to their position in the line. At one point the illustrations were taken from her and another performer would try to keep up, until another would take it in exasperation. Rosemary was to finally appear to understand, and she'd sing the last four lines by herself, complete with hand motions since someone else held the illustrations at this point. She had a wonderful singing voice and Nessa had begun coaching her individually. She shone. Just before she sang the last four lines as a triumphant solo, she stepped forward theatrically, as though she was stepping into an invisible spotlight. Even without an actual light to focus on her, she captivated the attention of the audience. She finished with a clear, full voice, stretching her arms out in an exaggerated flourish. They got a long standing ovation with shouts of *Encore*. Rosemary definitely shone that night.

Ben was the only eighth grader in school that year, and they knew he'd stay in school since his plan was to go on to law school after graduation. The next year they had five more children and in all of the students, three were eighth graders. Lily was overjoyed when all three showed up again for the following fall term. It looked like Lily's hope to keep as many students as possible in higher grades was working out. She realized some would need to leave school to work, but each one who stayed was a victory.

The first night together in their new home, Sophie, Billy, and John had read aloud to each other. They settled into the habit of reading every night, and most nights, all three would take a turn. Their first book was *Robinson Crusoe* by Daniel DeFoe.

Amos and John and Billy completed the fence sooner than the men projected. Billy proved to be a valuable asset and they developed a good working system. John surprised his new family one day by buying Sophie and Billy each a new horse. He took them to the saddlery and leatherworks shop and let them pick their own saddles. Billy was nearly overcome by emotion more than once that day. So was John when he saw Billy's reactions. When Billy decided to name his horse Friday after a character in Robinson Crusoe, Sophie named hers Crusoe.

The slaughterhouse was built just outside of town, as was the icehouse. The official name was almost the Big Rock Abattoir because some of the ladies of the town thought the word *slaughterhouse* held an unseemly connotation. But the *real men* of the town prevailed and named it the tougher word.

The slaughterhouse had connected cold rooms where the meat was frozen and wrapped in one room and stored in the other until it was ready for shipment or readied to be transferred to the butcher shop. For the sake of convenience, the men at the slaughterhouse wanted the icehouse close by. But the builders knew if the ice was close to the townspeople, they would buy more of it. There was a compromise, and the icehouse was built somewhere between the slaughterhouse and the town.

With a new icehouse in town, the Kellers at the mercantile sold out of kitchen iceboxes twice. They were a big hit. Some felt as though pretty soon Big Rock wouldn't feel like the west anymore; it was becoming too civilized. Too *easternized*, as they put it.

The butcher shop drew a bit of controversy before it was built, too. People argued about where it was needed most. It would be much easier for the slaughterhouse people if the butcher shop was at or near the slaughterhouse. But it would be easier for the townspeople if it were in town. The sheriff got tired of the bickering and told the main complainer, "Hang it up, Peterson, it's not like you're carrying all that meat yourself. The horse does all the work." It was built in town, a deep, narrow building not far from Mary's Restaurant, which became its first commercial customer and received a permanent discount in recognition of the fact.

Alice Stewart and Lettie thrived at the Bride & Board. Lettie even enjoyed helping her mother cook, but she didn't so much enjoy helping her clean. Mostly, she liked to draw, and most often in the quiet times she could be found tucked away unnoticed, drawing wonderful likenesses of the guests. Some even paid her to draw ink portraits of them to send to relatives.

Lily began incorporating an Introduction to Poetry segment in the curriculum, and the results were about what she expected. Some loved it, the rest tolerated it. Amos told her it was a pity she couldn't come out and say that poetry might well help them get laid somewhere down the line. She couldn't exactly use those words, but she did imply that most girls like poetry and throughout history, it's been used by men to romance women. It helped a little.

It was nearly two years later when Sophie and Lily both discovered they were pregnant. She kept teaching throughout —it was approved by the school board, which was almost unheard of. Most schoolteachers across the country weren't even allowed to marry. Will Wharton Cameron was born right at the end of the school year, about three weeks before Millie Maybelle Garrett was born. She was named after both her grandmothers. It was a little joke between their families that the two children would grow up and marry, but Lily insisted she wasn't joking. She knew they would marry. She had no doubt.

Sophie kept both children while Lily worked. Lily stayed home some, and Nessa substituted for her. It was a system that worked out well for them, given how much latitude they had from the school board. Some days Nessa even brought Liam with her to school. Other days he was kept by Opal Tucker, who adored the child.

As the town grew, the people recognized the need for a more formal form of government. They voted to adopt a mayor/town council structure, and Arthur Smithers was elected the first mayor. Suddenly Harriet had a new role to play, and she thrived in it.

Lily was asked to run for council, but she declined. She was flattered, of course, but quite happy with her roles as wife, mother, and schoolteacher. Although she couldn't very well say it to anyone, another reason she turned it down was because she also loved her recurring role as the disobedient, subservient submissive to her masterful husband. She liked to spend free time planning how she could instigate sessions and thinking about how they might pan out.

True to his word, John kept his promise to Billy, although he was never truly tested. Sophie and Billy were both naturally thoughtful, well-behaved people, and fun to spend time with. John adopted Billy, and Billy was overjoyed that he even wanted to. He started calling him "Daddy John," and in time, he dropped the "John." Never once was there a behavior problem that John couldn't handle with a well-reasoned man-to-young-man talk.

Alas, that wasn't the case with Lily.

NORA NOLAN

Nora Nolan is one of my pen names. It's nice to meet you! I love to read all kinds of books. All kinds! So far, though, I've only written one basic type. They usually have fairly normal, sexy, fun relationships between the main characters, infused with a little wicked kink. So if you like age play, strong D/s lifestyles, or women in chains who beg to be caned, you might want to look for other authors. I'm not there yet.

My newest joy is sitting at the keyboard letting the characters in my head write their stories. They often lead me in directions that surprise me. I never know when I start out what direction they'll take or where they'll end up.

I live in the southern central part of the US. My happier days find me with our family, or spending time with my wonderful alpha husband.

Email Nora directly at NoraNolan.books@gmail.com
Website: https://www.noranolanbooks.com

Don't miss these exciting titles by Nora Nolan and Blushing Books!

Operation Big Rock Brides (Historical Western)
Two Brides for Big Rock
Opal from Omaha
Ruby from Rawlins
Lacy from Laramie
Nellie from Newport

Lily from Lincoln

Big Rock Romance Series (Historical Western)
Marriage by Mail - Book One
A Badge in Big Rock - Book Two
Deputy's Dilemma - Book Three
Big Rock Rescue - Book Four
Bedlam at Big Rock - Book Five
Big Rock Romance Collection

BLUSHING BOOKS

Blushing Books is the oldest eBook publisher on the web. We've been running websites that publish steamy romance and erotica since 1999, and we have been selling eBooks since 2003. We have free and promotional offerings that change weekly, so please do visit us at http://www.blushingbooks.-com/free.

BLUSHING BOOKS NEWSLETTER

Please join the Blushing Books newsletter
to receive updates & special promotional offers.
You can also join by using your mobile phone:
Just text BLUSHING to 22828.

Every month, one new sign up via text messaging will receive a
$25.00 Amazon gift card, so sign up today!